PRAISE FOR

Elvis in the Morning

"A fanciful yet believable premise—a lifelong friendship that begins when an American teenager living on a military base in West Germany meets Pvt. Presley during the singer's well-known 1950s tour of duty in the Army.... Buckley uses his characters' lives to illustrate the times in which they lived and events ranging from university protests to the beginnings of the computer industry."

—*Houston Chronicle*

"It's gripping, stylish, funny, and moving. Who knows? Rolling Stone might even have to acknowledge its excellence."

—*The Oxford American*

"(A) quirky look at the life of Elvis and at an American era."

—*New York Daily News*

"In *Elvis in the Morning,* Buckley has crafted a warm, endearing and surprisingly intriguing fable about the wages of fame and the forces that shape our lives.... If you're too young to remember the Cold War, this is an excellent way to discover how it felt. If you remember the Elvis era, you'll have great fun reliving it."

—*The News-Press* (Ft. Myers, FL)

"It's a joyful read."

—*The Buffalo News*

"The erudite Buckley concocts a charmingly sympathetic tale tracing the fictional relationship between a young boy and the King. Buckley captures the hope, the yearning, the magic and pathos of the '50s and '60s as few authors have in this "Almost Famous"-like reflection on two turbulent decades.... The well-worn contours of Elvis's story take on a fresh sharpness when subjected to Buckley's surprisingly tender treatment. This is a low-key pleasure of a read, a nostalgic tale that eschews mush and a heartfelt tribute to the tragic figure who touched so many lives."
—*Publishers Weekly* (boxed)

"A breezy, Ragtime-style tale starring Elvis Presley, with cameo appearances by Richard Nixon, Barry Goldwater, Col. Tom Parker, and many, many more."
—*The Times-Union* (Albany, NY)

"William F. Buckley Jr's latest novel tracks a long-lasting friendship between the main character, Orson Killere, and his childhood idol, Elvis Presley.... Offer(s) an interesting, albeit fictional, glimpse into a complicated and fascinating life."
—*Roanoke Times*

"The publication of a novel by William F. Buckley is a literary event.... Buckley's payload is in the subtext of his gritty and unexpectedly darkly humorous 14th novel.... *Elvis in the Morning* is a tightly-woven tale that is enjoyable to read on any level that you care to approach it. Buckley has a knack for making us think and giving us pause no matter what, apparently, the subject matter."
—*January Magazine* (Canada)

"*Elvis in the Morning*—wistful with moments of subdued radiance—is a familiar story told in a strange and original way. The overall effect is immensely touching, and even has a quality of grace."
—*National Review*

ALSO BY WILLIAM F. BUCKLEY JR.

Elvis in the Morning

William F. Buckley Jr.

A HARVEST BOOK • HARCOURT, INC.

San Diego   New York   London

Photo on page 251 by Ollie Atkins courtesy of the National Archives
and the Nixon Presidential Materials staff.

Library of Congress Cataloging-in-Publication Data
Buckley, William F. (William Frank), 1925–
Elvis in the morning/William F. Buckley, Jr.—1st ed.
p. cm.
ISBN 0-15-100643-1
ISBN 0-15-600754-1 (pbk.)
1. Presley, Elvis, 1935–1977—Fiction.
2. Presley, Priscilla Beaulieu—Fiction. 3. Entertainers—Fiction.
I. Title.
PS3552.U344 E48 2001
813'.54—dc21   00-054484

Text set in Sabon
Designed by Cathy Riggs

Printed in the United States of America

First Harvest edition 2002
A C E G I K J H F D B

FOR JANE BUCKLEY SMITH,
WITH SPECIAL LOVE

ACKNOWLEDGMENTS

ALTHOUGH ELVIS PRESLEY IS A HISTORICAL FIGURE, THIS is a work of fiction and nothing written here about him or anyone else should be taken as factual.

I am indebted, in my own office, to Tony Savage, who did the typing and gave, throughout, critical encouragement; to Frances Bronson, who superintends my editorial life; to Julie Crane, who twice read the manuscript and helped with the copy editing; and to Dorothy McCartney, who helped with research.

At Harcourt, my thanks to André Bernard, my editor, and thanks also for his encouragement and stimulation. And to Marian Ryan for her extraordinary work as copy editor—her erudition is terrifying and enlightening; and to David Hough, managing editor, for his own work as copy editor.

I am especially grateful to James Ewing, who helped me day by day, month by month, and supplied such sophistication as is here on the subject of rock and roll. My thanks to Jack Soden, Chief Executive Officer of Elvis Presley Enterprises, who spent valuable hours with me at Graceland.

My thanks to those kind persons who read and criticized the

book, including my wife Pat, son Christopher, brother Reid, and sisters Carol and Priscilla. And to Professors Thomas Wendel, Chester Wolford, and Tracy Lee Simmons.

Above all, as is always the case, I acknowledge the inimitable advice and encouragement of Samuel S. Vaughan, about whom I feel as Baucis did about Philemon—when he ceases to edit, I'll cease to write.

Following are the books I consulted. In particular I am indebted to Peter Guralnick, the consummate scholar and unmatched chronicler of Elvis Presley and the Presley phenomenon.

Last Train to Memphis: The Rise of Elvis Presley, Peter Guralnick, Little Brown, 1994.

Careless Love: The Unmaking of Elvis Presley, Peter Guralnick, Little Brown, 1999.

The Elvis Encyclopedia: The Complete and Definitive Reference Book on the King of Rock & Roll, David E. Stanley, with Frank Coffey, General Publishing Group, Santa Monica, 1994.

Elvis Presley: A Life in Music, The Complete Recording Sessions, Ernst Jorgensen, St. Martin's Press, New York, 1998.

Good Rockin' Tonight: Sun Records and the Birth of Rock 'n' Roll, Colin Escott, with Martin Hawkins, St. Martin's Press, 1991.

Night Beat: A Shadow History of Rock & Roll, Mikal Gilmore, Anchor Press, 1998.

Elvis Presley, a Complete Reference, compiled by Wendy Sauers, McFarland & Company, Jefferson, North Carolina, 1984.

America Divided: The Civil War of the 1960s, Maurice Isserman, and Michael Kazin, Oxford, 2000.

America in the Sixties: An Intellectual History, Ronald Berman, Free Press, 1968.

Let It Blurt: The Life and Times of Lester Bangs, America's Greatest Rock Critic, Jim Derogatis, Broadway Books, New York, 2000.

On the Road, Jack Kerouac, Penguin, 1957.

The Elvex Pages (website) Lex Raaphorst.

WFB
Stamford, Connecticut
March 2001

Elvis
in the
Morning

BOOK ONE

1

Wiesbaden, 1951–1954

AFTER PLEADING FOR THREE WEEKS, ORSON FINALLY got permission: His mother would allow him to bicycle to his school in Wiesbaden. He had argued his point persuasively and, finally, irresistibly. True, he would average on his bicycle only sixteen miles per hour. True, the bus traveled at a greater speed. But Orson presented his patient mother with stopwatched documentation filling six pages, including diagrams. The research extended over a trial period of two weeks and concluded that, on a bicycle, he would arrive at school at the same time as the bus. "The bus driver, Mum, has to zigzag his way. He has to pick up nine other kids before arriving at school. On my bike I could leave the house *twelve minutes and twenty seconds* after the bus."

Francie Killere had intentionally stretched out the interval between hearing Orson's request and acquiescing in it. She liked watching her precocious boy lower his eyes in earnest frustration over the law's delays. He wore his eyeglasses, with the trim tortoiseshell frames so tightly against his face they seemed more like frames around his eyes than eyeglasses. Looking through them at his eyes, she saw, magnified, the light hazel of his irises, intensifying the ardor of his petition.

Orson had needed glasses since age five and seldom took them off. His unruly hair fell down over his eyes, especially when engrossed in a book and absentmindedly running his fingers over his head, managing somehow to see through the forest to what he was reading. "Orson," his exasperated mother once said to him, "I assume you have eyes, otherwise you would stumble down the stairs. But I certainly can't *see* any eyes, the way you let your hair fall down over your face."

Orson returned one afternoon from school with what seemed no hair at all. He had told the barber—as later reported to Mrs. Killere by his pal Priscilla, who had sat waiting for him until he was finished—to "cut it all off. My mother does not like my hair." Francie thundered at him, and Orson smiled, unrepentant and defiant. She didn't criticize his hair again, after it had finally grown back. And when she mentioned the episode to Amos Hoffritz, her boss at Camp Pershing, she did not conceal her amusement. Amos commented, "He's headstrong. Maybe you should send him to Parris Island for training when he gets a little older."

Orson a United States Marine! Francie shuddered at the thought. But Orson was growing up. He had grown several inches in the year since his mother moved from Paris. She had come to Camp Pershing to take on her new post, personnel administrator with the freshly promoted General Hoffritz, Seventh Army, Frankfurt. Orson would probably be lean, she speculated, if he grew much taller. He would be handsome; he was already alluringly good-looking. But she arrested herself in midthought—mothers tend to think nice things about their boys. She allowed herself a modification: Orson would never be as outrageously handsome as his late father. That was inconceivable. She looked over at the photograph of Jean-Jacques taken in London, twenty-four hours before he left to return to rejoin the French resistance and do as commanded by the representative of General Charles de Gaulle after D-Day.

The Allied High Command knew that when the American and British invasion was launched, the French resistance working behind the lines would be critical. They would proceed with such disruption as could be effected on the Nazi military machine. Jean-Jacques Killere, who had trained in England under the banner of the Free French, would be a leader in that support movement, gnawing away as could be done at German installations.

He left London three days later, after a passionate night with Francie, now Mme Jean-Jacques Killere. She never saw him whole again. After V-E Day, recovering as best he could from his deprivations in a German prisoner-of-war camp, he was detained in a U.S. military hospital in Belgium for five weeks. He had arrived at the Saint-Lazare Station in Paris just in time to participate, though haltingly, in a victory parade down the Champs-Elysées. In the years after Jean-Jacques died, his shattered body finally giving way to the tuberculosis, Francie had succeeded in obliterating from memory his disfiguring, consumptive features, first viewed on the day he climbed down from the train. She was waiting on the platform with their child. Mother and son would keep him company for the two years Jean-Jacques Killere had left to live.

Orson Peter Marye Killere was the name his mother had put down when applying for her son's passport. Orson now focused on the question of his surname when on the visit to Poissy, a monthly outing to his grandparents' farm. He had only just learned to write out his name, and today, arriving in short-sleeved

shirt, gray cotton shorts, and ankle-high canvas shoes, he straight-
ened up his five-year-old frame after deciphering the neatly
painted surname of his grandparents at the gate of their farm-
house. The mailbox spelled out K-I-L-L-E-R-E, leaving out the accent mark on the E. Proudly, Orson called his mother's attention
to the omission. "He must be a very blind painter, the man who
painted that," he remarked, peering through his own tight glasses.

Walking with him hand in hand to the solid, white-framed,
oaken door of the cottage, Francie explained that *that—
KILLERE, without the accent mark—*was the way the French
spelled Orson's father's name *when using capital letters*. Orson
pondered what she said.

He already knew how he had come by his first name. He liked
to tell his classmates the story. His mother, in the Paris hospital at
the birth of her child, had sent a handwritten letter to the father.
She had written, *"Our son arrived this morning, and he is seven
pounds."* Congratulatory word came back from the father, who
read the message as announcing the birth of "Orson."

The name stuck, though at baptism time the old priest at
Neuilly was skeptical about it, wondering out loud whether there
had ever been a Saint Orson. *"Orson Welles, celui n'est pas très
saint, je pense pas."*

Francie now explained to Orson that the French spelling of
his surname, including the grave accent, would confuse Americans. "That's why I didn't put it on your passport. Your passport
is exactly like that sign."

"Why would that confuse Americans, having the accent?"

"Because they don't use accents."

"How will they know how to pronounce my name? I mean, I
am Orson Kill-air, not Killer-EE."

"There'll be some confusion, dear. But what's important is
that you still have your father's name. And some people will pronounce it just 'killer.' Like someone who kills people."

"I like that." Orson pulled out his toy pistol to kill off the hand-painted *KILLERE*. Francie obliged by falling to the ground, clasping her heart. Orson went wild with glee and laughter.

Francie reminded the boy, clutching his little wrist with fierce maternal affection, that as the son of an American parent, he was by law entitled to be American. "But when you are twenty-one, Orson, you can choose to take French citizenship, if you want to."

Seated at tea, Orson reflected on the point and then commented to the indulgent assembly, parent, grandparents, and cousins, that when the moment came he would almost certainly choose to be a French citizen, because he liked his French teachers, in particular Mademoiselle Bouchex. Francie commented that perhaps in later years he might also come to like American teachers.

Accepting with a slight nod of his head the raisin cake his grandmother handed him, Orson opined that this was indeed possible, inasmuch as—he lapsed now into quietly rendered English; Orson would always avoid a public display of affection—he liked his American *mother* very much, and therefore could imagine liking American *teachers*.

"You could be an American teacher, if you wanted." He pointed to his mother. "Because you know French and German just as well as you know English." And if she became a teacher, he would like her very much. He concluded that he could like American teachers who weren't also his mother.

Francie laughed and instructed her son to tell Grandmère Claudine what he had just now said, "because Grandmère does not speak English." Orson obliged, and was given more cake. Francie sent the boy out to play with his cousins.

She then informed her in-laws that she and the boy would be visiting in Camden, South Carolina, for a month, "to meet his other grandmother." After that they would move to Germany, Francie continuing in her profession as personnel administrator. "General Hoffritz is being sent to Camp Pershing, which is near Frankfurt, to command the Seventh Army's Thirty-seventh Division. He wants me to take charge of the personnel center. That is a big promotion. And I am glad to continue to work with Amos Hoffritz. It's an advantage that he worked on the staff of General Eisenhower at the end of the war and remains on personal terms with him."

"Is it true General Eisenhower is going to run for president next year?"

"That's what they say," said Francie.

"Do you have a place in your heart for this General Hoffritz, to take the place of Jean-Jacques? I hope so. So would my son in heaven hope so."

Francie spoke back sharply. "General Hoffritz is married."

Grandmère sighed. She said she would be very sorry to see Francie and Ohr-sohn move away, but she trusted Francie to make the right decision for herself and for her grandson.

2

Wiesbaden, 1959

EIGHT YEARS LATER, AT THE ROOSEVELT SCHOOL IN
Wiesbaden, Orson competed for the debating team. He proved,
even at age fourteen, a formidable talker, speaking and arguing
confidently. Though only a freshman, he won a place on the team.

His German debate coach, a stolid, one-legged teacher of English, explained to the six debaters what would be expected of
them. The intramural contest was to take place in May, on the afternoon before the school's commencement exercises. The debate
would be conducted in English, the rebuttals in German.

Now, Mr. Feiffer went on, the debate topic would be: "Resolved: Medical services should be free." The procedure, he explained for the benefit of the three younger speakers, unfamiliar
with the rules, required that the debaters prepare to defend both
sides of the resolution. "Then, when everyone is assembled for
the debate actually to begin, I will draw from a hat"—dramatically, he opened his drawer, pulling out the blue beret he wore to
school—"three slips of paper. They will give the names of the af-
firmative team."

Orson raised his hand. "Sir, I would not argue against free
health care."

Mr. Feiffer smiled. "This is a *debate,* Orson. The purpose of this exercise isn't to postulate a right and a wrong. It is to develop skills in arguing."

"I don't think it's right for people to develop skills to argue wrong positions."

Mr. Feiffer paused, then said he would talk to Orson after class.

But after class he resolved, instead, to have a chat with Mrs. Killere. She'd be at school for the monthly parents-teachers meeting at five.

Mrs. Killere listened to Mr. Feiffer. She agreed that she would tell Orson as a matter of discipline that he would need to submit to the rules of the game. "But Orson makes up his own mind about things these days. He might actually withdraw from the debate," she warned. "There is no way Orson will speak out against free medicine—unless Elvis Presley comes out against free medicine."

3

Camden, South Carolina, January 1956

ORSON WAS ELEVEN WHEN HE SAW THE TELEVISION program. He was staying with his mother at the home of Alice Marye, his grandmother, a matronly woman of aristocratic manner, her gray hair conventionally worn, just past the ears, slightly curled. She was now a widow and looked after the retired doctor, her aging father, in the same house she had grown up in, into which Francie's father had moved, after their wedding, to effect an economy.

Like so many Southern-style houses in Camden, the house on Lyttleton Street was worn in appearance, outside and inside. Camden had a lively history, with a role in both the Revolutionary War and the Civil War. Battles had been fought in Camden—fought bravely and lost, against the British in the eighteenth century and, a hundred years later, against the Yankees. The effects of the long long economic drought that parched the South after General Lee's surrender were still detectable, in 1956, in Camden. The big old houses were still lived in but they were mostly underpainted and undermaintained. The long, tree-lined avenues without any trace of commercial life suggested a vigorous economic community sustaining the pastoral scene, but in Camden there was nothing, really, except the monuments to the Revolutionary War and to Baron de Kalb and to the Civil War. There were two movie houses, the older one admitting black customers, but only to the balcony. There was the sense of historical memory suspended, an unarticulated domestic pride in something or other, and a patient expectation that something would come around one of these days to revive Camden, and give it economic life.

Mrs. Marye's husband had earned only the modest salary of a professor at the University of South Carolina, in Columbia, dying of cancer at age forty. At Number 8 Lyttleton Street, Dr. Caleb Whittaker, the father of Alice Marye, lived on. He had been born in the last year of the Confederacy, attending medical school in Charleston, and was renowned for his frugality and the correlative modesty of his fees. He charged his patients one dollar per visit, five dollars for delivering a baby. He did not adjust his rates to the inflation of the war years, and at last he had retired, further reducing the household income.

Even so, Mrs. Marye had managed to buy a television set the year before Francie and Orson came to visit. She enjoyed showing it off to those of her neighbors who didn't yet have one. She was eager to display it to Francie and her grandson, whom she had last seen as a six-year-old, when they came to Camden after the death of Francie's Jean-Jacques.

Now Alice Marye, smoking her beloved Lucky Strike cigarettes, waited in her six-year-old Ford at Camden's old train station for the Seaboard Line's Silver Meteor. Camden was one of the many stops on its nightly journey from New York to Miami. When she heard the whistle she had grown up listening to—you could hear it all the way over at Lyttleton Street—she put out her cigarette and opened the door to what passed as wintry weather in South Carolina. When the train stopped she was standing, waiting, at the platform. She hoped Francie and Orson would be stepping down from one of the Pullman cars...but no; they climbed down from a coach car, up front.

Francie Killere stepped down first, wearing a beret-style hat. She was balancing a package and a large suitcase in her hands. Alice Marye was hugging her daughter joyously when she felt a thud on her rear. It was the impact of a second large suitcase, propelled by Orson Peter Marye Killere. In his other hand the boy held a bulky briefcase. Alice Marye closed her arms around her grandson, who stood mutely, the bags still suspended in his hands.

"You sweet boy, little—*growing big*—Orson, you're just the *apple* of mah eye. Oh darlin' Francie, how much I've missed you!" Mrs. Marye signaled to a porter standing by. He took the bags, and in ten minutes they were in the big old house.

Alice Marye had lots of friends, and some of them owned horses. One neighbor, Bill Woodie, ran a riding stable for guests at the Kirkwood Hotel. In Camden everybody did things for other people, that's how they acted, and Bill Woodie, sizing up the situation at Number 8 Lyttleton Street—an eleven-year-old boy with a thirty-five-year-old mother, a sixty-five-year-old grandmother, and a ninety-year-old great-grandfather—volunteered to teach Orson how to ride. Camden was a horse town, with miles and miles of bridle paths through pine woods and soft hills. Besides, Camden was the center of American steeplechasing, and, at many intersections on the unpaved roads the injunction was displayed: Motorists Must Give Way to Horsemen.

Orson delighted in his new sport. Bill Woodie assigned whichever of his grooms was not engaged with paying guests of the hotel to take Orson riding for two, sometimes three, hours. At the end of the week, Orson told his mother he thought he would join the cavalry after finishing school. Francie nodded her

head gravely. She had learned to indulge Orson's serial enthusi-
asms, which only last summer had inclined him to marine biology, after visiting the North Sea coast of Germany and marveling
at the huge mudflats of the Wattenmeer.

Old Dr. Whittaker didn't hear very well. He sat every evening
close to the television set, his hearing aid turned on, the volume
turned high. His daughter and granddaughter sat back from the
screen, distancing themselves. Orson sat by his great-grandfather,
impervious to the loud sound. Tonight they would listen to the
program produced by Jackie Gleason, the comedian, with hosts
Jimmy and Tommy Dorsey.

"Do you know who Jackie Gleason is?" Alice Marye addressed her daughter. Francie had read that he was a gifted actor
and comedian, but knew nothing more. "You'll like his show. So
will you, Orson."

Gleason, robust, good-humored, teasing in mannerisms and
in voice, would come on the black-and-white screen and do
comic skits with his TV wife, Audrey Meadows. Now it was
Tommy Dorsey who announced the featured guest of the evening.
"A very special guest, ladies and gentlemen, he is that singing—
no, *singin'!*—sensation from Memphis, Tennessee. Tonight will
be his debut on national television. I'm talking about—I mean,
I'm talkin' about—EL—VIIIS PRESLEY!"

Orson looked curiously at the twenty-one-year-old who appeared, with the angel face, broad smile, and pompadoured hair.
With him were a guitar player, a bass man, and a drummer. The
singer opened his mouth and began to sing his heart out to a
brand-new, hypnotic beat.

Four minutes later Orson thought it was the end of the world:
Nothing, ever, could match the excitement he felt. The rapturous
sound, the beat, the joy on the godlike face of the performer.
That man saying: *Do what you want to do and enjoy, and don't*

give a—shit what others say. That, Orson knew, feeling the sense
of the fugitive word he had only just learned—that was the senti-
ment Elvis Presley obviously had in mind when he sang "I Got a
Woman." It spoke of a woman's devotion to a man, who sang
out his elation. It was clearly Elvis's woman he was singing for,
nobody else counted.

His mother turned to say something and stopped, startled
when Orson let out a firm, pleading *shhhh!* There came another
song, with a faster rhythm, the beat more insistent. He heard
"Shake, Rattle, and Roll." Without a pause singer and accompanists turned to "Flip, Flop, and Fly." Orson could not make out
exactly what Elvis Presley now celebrated, but he caught the last
line, enjoining against his woman ever saying good-bye to him.
How could anybody say good-bye to the man who sang that
song?

Orson joined in the applause of the studio audience. They
clamored for one more song, but Tommy Dorsey said that the
time was up, wonderful though Elvis was, singing—singin'—like
a true son of the South, of gospel, of Dixie and blues and—
"maybe they'll just call it Elvis music! You're really great, Elvis!"

When Elvis departed the stage, Orson got up and headed toward the staircase.

"Turning in, dahlin'?"

He nodded to his grandmother, who blew him a kiss, which
he returned.

An hour later Francie saw that his light was still on. She
knocked softly on the door. Orson's soprano voice told her to
come in.

He was seated at the old desk in what had been the study of
Francie's father. The desk light illuminated the pad of paper
under his pen.

"Who you writing to?" Francie asked.

"To Elvis Presley."

She paused. "That's fine, dear. Are you telling him you liked his songs?"

"I'm asking him if I can go to work for him this summer. After school gets out," he added. Orson did not want to sound reckless.

Francie said good night, closed the door, and walked down to the kitchen, where her mother was washing dishes.

"What did you think of that singer?" she asked Alice Marye.

"The one just now? With Tommy Dorsey?"

"Yes."

"I think that young man should be—I don't know. He can certainly sing. I was thinkin' maybe he should have a belt tied around his knees. Did Orson like him? I'd guess so, the way he carried on."

Francie laughed. "Orson wants to go to work for him. Maybe tomorrow he'll ask for singing lessons."

"He could sing while riding a horse!"

"Gene Autry, next generation."

Early the next day Orson, after a few minutes on the telephone, told his mother that he intended to take a bus to Columbia, an hour's journey. He would be going to a music store. "There's a bus at 9:40. I'll be on the 6:10 getting back. Remember, Mother, I have over thirty dollars of my own money." Reflecting on the bus schedule, Francie objected that Orson would be stranded in Columbia a full five hours.

He replied that he didn't care. "I can always go to a movie." There was a pause, and Orson said, "Maybe they're showing *Gone with the Wind*?" Orson smiled condescendingly at his reference to his mother's continuing enthusiasm for the movie, which she several times remarked on having first seen in Columbia in 1939, before the war.

Francie bit back. "*Gone with the Wind* has lasted... almost twenty years. Let's see if your new hero, Elvis what's-his-name is around in 1976."

Orson accepted the challenge. He was even willing to joke a little about it. "Maybe in 1976 he'll be in heaven."

Orson came back weary and disappointed. The store didn't have the songs he had heard the night before. The Columbia Record Shop had only a single song by Elvis Presley. He opened his brief-case and took out a 45-rpm record. It had Elvis Presley singing a song called "Heartbreak Hotel."

"They let me play it in the store. I tell you what, Mum. They'll be listening to this song in 1976, I promise you."

Francie would not argue with him again, nor disparage his new icon.

She said she was sure that would be so, and she very much wanted to hear it. She'd ask his grandmother if she knew some-one who had a 45-rpm player.

4

Wiesbaden, May 1956

BACK HOME IN WIESBADEN ORSON HAD PLAYED AND replayed the one record on his mother's record player, waiting for a package to arrive. He'd heard about the great music store in New York City called Sam Goody and its fabled inventory. By March the single Elvis record had become an album of twelve songs. Orson heard of it from his own mother. Francie Killere, on duty at the personnel office, had authorized purchases of the new album by the camp's PX, which stocked everything of likely interest to soldiers and their families. But acquisitions were slow. Orson urged his mother to order the Elvis Presley album expeditiously. Buying records at the PX was cheaper for him, using his mother's GI discount. Meanwhile, he'd wait for the package from Sam Goody.

It pleased him that, not long after the record finally came in, Elvis Presley's name had become familiar to many others at school, who heard his songs over the radio and were carried away by them. "Carried away? By what, exactly?" his mother had asked, a little impatiently, after a few months of good-natured acquiescence in the post-Camden days. Orson struggled to define the mix of energy, joy, and love he said he was listening to. He was hardly alone, he said. Consider Priscilla Beaulieu.

He was embarrassed that his neighbor, Priscilla Ann Beaulieu, had taken the initiative from him in founding the FDR Presley Fan Club, EPFC, for short. At school Priscilla was his closest companion, a young girl of great beauty, whose smile and warmth made Orson happy whenever he was in her company. What Orson did not tell his mother was that when he was a little older he would propose marriage to Priscilla. He hadn't yet acquired a sense of the comic in his serial commitments to marine biology, his teacher Mr. Simon, horses, Elvis, and now Priscilla. He was old enough to see that in others' eyes his behavior was dismissed as juvenile infatuation, but this didn't mean he doubted that Priscilla and he would one day be united in marriage. His curiosity about the mechanics of conjugal life was provoked and, in his habitual way, he satisfied it comprehensively by finding out what to read and finding out how to get what he wanted to read, until he thought himself amply informed.

But although he and Priscilla discussed many things, including all the lyrics in all the songs of Elvis Presley, Orson drew a line at any mention of what exactly some of those words implied. When news got out that Elvis would not be permitted the habitual exposure of his body in his forthcoming appearance on "The Steve Allen Show," Orson and Priscilla had to face the question of Elvis's "sexuality," as the GI daily, *Stars and Stripes,* had referred to it. "It's mostly people objecting to him because he's so, sort of, passionate, you know. They're puritans," Orson concluded. But his physical gyrations to one side, Orson and Priscilla declined to find anything reprehensibly suggestive in his lyrics.

It was enough that they were words used by Elvis Presley. They were, for that reason alone, really immaculate. And both he and Priscilla spread the gospel. By mid-May their fan club had over twenty members. Club dues consisted of bringing in for the FDR scrapbook any notice about Elvis Presley, in any newspaper the cosmopolitan students came upon or could dig up—in English, French, or German. Members were invited to formulate, write out, and contribute to the scrapbook accounts of their devotion to Elvis and his work. Orson advised that the daily twelve minutes he saved up by bicycling to school instead of taking the bus were allocated to listening to Elvis.

The scrapbook filled quickly. There was news of yet another appearance with Gleason, in which Elvis sang "Baby, Let's Play House" and "Blue Suede Shoes." The starstruck cultural reporter Corporal Stan Machlup wrote twice a week for *Stars and Stripes*. In his column he reported that Presley had traveled to Hollywood and was contracted to appear in a movie! Machlup's assignment was to review for the army daily "cultural activity," which included movies and television and music. He confessed his anxiety to see an Elvis Presley movie. His column now almost never appeared without some mention of Elvis Presley.

Some months later Orson and Priscilla learned with horror from Machlup's column that the aircraft bringing Presley back to Memphis from a singing date had the next thing to a crash landing when the rear wheel buckled. Imagine, Corporal Machlup wrote, if there had been a casualty! Elvis, he recorded solemnly, was now perhaps a contender to be the major entertainer in the United States, the rival of Frank Sinatra. "Heartbreak Hotel" had sold 1,250,000 copies. The album called *Elvis Presley* was now RCA's biggest-selling LP ever. When it was reported that Elvis, having performed once on "The Milton Berle Show," was booked to perform again, the FDR Fan Club sent a delegation to the office of Captain Haley Laswell, requesting that a movie reel of the two performances be procured for showing at the camp on Saturday night, preceding the weekly movie. Captain Laswell threw up his hands in frustration.

"Priscilla Beaulieu. Orson Killere—" Seated at his desk confronting the delegation, he singled out the most familiar names on the petition and addressed them directly. "We can't *keep up* with your guy. Elvis Presley has been signed to do *three* performances with Ed Sullivan. Are we supposed to get copies of those?" Captain Laswell paused, distracted. As though speaking to himself, he added, "The paper says that Elvis will be paid fifty thousand dollars for his appearance on Ed Sullivan. That makes him, according to the story, the highest-paid guest star on a variety show in television history—" He paused.

"I like Elvis," the captain quickly added. "But I'm not going to make the entertainment program of the Thirty-seventh Division in Germany an Elvis Presley world's fair." He turned to Orson. "Your mother knows the records are flowing into the PX. They probably have fifty of them in there now. So it isn't like you're, you know, starving to death…"

Priscilla wrote a report of the delegation's reception for the EPFC scrapbook and read it out loud at the monthly meeting. Then she and her classmates listened—silence was required while Elvis sang—to "Hound Dog," "Don't Be Cruel," "Love Me Tender," and "How Do You Think I Feel?" Afterward Priscilla and Orson walked from the recreation hall hand in hand to the gas station, where, every school day, Orson's bicycle was protectively chained to an old rusty gate in the back, under the obliging eye of the gas station owner, Herr Hafner. Priscilla walked on to the waiting bus.

"I'll call you later."

"Good." He waved his hand. "Maybe I'll come on over, after homework. Before supper."

She gave her big smile.

5

Wiesbaden, 1960

ORSON WASN'T SURPRISED WHEN HIS MOTHER, BEAM-
ing, showed him his year-end report card from tenth grade. He
had earned A grades in English and German Literature, Mathe-
matics, and Geography. What gave him special pleasure (he didn't
reveal this to his mother—it's not right to boast, he reminded
himself sternly) was the penciled note after the A grade in Government. Mr. Simon had written, "I'd have made this A plus, except the school doesn't allow it." The note was initialed *SiSi.*
Siegfried Simon.

Mr. Simon was Orson's favorite teacher. Orson greatly re-
sented it that, next year, his junior year, the school would offer no
third-year course by Mr. Simon. He resolved to approach him at
the midmorning break, when milk and cookies were served and
the faculty mingled with the students. Orson would ask Mr.
Simon for a reading program he could pursue on his own time.

Siegfried Simon had been drafted into the Wehrmacht in 1943, at
age sixteen. The German army was bleeding from staggering
losses deep in the Russian interior. A year earlier he and his Jew-

ish father had been rounded up and placed in a processing camp at Breslau, the first leg on what was widely suspected would be a fatal trip to a concentration camp.

What came then was the scene with the major at German Army headquarters. Anita Simon arrived at the bustling office of Major Eristoff, the harried chief of personnel movements. His instructions from the chief, Army Command, were straightforward: He was to apprehend all Jews and Gypsies and send them to Gross-Rosen, an extermination camp. The second order was to examine the birth certificates of all boys in the area to ascertain if any were in fact already sixteen, disguising their age to stay out of the draft. Sixteen-year-olds, once detected, would go to basic infantry training.

The elderly corporal sitting at the desk in the crowded corridor and directing the traffic center would not admit Frau Simon to the office of the major. "He is too busy—"

"I must see him."

"Frau Simon! You can *see* how occupied we are here."

Uniformed men and women walked briskly through the reception area as they spoke. The narrow corridor was thick with cigarette smoke. A continuous sound came in from the radio, giving out national news in a melancholy monotone. One helmeted soldier came by leading three disconcerted teenage boys. Their true age would be verified at the town records office, adjacent.

Anita Simon declared that what she had to say to the major was a question of life and death and that she would not move from the personnel office until she had had five minutes with Major Eristoff. She told the corporal that she was entitled to a brief audience. Her father had died fighting for the Fatherland in the First War and she had supported the current war effort by working three nights every week in the hospital, on top of her regular work as a teacher at the grade school.

"Sei ruhig!" she was told. Shut up!

But the white-haired corporal then rose, turned, and entered the major's office, closing the door behind him. He pleaded with Major Eristoff, who was half the age of the corporal, a veteran of the earlier war, to give the adamant woman outside a couple of minutes. "Otherwise, Herr Commandant, the war effort will quite simply stop."

Even at his young age, Major Eristoff knew something about extreme tensions at personnel centers. Sometimes one has to give way a bit.

"Show her in. And stay here while she has her say."

Anita Simon entered the room. She was dressed in her hospital apron. She bowed her head, then thrust her hand down to her purse. The corporal, alarmed, lunged at her, grabbing her arm.

"I'm just reaching for a piece of paper, Herr Gefreiter. I did not come here to make war."

Cautiously he removed his hand.

Anita Simon brought out an envelope and drew from it a baptismal certificate.

Her son Siegfried, she explained through tears, was not in fact the son of her husband, Hendrik Simon. She had had a . . . love affair when her husband was away at his studies at Cologne. She had never confessed to her husband that the boy was—another man's son. But—she thrust the certificate onto the major's desk—she had had Siegfried baptized and had given the name of his real father.

"There, sir, you can see that the father is Walter Fahnstock. He is the headmaster, sir," she lowered her head, "at my school. If you insist on calling him in here, he will not deny what I am saying, sir. And of course Herr Fahnstock is Evangelical, not a Jew. But don't call him in. I would not want Hendrik, after all this time, to find out he is not the father of my son. He is . . . a Jewish *patriot* . . . terrible days ahead of him, I know. Sir, let my son grow up here. In two years he will be old enough to fight for the führer."

Major Eristoff stared at her through tired young eyes and ran a finger over the baptismal certificate. And then, to his subordinate, "Bring me the boy's dispatch order."

Anita stood while the clerk left the room. Major Eristoff looked up and smiled wanly. "The rewards of indiscretion, Frau Simon."

The corporal returned with the file. Major Eristoff withdrew the dispatch order, wrote over Siegfried Simon's name, crossed out Simon, and replaced it with Fahnstock. He nodded to the corporal to call in an orderly to take the paper to the compound and release Siegfried Simon.

He raised the baton from his desk. He took the precaution of warding her off in the event the woman threw herself at him in gratitude. Major Eristoff needed approval only from Adolf Hitler.

6

Wiesbaden, 1958

THIRTEEN-YEAR-OLDS AT THE FDR SCHOOL WERE AS-
signed by Mr. Simon to read about the founding of the United
States. He traced the evolution of the Bill of Rights back to the religious persecutions in Europe and determined efforts in the
colonies ("with some exceptions") to assure freedom of religious
practice. Collateral readings introduced the students to the evolution of constitutional practices in Great Britain and to the "great
theoretical leap" to the formulations of the Declaration of Independence, all of this alongside retrograde practices in France. "It
became too much for the French people to stare at the luxuries of
the ruling class, while they struggled simply to stay alive," Mr.
Simon lectured.

The Franklin Delano Roosevelt School had been organized
soon after the fall of Hitler. As fighting ended, peacekeeping
began. But over forty U.S. divisions remained in the liberated
areas. Military personnel gathered in Wiesbaden constituted the
army's Thirty-seventh Division. The Soviet Union governed the
East and its eleven million captive Germans.

At Wiesbaden the full fighting division trained and lived. The
division was made up of fifteen thousand men. Half of these were

recruits, drafted in America and sent to Germany to do eighteen months of duty. These men were trained to fight and to clean toilets, to repair tanks and to dig ditches. The other half were career military, most of them married, many with children. The substantial building on Frankfurterstrasse that had served the German army as an emergency hospital became now a military-sponsored schoolhouse. There, 275 students, sons and daughters of the military, worked toward high school diplomas. At age five Orson Killere became a member of the class of 1962 at the FDR School.

The organizer of the school had accepted the assignment when he was a young army field officer. Major Bruno Brennan had earned his discharge from the army after four years' service. Engrossed by the FDR School, which he had begun to serve while still in the army, he applied for reassignment there as a civilian principal.

Major Brennan (everyone continued to refer to him as *Major*) had graduated from Cornell University, in New York, in 1936, studying German literature. His German mother, having settled with his American father in Utica, had ensured the boy was fluent in German, the language she used at home. At his weekly visits to the Utica speakeasy he patronized, Bruno's father, John, expressed his frustration at hearing only German spoken by his wife and son. He would give way to his exasperation, referring ruefully and ungallantly to his libertine practices in postwar Germany as an American veteran working with the Red Cross. "I had to go and marry my whore," he'd say. Pause. "I guess it was her name I fell in love with." He would turn, when practical, to whoever was seated at his side. "My wife's name is Brünnehilde." When there was no reaction, he would push the point, asking "What is *your* wife's name?" Then he would return to his beer and order a second.

John Brennan's credit was good. He was a paid-up member of the Brotherhood of Locomotive Engineers, working the

New York Central line, Buffalo-Syracuse-Utica-Albany-New York. Under union rules he did one round-trip (sixteen hours of travel), then had two days off, spent at home in Utica with Brünnehilde and Bruno, except when he'd get snowbound in Buffalo, which happened every year or two. He was proud of Bruno's record at Cornell, and in deference to his son's interest in German, finally adjourned his objections to Kraut talk at home.

Major Brennan was not yet thirty when put in charge of the little school for army children. There were many applicants for positions on the faculty from the huge pool of unemployed Germans. Brennan didn't insist on English in the classroom. He wanted his students to wrestle with a foreign language, even if they were made uncomfortable at first. When he interviewed Siegfried Simon, whose English was astonishingly fluent, he quickly knew that he was talking with a natural pedagogue. Mr. Simon was only twenty-three, but looked ten years older. He had been captured by an American unit in the closing days of the war. Upon release he studied history at the university at Essen, his way paid by his school-teaching mother. Major Brennan was much taken by Simon's captivating dignity and hired him probationarily to teach Government, replacing a teacher who had decided to emigrate to America.

Orson was twelve when first exposed to Mr. Simon. His impression of the thin German with a full command of English was that of a monk in mufti. Mr. Simon was bald or else had shaved his head. He wore a shirt and tie, but Orson sensed that in doing so he was merely complying with the school dress code. This was confirmed when, visiting the new wing of the museum in Sachsenhausen, Frankfurt, he ran into Mr. Simon in the ticket line, wearing the same dark shirt and coat, but tieless. Orson was surprised at the pleasure he felt on bumping into the gentle teacher off school premises. Mr. Simon invited Orson to tag along—"or is someone waiting for you?"

"Actually, Priscilla, Priscilla Beaulieu, is supposed to be here"—he looked at his watch—"in five minutes. She's always prompt. Would it be okay if she came, too?"

"Of course."

Orson and Priscilla listened with awe as Mr. Simon, moving from room to room, discussed the paintings, the painters, their motives in painting, the pressures they felt living when they did, where they did, doing what they did. When three hours later they were back at the museum's entrance, Orson asked Mr. Simon whether he would like to come home and have "some tea, or something—whatever you want—Mum should be back home by now." Siegfried Simon thanked him and said no, he had some reading to do. Riding home on the bus, Orson said to Priscilla that Mr. Simon had to be something of a saint, speaking as he had with such understanding and insight of all the artists whose lives he had reviewed.

She agreed. "I bet he'll actually *be* a saint later on."

Orson nodded.

In his class on government, Mr. Simon devoted a month in the second semester to the events that led to the First World War. When, in May, he arrived at the year 1917, he said that a light had been lit in Leningrad that year but that it had lasted for only a very little while. Mr. Simon recounted with quiet excitement the events leading to the birth of a movement based on the idea of common property and common human concerns. Priscilla Beaulieu asked whether the rule of Lenin and of Stalin—the students had read the chapter on Soviet history—hadn't defiled the whole idea of communism. The textbook itself, edited by Elihu Estridge, was one of several favored in 1957 for American secondary students studying abroad, and passed no moral judgment on the rule of Lenin and Stalin. In addressing Priscilla's question, Mr. Simon explained that standards of conduct differed from country to country. He wished to correct for this, he said, and to devote time now to societies other than that of the United States. It was important to bear in mind, Mr. Simon never tired of reminding them, that America was only a single country, "that what distinguishes it, when all is said and done, is its capitalist wealth and its nuclear armory."

Orson wanted to know whether Mr. Simon thought it was wrong to use the atomic bomb at Hiroshima. Mr. Simon replied that the decision to use it was made by an American president who was eager to end that war in order to pursue another war, the Cold War. He explained that by August 1945 the war against the Nazis and the fascists had been won, the war against Japan visibly ending. That left Washington with the awesome prospect of massive unemployment of the kind that had crippled America in the 1930s.

Though he had no lack of respect for the military, Mr. Simon explained, history had acknowledged the special problems of America, with ten million soldiers returning from the wars. Something was badly needed to keep the economy humming. What that was was the pursuit of another huge national project. That national project, he explained, had developed into an obsession with communism. In some ways understandable, Mr. Simon acknowledged, because communism, in pursuit of its own concerns, had here and there used a heavy hand. "The great loss to the entire world," he noted, "has been the dilution of the new vision, the great vision of the Soviet revolution." The vision, of course, "before it lost its way under Lenin, and then Stalin, mercifully dead these past five years."

Mr. Simon read to them passages from Sir Thomas More and Daniel De Leon and more contemporary utopians, especially the American socialist Dorothy Day. He spent time describing the life of Henry Thoreau and reading from his work. Thoreau, Mr. Simon said, his eyes alight from the mere thought of it, wrote that his ambition was "to live every day with less and less."

That would not have made him a very good capitalist, he con-
ceded. But then capitalism feeds on a single aspect of human nature, which is the desire for more. It is fine to desire more. It is
altogether understandable to desire more—unless this is done at
the expense of others. Henry Thoreau was in the tradition of the
stoics, Mr. Simon explained. The Cold War, he said finally, is a
very great distraction, away from the pursuit of a world in which
property is, like the air and the water, commonly owned.

By the end of the spring term, Orson was not only a student
of Siegfried Simon's, but a disciple. Over the next year he read
eagerly from a collection of utopian works especially assembled
by his teacher for interested students, and his views on property
began to change.

When his mother asked him what he wanted for his thir-
teenth birthday—"apart from the latest Elvis Presley, assuming
there is a record out you don't already have, dear"—Orson
thought hard. He had for two years taken a special joy in his
birthday because, falling on January 9, it came one day after Presley's birthday, January 8. At Wiesbaden they were seven hours
ahead of local time in Memphis, Tennessee. That meant that for
seven hours he and Elvis would be celebrating their birthdays simultaneously! It would be January 9 in Germany and January 8
in Memphis.

He had asked his mother to serve his birthday cake at midnight on January 9, at which hour Elvis and he would be celebrating the anniversary of their birth; never mind that Elvis was
born in 1935, ten years earlier than Orson.

Francie Killere indulged her son but flatly refused to invite
Priscilla and Danny and Helen to come to the house at midnight.
"You'll just have to eat your cake by yourself." She relented a
little. "But I will be with you, darling. And we can send a tele-
gram to Mr. Presley." That had greatly cheered Orson.

But now, as he turned fourteen, he wondered at the very idea of asking for a birthday present. To ask for something was to exercise the impulse Mr. Simon had identified, the impulse for self-aggrandizement at the expense of others. It occurred to him, a week before his birthday, to ask at the meeting of the Elvis Presley Fan Club how many of its members knew a German boy or girl who would relish owning an Elvis Presley record but could not afford to purchase one, especially since the price of imported records, in a Germany starved for U.S. dollars, was a singular sacrifice.

Almost all the students knew some teenager who had come into their houses and apartments to listen to Elvis's songs. "Anita Jutzeler," Priscilla Beaulieu had told them, "comes to see me every Saturday morning and listens for two hours, until her mother comes and gets her. One time she borrowed one of my records, but when her mother found out, she made her bring it back. All Anita can do is sit with the radio on and wait for Elvis."

Orson brooded on the matter. An exalting idea evolved. He considered taking Priscilla into his confidence but decided against it. Impetuously, after class one day, he thought of confiding to Mr. Simon what he had in mind to do. Again he stopped himself. What he proposed to do had to be a totally private deed. His personal tribute to an idea. A modest effort at sharing the great wealth he had discovered that momentous night in Camden, almost three years ago.

7

Wiesbaden, January 1959

ORSON KNEW THE AREA WELL. HE REASSURED HIMSELF
that if blindfolded at the entrance to Camp Pershing, he could
make his way to the PX.

He closed his eyes and rehearsed the geography of Thirty-
seventh Army Division headquarters. Passing the (armed) gate,
you would walk 120 steps (he had paced the distance) north
(northeast, actually). You would then have reached Barracks 16.
Eighty paces on, Barracks 14. And so on, until you reached Barracks 2.

Then there was the string of hangars, each of them fifty-two
yards long (and twenty-five yards wide—but that was irrelevant).
Between the hangars that lay on his route there was a stretch of
grass and roadway, sixteen yards across. At the far end of the
third hangar, you turn east (actually, southeast). You go twenty-
five yards and zag left to avoid walking up into the army chapel.
Duck back behind the chapel, turn left again, and you are: *There!*
At the army PX of the Thirty-seventh Division.

Orson liked to bicycle about Wiesbaden and so knew first-
hand the scarcities of postwar Germany. He himself had never
suffered from them, because anything his mother couldn't buy at

the local market she would pick up at the PX. Not that Francie Killere could afford luxuries, but they were certainly there. Watches, champagne, comic books...Elvis records.

He made a surgical study of the target building. If this were summer, it would be easier to slide one's way painlessly to the trapdoor that lay under the large one-story wooden structure, which sat up twelve inches from the ground on steel studs. Now the ground was frozen, and he would expect to be scraped by the hard earth. He removed his woolen jacket; he could not afford the extra girth. But he'd have only eight feet to go. In the sack he dragged alongside, he had a brand-new electric drill, borrowed from his friend Andy, a little flashlight, a claw hammer, and other necessary tools.

The PX closed down at eight. The camp library didn't close until eleven. At eight Orson was at the library, reading. The librarian was not especially surprised, though Orson usually came in the late afternoon. When, at 8:45, he left the reading room and said good night, Sergeant Angela Humphreys commented, "My, Orson, you read more than I think anybody in the whole camp. Are you trying to catch up?"

Orson smiled pleasantly and said there was always a lot to catch up with.

He walked to his bicycle and, his tool sack padlocked to the basket in front, he biked along M Street. Reaching the PX, he circled it twice. It was too cold for army strollers, the one advantage of the winter night. He went to the chapel and parked his bicycle there. He walked back to the PX and ducked under the end of the building adjacent to the trapdoor that was opened when heating fuel was pumped into the PX's furnace.

Quickly he took off his jacket and crawled on his back toward the trapdoor. Dirt and pebbles, scraped up by his belt, lodged under his trouser waistband when he turned and inched his way around to face the outdoors. He had only just enough space to turn his head laterally. Drawing the flashlight from his sack, he looked up at the trapdoor. The iron hinges lay on the side closest to the outside wall. The locking bolt was on the side opposite. He planned to drill a hole through the trapdoor boards near the hinges. The hole would need to be wide enough to let his arm go through, to reach the bolt with his fingers and unlatch it.

He raised his left forearm up against the trapdoor. Shifting his body back and forth to reposition his elbow, he located the hole in the planking that would let him reach through to the locking bolt. It was very cold, but he was sweating.

The pebbles inside his waistband ground against his hip and spine. He twisted about, feeling for the auger with his free hand. It was slow and tiresome work. Sweat carried grime into his eyes. But spirals of wood shavings smoothly lengthened as the drill sank deeper and faster through the plank. Finally a faint splintering sound came as his pressure on the auger broke through the trapdoor's top side. He was able to slide back the bolt and push open the door.

At last he could sit up. He did that, pulled out his wadded handkerchief, shook it out, and wiped the sweat and grime from his eyes. He blew his nose. He'd inhaled dust, dirt, and bits of wood. Flashlight between his teeth, he reached into the cellar of the building, his head up against the fuel tank.

Now he could make his way, carefree, to the record counter and the sought-for treasure. He would take twenty copies of the *Elvis's Golden Records* compilation and slip them through the trapdoor. After getting himself through, he'd put them into the sack, crawl out, and walk over to his bicycle, nonchalantly. The discs would just fit into his bicycle basket.

He couched ten under each arm, and then the lights flashed on.

Orson had to close his eyes against the glare. When he opened them he saw the four military policemen, their M-1911 pistols pointed at him. The voice from the rear of the room said:

"I'll be damned! It's a kid. What you got there, boy?"

The lieutenant walked over. Orson still held the records under his arms. The officer started to reach for them. But then he paused. "Ellis. Quick, take your shot."

The camera flashed. "That'll go for the record," said the lieutenant. "That's what you call getting caught with your pants down."

The military policeman put the records on the counter. He noticed they were all copies of a single album by Elvis Presley. He thought quickly about a more permissive way to handle the problem but decided the boy needed a lesson. He nodded to the corporal and said gravely, "Put the cuffs on him."

They led him away to the guard office. It was just after ten o'clock.

8

Wiesbaden, January 1959

FRANCIE KILLERE PULLED FRIDAY'S ISSUE OF *STARS*
and Stripes from her mailbox at headquarters but didn't open it,
stuffing it into the reticule she brought with her to work every
day. It lay there in the gratefully deep bag, the whole of the folded
GI paper out of sight, if only for the blessed half hour before she
reached home and had to open it, and read it.

The call the night before had been, as she'd have expected,
from General Hoffritz himself. He called not from his home—his
wife, Gracie, was jealous of Francie, and Amos was careful not to
antagonize her. On the office phone, General Hoffritz explained.
Orson's name had been identified by the MP's office as, obviously, the son of the only other Killere the MPs had ever heard of,
the personnel manager and close personal assistant of the general.
"Let me just tell you this." Hoffritz put her at ease. "Your son is
here and he is okay."

"Oh...dear. Oh. I *have* been a little worried. He is sometimes late but not this late. What is this all about, Amos? Where
is he?" Officially, he was General Hoffritz, but in private it had
been Amos ever since 1945, when she had met him as Captain
Amos.

She repeated: "Where is Orson?"

"Well, Francie, he is in the guardhouse. Under detention." He hurried the story, to get it off his back. "What he did, Francie, was break into the PX. The alarm went off, the MPs moved in—and detained him. Word got to me here at home. There aren't that many people around called Killere. The duty officer called me. And I'm calling you."

"I don't understand. Orson breaking into the PX? Amos, can I come down now and straighten it all out?"

"No. There's a problem, the obvious problem. You work for me, and your son has committed a Grade C offense. It helps that he's just fourteen. Now, we don't—if you follow the book—have any formal authority over a civilian. The proper thing to do would be to turn him over to the German police. My idea is to go for a hoked-up summary court-martial as if he *were* military. You'll have to pick up the costs for repairing the trapdoor. I have to keep my hand out of it exactly because you and I are friends and associates. But I know that the judge advocate will—well, I know he won't try to send Orson to Devil's Island."

"Why can't I see him?"

"Because I would have to waive the visiting hours to make that possible, and that's the kind of thing I don't want on the record. You understand?"

"Yes. So when *do* I see him?"

"I have ... got the word to Lieutenant Armour—he's the JA—that it makes sense to get the thing done, over with. A summary court-martial in form. That's the court-martial for minor offenses. Francie, be here at 8:45 in the morning. The trial—the hearing—will be at the adjutant's office. I will not, repeat, *not* be present."

"Who else will be? I mean, other than Orson and the—"

"The MPs who caught him. And, I'm afraid, a reporter from *Stars and Stripes*."

"Amos, thank you. Thank you ever so much, dear. Now forgive me, I have to hang up."

She did, and twenty minutes later she was at the gate. She didn't recognize the sentry, but her working pass and photograph sufficed and he waved her through.

At the guardhouse, a corporal was at the desk, reading a magazine.

"Ma'am, these aren't visiting hours—"

"I know. But I am Mrs. Killere, chief of personnel. And I have an envelope and would be very grateful"—Francie smiled warmly—"if you would just get it to the...young man...my son."

The corporal, a black man only a few years older than Orson, looked down at the envelope addressed to Orson Killere.

"Okay, ma'am. I guess I can do that."

Orson was grateful for the message. A single line. "I'll be there tomorrow. With love always, Mum."

Orson was released at ten the next morning, a Friday. The presiding officer, a major in the regular army, had given him a severe tongue-lashing and handed down his sentence. The hearing was over.

The following morning's issue of *Stars and Stripes,* which Francie now opened, featured Orson Killere, eyes wide-open to the flashbulb, each of his arms gripping phonograph records. The boldface caption read:

Elvis Fan Breaks Into Pershing PX
Lifts 20 'Elvis's Golden Records' Albums
Military 'Court' Imposes Harsh Sentence

And the text of the story:

S/S CAMP PERSHING, JANUARY 25. At what passed as a summary court-martial today, Major Angus Leavitt of the Judge Advocate Division heard evidence against Orson Killere, age fourteen.

Killere, the JA asserted, on the night of Thursday, January 24, broke into the PX at Camp Pershing at about 2100 hours. The military police were alerted by a burglar alarm and surprised the defendant with the goods he was trying to steal.

The defendant, Killere, had ten copies of the latest Elvis Presley album, *Elvis's Golden Records,* under each arm when he was apprehended.

Orson Killere is a ninth-grade student at the Roosevelt School in Wiesbaden. His mother, Mrs. Frances Killere, is a war widow. She is chief of personnel at Camp Pershing headquarters.

Major Leavitt questioned the defendant.

"How do you plead, young man?"

"Guilty, sir."

"Why did you attempt to steal the records?"

"Because I wanted to give them to people who don't have them."

"Have you not been taught, at home or at school, about theft?"

"Yes, sir. But some things, I think, are . . . well, sir, like common property. Like the air and the water."

"You are telling the court that the music of Elvis Presley should be free, like the air and water?"

"Yes, sir, that's my opinion."

The court recessed for fifteen minutes.

Major Leavitt ordered the defendant to stand. He lectured him about theft and passed the sentence:

"Orson Killere is sentenced to thirty days' confinement. He is released on probation in the custody of his mother, Mrs. Frances Killere. Any recurrence of criminal activity in the jurisdiction of this command will result in the immediate activation of detention."

The judge then gave out a further sentence: "The probationary sentence further forbids the defendant, Killere, from listening at his home to any music by Elvis Presley for the probationary period of thirty days."

Major Leavitt's gavel fell, and the case was closed.

A reporter sought to interview Orson Killere, but his mother told him to keep quiet, and walked with him to her car outside.

Francie read it again. She picked up the telephone and called her mother in South Carolina. They laughed together over the telephone.

"What's the dahlin' goin' to do, Francie, thirty whole days without Elvis in the morning?"

But Francie did not laugh about it when she sat Orson down in the kitchen.

"Do you know what you did? Suppose everybody felt they could just take things, whatever they wanted. You have some hard thinking to do."

Orson said he was terribly, terribly sorry to have hurt his mother and caused such commotion. What he was telling himself, he didn't tell his mother. It was that the pursuit of the revolutionary cause would inevitably bring on bourgeois disruptions and that these would weigh, on those afflicted, at an emotional level. He truly loved his mother and told himself quite convincingly that he would die for her if necessary; but he would not undertake to explain to her why such a gesture as he had made at the PX was integral to the revolutionary idea. No, he'd bury that. He'd just tell her that he was pained at—the pain she had been submitted to.

And he was, very much so. But Francie Killere sensed her son's aloofness from the implications of what he had done. Orson was sorry, she had to face it, primarily for having been caught, and for distressing his mother.

The next morning, before his Saturday classes, he faced the music at school. He was not surprised to find a note on the bulletin board summoning him to the office of the principal.

Major Brennan didn't even ask him to sit down. "On the business at the PX two days ago, Orson, I have instructed the faculty not to raise the matter with you. You have been publicly reprimanded and punished, and I can only hope you are coming to your senses. You are on probation for the balance of the winter term."

That was easy enough. But what he most eagerly sought was a few minutes with Mr. Simon, who would surely applaud his enterprise.

After the compulsory exercise period—Orson's sport was boxing—he walked to the office of Siegfried Simon and knocked on the door.

"Come in."

Mr. Simon was alone, correcting papers. "Sit down, Orson. You've sat in the same chair the last twenty times you've been here. Why are you looking at the chair so questioningly?"

Orson let out a nervous smile and sat down in the austere, straight-backed chair in the small unadorned office he had come to know so well. The office of his mentor and, now, his confidant.

"I wanted you to know I didn't tell them—not *anybody*—not

the judge advocate, nor the press guy, nor my mother, even...
about you and your ideas—our ideas—about common property."

Mr. Simon nodded his head. "It would have been all right,
Orson, if you had told them what my private ideas are. Mc-
Carthyism isn't going to get me fired because I'm a utopian socialist. And anyway, Senator McCarthy is dead. What would not
have been all right is if you had told them that I urged you to
steal the records. Urged you to steal *anything*. I think property
should be commonly held, but I don't believe you can set aside
laws as a matter of opportunity."

Simon looked over at his library. "If—to use a fancy word—
if the tocsin sounded and its summons moved everyone to act
together—like the men and women of Nineveh, united in repen-
tance—or like the hungry and war-ridden in Petrograd in 1917—
that's one thing. I hate to quote Lenin, but he'd have described
what you did at the camp as 'infantile behavior.'"

Orson looked away. He had thought that Mr. Simon, even if
he did not say so publicly, would have approved his initiative. He
was now sorry in a very different way from what he felt about
upsetting his mother. He felt he had misunderstood, and perhaps
traduced in some way the ideals he held in common with Mr.
Simon.

At two on Saturday afternoon, a white BMW sedan drove up and
parked outside Francie Killere's house.

The driver, in uniform with a private's insignia, opened the
door, walked up the pathway, and rang the bell.

Francie opened the door. Orson was sitting in view at the
kitchen table, playing solitaire.

"You Mrs. Killere, ma'am?"

"I am Mrs. Killere. What can I do for you?"

"Well," said the private, smiling over at Orson in the kitchen, "I'm Elvis Presley. And I've come to sing to Orson, on account he cayunt hear me on the record player."

Francie Killere gasped and looked back at Orson.

Orson was frozen, a card in his right hand.

"Can we come in, ma'am?"

Francie nodded.

Elvis signaled to the car. Another soldier opened the car door, wrestled out some equipment, and walked up to the house, carrying a guitar.

"Here you go, Elvis." He handed it over.

Elvis took it and smiled at Mrs. Killere. "This is my long-time buddy Charlie Hodge. Charlie, this is Orson's mother. Can we come in, ma'am?"

9

Wiesbaden, January 1959

ELVIS STAYED FOR TWO HOURS. TWO ENCHANTED HOURS, Orson thought. There was the beautiful music and the world-famous voice, but there was also the animal proximity. To be in the same *room* with Elvis! In *my* house! Singing for *me*! Did this alone justify the PX adventure? Was God rewarding Orson for his concern for the underprivileged who had no Elvis Presley records? And how long would he sit there on that kitchen chair playing?

"He just loves to sing, ma'am," Charlie told Mrs. Killere when she went in to make coffee. "It's his day off—we get off at noon Saturday, not due back till eight A.M. Monday. Elvis got a real bang out of that story in the paper. He just said to me, just said, 'Charlie, you figure out how to get to that kid's house. I'm going to go and play for him myself!' Then Elvis went to the phone and put in a call to Colonel Parker. He's not a military gentleman, ma'am. He's our—he's Elvis's—manager. He calls all the shots."

Charlie laughed. "I'd be surprised if the Thirty-seventh Division would *move* without checking with Colonel Parker. I was kiddin', ma'am. But Elvis relies on him, and over the telephone—he doesn't care who's in the room when he calls: I was there,

Lamar was there, Vernon and Red West were there, and he gets through to the Colonel in Nashville. Now, that means," he ducked to one side so that Francie could reach into the cupboard for the cups, "that means the phone rings in the Colonel's hotel—he always stays in a hotel, never mind where he is at—at 6:30 *in the morning*."

Charlie moved over to the door and closed it, so Elvis wouldn't hear. He was singing "All Shook Up" and banging on the floor with his right foot.

"Easier to hear now, ma'am. So Elvis says to the Colonel, after the Colonel gets through chewing his ahhh...chewing him out for calling so early. Elvis wants to know if the Colonel didn't think it was *unconstitutional* for the major out there, at the court-martial, to tell your boy he couldn't *listen* to Elvis. Well, that's not accurate, because he's listening to Elvis right this minute—Elvis *loves* that "One Night I Got Stung"—I mean, ordering your boy not to play Elvis on his record machine! That's like...that's like saying he couldn't read a book! And the Supreme Court has ruled *that's* not constitutional, you bet. Here, let me help you, ma'am."

With coffee on a tray, they opened the door from the kitchen to the living room. Orson was sitting on the edge of his chair, his glasses embedded even more deeply than usual into his face, eyes lit with pleasure and fascination. Elvis had one foot on the bottom rung of the stool by the small dining table, singing the last words of the song, *Missin' you dahlin', missin' you.*

Elvis put down his guitar and took a cup. "Well, that's real nice of you, ma'am, don't mind if I do. I take a lot of cream and sugar. Charlie knows how much. And yes," he reached over to the plate Francie held out to him, "I'll take one of those nice cookies. No, I'll take *two* of them."

Elvis set the cookies down on the table, then took the plate from Francie and held it out to Orson. Orson just shook his head.

"No, sir, Mr. Presley. I don't want anything, nothing... to get in the way of this dream."

Elvis's face lit up. He gobbled first one, then the second cookie, and reached for the guitar, which he hoisted up on his thigh.

"Want to hear something I bet you haven't heard before? I'm gonna tape it just as soon as I get back to the States. I wish Scotty and Bill were here, don't you, Charlie? Scotty," he addressed Mrs. Killere, "is—"

Orson interrupted. "That's Scotty Moore, Mum. Mr. Presley's guitarist." Orson went on, speaking at rapid speed. "Bill Black is his bass player. They were with him from the beginning, in 1954, at the Sun Records Studio."

Elvis let his hand down from the guitar, looking over at Orson with a grin of surprise and pleasure. "You're a bright boy, Orson. I'm really glad I met you."

Orson Killere's face broke out into a jubilant smile of pleasure. He stared at Elvis Presley, unbelieving.

Elvis continued. "I'll play you this one song. Then, I guess, Charlie and me got to go on, the boys will be wonderin' about us. But, Orson, you must come and visit me and the gang at my place in Bad Nauheim. We have our own house, you know. Me an' Dad an' Granma. Charlie here will write down the address. It's only like a half hour or so from your camp, depending on how fast you like to drive."

Orson stood up. Elvis, about to stroke the guitar, stopped. "Something wrong, boy?"

"It's just, sir, could you just let me—it won't take five minutes... *three* minutes, I promise. But I have a friend, and she'd kill me, kill me with her bare hands, if you went without her saying hello."

"Sure, sure," Elvis smiled. "You go on ahead. I'll chat with your ma, an' maybe have one more cookie."

Orson sprang from the chair, moved to the door, wrenched it open, and ran across the yard to the sidewalk.

He was back in minutes, throwing the door open. "This is Priscilla, Mr. Presley. Priscilla Ann Beaulieu."

Elvis now put the guitar down on the table. He stared at her. He said nothing, but his eyes widened.

"Priscilla. Priscilla whatever-your-last-name-was. You gotta be the most beautiful little girl in the *whole* world."

Tears escaped her eyes as she took his hand.

10

Wiesbaden, May 1959

WHEN, AFTER A FEW MONTHS, ORSON'S PERSPECTIVES on the exciting friendship had broadened, he allowed himself to ponder Elvis's manifest attraction to Priscilla. The episode of January had evolved into a friendship, something very different from the mere stunt of that first visit, and Priscilla was an organic part of it. It had begun rapidly.

On the Monday after Elvis's visit, when Orson was back from school, the telephone rang. The caller announced himself as Vernon Presley.

Orson stumbled a bit over the line. The voice on the line helped out by saying, "I'm Elvis's father. He wants to talk to you."

"Yes, sir. I'm right here."

"I know you're right there, son, because I'm talking to you. But the thing of it is, Elvis right now is on the other line talking to... talking to the United States. He doesn't much like to wait on the calls, so can you stay on the line?"

Orson said he would be glad to stay on the line. "You can take all the time you want, Mr. Presley."

Elvis came on after a bit and began by saying: "Now, let's get this straight, Orson. I'm Elvis, not Mr. Presley. I don't like *Mr.*

Presley. I can't do nothin' about the United States Army. They're callin' me Private Presley—" He broke into song. "*Private Presley went to town/ Ee-ya-ee-ya yo/ And when he got there wha'd he do?/ Came on, came on back*—You like that?"

"I sure do. Elvis."

"Well now, look here, I thought it would be nice if you and your girlfriend Priscilla—"

"She's not *exactly* my girlfriend, she's just my *best friend*."

Elvis laughed. "That's nice. Yeah, you got to be careful of this *girlfriend* business. Why can't we jus' have *girls* who are simultaneously *our friends*? You agree, Orson? I mean, I'd like to be a *friend* of Priscilla—and of you. Without, you know, people sayin' I have a new girlfriend."

"Elvis, Priscilla is only fourteen years old."

"I like that about her. I wish she'd never grow any older. Well, I'm not sure. I'm not sure I wanna say that. If she was jus'—like *six weeks* older—I'd like to give her a real sweet kiss. You ever kissed Priscilla?"

Orson was at once taken aback and provoked. Would it be unmanly to say no, he hadn't actually ever done that? He hadn't ever kissed Priscilla?

"Well, Elvis, Priscilla and I sort of grew up together, and people who grow up together don't kiss. 'Least, that's how I understand it."

Elvis laughed. "Well, maybe you'll want to experiment. When *you* get six weeks older. But before that happens, I want you and Priscilla to come on around and have a little dinner at my house. I got a nice big rented house an' I come back to it every night after my army duty. Nobody bothers me, though every now and then there's a photographer hangin' around, but my people, they're careful not to give out my address. I tole you I'd have Charlie— you know, Charlie's a pretty good musician on his own. He writes songs, and every now and then I try out one of his songs. I said I'd have Charlie give you my address. Well, I'm gonna give it to you mahself. *Dad?!*" He yelled for his father. "Remin' me, what's our address? I mean," he now returned to Orson, "we've lived here nine months, but I'm *always* forgettin' those German spellings."

Finally he called out, "Fourteen Goethestrasse. Want me to spell that?"

No need, Orson told him.

"Now, what I'm proposin' is you and Priscilla come here for dinner on Friday night. I'll send a car for you, now I know where you are. I don't want your Ma to have to worry about anything. I'll have you picked up at 5:30."

Orson couldn't think what to say. He tried to be urbane about this invitation to have dinner with the most illustrious person in the whole world, with maybe the exception of Winston Churchill and President Eisenhower.

"Can I—can I bring anything along you'd like? Mum makes great lemon meringue pies."

Elvis hesitated a moment. "Sure. Tell your mum we'd be happy to have one of her lemon meringue pies. Unless she's given out so many to the court-martial people she's jus' plain tired of bakin' them!"

Orson said he was certain his mother would never be so tired she couldn't make a pie for Elvis Presley.

It was a memorable evening. Orson established, in conversation, that the driver, Erhard, was a German who drove regularly for Elvis. Orson sat in the front seat, next to Erhard, Priscilla in back. He eased into his questioning. When he thought he was going too far, he would revert to Priscilla in the back seat, talking to her in English. Erhard didn't know any English.

"Do you think it's okay if I ask him how many people bunk down at Elvis's place?"

"No. I don't think it's okay. But you can ask him, oh, how many people does Elvis usually have for dinner on Friday nights? That would be okay, if you put it that way."

Orson tried out the question, and Erhard willingly answered it. Sometimes only four or five, he said. Sometimes ten or fifteen. "He likes to give his guests Southern cooking, especially when it's Germans he invites. But he doesn't like to have them unless they speak in English. He doesn't even *try* to speak our language. Why is your German so good?"

"I've been at school here for nine years."

"Ah, I understand. And you, Miss Priscilla?"

Priscilla had no problem in German. "I've been here the same time."

Erhard, who looked thirty or thirty-five, said he was going to try to learn English. He and his wife were going to study it together. Elvis had told him he would pay if they would learn from the sergeant in his platoon, who gave English lessons on weekends. "Mr. Presley said he didn't mind if I used his car to go to where the sergeant teaches."

Priscilla spoke now in English. "Do you think, Orson, I could ask him if he was in the war?"

"Priscilla!" Orson spoke impatiently. "Of *course* he was in the war. *Everybody* in Germany was in the war, unless they had no legs, or three legs. Mr. Simon was in the war, you know. And he was wounded. That's probably why's he's alive."

"You know a lot about Mr. Simon. What do you do, all those times you go to see him in his study?"

Orson was mysterious in his response. "We talk about world affairs," he said sniffily. "Like what's going to happen when Khrushchev travels to America to meet with President Eisenhower. And what are they going to do when unemployment and inflation in America get *really* bad. That kind of thing." He felt he was rudely excluding Erhard from the conversation, speaking in English to Priscilla. He turned to face the driver. "Erhard, when you were in the war, were you captured? Or were you in one of those divisions that surrendered?"

Erhard snapped, "I was a prisoner of war, from January 1945."

Orson wondered if Erhard and Orson's dead father had once shot at each other.

They slowed down as they approached Goethestrasse, with its substantial buildings, still in need of repair. The house at the corner was Number 14, stucco, solid, plain, dirty white. A man dressed in plain clothes looked out from in front of the garage. The day was warm, and his tie was loosely worn. He nodded at Erhard and motioned him to drive in. Then Erhard bounced out of the driver's seat and opened the rear door for Priscilla, who got out and, when Orson came around to join her, extended her hand. He took it, and together they approached the front door.

11

Bad Nauheim, May 1959

IN MAY ELVIS ASKED HIS FATHER, VERNON, TO TENDER the invitation. "Better chance they'd say yes to you than to me, right, Dad?"

Vernon Presley was remarried now, after the painful death of his beloved Gladys, buried at Graceland only weeks before Elvis had shipped out to Germany. He now lived in a corner of Elvis's house in Bad Nauheim, occupying himself with Elvis's personal finances, entering the profuse royalties paid him every month and writing checks for his son's expenses and extravagances.

He generally did, unquestioningly, what his superstar son asked him to do, and he agreed to undertake this latest mission. Elvis had decided on a trip to Paris, to be taken during his five-day furlough coming up. It would be a sightseeing trip and a fun trip, with Charlie, Joe, and Lamar, and his idea was to ask along Orson and Priscilla. Orson, of course, knew the city well, after visiting there often. But Priscilla hadn't ever been in Paris.

"Tell the captain"—Elvis was referring to Captain Beaulieu, Priscilla's stepfather—"that she'll be very well looked after."

They had visited together frequently, at Elvis's home in Bad Nauheim, and at Orson's, in Wiesbaden, in the past four months.

Elvis was passionate in conversations with his entourage, the so-called Memphis Mafia, on the subject of Priscilla and the singular beauty of the girl with the deep blue eyes and the oval face and bright, shining expression.

"You watch, Dad," he said joshingly to his father. "One day I will marry Priscilla Ann Beaulieu. But I wouldn't touch her before that, never, not for a hundred gold records. Not for an Oscar Award."

The answer from Mrs. Beaulieu to the suggestion that Priscilla go to Paris with Elvis was delivered in her living room to Mr. Vernon Presley, the petitioner, in the presence of a startled Captain Beaulieu, who had come in from the side door, carrying the wood for the fireplace.

"Excuse me, Mr. Presley, but is your son crazy? I don't mean that...insultingly. Priscilla is fifteen years old!"

So that idea was abandoned. But Elvis still wanted the company of Orson, even if he came alone.

The approach to Mrs. Francie Killere, at the other end of the Frankfurterstrasse, was differently handled. Vernon Presley, addressing his only slightly younger contemporary, said, "Elvis needs somebody he can completely trust and who knows French to help him get around. Sure, Paris will be looking out for Elvis, and sure, he's got the two bodyguards and he's got three, four of his pals. But he really would like Orson along. He thinks the whole world of your son."

Francie was not entirely surprised. She liked Elvis Presley, and she had observed with amusement, curiosity, and approval the hardening friendship between her fifteen-year-old son and the King of Rock and Roll, the entertainer whom, it seemed, the entire younger generation was prepared to adore. She knew there wasn't any chance she could just say a formulaic no and let it go at that. Not with Orson. This was an invitation he would hear about, perhaps directly from Elvis, never mind that Vernon was being used to make the whole thing a little more conventional, the invitation being to a fifteen-year-old boy. She told Vernon she would think about it, but she doubted it was the right thing to do.

Elvis had several times visited at Wiesbaden, and Orson and Priscilla had three times traveled to the house at 14 Goethestrasse. Francie herself had come close to experiencing the Elvis House at Bad Nauheim. Just two weeks before, sharing the front seat of the Fiat, Priscilla's mother at the wheel, she and Ann Beaulieu had dropped off Orson and Priscilla at Goethestrasse at six. The mothers had dinner and drove to the movie theater at Friedberg to see *Some Like It Hot.* They were back at ten, as arranged, to pick up their brood. The plainclothesman outside motioned them to stop, as usual, at the street in front of the house. He ducked in and, a moment later, Orson and Priscilla came out, followed by Elvis. He trotted over to the car and shook hands with both the ladies, inviting them to come on in. Orson froze, for fear his mother would accept—it just wasn't her scene in there. But Francie declined, pleading the lateness of the hour.

That much amused Orson, the lateness of the hour in deference to Elvis! But he thought better of discussing Elvis's hours with his mother. Ann Beaulieu took advantage of the autobahn, where there was no speed limit, and drove at a fast clip. Orson was agog with it all. He tried to sing one of Elvis's new songs, but gave up.

"You try it, Priss. I'll give you the beat."

She launched into the ballad "Willow Weep for Me." She had got the song's title right but couldn't remember the lyrics, and made do with just the melody, while Orson clapped his hands in syncopated accompaniment.

Orson laughed. "Elvis's accompanists did better than I did! The two guys, Mum, who play in the army band were there tonight, Corporal George something or other and Warrant Officer Elmsley—"

"Elmley," Priscilla corrected.

"Whatever, he's a hell of a drummer." Orson practiced a drummer's exercise on his mother's head with his fingers until she lightly brushed them away. He moved his fingers to Priscilla's head.

"Did you have a nice dinner?" Francie wanted to know.

"Oh yes!" Priscilla used her index finger to count out what they had been given, item by item. "There was biscuits, corn, fried chicken, beans, yams, bacon, jam, jelly, apple pie, and peanut-brittle ice cream. What a feast."

"What did you have to drink?" her mother wanted to know.

"Well, the guys had beer, but Elvis—"

" 'Elvis' you're calling him?"

"Mum, you know that. From way back." Orson could hardly remember back to when he hadn't known Elvis. "No way you could call him 'Mr. Presley.' Not except for that first time."

The car stopped. Francie and Orson stepped out. Before closing the car door, Orson gave Priscilla's hand a hard squeeze.

What would Jean-Jacques Killere have thought of it all! Five prospective days for Orson in his beloved Paris without any thought of buses and subways and waiting in line. She wavered for one moment. Then shook her head. Of course the trip was out of the question. Orson was simply *too young,* never mind how precocious he was, how tall and good-looking and well-read.

She did have one development working for her. The thought crossed her mind: Orson's adored Mr. Simon had scheduled his annual three-day history-and-art trip to Munich, for which Orson had enthusiastically signed up. Francie walked nervously to her desk and opened her calendar. *Praise the Lord.* The two trips were both scheduled to begin on the same day. That would make life easier for Francie Killere.

Orson learned of the invitation. When Vernon reported discouragement after visiting Francie, Elvis called Charlie. "You tell Orson, Charlie. Figure out a way to get him to go."

Orson and Charlie Hodge were now good friends. Elvis had taken to relaying through Charlie both his invitations to come to him at Bad Nauheim and Elvis's occasional self-invitations to drop by at Wiesbaden. Now Charlie arrived at the FDR School, bringing his own sandwich to share with Orson at lunch, as arranged over the telephone the night before.

Charlie reported first on Elvis's invitation for June 16. Then on Vernon's unsuccessful mission "to the ladies, Mrs. Killer and Mrs. Beaulieu," the afternoon before.

"What did my mother say?" Orson's voice strained with excitement.

"Vernon said she didn't say much. All she said was that you are only fifteen years old."

"Is that all? She didn't just say no?"

"I'm afraid, Orson, that's what Elvis's pa makes out of it. It was more than just no from the Beaulieus. Captain Beaulieu almost went to the closet for a shotgun."

"Thanks, Charlie." Orson's mind was racing. "You'll hear from me." He had to talk with Mr. Simon. At four that afternoon he knocked on the door, sat down, and came to the point.

"Mr. Simon, you've heard about my friendship with Mr. Presley? With Elvis?"

"Yes. I think everybody has heard of it."

"Well, what he did, coming to my house and singing for me,

that was a kind of stunt. One-time stuff. But what people don't know, and I'm not going to go around telling people, is that Elvis and I are—friends now. He comes over to my house, and he likes Priscilla a lot. Well. He's asked me to...to be his guide in Paris. You know, translate for him and stuff."

Mr. Simon nodded his head, then tilted it to shield his eyes from the sun coming in through the high window of the office, once a horse barn.

"Well, that sounds interesting enough. Orson, what do you want to talk with me about? You know I'll be glad to talk with you about any of your concerns."

Orson flushed and looked down at the desk, with the blue examination books neatly assembled there. "There are two problems, Mr. Simon. One of them is that Elvis is leaving on the same day we're...you're...booked to go to Munich—"

"And the second problem?"

"My mother isn't going to let me go."

"Well, the first problem is easy. Munich is seven hundred years old, has seen a lot of war, plus a Hitler-attempted putsch and then another world war. It will be there when next you want to see it."

Orson interjected his gratitude. "That's swell of you. But I would want to see it with you."

"Perhaps that can also be arranged. Munich is not far. Now, on the second matter, it's up to you to persuade your mother that a trip to Paris with the most celebrated living popular musician would be—well, would be a unique experience."

"What if she says no?"

Siegfried Simon drew back and, with his index finger, stroked the eye with the scar over it.

"Tell her you're either going to go with Elvis to Paris, or you are going to Paris on your own and connect up with Mr. Presley."

Orson stared at him in disbelief.

"Look, Orson, you are only fifteen, but you are more advanced than most seventeen-year-olds. In this world you can't tell other people what to do, unless you are a dictator—"

"Or a court-martial judge."

Siegfried Simon smiled. "Sure, there are lines of authority that stretch right down to presidents and mayors and city councilmen and policemen and schoolteachers—and parents. But there is even biblical authority for taking control, when the time has come, over your own life."

Mr. Simon paused. "I know you, and I trust you not to repeat what I've said. I wouldn't give the same advice to any other boy of your age. Now run along. I have work to do."

Orson got up from his chair. He stopped, then lowered his head slightly, his eyes, behind the tight tortoiseshell glasses, wide with mute thanks.

12

Wiesbaden, June 1959

FRANCIE KILLERE FELT KEENLY THE ABSENCE OF A husband, a father who could help provide guidance. She knew that Orson had developed reserves of determination on which he might be willing to draw, even mutinously, on the matter of Paris with Elvis. Back from work, she put off talking to him about it when he arrived on his bicycle. She knew the invitation had been conveyed to him personally. He had told Priscilla, Priscilla told her mother, her mother called Francie at work.

Orson made his way directly to his own room. She hadn't detained him except with a formal greeting and the routine kiss. But after preparing the meal and putting it to one side, she resolved to face it. She called him to come down.

"Why is it so important to you, darling? This trip."

Orson spoke slowly but didn't turn his head.

"I've been thinking ever since—ever since January—that Elvis had me along only on account of Priscilla. When Captain Beaulieu said no to Priscilla going and Elvis said he still wanted me along, that was terribly important."

Francie said she understood.

"I felt for a while"—now there was a tremor in his voice—"that Priscilla really wasn't interested in me anymore, just in Elvis; and that Elvis wasn't interested in me, just Priscilla. Now I know that Elvis is really my friend and I'm not, just, you know, the guy who brings Priscilla along. That's why I just—can't—really—say no, Mum."

Francie said again that she understood. She left for the kitchen to stir the soup. Five minutes later, setting the kitchen table, she said he could go. He embraced her and, in his excitement, couldn't get to sleep until well after midnight.

Orson stood outside the waiting room at the railroad station at Friedberg. Charlie Hodge had told him their train would leave at 2:13. Orson left his bus just after 1:30, carrying his navy blue sea bag, inherited from his father. At a quarter to two, he noticed the policeman who came by, stationing himself conspicuously on the platform. A metallic woman's voice, in flat Hochdeutsch, came in over the speakers, announcing periodic arrivals. *"The 13:37 to Stuttgart via Frankfurt and Mannheim coming in on track three...The 13:42 Hanover via Gottingen is next on track four."*

A police car drove up, pulling under the majestic, leafy oak tree in front of the building. The policeman began to ward off cars coming in routinely to discharge passengers, as also cars coming in to meet incoming passengers. The arriving cars were directed to an area well away from the busy part of the platform. Orson moved out to the incoming end of the platform. He heard a woman's voice protesting. "But, officer, I always come exactly here to meet my husband, he's on the early shift, and comes in on the 14:02." The policeman muttered: "Security," and motioned her to the recessed parking lot. Suddenly Orson realized that yet another policeman was there, addressing him.

"Where are you going, *junger Mann*?"

"I am going on the 14:13, Herr Polizist."

"You will have to wait there—" He pointed to a far end of the platform. "From here down it is reserved."

Then they started to come quickly, from all sides. Boys, too, but mostly teenage girls. They appeared in the dress of students and the working young. There was a sound of anticipation. One young man leaned back on the tree and held up his Grundig portable, turning up the sound on the radio station and chanting "El-*vis*! El-*vis*!" The word caught on, and the demand now came rhythmically from a chorus rapidly growing in size. Three more policemen materialized, and soon they had strung out a rope designed to segregate the eastern side of the station.

It was two, and the crowd turned now away from the young man and his radio, edging toward the station and the policemen. The cry had now changed. "*Elvis kommt!* Elvis is coming!"

It wouldn't be easy for Orson to join his party, he reflected. He might have to board the front end of the train and then make his way back.

Three cars approached slowly. In the first were four men in mufti. Authorized officials, evidently. The lead driver flashed the badge in his wallet and was acknowledged by the security policeman in charge. The first car moved forward to the platform, and the second car drew alongside. The third car backed up at right angles to the other two, blocking access. Two men left it and stationed themselves alongside. The three vehicles formed a T with two vertical stems.

The shouting grew louder. But the doors of the second car remained resolutely shut, though Orson could detect a window lowered in the back seat.

At 2:05 the car door at the right opened.

It was Elvis. The trim soldier, sideburns gone, uniform pressed, jacket tailored, with a corporal's chevron, conspicuously new.

The crowd was instantly delirious. He walked to the cordon and started to shake hands. The police kept the barrier firm. The approaching train's whistles blew. Elvis raised both hands saluting his fans with a face-splitting smile. He tried a few words in German. "*Vielen Dank!*" Thank you very much. "Thank you very much, my *geliebte Freunden.*" As he backed up to the railroad car now alongside, he repeated the words. Four men had emerged carrying baggage. A conductor pointed to the reserved rear car. Orson attempted to break through, but the cordon was firm. He shouted out desperately: "Elvis! Charlie! Lamar! Joe! It's me! Orson!"

Joe Esposito spotted him, walked over to the policeman, and spoke the necessary words.

The cordon was lifted and Orson, sea bag in hand, ducked under and rushed aft. He waited for the others to mount the gangway, then turned to look out to where they had come from, hoping wistfully that Priscilla, or his mother—or Mr. Simon, or—he smiled to himself, General Hoffritz!—might just be there to see Orson Killere going off with Elvis in his private compartment. With Elvis Presley!

He climbed the gangway into the private railroad car the Colonel had arranged for Elvis and his traveling companions.

13

Friedberg, June 1959

ORSON HAD NEVER TRAVELED IN A COMPARTMENT ON a train. Not even a shared compartment, let alone a private one. There were eight in the private car, equal in size. The first two were reserved for Elvis. Then Lamar Fike, then Charlie Hodge, and Joe Esposito. Beyond the cabins, in the rear car of the train, were two saloons. At the first a porter stood behind the bar. There were seats for six people. Adjoining it was the second, larger saloon, with a broad window and a tray platform, permitting a view of the early, full-blown central Rhineland spring. At the forward end, abutting the bar, was an upright piano. The porter had handed Elvis an envelope. It enclosed a note from the Colonel: *Elvis. You'll be met, of course. Thought you'd enjoy the piano. Cook me up a couple of nice new songs. Yrs, Tom.*

Elvis was overjoyed. He pulled out the stool and started to play and sing. He began with "Mystery Train." Charlie picked up two ballpoint pens, went into the bar, and came back with a bottle of Red Label scotch. Using the pens he beat out an accompanying rhythm. Elvis sang at the top of his lungs. There was applause. Orson having sidled up, he could join happily in it. Elvis stood beaming, his hands outstretched as though the applause had come in from a packed house at Ryman Auditorium in Nashville. He bowed his head and turned it left to right. "Thank you, thank you." He sat down and sang "Hound Dog." Again the applause, now routine. He sat down a third time but stopped and turned his head. "Lamar. Lamar? For this one I want my guitar. Fetch it here for me, attaboy." Lamar returned with the guitar, and Elvis sang.

It was endlessly so. The porter took orders for drinks. Elvis called for a beer. Orson asked for a Coca-Cola. When time came to eat, a record player was turned on. And there, stacked on three shelves, courtesy of the Colonel, was a full collection of Elvis's records, including the just-released *Elvis's Golden Records Volume 2.*

They talked of Paris. "Poontang city," said Joe, face alight.

"Say that in French, Joe," Lamar challenged.

"Ask Orson how to say it."

Everyone turned to Orson, sitting with his Coke, his eyes and glasses barely visible through the hair that had fallen down when his head bobbed along with Elvis's songs. Orson blushed. He began to stammer. Elvis delivered him. "I'm gonna see *all* the sights in Paris," the King announced. "Not just the kind of thing you dudes are thinkin' about. An' you know, I know you know, I've got myself a *private* guide here who's just as good when he speaks French as he is when he speaks English. Right, Orson? Let's have a drink to the first person in history a military judge told he couldn't listen to Elvis records."

"Now that is *capital* punishment," Lamar broke in, raising his glass of bourbon and ginger ale.

Elvis addressed Orson. He had taken to calling him, pure and simple, Killer. "You don't sing, do ya, Killer? I know you don't because Priscilla tole me she does the singin' when you're together."

Orson spoke now. "Can't say I do, can't quite hit the notes. Priscilla, she's very good." Orson thought to stress his familiarity with her. "She's working on a couple of German songs. They call them *Lieder*."

"Maybe I'll train you. You'll be able to say you had the most expensive music teacher in the history of the world! Now, sing after me... *Twinkle, twinkle lit-tul star, how I won-der what you are*. Okay. Come on now, Orson. Give him a hand, guys."

Orson closed his eyes and raised his hands to his collar, as if to liberate the sound.

"Twinkle twinkle liiiiitl star—"

Elvis's face was wreathed with pleasure. With one hand he restrained his companions, with the other, urged Orson on....

"How I wonnnnn-der what you are."

They all burst into applause, and Orson opened his eyes. Suddenly he said, "Elvis, could I maybe have a beer?"

"First beer?" Elvis asked, eyebrows raised, his upper lip raised, quizzically.

"Yes, sir."

"Just yes is good enough." He motioned to the porter. They all raised their glasses, and Orson was given a tall, foaming glass of Jever. Elvis raised his guitar to his lap. And the song came out in his own bel canto.

> *Twinkle, twinkle, little staahrr,*
> *How I wonder what you aahrr,*
> *Up above the world so high,*
> *Like a diamond in the skyyye!*
> *Twinkle, twinkle, little starahrr,*
> *How I wonder what you aahrr*

There was silence.

Quietly, then, Charlie said, "That was fine, Elvis. Real fine."

Had he ever been so happy, Orson wondered?

14

Paris, June 1959

THEY WERE MET AT THE STATION IN PARIS BY THE
French producer of Elvis's records. Jean Aberbach took them to
the top-floor suite at the Prince de Galles Hotel. This gave them
a panoramic view of the city, the grand ten thousand acres that
had been the center of civilization for three hundred years, had
been fought for and conquered twice, and were pulsing now with
the energies of a reborn spirit, with a new constitution and a new
president.

"I know this is a vacation trip," Jean said. "So I haven't laid
out a schedule. We can do anything for you you like."

Elvis said he was interested in the historical Paris, but also in
the nightlife. "Orson here can take care of mah daytime education, right Orson?" Yes, he would like to see some of the regular
sights, and perhaps he could get about unrecognized. Aberbach
was skeptical.

They walked out together to a sidewalk café for late coffee
and refreshments. Elvis kept on his uniform, which contributed
to his anonymity. Orson motioned to the waiter.

"Ask if they've got any bacon," Elvis said to Orson. "You
know, I like bacon burned to a crisp. Maybe a fried egg or two,

over light, maybe three." Orson talked with the waiter, who began to examine Elvis. He kept one eye on him while writing down the orders from Lamar, Joe, and Charlie, relayed through Orson.

Then it happened. A girl came over with her school pad. Could she have an autograph?

Elvis's rule was never to decline a request for an autograph or a handshake—or even a joint photograph. On the other hand, he had no illusions about what was now likely to happen.

And, indeed, a line began to form. Elvis turned his head from the boy whose hand he was shaking and, the smile on his face unbroken, rapped out his instructions.

"Joe, Lamar, you stay on. Orson, you take me back to the hotel. Jean, you send a car at nine."

Jean nodded. Elvis rose. Orson led him at a rapid pace across the street and down to the hotel. Back in the suite Elvis ordered lunch, then addressed Orson: "Order us a car and show me Paris from inside the car, okay, Killer?"

They were off. Orson directed the driver to the Quai d'Orsay and the Tuileries. ("It's prettier," Elvis commented, "than our own capital. Or that's my impression, anyways.") And then to the Eiffel Tower ("Maybe I can go up it at night?"). No. Orson told him that the elevator of the Eiffel Tower didn't go up past the second floor any later than five in the afternoon. They made their way out of town to Versailles.

It was after six when they headed back to Paris. Elvis was stupefied by the size of the palace and the beauty and expanse of the gardens he surveyed from the gate. He considered entering, but was put off by the density of the tourists on this Monday afternoon in June. "Let's just go on back to the hotel," he said finally.

An hour later, after fighting the traffic, they were in the Prince de Galles. In the large salon servicing their four bedrooms, Charlie and Lamar were reading American magazines. Joe was asleep. Elvis said he would nap too, and went into the presidential room.

Orson had been assigned the small room set apart for valets and aides of visiting dignitaries. From there he placed a collect call to his mother. He tried to express the excitement of the last twenty-four hours, but settled for enumerating the things he had done and the sights he had seen since leaving Wiesbaden. He said he would not have time to visit his grandmother at Poissy, but that he would try to get to Père Lachaise cemetery and visit his father's grave, and offer up a prayer for him. "And for you, Mom. I love you a whole lot." He promised to call her again "if there's time."

He lay down on the bed, closed his eyes, and slept.

Two hours later, Orson still asleep, Elvis emerged. Jean Aberbach and his companions were waiting for him, seated on the sofas circled about the large marble coffee table.

"Now," Elvis addressed Lamar and Aberbach, "we got a problem here. Orson. I mean, he's only what, fifteen? Do they let minors go to the places like where we're going tonight, Jean?"

"They let them in if they're with you." He winked.

Elvis brooded on the quandary. "I don't want to do nothin' wrong with Orson along."

"*Come on*," Lamar said, stretching his huge frame. "He's near-on sixteen. It's time for him to get laid. An' anyway, he's a good-looking kid, they'll line up for him."

Elvis was angry. He snapped. "Look, we're *not* headin' out for a whorehouse. Can you understan' that, Lamar?" He turned to Jean. "You tell us, Jean, what you've got lined up for us."

Jean Aberbach told him they would go first to the world-famous Folies Bergère. "That's really great entertainment, Elvis. Beautiful girls—they don't wear much, that's true. Great food and wine. Great music."

"Then what?"

"Then we'll go to the Lido. The girls there are mostly English. Tall, beautiful ladies. Great nightlife."

"Then what?"

"*Eh bien.*" Jean said that foreign visitors—and indeed, he himself—loved Le Bantu. "Le Bantu doesn't open up until three A.M."

"Okay, then. We'll take Orson with us and maybe also to the Lido. But after that we send him home before...going on."

Jean Aberbach nodded his head. "That's easily arranged."

Orson was roused by Charlie. "Time for chow."

Orson changed his shirt and came into the salon. Elvis was in high spirits. The food was lavishly served. He sipped champagne, while watching his companions drink more deeply. Twice he got up to view the lights of Paris from the large penthouse windows. "What's *that*?" he asked Orson, pointing.

"That's the Place de la Concorde. That's where they chopped off the head of Marie Antoinette."

Elvis said he'd want to see that "up close tomorrow."

They went down to their small, luxuriously appointed, topless bus and toured Paris, hearing the special sounds, breathing the early summer air. They stopped when Elvis said he wanted some fresh roasted chestnuts from the street vendor.

They were behind schedule and Aberbach suggested they skip the Folies—"we will do it tomorrow"—and go directly to the Lido. It was lively and colorful, the girls sophisticated and enticing. The bandleader came down when the curtain closed on the Lido's act and asked Elvis please to sing just one song. Much of the dinner crowd, among whom rumors of the great presence had circulated, took note of the solicitation, stood and applauded louder and louder in anticipation. Elvis was rattled. The bandleader had addressed him in crippled English. Elvis turned to Orson. "Tell him I ain't performed in public for fifteen months."

There were rapid exchanges, Orson acting as simultaneous interpreter. Elvis agreed to a single song.

To clamoring applause, Elvis walked up to the stage. He hummed a few bars to the lead violinist, who picked out the tune and signaled the key to the eighteen-piece orchestra. Elvis picked up the microphone and sang the plaintive "Willow Weep for Me."

Everybody loved it. Elvis stuck to his word, and the conductor didn't argue with him, however vociferous the audience was in wanting more.

Two hours later the maître d'hôtel declined to present Jean Aberbach with a bill for Elvis and his company. But Elvis wrinkled his face. He was reluctant to encourage any suggestion that he had calculatedly exchanged one song for one dinner. He reached into his pocket and drew out a butane lighter. These had only just now arrived at the PX and were an overnight sensation. Elvis turned its dial and flicked the flint. A six-inch spurt of flame shot out.

"Here," said Elvis, "this is for you." Impulsively, he drew out a second lighter from the half dozen in his pocket. "And this one is for the bandleader." The maître d' thanked him with a deep bow.

"*Alors*," said Jean. "On to the Bantu?"

It was after three in the morning.

"Okay. But," he pointed to Orson, "you gotta get home, kid."

Orson thought to plead his case. "I feel real good, Elvis. You know, I had a *real* sleep this afternoon. A long sleep. Couldn't I stick with you?"

Elvis pursed his lips. He looked over at Lamar. Then at Jean.

"No. It might get a little rough." To Jean he said, "Get somebody to drive Orson home."

"I can walk, Elvis. I know the way. It's just a few blocks."

"Is that safe?" Elvis asked Jean.

"Oh yes, Elvis, all of Paris is asleep or making love at this hour."

Elvis motioned to Orson to get on, and to the others to follow Jean to the car.

Elvis's plan, realized after the first night in Paris, was to sleep until
very late in the afternoon. On day two at six P.M., Lamar was still
in his own bedroom, asleep. Charlie had gone out, and Orson was
in the living room, with a book. Elvis nodded at him and disap-
peared into the shower. He returned in shorts and a T-shirt,
shaved, his hair composed. "That was good last night, real good."

Orson nodded. "What I saw of it was good."

"What you didn't see was even better." Elvis laughed. "I
promised some of the ladies at the Lido I'd take them tonight to
the Bantu after their performance. Maybe...no. You got enough
nightlife. Hey, I want to order chow. We'll order for everybody.
You ready? Here's what I want, Orson."

The first meal of the day came at eight. Eggs and bacon and
sausage and sweet rolls and fried potatoes and fried tomatoes,
with coffee and milk and Coca-Cola and champagne. "Tell the
waiter," Elvis directed Orson, "to bring some candles. I like
candles at night. It's almost dark outside." He peered out over
the city. "That's the Eiffel Tower over there, Charlie. 'Case you
didn't know." Charlie grunted and resumed his reading of the *International Herald Tribune*.

At six in the morning, Orson woke, though he had been asleep
only three hours. He had heard the voices, men's voices and
women's. Dressed in shorts and a T-shirt, he opened his door
cautiously. He could see three statuesque women munching on
sandwiches and sipping champagne. Elvis was wholly awake on
the sofa. One woman—he called her "Maman"—ran her hand
up and down his hip. He fondled her behind the ear. Charlie rose,

took the hand of the tall redhead, motioning her to the door of his room. Lamar took a bottle of champagne and signaled to the second girl to follow him. There was only Elvis now, and Maman. He stretched out on the sofa. He reached out his hand to hers and guided it to his zipper.

Orson opened his door wider. Breathing hard, he traced with his eyes Elvis's own hand reaching to her dress, which came down, exposing the full breasts. She worked her hand down into Elvis's shorts and moaned her pleasure.

Elvis shook his head and sat up. "Hey, Maman, you-all come on to my bed, let's—let's make it like at home."

She gurgled her assent and followed him away, trailing her long dress at one side.

Orson Killere walked into the large room. Dawn was breaking. He looked at the champagne and emptied glasses. Absentmindedly he picked up a sandwich and nibbled on it. He did not taste anything. He sat on the sofa Elvis had just vacated and looked down on his stretched shorts, excited and apprehensive. His hand was moving down when he heard the tinkle of glass. In front of him was a small, smiling, blond girl with wide blue eyes, and a half-filled glass in her hand.

"How-dee-do, lovey. I'm Pearl. I missed the last of the party. I was asleep over there." She walked with her glass and sat on the sofa by Orson.

"You're a real cute boy."

She put her glass on the coffee table and plunged her hand under the waistband of Orson's shorts. She fondled him tenderly; and now passionately. Orson Killere gave way.

His mind cleared after returning her deep, languorous kiss.

"Let's us go. To my room. My little room. All right?"

"You bet, yes, lovey, let's just go and…do it till…" She looked out at the increasing light. "Do it until the sun goes down again!"

15

Wiesbaden, 1961

IT WAS AFTER THE PARIS TRIP THAT ELVIS BEGAN TELE-
phoning Orson, usually late at night.

Orson saw at first a design in this attention from the King.
Elvis had no apparent agenda in calling, but Orson knew that
Elvis was simultaneously wooing Priscilla. Not in any connubial
sense—Priscilla was not yet sixteen. Elvis did request Orson, in
the second or third phone call, to intercede with Priscilla's mother
to permit Priscilla to visit more frequently at his house in Bad
Nauheim; to accompany Orson, as she had twice done before the
Paris trip, but also to feel free to come on her own. He would
send Joe Esposito or Lamar Fike to pick her up and to return her
home—guaranteed before eleven o'clock.

Orson, for the very first time in their dealings, showed a trace
of impatience, advising Elvis that, really, he would have to nego-
tiate whatever he had in mind directly with Mrs. Beaulieu. Elvis
agreed. "Of course that's the way it goes." He just wanted Orson
to put in a good word for him.

When he put down the phone, Orson asked himself: How
could he honestly put in a reassuring word about Elvis to Mrs.
Beaulieu, let alone to Captain Beaulieu, in the context of what he

knew? He liked, even loved the King. But Elvis was a flower child. Like Adonis, Orson thought with some satisfaction—he had read about Adonis; beautiful, coddled, self-indulgent. When Elvis declared that he would under no circumstances "harm" Priscilla, Orson thought his word good for it—that far he could go. He told his mother as much, that Elvis was to be trusted as a man of honor; and she reported as much to Ann Beaulieu. Prior to Elvis's discharge and return to the States, regular visits by Priscilla to Goethestrasse were, rather grumpily, authorized by Captain Beaulieu.

Orson's pride in Elvis and his fascination in their conversations he confided only to Mr. Simon. It had been almost two years since Orson's first purely extracurricular visit with the teacher of government and world revolution. Now, in his senior year, Orson found himself leaning on Mr. Simon less as a revolutionary mentor than as a general adviser and seer. The relationship had evolved very naturally. Orson found that when he brought up a subject that had, really, no bearing on his studies, or on world history, or on a new and better world, Siegfried Simon conversed as responsively as if Orson had brought up the labor theory of value. There was never any sign of reluctance in Siegfried Simon to help Orson to square off on his problems. In April it occurred to Orson to ask Mr. Simon whether he had any favorite song among Elvis's. He was dismayed, and even a little put off, to hear Mr. Simon say that he had never heard *any* song by Elvis Presley. On saying this, Simon sensed the impulse in his protégé to bolt from his chair, rush out, and return with a Presley record. Mr. Simon raised his hand, smiled a companionable smile, and said that he had no "ear" for modern music, and did not wish to cultivate any composer later than Richard Strauss— "and he died twelve years ago." But that did not mean he was less than interested in the human relationship—Orson, his student and friend, and Elvis, the great international star ten years older. "He remains an icon, Orson. I acknowledge that. But I'd say, from what you have told me of your conversations, he has become, also, a friend. And that isn't so unusual, that you should be befriended by someone ten years your senior. I am what, sixteen years older and think of you as a friend." Orson liked that formulation a great deal, and repeated it to his mother at dinner.

The next time Orson went up to the little study, two weeks before graduating, Mr. Simon hung a Do Not Disturb sign outside his office after asking him in. Orson thought to confide in Mr. Simon about Priscilla and her obsession with Elvis. She was now visiting Goethestrasse two or three times every week.

"You say you are certain it is a chaste arrangement?"

Orson said he would swear by it. Priscilla was no longer his own girlfriend, he acknowledged to Mr. Simon; but she continued as his very close confidante. She would have told him, or he would have sensed it, if something was ... improper.

Mr. Simon said that to use that word—improper—was to introduce conventional perspectives. Those were suspect in any cosmology that welcomed fresh thinking on every subject: property, war, imperialism, and, well, social habits. Mr. Simon paused. "I don't listen to his records, but I see public references to Elvis Presley, and he is what you call a lady-killer." Mr. Simon paused again. "We all have appetites."

Orson looked up at him through his glasses, a flush of confessional candor prompting him. Would he tell Mr. Simon about Paris? About what happened there? At the hotel? At six in the morning?

Talking with Mr. Simon was more comfortable, in a way, than talking about such things would be, hypothetically, with his father. Orson would have hesitated, he knew, to describe to his father—let alone to his mother—what went on in Paris. But Mr. Simon was wholly uncensorious and detached. That was his way.

He hated capitalism—and Adolf Hitler—and the Cold War—but he would never deplore them in any but an abstract framework. Orson Killere was prompted to examine the Paris experience, to ventilate his thoughts and memories as, he had reason to believe, some of his male classmates would do in excited conversations among themselves. Orson would never participate in such conversations. That would be to betray Elvis, and Orson would never do that. He felt even more strongly on the point after Elvis's discharge and return to Memphis. But talking with Mr. Simon about it all was safe because Mr. Simon operated in so detached a way about things. People did as people did, and one regretted unemployment and Auschwitz and arms races and Jim Crow, but thundering about these things and seeking casual changes in human and institutional behavior just wasn't something Mr. Simon went in for.

So, turning his head slightly to one side, Orson told him. Told about the nightlife in Paris, and told him—with some hesitation, but then, high in the confessional mode, with graphic candor—about his first time.

His first time had been his single time, he thought to add; but that would presumably not be so for very long.

"No," Mr. Simon concurred, "presumably not, that being how we are."

We! Orson concealed his surprise. Could Mr. Simon *also* have such appetites? Such weaknesses? Or *were* these weaknesses, in the world of Mr. Simon?

Orson would certainly not inquire. He doubted that Mr. Simon would volunteer anything of that order about himself, never mind the intimacy Orson felt with his mentor, his de facto father.

Mr. Simon agreed that there was nothing to be done on the matter of protecting Priscilla. "Just keep her as a friend, and give her advice as she seeks it. You are a year older than she is, and much better read."

"Gee, Mr. Simon, thanks"—Orson would from time to time relapse into the language of a teenager. Siegfried Simon loved that in him. He looked up at Orson and said it would be nice if some evening he could arrange to have dinner with him at his apartment. "And perhaps listen to some of *my* music."

Orson stammered his willingness—eagerness—to accept the invitation. "I'll see if I can arrange that with my mother."

He looked at his watch, got up, smiled, and said thanks again. "Got to go now, Mr. Simon."

At supper he cheerfully related the invitation he had had to his mother, omitting details of the conversation that had preceded it.

Francie Killere's reaction was flat and authoritative. "The answer is no. You are *not* to visit with Mr. Simon in his living quarters after hours. And now listen, Orson Killere, that is my last word on that subject. You're going in a little while to college. You can do what you want there. Here I have some responsibility for you and I'm exercising that responsibility."

Orson was shaken by his mother's mood and firmness. He said nothing. She walked out of the kitchen, into her room.

Orson wasn't tempted, he discovered on reflection, to defy her. He did wonder what he would say to Mr. Simon. Probably best to say nothing. That was easy because two days later classes ended, and Mr. Simon had suddenly been called away to be with his ailing mother in Bayreuth. Immediately after graduation Orson went for the summer to Bern. General Hoffritz had got him a job with the U.S. Embassy immigration office, deciphering visa applications. The ambassador was a retired wartime colonel, a college classmate of Amos Hoffritz.

Orson did his work in the Swiss capital industriously. He trained himself to type out English translations of German text. It was very impressive, the number of people who wanted to travel to America. He reminded himself, with some satisfaction, that *he* wouldn't need to apply for a visa to travel to Amerika, as an underground paper from Boston he read referred to it. At the University of Michigan, he had established by correspondence, he would find some students who really knew what was going on in Amerika, the bastion of capitalist imperialism.

BOOK TWO

16

Ann Arbor, May 1964

IT WAS ALWAYS A PROBLEM AT ANN ARBOR, THE PHONE calls with Elvis. Orson guarded fastidiously the sacred, private friendship. Only Lizzie knew. But maintaining a friendship with Elvis meant frequent calls. Usually they were initiated by Elvis. They came in from Memphis or Hollywood—he was now dividing his time between the two cities. And there was only the single telephone in Orson's college quarters at Ann Arbor. No way he could—*Jeezus!*—just imagine! *lie in bed talking with Elvis Presley* while his three roommates were just, well, around.

The calls almost always came in through Lydia, Elvis's personal telephone operator. So what Orson did, when the phone rang for him in his college quarters, was to say: "Hold that, Lydia. I'll call you back in a couple of minutes." Orson would climb down the stairs of the dormitory to the public phone booth by the Coca-Cola machine. He'd dial the operator. "I want to put in a collect call to anyone who answers. The number is Essex 7-7224. This is Orson Killere calling. Yes, Killere. K-i-l-l-e-r-e, ma'am." Lydia would come on the line. "Hang on, Orson, he's on another call. I'll tell him you're there."

Orson always brought along a magazine or book to read because sometimes he'd be waiting on the line for ten minutes or
more before Elvis got on. But eventually the magic voice would
come in.

"How you doin', Killer?"

Telephone calls with Elvis were always a problem. They had
been a problem well before Orson left Wiesbaden to come to
America. It was soon after he arrived at Ann Arbor that Priscilla
had communicated her exciting news: She would leave in one
month to go to live at Graceland—"properly chaperoned, need-
less to say."

In Germany there had been the long struggle with her parents.
But now Priscilla had prevailed. The captain had capitulated
after his wife announced that she could *no longer* put up with
the existing situation—Priscilla moping all day long, dreaming of
Graceland, and weeping tears every day or two over her absence
from Elvis.

Priscilla had had an average of three calls a week. But, she'd
reminded Orson at school one day, she had the advantage of the
time zone: Elvis called late in the day from the United States,
Priscilla rose early in West Germany. "I've tried to get him used
to calling me at nine P.M. his time when he calls from Hollywood,
midnight his time when he calls from Memphis. That way I can
stand by, and quickly pick up the phone before it wakes up Mom
or Dad." Now, of course, Elvis's calls to Priscilla were to
Graceland.

Lydia, of course, was familiar with all the numbers of everyone Elvis ever wanted to talk to. But getting through to Orson at
Ann Arbor was difficult, living as he did in a dormitory. If Lydia
could get to him within a reasonable time, Elvis didn't mind. If
more than a week or two went by without a conversation, he
could be saddened, and a little cranky. "For heaven's sakes,"
Charlie Hodge said on the phone when Orson got back from a

canoe trip with Lizzie, "give him a ring, will you? He's tried three times to get through."

"I did tell him I'd be gone for ten days."

"Orson. You know better. The King doesn't have any *idea* of time. How's everything?"

Orson told him things were okay except that we were heading into an economic depression, a thermonuclear collision, and a race war.

"I mean, apart from that, Killer?"

Orson promised to call Lydia. "Where you at, Charlie?"

"We're in Hollywood."

"Okay. In that case I'll call in at ten P.M. your time. Will Elvis be back from the studio?"

"I expect. Give it a try. Lydia'll know."

Orson sat now in the public booth with a Coca-Cola and the current issue of *Time* magazine. Its cover was given to Governor William Scranton of Pennsylvania, who had entered the race for the Republican presidential nomination against the favorite, Senator Barry Goldwater. After a bit Elvis came on the line.

"Well, where you been, Killer?"

"I got back from that canoe trip I told you about. I went with Lizzie, just two of us, camping equipment, and stuff to eat—"

"Like what?"

"Well, we had ham, canned tomatoes, and peas—"

"Sounds awful."

"Not good Elvis-food. But we had breads and cakes and chocolate and a bottle of good hootch."

"There's no such thing as good hootch. I've told you that. You shouldn't drink and you shouldn't smoke. But I've been telling you that since you were what, ten?"

"Fourteen."

"Well, fourteen—and how old are you now?"

"Nineteen."

"Well, the rules don' change. It don' change, no more than there are always people tryin' to do you in. That ever happen to you?"

Orson said it had. But Orson knew that Elvis wouldn't have framed the point in that way except that he wanted to lodge a grievance.

"You heard anything about the article? The one in the *Las Vegas News*?"

In fact Orson had heard about it, from Priscilla. But he knew Elvis would like to tell him about it in his own words.

"You know Hal Wallis has been doin' my pictures. This is like maybe three I've done with him. Well, he likes to do them real fast, tight budget kind of thing. So last year he takes time off to produce *Becket*. You seen it?"

Orson had seen it. "It was a terrific picture."

"I know. I'm not sayin' it wasn't a terrific picture. But the shit who wrote that article said that I—*I*—was responsible for makin' it. You know how he figured that out?"

"No," Orson lied.

"That writer said it's as simple as this. Hal Wallis makes lousy pictures with Elvis Presley in order to bankroll a good picture like *Becket*. So...that means that Peter O'Toole and Richard Burton—they were the stars of *Becket*, remember? That means they owe their careers to Presley. If we didn't have bad actors to make bad movies, Hollywood wouldn't have good actors who make good movies. What you think of that?"

Orson said it was silly and unfair. He asked what Elvis thought of his current movie.

"It's called *Roustabout*. I get to sing twelve songs, which is okay, but also, I'm supposed to act unpleasant. Sort of surly. That takes a lot of practice."

Orson laughed. "Well, Elvis, if you're going to become a great contemporary actor, you have to know how to act *surly*."

Elvis laughed loudly. He said he was working hard and hoped to be able to complete the picture in two weeks, and then "get back to mah Priscilla. Now she's in Memphis I can be with her easily. You heard from her?"

"Yeah. We talked just before the canoe trip."

"Is she happy?"

"Well Elvis, I mean it's a kind of crazy situation. Leaving her family and living now with Vernon. But you're still unmarried—"

"Nobody believes it, but you know, I haven't *touched* her. And don' think that's been easy. As a matter of fact, Killer, and this is just for you to know, Priscilla *eggs me on*. She'd...do it tomorrow, if I let her. But I won't. I gave my word to that stiff-necked father of hers that she'd be okay, livin' with my father in a separate building. But this way I do get to spend time with her, lots and lots of time."

Orson asked how the album *Viva Las Vegas* was doing. Elvis said it was hanging in there at Number 13. "That's good, but that's not good enough. I told the Colonel—told Tom—that someday I'm goin' to have to say good-bye for a while to Hollywood—even though I'm the highest-paid actor in Hollywood right now—and do some good stuff. Maybe live performances—"

"It's been a long time, Elvis. And you haven't done television since Frank Sinatra. I know that's right, because even though I study other stuff, too, Elvis Presley is my specialty. I never saw that great program—"

"You were still at school in Germany—"

"Yeah, finishing up. They tried to get it to show at the camp, but they couldn't get the rights."

"Why didn't you just steal a copy, Killer?"

Orson laughed. "You'd better not encourage me. If I made

the laws, you'd get a salary, that's all. No royalties. Your music belongs to everybody."

"You're still on to that horseshit, Killer?"

"Well, yeah. But don't tell the Colonel. He'll put his uniform back on and hunt me down."

"I promise." Elvis yodeled a bar from "Promises, Promises."

"You make me feel good, Elvis. That's why I look after you," Orson jibed.

"That's nice to know, Killer. Now next time you go on a canoe trip, call me and I'll send you somethin' you can *eat* on that trip. Bye-bye."

With Orson it was as if there hadn't been any physical separation since the days at Friedberg, never mind that since then Elvis had left the army, come back to America, made the big hit as the TV guest of Frank Sinatra, and signed a gaudy contract for yet more Hollywood movies. It was very different from his other grown-up friend back at FDR: He just didn't hear at all from Mr. Simon.

17

Ann Arbor, May 1964

ORSON PICKED UP THE TELEPHONE AND SAID HE wanted to speak to Lizzie.

"Lizzie who?"

Orson paused. He had never been asked that before—Lizzie who?—when he dialed this number. Was there more than *one* Lizzie at Humphrey House, University of Michigan?

"Uh, Lizzie Borden," he elaborated. Nice way to handle *that,* he thought. He could expect now to hear from the girl on the phone that (a) "There is no Lizzie Borden at Humphrey House"; or (b) "Are you playing games? In which case, please don't." Or (c) she'd go get Lizzie.

It was as he thought. There was no other Lizzie at that number. His Lizzie came to the phone.

Orson was lying on his bed, head propped up above the headboard, the telephone with the long extension cord sitting on his tight stomach. He had come from the shower and wore only shorts and the F.U.M. (Fuck the University of Michigan) T-shirt. One of his roommates occupied the desk across the way. The other two were out. And why not? In the wonderful May weather, Ann Arbor was resplendent.

"Liz? You okay? Just checking."

She replied in something of a whisper. Other girls were obviously within earshot. "Yeah, I'm okay. A little nervous, to tell the truth."

"Well, why? There's no capital punishment in the State of Michigan."

"Don't be funny. I was talking to Alice. She has cold feet. I'm not sure we can absolutely count on her."

"Doesn't matter. Even if she pulls out, we've still got fifteen. It does matter, though, that if she pulls out the guy or girl to the right and the left of her position should know about it."

"She agrees to tell them if she decides not to turn up. Maybe she'll come through."

Orson became serious. "It's a problem for us to get used to a totally different cultural orientation. It isn't unexpected that the ruling class will exert its power. But there'll be that nice time of seeing them, well, *paralyzed,* when they just don't know what to do. Don't *quite* know *what* to do."

"They can call the police."

"Yep. They'll do that, all right."

Mr. Simon had made the point that capitalist exertions in defense of their own interests were a "spastic thing." Orson remembered the word he used. Such reactions were to be expected. But, Mr. Simon argued, when there was a withering away of true conviction by capitalists—and, he counseled, such an erosion will certainly happen—then capitalist self-defense will become formalistic, and a revolutionary breakthrough becomes possible. At meetings of their committee, Orson and the others had talked endlessly on these points.

The final decision had been reached after midnight on Thursday. The University of Michigan branch of the Students for Democratic Peace would act on its own to protest the corporatist makeup of the university's administration and trustees. It would not do to inform other branches of the SDP in neighboring universities about the proposed initiative. Any leak could ruin the impact of the whole demonstration. Let the Ann Arbor campus strike out; others could follow. Or, if too timid, they would at least simply admire their more venturesome affiliate. The idea of cordoning off the president, the provost, and the entire board of trustees of the university on the day before commencement! A galvanizing idea, really bracing, Orson thought. Now the moment was at hand.

It was Barry Schmidt, the engineering student with the dark eyes and long brown hair, who had come up with the idea of the handcuffs. The grand entrance to the president's building was bordered by ornate ironwork railings, curving up on each end of the broad stone steps. At exactly the right moment, when the first of the trustees was seen coming out of the building, the student at the far right, Elsie, with the braces on her teeth and the perpetual smile, would attach the manacle on her wrist to the iron railing. At the other end, Jonathan, the rugged athlete, would do the same thing. The fifteen students apparently just loitering about the building would get the signal and immediately fan out, each one manacling himself to the next student in the semicircle. The effect of it would be sixteen students forming an impenetrable barrier to the departure of anybody in the building—president, trustees, anybody.

It was the job of Harry and Eleanor, both from the tiny village of Mecosta, in the north, to telephone the Ann Arbor bureau of the *Detroit Free Press,* the *Michigan Daily,* and the television station at the climactic minute. The planners had given much thought to the text of the message to be given out. It had to be short but electric. Finally they'd resolved on: *The Students for Democratic Peace will forbid university trustees to leave Fleming*

*Hall until the trustees have acted on student demands for eco-
nomic justice, nuclear disarmament, and racial equality. The students will form a human chain outside the hall.*

A key figure was Henrietta Foley, with the straight hair and
blue eyes, a native of Brussels, who spoke in French to Orson.
The hour at which trustee meetings ended was about six. Her assignment was to stride nonchalantly, beginning at five-thirty,
along the corridor outside the meeting hall, as if looking for
somebody or something. When there was outward movement
from the inner sanctum, she would duck into the public telephone
booth in Fleming and call Orson, who was standing by the telephone across Plymouth Road. He would ring Harry, who would
ring Eleanor, and they would issue the bulletins to the papers.
Orson would then run across the road and join his apparently innocent companions sitting and standing about the public benches
outside the hall. They would spring into action, clip on their
handcuffs, and so forge a resolute human chain.

Inside, Henrietta saw the great door opening. She easily made
out the robust profile of President Vernon. He was ushering the
trustees to the exit. Quickly she reached the phone booth, in-
serted a dime, and dialed Orson.

"They're coming out!" She spoke in an urgent whisper.

No more needed to be said. Orson hung up, put in his dime,
dialed Harry—and got a busy signal.

How could that be! Could he have misdialed? Inconceivable.
Still...he put the coin back in and dialed the number again,
carefully.

Busy.

Eleanor! He would call Eleanor. He had her phone number...
somewhere. He fumbled in his pocket for his pad. He flipped
through the pages...Eleanor Holmes, Branford House. AR4155.
She answered immediately. "Ready to go, Harry?"

"No! This is Orson. Harry's line is busy! I got to run now.

Get through to the press, or it's no use. Call Harry when you can, and after that, get him going."

He raced across the road and summoned his comrades. They had rehearsed the maneuver in the empty gymnasium the night before. Elsie and Jonathan, the anchors, went instantly to the railings. Elsie brought out the handcuffs, purchased at the toy department of Woolworth's in Detroit, and snapped one end onto the iron railing. She looked to her right. Joshua was waiting, his cuff open. It snapped around her right wrist. She looked over to the other end. The chain, beginning with Jonathan at the east end, was crystallizing. Orson was at the center, extending both his wrists to be incorporated into the chain.

A startled secretary descended the steps from the door. "Oh," she said, bumping up against Josh. "Hey. What's going on? Let me through!" Orson nodded okay to Joshua. She was not the enemy. Joshua and Eleanor raised their arms to let her pass.

But not the next two gentlemen, wearing suits and ties and carrying briefcases. Time to begin the chant. Orson raised his voice:

"We demand justice!"

They had practiced that, too. It made a difference to say it in unison. They would follow Orson's beat.

"We—demand—justice!"

There were now eight or ten figures, obviously men of senior status, clotted about the entrance. They began to look behind for directions from their leader.

And then he emerged, President Dwight Vernon, with the gray hair and trim mustache.

He scanned the student line and went to its center.

"What is your name?" he asked Orson.

It had been agreed that no one accosted would permit their chant to be interrupted.

"We want justice!" was all that the president could get from the ringleader.

Dwight Vernon, as an undergraduate, had been the fullback on the UM football team. He felt a temptation, very nearly over-powering, to lower his head and charge into Orson, driving him to the ground, and also the attached students at either side. *And who knows, maybe the whole line!*

No: No charging. He was the president. He would behave with appropriate dignity.

He walked back to the doorway and motioned to the trustees to go back into the building.

Finally! Orson thought, the television camera team had ar-rived. The protesters permitted the man with the camera to duck under the line and begin to film. The accompanying reporter tried, unsuccessfully, to get Orson to respond to his questions. Two more reporters came, with still cameras. One was Maggie Alling-ham, who covered student events for the Ann Arbor edition of the *Free Press.* She gave up on Orson and went to Jonathan.

"How can we report on what you are striking for, if you don't tell us?"

Jonathan motioned to Henrietta, who brought out the printed flyers from her large handbag. Miss Allingham ran her eyes over the list of SDP demands. She pocketed one of the flyers and ducked back out under the chain. *What now?* she asked herself.

President Vernon had led the trustees down the old stone steps to the ground floor, then to the rear of the building. He calmly broke the seal to the fire door, opened it, and let the group out, with apologies. They would meet for cocktails and dinner at 7:30.

Orson, fifteen minutes having gone by without any more con-frontation, discerned a danger of a loss of morale among his troops. The press had done their work, and only Maggie and her cameraman lingered to see what the next chapter would be.

Henrietta talked with a clerk who had come around the cor-ner of Fleming Hall. Then she gave Orson the terrible news: The trustees had escaped their trap. They had left the building using a door the planners hadn't known existed. What now?

The students on the chain all looked over at Orson. He passed the word along to his edgy confederates. "Quitting time on this exercise," he called out.

They set about fitting their keys to the handcuffs. Esther and Josie could not get theirs to open. Worse, Elsie could not free herself from the iron railing. "Let me try it." Orson took the key and tried to turn it. No luck. Esther and Josie had walked away still manacled to one another. Josie told Henrietta they were going to try calling the fire station for relief. The flashbulb went off again as Orson pounded on Elsie's handcuff with a rock from the garden. But it would not yield, and now Elsie was crying. Lizzie stayed on with Orson, but the others left. Fire ax! he thought. He rushed into Sprague Hall and looked about for fire-fighting equipment. He spotted the glass case at the end of the hall and broke it open.

But outside, the firemen had arrived. One of them used a huge cable cutter and bit through the end of the manacle, freeing Elsie. She rushed to embrace Lizzie, relieved, and then bounded back to her room.

The scene had now attracted fellow students in addition to the firefighters and the police. Orson gestured to Lizzie, and they made their way out, to the bar across the quadrangle and down Church Street. She didn't wait. "Give me a beer," she said to the bartender. "Two beers."

"Well," Lizzie said after a prolonged silence, lifting her glass. "Long live the revolution."

Orson permitted himself a smile. After a while they giggled, then laughed and laughed with nervous relief.

18

Ann Arbor, May 1964

THE SUMMONS TO THE OFFICE OF THE DEAN WAS NOT a laughing matter. John H. Revercomb was an old-school administrator. A child of the Depression, he had worked in a factory during the daylight hours and studied and attended classes at night. The war's interruption had meant three years' service with the Marines. All of this together had amounted to an interval of fourteen years between his matriculation as a freshman and the award of his doctorate in physical education in 1952. Fourteen years of hard work in the foxholes of the Pacific and the academy had taught him that, simply put: Rules are to be obeyed. Like the rules in the Marines. It was so with the rules of life.

With it all, Dean Revercomb was always curious about the motivation of student miscreants. He was pleased that, in the three years he had held the office, there were very few, given a student body of twenty-plus thousand, whose offenses were so serious as to require his personal attention. But there was no question about the gravity of the offense committed by the student waiting outside.

Revercomb had had prolonged exposure to barracks language, from Parris Island to Camp Pendleton. Even so he was surprised by what he had just now read. The letter, discreetly resealed, was on his desk. He had opened it to find, clipped out, the front page of that morning's *Detroit Free Press*. In the easily recognized, green-inked broad stroke of President Vernon, he read: *Revercomb: Find out who this motherfucker is and get his ass out of UM. Confirm. DV.*

The green ink line descended to the large photograph circling the head of the student President Vernon had addressed the afternoon before. The photo, stretching right across the page, showed the human chain. The caption read: UM PRESIDENT DWIGHT VER-NON TRIES WITHOUT SUCCESS TO BREACH THE STUDENT WALL, HANDCUFF-TO-HANDCUFF, HEMMING IN UNIVERSITY TRUSTEES AT FLEMING HALL. PROTESTING STUDENTS DEMANDED PEACE AND RACIAL AND ECONOMIC JUSTICE. The ensuing news story gave the text of the demands of the Students for Democratic Peace.

John Revercomb rose to full height and went to the door, summoning the sophomore student seated in the waiting room to come in. He studied the trim nineteen-year-old with the tight glasses over his blue eyes and the mouth slightly parted to show bright teeth, wearing a T-shirt with the not-very-enigmatic acronym, F.U.M.

"I see from your records here, Mr. Killere, that, nearing the end of two years, you have done well in your studies. You have also engaged in extracurricular activity, including debate and student journalism. Now, let me ask you this: What in the name of *God* did you think you were up to yesterday?"

Orson knew he didn't have a chance. He'd engage, under the circumstances, in only minimal civility.

"Our committee thought we needed to take a stand. There's the Cold War, nuclear armament, poverty, race—"

"*Quiet!* I don't want a catalog of everything going on here and in other parts of the world that displeases me, let alone displeases you and your committee. I'm not asking you how come you are in favor of peace and racial justice. I'm asking why you thought you had the right to tell the people responsible for the university where they can enter and exit campus buildings. Out of curiosity, Killere, why didn't you and your platoon—why didn't you string out some barbed wire? And maybe, though this would have taken a little time, maybe land-mine the area? Also, why didn't you cut off the north area? Or you might have got some sniper rifles and knocked a few of them off, right? Assuming you could aim and hit anything you aimed at. What a half-ass demonstration that was..."

Orson started to form a word, stopped, started again, stopped. Dean Revercomb didn't give him any help.

"Just out of curiosity, did you think your demonstration would affect the policies of the University in any way? If so, how?"

Orson's temperature was rising. "There's a course here in nuclear physics. That should be eliminated... There are six percent Negro students, proportional would be more like twelve... double... There are only two courses in Marxist studies—"

"And all those things would be corrected by your human chain demonstration?"

"That's how protesters attract attention. You know, like burning yourself up, the way the monks did in Saigon to bring down Diem."

"How old are you?" Revercomb snapped. "Never mind, I can see here you were born in January 1945. In January 1945, I was in the Pacific. I was there because that's where I was sent. I killed people I was told to kill. Told by superior officers appointed through a democratic chain of command. This is a state university. Its officers are democratically elected. I am a dean with designated responsibilities. I am exercising that responsibility by expelling you from the university. You may reapply in one year. I hope between now and then you will grow up a little. Strike that. I hope between now and then you will grow up a lot."

Dean Revercomb pointed to the door.

19

Ann Arbor, May 1964

ORSON LEFT THE DEAN'S OFFICE AND WALKED ACROSS the green to the student center. A room in the center could be booked by any student group. Word of the meeting had got out to survivors of the great-human-chain event of the day before. Lizzie had told them that the dean had hunted Orson down and called him in, though she didn't know what had come of the meeting. They'd find out now.

Lizzie was there waiting, with a half dozen conspirators-at-arms. They knew the story immediately from the look on Orson's face.

"Is it curtains?" Lizzie asked.

"Yep. I can reapply in one year. Just send in an application. Readmission Department, Department of Admissions, University of Michigan."

Todd asked: "Did they want to know who else was there? You figure we're going to get the same treatment?"

Orson said he doubted it. "I think they wanted exemplary action for one guy, and I was the most exposed guy. It was that easy for them."

Josh broke in. "What are we sitting here bitching about?

What would we expect the Man to do? Give us honorary degrees? You're kicked out, Orson. Me, Josh Burton, I'm leaving town."

"To do what?" Lizzie wanted to know.

"Fight the fight wherever. Head east. The center of power of the military-industrial establishment is at the Pentagon."

Orson agreed. "The Pentagon is the central concentration of the Dean Revercombs of America. That's where the dean was trained." He paused, but only for a moment. His mind turned involuntarily to Wiesbaden, to the apparently civilized military friends of his mother's, not least General Amos Hoffritz, with whom, Orson guessed, his mother was in love. They were all a part of the military.

But that was no reason to excuse them from what had to be done, which was to overthrow the military-industrial complex. He must guard against sentimentalizing the problem. Josh was right. What should he expect, when an operation goes sour?

Still, it was true that he had made no contingency plans. It wasn't quite as simple as moving from one resistance center to an adjacent resistance center. Ann Arbor had stepped forward— substantially under his direction—to act as a prototype of what he had to believe would be a burgeoning student revolution against the establishment. Not much thought had been given to protecting individually the revolutionary practitioners against the consequences of their enterprise.

Tim, a senior, admitted that it had crossed his mind to wear a mask when he signed up for the human chain. "I figured, shit, I'm in line to get a diploma tomorrow after four years of hard labor, not much point in throwing *that* away."

"They're not going to keep you from graduating." Lizzie was reassuring. "That would mean a civil liberties case. That's the *last* thing they'd want on their hands."

Others among the activists-conspirators raised their voices. One said: "Let's face it. It was a snafu and it's *our* fault—"

He was interrupted. Tim said, "You weren't exactly egging us on to take extra precautions, Harry. I mean, you were prepared to quit before we even got *word* about the rear entrance—"

"What the hell, obviously we had to quit *sometime*, I mean, we weren't planning to spend the *whole fucking night* there—"

"Hang on, hang on," Orson said. "We've got to think this through—"

There was a knock on the door. Orson turned to Lizzie. "Is it on the center bulletin board that we're meeting here now?"

"Yep. Students for Democratic Peace reserved what we're sitting in. There was no other way to get a room. I couldn't just make up a name—"

"Why didn't you use the glee club's name?" Orson taunted her.

But that didn't save him from the business at hand, which was to answer the knock on the door, whoever it was out there, gunning for them.

It was Maggie Allingham, of the Ann Arbor paper. She was dressed in a floral blouse and tight chinos. In her left hand she clutched her purse and a secretarial pad.

"So! This is the brain trust of the Students for Democratic Peace! Where do you keep the brains? I couldn't find any yesterday afternoon."

She was greeted with silence. "Sorry to interrupt the revolution, but this is business. I've got a story to file. Which one of you dudes is Orson Killere—how do you pronounce that?"

"Kill-air," Lizzie volunteered.

"I guess after what happened at the dean's office this morning, from what I hear, I should refer to him as an 'ex-student' at the University of Michigan?"

Everyone's eyes turned to Orson, still standing by the door. "I'm Orson."

"You're a nice-looking kid. Strike that. It's unprofessional. How old are you?"

Josh intervened. "Hey wait a minute. Orson, remember, you don't have to talk to her."

Orson thought a moment. "Look, Miss Allingham. Could you step back outside? We'll confer. And then if we decide to go public with our end of the story, we'll give it to you."

"You guys are funny. Suddenly you don't want publicity. Yesterday you did everything except set yourselves on fire in the middle of the campus to get publicity. Okay. I'll wait outside."

They took to talking to one another in whispers. The steam had gone out of their big idea. Barry put it quickly into words: "Whatever we decide to do next semester, there isn't any point in giving out the names of the whole gang. All they've got is Orson."

"Hey, wait, we're not going to chicken out on this and just leave Orson to the pigs?" Harry, finishing out his freshman year, was afire. He put a practical edge on it: "They can find out who we are anyway, so why try to hide?"

"Sure, they can find us," Barry agreed. "If they want to put the FBI on it, they can probably get all sixteen names from photographs. But I don't think, except for Orson, they're turning on that kind of heat. Let's just tell her a protest will be filed with the student council about Orson and that the Students for Democratic Peace are proud to have made a public demand on the trustees to advance—"

"Peace, democracy, economic equality, and racial justice." They all looked at Orson. Was he trivializing the movement?

"Look," he said, "there are two questions: The first is what to do about the press. I have the answer to that: I'll go talk to Allingham, answer her questions about me but say nothing about our committee. I won't even mention whether it will reconvene next fall. And I'll say, yes—that we're concerned about peace, democracy, economic equality, and racial justice.

"The second question is: Where do we go with the big movement, which is—should be—international, but can't be just a revival of the Old Left. Me, I don't have the answer to that, but I know that I'm going to give it a lot of thought. But none of it"—he managed a smile—"on this campus."

Lizzie approached and flung her arms around him.

He embraced her and then shook hands, one by one, with his confederates.

He opened the door and motioned Maggie Allingham in. As arranged, his accomplices filed out without a word.

Back in the dorm all but one of his roommates had packed and left. Elmer had written a note: *Heard about what they did to you, Orson. Real sorry about that. I'll be back late.*

He was alone, which was as he had so much hoped it would be.

He'd have to call his mother. What would he say?

In fact, what would he do?

20

Billings, October 1964

ORSON LAID DOWN HIS BACKPACK AND LOOKED AT the posted offerings. Each item and its price were chalked on the blackboard hanging under the sign that said Sam's Eatery. The neon letters glistened even in the early light. They were sparkling new, in contrast to the flaking, once white-painted truckers' restaurant they advertised.

It was pleasantly cool in Billings, and the air was good, in grateful contrast to the airlessness of the boxcar on the Northern Pacific line. The sun was rising as though personally to welcome him to town. The highway and the railroad line evidently lay in parallel, he had observed after walking away from the tracks. Both headed through Montana in the general direction of the Pacific Ocean. The four trucks strung out limply in the parking area behind the fuel station established that the highway was largely a commercial thoroughfare. Orson had gone only a hundred yards to get to Sam's, and the railroad tracks were still in clear view. Maybe the railroad builders were in cahoots with the road builders and had used the same surveyor, in good oligopolistic fashion.

To business. There was the Big Beefburger, at 35 cents. Beef entered into most of Sam's Eatery's inventory, though there was also spaghetti (30 cents) and Fried Irresistable Shrimps (45 cents).

Orson had never had what the bourgeoisie would call cash reserves. He did remember, with the smile of an old roué, that when he was twelve and crossed the Atlantic Ocean with his mother he had a *gros paquet,* as he and his Paris classmates would have described it. He had brought with him to South Carolina his life's savings. To protect them he had inveigled a money belt from a security officer at Camp Pershing. Strapped about his waist, it proved cumbersome when, the first day, he had wanted to pull out some change for a chocolate bar.

But poverty had become something of a stigma, reminding him now of the tenuous hold he and his mother had on middle-class life. Even when, under the influence of Mr. Simon, he had arrived philosophically at his view that all property was properly common property, he derived little comfort from the knowledge that he had very little of it. His sick father died destitute, never mind the pension provided by the Fourth Republic for veterans who had been fatally wounded or treated. That pension, to use his mother's term, had been "nominal." She herself, Frances Marye Killere, was splendidly educated, fluent in German and in French, but her pay as civilian personnel head in the Seventh Army, Thirty-seventh Division, had left little to put aside after food and rent and school fees. Francie sent a check to Camden for fifty dollars on her mother's birthdays and at Christmas; gratefully received, but the traffic was one way. Alice Marye had the large old house to look after, and also her aged father.

But Francie Killere, without any wistful thought of sacrifices made to do so, had deposited five percent of every check into a fund to help pay, in the years ahead, Orson's tuition at college. That was it: the short, spare financial story of the Killere household.

Orson began early in life to look for opportunities to earn some money for himself. At age fourteen he was giving ten hours a week to the army hospital at Wiesbaden, working in the laundry room at the minimum wage. Arrived at Ann Arbor, Orson promptly checked in with student financial aid, which found him work—again, ten hours a week—as a bursary student. The emolument was passed directly to the college bursar toward his boarding fee: exactly enough to pay his meal ticket.

And of course his fifteen-hundred-dollar scholarship at Michigan (he had graduated first in his class at FDR) was critical. Elvis had twice asked him whether he needed "some help at school—I sure did, when *I* was schoolin'." Orson declined both times, accepting from Elvis only free copies of his new record releases. But on his birthday Orson was tracked down by the local Buick dealer, who advised him grandly that his "new car" was ready! Orson acted quickly. He hadn't, practically *ever*, written to Elvis—Elvis was a telephone friend. But this time he wrote. *Elvis, he typed out on the Hermes his mother gave him on his fifteenth birthday, you are a super friend, but I told the dealer to give you back the money for the beautiful Buick. No way I could use it. Wish I could give you something, but can't think what. Maybe someday.*

His mother's college fund was programmed to phase in over four years. That fund had now been dormant for the five months since Orson had left Ann Arbor. He was relieved when Francie told him she would be marrying Amos Hoffritz, a widower since Christmas. Orson liked the old man (General Hoffritz was forty-seven), but mostly he was glad for the security it meant for his mother.

A curious by-product of his experience on the road was that Orson nowadays knew exactly how much money he had on him. When he got off the train at Billings, he had $21.50. Anytime he bought anything an automatic deduction was triggered in the ledger he kept in his mind. He knew now that if he selected the spaghetti and the pie, and a Coca-Cola, his capital would reduce to $20.50. He trusted there would be a new chapter to translate, waiting for him at General Delivery in the post office. That would bring him some cash.

It had taken him a while to reorient his ingrained metabolic impulses. Except during those idyllic hours when he was riding a horse on the endless, captivating bridle paths in Camden, South Carolina, wishing the afternoons would never end, he had always felt rushed. Washing the dishes, going to school, doing homework, reading those books and newspapers and magazines, Orson was always parceling out his time. He had applied himself to save those twelve minutes getting to school. To do what? More time with Elvis in the morning.

Was that a waste of time? Time spent listening to Elvis? He dismissed the thought, first out of impulsive loyalty, but then, with conviction, after what he deemed mature philosophical self-examination. It was Elvis, he was convinced, who had sown the seeds of Orson's political vision. It had taken a year or two, and Mr. Simon was the catalyst, but Elvis had freed up Orson's mind that night in Camden. Elvis was his epiphany. When he heard him sing—saw him sing!—"I Got a Woman," Orson was instantly, *at that very moment,* jolted into a carnal understanding of the opposite sex. And the movements of Elvis! Self-evidently Elvis cared for nothing else than his song. He sang it out as if he were addressing paradise. An appropriate princeling of paradise—because Elvis was the handsomest man Orson had ever seen, a Greek god alive—swinging his hips on Jackie Gleason's television program to encourage a national jauntiness. Elvis was addressing the sadness of the world and the desires of the world, as if to say that none of the traditional restraints were bearable or—here Mr.

Simon's perspective was critical—justifiable. No, Orson thought, still deliberating between the spaghetti and the beefburger, Mr. Simon had truly penetrated these problems, illuminating the crying need for the world revolution so universally scorned.

He ordered the beefburger and a soda and logged in his memory what he now had left.

He sat down on the bench with his burger and Coke at the broad outdoor table, tilting his head slightly to shield his eyes from the sun. He ran his finger over his face. *Time to shave.* One resolution, on setting out, though, was not to ape the archetypal dropout. Jack Kerouac, he knew from loose talk about his book, had set protocols which some true believers observed as though they were sacred oaths. *Forget it.* Orson Killere would shave when there was hot water, and there was almost always hot water, when you came down to it. In public men's rooms, in the pretty-much hygienic culture of trains and buses and restaurants. One blade would last him twenty days, provided he had soap.

He had taken with him two pairs of pants, one light khaki, army-style, the other, a brown corduroy suitable for cold weather. He carried three sports shirts and two pairs of boxer shorts, four socks and a jar of Woolite cleanser. In the small leather kit, along with his razor, there was the comb, toothbrush, toothpaste, a soapbox, and a precious replacement pair of eyeglasses. And of course the sponge, the all-purpose cleaning instrument Mlle Bouchex had taught him to use when at school in Paris. He had added to the assortment, because of his night in the fetid swamp on the canoe trip, a can of fly repellent. And, in his sack, a compass and two books. When he finished one book, he would filch a replacement from any appropriate library, giving up the one he had read. A rough trade; a form of barter. The bulkiest item in his case was the thick sheaf of blank papers appended to the clipboard on which he wrote out his translations. The paper and the two ballpoint pens. So far, these tools had kept him free, free on the road.

Orson assumed that the post office in Billings would be open until five, local time. He walked back into the diner and looked up at the calendar above the counter, to make certain today wasn't a holiday. If today was Sunday, why, he'd simply wait until Monday to check the post office. But it was Friday. He asked the waitress: "Does this road out here take you into town?"

She nodded. "Yep."

He would not ask her where in town the post office was. Obviously it was somewhere. He'd wait to ask more specific directions when he got into the business district.

He needed shade for his eyes and pulled out his cotton, cowboy-shaped hat. He kept it in the pocket of his denim jacket. He could shape it so as to give him some protection from the sun, to one side, in front, or behind.

All the traffic was vehicular. Very few people traveled on foot. As he walked down the road with his backpack, his eyes took routine note of possible shelters of opportunity for tonight. Probably he would return to the train station and find another boxcar. But there was always something else, if you used your imagination. He noted the For Sale sign on what had evidently been a barber shop. That would qualify for overnight. He preferred to avoid forced entries, but he had developed rudimentary skills.

After all, as Mr. Simon had remarked one day to the class, by theological reasoning, you aren't stealing if you requisition an apple to avoid starvation. By extension, if you need shelter and there's shelter there, not being used—wouldn't it follow that you aren't trespassing? In Fargo, asleep under a construction platform alongside the city tennis courts, he had been poked awake by a sheriff with a baton. The sports shop, the sheriff told him, had been broken into. A large supply of golf and tennis balls had been taken, he said insinuatingly. He blurted out, "We're going to search you," before it registered on him that Orson could not effectively be hiding a store of golf and tennis balls. A few, perhaps, tucked away in his sack and pockets, but not more.

The officer struggled to avoid appearing wholly foolish. He changed his line of questioning and asked whether Orson had seen anyone trifling with the sports shop next door.

"No, sir, I haven't," replied Orson helpfully.

"Where do you live, young man?"

"In Germany."

The sheriff, a middle-aged man with serious eyes and cast of expression, wondered whether to interpret Orson's answer as insolent.

"What are you doing here?"

"I'm sort of exploring. I'm on vacation from college."

The sheriff was relieved by the plausibility of the explanation. People did go about the country exploring, after all, and some Americans did have parents in Germany.

But he was once again provoked when, in answer to the question "Where are you headed?" Orson replied, "I don't know, actually." Orson relieved the tension by asking, "Could you tell me which way to the railroad station?"

The sheriff gladly volunteered the directions and drove on.

Maybe he should write Mr. Simon and ask him where in Thomas Aquinas he could get clarification on the matter of requisitioning shelter. On the other hand, *fuck St. Thomas....* No, he took that back. *Well then, fuck Mr. Simon.* The idea made him smile.

Orson had had to accept his exchange, or lack of it, with Mr. Simon. A few weeks after he'd first come to Michigan, he had written to Mr. Simon, a letter full of campus detail—the courses being offered, the constitution of the student political assembly, the extracurricular diversions—that pleaded for advice and encouragement. He told Mr. Simon that he had felt his way through to five students "who feel the way we do about the capitalist order." There was no organization on campus that faithfully reflected the total anticapitalist position, and Orson thought he would not join the progressive party of the UM political assembly—"when you get right down to it, they're just a bunch of Democrats, and if President Kennedy told them to join the Green Berets and force capitalism down the throats of the Third World, they'd probably do just that. No hard resolution there, Mr. Simon. No really informed theoretical training."

That was almost two years ago. Mr. Simon hadn't replied, not even a postcard. And Orson would not be seeing him during that Christmas. He couldn't afford to return to Germany for the holidays, so he'd taken a two-week job with the post office, which always needed extra help during the season. Most nights, after work, he spent in the library. He found, in German, the new book of Günter Grass, *Dog Years,* and rejoiced in it, as much for the splendor of the language as for the independence of thought and the blistering indictment of the Christian Democratic government. He allowed himself to wonder whether Grass might be, at heart, a revolutionary. He picked up his courage, one night, to write again to Mr. Simon. He drank a beer before putting a sheet of paper into his typewriter. Then a second beer. He was not, this time around, his old docile self. The opening line, right after *Dear Mr. Simon,* suggested the mounting self-assurance.

> *I wrote to you two months ago and told you how it was going for me here, and how the situation was in terms of our common interests. Well, what do you know, I heard not one word back from you, not even* Alles gutes. *You know, Mr. Simon, I let myself think for a minute that the post office, which is half-breed socialism, let me down. But I've had*

*a lot of experience with it at a pretty intimate level in the
past week or two, and letters do get through. Mine had a return address, but it didn't come back, and I'm wondering
whether you've lost interest in your past protégé. I hope it
wasn't anything I told you the last time we visited, about
what happened in Paris. But now I'm wondering. Wondering
about a lot of things. Like West Germany—my Germany—
going for European political unification even though de
Gaulle is opposed. I'm wondering what you think about it.
Do hope to hear from you.*

He hadn't.

In Billings Orson felt briefly an activist impulse he had mostly
freed himself from in his six months of deracination: an impulse
to do something. How busy he had been—he thought back, as if
reflecting on a different person—for as long as he could remember. But that one day at Michigan convulsed his perspective. In
that one day he had engineered a farcical protest and gotten
booted out of school. He cared—he thought—that others should
continue the struggle, on the campuses and elsewhere. But he had
to let those programmatic ideological energies reassemble, in
their own way, in their own time. All that he felt he needed to do,
after his meeting with Mr. Revercomb and his good-bye to
Lizzie, was to do nothing. Doing nothing required very little pur-
posive thought, but from time to time there were specific problems, clerical problems, mostly. Like where's the post office?

Lars Woerward, his classmate at FDR, would have received
two weeks ago the postcard from Orson, giving Billings as the
site for the next package. Orson had received chapters in Madison, Fargo, and Bismarck. There should be a package waiting for
him here. If not, he'd forward another address to Woerward. Be-

fore that Orson would need to study the rail lines and figure out where to go. Maybe Phoenix. Maybe San Antonio.

He walked up the broad stairs of the post office, took off his malleable hat and stuffed it into his jacket pocket. At the window he asked, was there anything for Orson Killere?

The clerk returned in a few minutes, a package in hand. "You any relation to Gaymar Killere, Salt Lake City?"

Orson shook his head. "My people are all French." He signed for the package and walked two blocks to the large gray-stone public library.

There he went first to the men's room. He brought out his razor and shaved, washed his face, underarms, and torso with the sponge. Then he put away his pack and, jacket over his arm, went up to the second floor, to the large reading room. He sat down at one end of a long table and opened the package.

His eyes focused immediately on the money order. He felt a pang of relief: the seventy-five dollars would take him a long way. Before reading Lars's covering letter, he thought to give a moment to examining the reason for this jolt of satisfaction....

Mother Greed! The material imperative! Always present!

There had to be money, just to get by, granted. Was he being tempted to deflect from principle? No. By doing what he was doing he was not violating any of his deeply felt principles. Just as he was willing to wash dishes in exchange for food and shelter—an honorable exchange—he was willing to translate Lars's biography of the mad Bavarian king, Ludwig II, for a fee used to buy food, and occasional shelter. Not as a program of capital accumulation.

Lars had been a senior at the FDR School when Orson was a sophomore. They became friends, and Lars, uneasy in English, enjoyed talking in his native German with the precocious younger boy. Lars was now at Fordham University, in New York, and was writing the biography as a dissertation. It had to be presented to the faculty committee in English. From long habit, dating back to Wiesbaden, Lars relied on Orson to come up with idiomatic, even engaging translations. Orson looked down now on fifty-five pages of handwritten text in German. The working arrangement, made between old friends, had been $1.50 per translated page. He figured one hour's work per page. Lars had shortchanged him a bit, Orson smiled inwardly, given that it took more than one hour per translation of a single-spaced page.

But we college dropouts should not stoop to such materialist reckoning, he reproached himself, amused. He thought it entirely innocent to be pleased that he was actually enjoying the translation work. The last chapter he had worked on took Ludwig to the great state financial crisis in Bavaria of 1885, and he looked forward eagerly to the succeeding chapter. He got to work.

But it was a pity that he had no typewriter to work with. Still, he had fresh white paper, and his script was neat. He did require, for arcane words, the use of a German-English dictionary, and he had always found one in the public libraries.

Waiting for the librarian to free herself from a reader asking persistent questions, he ran his eyes over the *Billings Gazette,* which lay on the reading table (attached to the wooden spindle), along with day-old copies of the *New York Times* and the *Wall Street Journal.* He read hastily the lead news items in the Billings paper. The Warren Commission found that the assassination of President Kennedy had been a one-man operation. Republican nominee Senator Goldwater was campaigning in the South. President Johnson had denounced Goldwater's speech of the day before as "nuclear rhetoric." Orson had no interest. He turned to the next page. It carried the television, radio, and entertainment schedules.

His heart stopped beating. At the Loew's Theater: *Roustabout.* "The unforgettable new movie featuring Elvis Presley!"

He looked at his watch. He had been at work for four hours. The library closed at nine. The first showing of the movie was at

six, the second at eight. He felt a deep yearning to see his friend
and idol on the screen, but felt also the fear aroused by the conversation with Elvis back in May about the caustic Las Vegas
critic. Would he be viewing the same movie the critic had singled
out as an example of Hal Wallis making bad movies with Elvis in
order to bankroll good movies with Richard Burton?

"*Unforgettable*," the advertisement had described it. He
doubted that the people who wrote such things had ever actually
viewed the movies they were hyping. That's the way capitalism
works—sell it. Sell everything. But Elvis, surely, was selling himself? He'd see.

And then another pang. He hadn't called Elvis in a month. In
St. Louis he had rung from a motel room and spoken for almost
an hour. During that call he told Elvis that he was on a college
"field trip," and Elvis hadn't asked for more detail. He never did,
actually. Because he wasn't interested, really, and because Elvis
had come to believe that details were for other people to worry
about; and that, with Elvis, was in fact usually so. Elvis talked
during that call about Hollywood, about his planned return to
Graceland, about his conversations with Priscilla, about the stern
schedule the Colonel had set up for him, about the affair of the
heart of his Mafia companion, Red West. Orson said he would be
in wild country during the next weeks, nowhere near a telephone,
but would certainly phone in as soon as possible.

Had Elvis, back then in that phone call to Orson at Ann
Arbor, given the name of the movie in which he was having
trouble appearing as a "surly" character? Was that *Roustabout*?
Orson couldn't remember.

The elderly, obliging librarian arrived with the dictionary
Orson had asked for. Suddenly Orson felt overwhelmed by simultaneous pressures. Like the old days. *Obligations! Stress!* He
had to get started on the translation. He had to see the movie.
And he had to write to his mother.

He looked about the reading room. There were eight or ten readers there, two old women, two girls, a male student or two, one of them a young man at the other end of his reading desk, wearing red suspenders and taking notes. Orson had skipped lunch and was suddenly hungry. He asked the librarian, who wore a name tag—*Miss Mackey*—if there was a vending machine in the building. The man with the red suspenders interjected. "There's one outside, across the street at the Loew's Theater."

"Want me to pick up something for you?" Orson asked.

"Well yeah, a Milky Way." The student began to reach into his pocket for the money.

"Never mind," Orson said. "I'll treat." Ten cents for that guy's Milky Way, ten cents for Orson's, that meant he'd be down to $20.80. So? When he went to the post office tomorrow with his money order, that would increase his capital by $75, to $95.80.

He was back in a few minutes. He delivered the candy bar, opened his own, and, munching on it, began to read in German about Ludwig's bankruptcy and the state's expenses, significantly augmented by the king's support of the extravagant Richard Wagner.

He got to work. "*Die Verringerung des Kapitals war Ludwigs eigene Schuld....*" Ludwig's depleted capital was his own fault.

He crossed that out. Better: "The depletion in Ludwig's capital was his own responsibility."

He did a third take. "The depletion of capital was Ludwig's own fault." Okay.

It was 7:15, and the young man at the end of the desk rose and addressed Orson. His face was relaxed, now that he was away from his concentrated note taking. "You want to go get something to eat? Or you got plans?"

"I, er, I've got to see the movie. Across the way. It begins at eight."

"I'd like to see it, too. I've had enough of First World War battles."

"College paper?"

He nodded. "I'm Brian."

"I'm Orson." He looked down at his manuscript and carefully tucked the work away. He had got almost five pages done. "Where do we go to eat? I'm on a limited budget."

Brian put his light jacket over his suspenders. "Is that why you're giving away candy bars?"

Orson laughed. "That was thoughtless of me, I guess. Reflex action, return to old bad habits."

"I've got a car. But since we're going to the flick across the street, no point in using it. There's a café down the block. You know, Orson, you look kind of—thin."

"I'm okay, thanks. Just ... seeing the country on a nickel."

They entered the fried chicken place, and in fifteen minutes Orson found himself very happy for the company of a good-natured contemporary. Brian tried to pay for the chicken, but Orson said no.

"Wait a minute, this can't be just a one-way street," Brian protested. But Orson refused. "Okay, then. But I'll pay for Elvis."

Orson had to close his eyes and concentrate to fight down the awful temptation to blurt out his tie, the tie of this impoverished nomad, to the great public figure: *Elvis is my close friend ever since I was fourteen years old!*

He thanked the good Lord for his restraint. He repressed the impulse to such a bout of exhibitionism.

But after the movie, at the little bar, after two bottles of beer, he couldn't hold it all back. He trimmed the story a lot. What he said was that he had *met* the singer when Elvis Presley was a soldier in Germany and that he was a very nice guy and that Orson had ever since paid a lot of attention to all of Elvis's music.

Brian was himself an Elvis enthusiast, and they talked about the disappointing movie and about Elvis's career in the past few years.

Orson was discussing the new song, "Viva Las Vegas," when Brian interrupted him: "You don't have any place to stay the night, do you?"

Orson paused. "I'll find someplace."

"I'm in the dorm. I'm back to college early. There are maybe three empty rooms there."

Orson's full, surprised smile was like the one he'd worn when Elvis Presley showed up at his house almost six years ago.

He accepted the invitation instantly. "Make that *two* empty rooms."

He spent six nights as Brian's guest.

On the last day Brian invited him to an evening at his fraternity, Delta Sigma Chi. Everyone was back, and there'd be a celebration in honor of the football team. Orson borrowed a shirt and tie—"I don't need red suspenders, thanks"—and was indistinguishable from the forty fraternity brothers who toasted, and retoasted, the victorious football team. After supper the fraternity members brought in their girlfriends for the show. Brian invited Orson to sit with him and Phyllis—Phyllis was from Detroit. Orson acknowledged the home of the *Detroit Free Press* and told them that that was the paper that had memorialized the great human-chain episode and got him kicked out of school.

They sat together on the floor with sixty-odd other couples. DSC's living room was large and comfortable, but students needed all the floor space to crowd in. The area by the chimney had become a stage of sorts. They were silenced by the master of ceremonies, whose voice boomed through a commanding set of loudspeakers.

The tall, redheaded emcee with the agreeable features wore his hair down to his shoulders. He had on a checkered blue jacket, a yellow handkerchief neatly in place in the breast pocket. His broad yellow tie was held in place by a large clasp displaying the proud initials of Delta Sigma Chi.

"That's Slim Castle," Brian whispered. "He's *really* good. Real showbiz."

Castle used a lavalier microphone and spoke in jovial tones, without pause. He would begin the evening, he said, by presenting the great touring magician from Transylvania, Count Dracula.

While the drummer did the executioner's roll on the drums, Slim Castle ducked back from the large overhead light and reappeared wearing a shawl, a mustache, and an opera hat.

In an exaggerated German accent, he thanked "my American friends," complained of his ill-fitting hat, drew it down, and extracted a white rabbit from it. Half the assembly applauded, half booed lightheartedly, and Count Dracula proceeded to juggle four tennis balls.

"What's great about Slim," Phyllis whispered to Orson, "is he can do all that stuff and never stop talking." Which indeed Slim did not, his rambling, buoyant, pep-party talk generating, after a little while, a mesmerizing effect, sheltering Slim from insubordinate rabbits, dropped balls, and failed jokes.

Never drawing breath, Slim now signaled to the band. The student on the guitar led off, the drummer provided the enthusiastic beat, and the girl on the piano hit the chords as Slim began to roar out his imitation of Elvis Presley's journey to "Heartbreak Hotel." He howled out the words with the abandoned melancholy of the master, hitting the tremulous blues of a soul song. Orson closed his eyes, and heard the King himself singing, singing plaintively that he got so *lo-hne-ly* he could *diiie*. The words hit Orson hard, and he gave a fleeting thought, even before Slim ended, to the lonely road he had traveled in the months since leaving Ann Arbor. He swallowed hard. His eyes misted. But then he joined happily in the applause.

"What did you think?—" Brian interrupted himself, turning to Phyllis: "Orson here, *saw* him once, saw Elvis in Germany." Phyllis was much impressed, but they were quickly silent again. Slim was doing a monologue, imitating Jack Benny.

It was after midnight, and Phyllis said she'd be going back to her dorm. Orson looked up at Brian, whose lead he would follow. He motioned to Orson to wait, went off to the door with Phyllis to say good night, and came back.

"Let's have a last beer."

He drew two bottles from the ice in the aluminum tub alongside the bar, sat down on the rounded sofa at the corner, and said, "You know, if you want, you can tell me what you're up to."

Orson didn't want to sound aloof. So he had to come up with something more than mere routine. Something better than that he had an ingenuous curiosity about life and travel alone. It would be cowardly to say just that. He wasn't talking to Dean Revercomb.

So he answered, "Well, to tell you the truth, I think capitalism is shit and we're risking nuclear war. But let's not," he smiled fully at Brian, "you know, let's not *push* it."

But, Brian wanted to know, what did he intend to do in the time ahead?

"That's a problem, I'm not sure, but I want, you know, to let my thoughts come together. I don't even know whether I'll *want* to go back to school."

Had he read Kerouac's *On the Road,* Brian wanted to know?

In fact he hadn't, though of course he had heard about it, said Orson. Did the book have a key to everything? A key to *anything*?

"I don't know," Brian said. "Maybe if I had your itch, I'd find something there."

Orson said he'd pick up a copy.

"Don't *move*. I'm talking about—I'll be gone three minutes."

In five minutes Brian was back, out of breath from the round-trip sprint to his room. He handed Orson his own, marked-up copy of *On the Road*.

"Here's my candy bar."

21

Billings, October 1964

IT HAD GOT COLD, SO WHEN HE WROTE TO LARS WOER-
ward he gave him Phoenix as the address for the next manuscript
shipment. Arizona is always warm, Orson had read. And he had
the Rockies yet to cross. In his conversations with Brian, the
question arose, How was Orson to protect himself from such
cold? "Kerouac was on a truck and he said it was ice-cold, and
what he did was drink whiskey every little while," Brian grinned.

Well, Orson would face that problem as required, and he was
in no hurry: The next chapter wouldn't be coming in for several
weeks. Lars had notified him, when he'd sent the Billings install-
ment, that Orson was well ahead of him. "You may have to wait
a little before Ludwig gets to be terminally insane." So...while
the Emperor Ludwig was taking a bit of time to go cuckoo,
Orson would take a bit of time, Your Royal Majesty, to go where
the weather would be warmer.

When he got ready to say good-bye to Miss Mackey, after the
sixth day, Orson permitted himself to wish that he had lots of
money to spend. She had greeted him every morning with a
mother's smile, handing him the dictionary and wishing him a
"good writing day."

On the fifth day she had brought him chocolate-chip peanut butter cookies. "I hope you like them. I made them once before for my sister, who hated them, but she hates most things."

If he had a magic wand, he'd have given her, he played with the idea, a pearl tiara, because her head and the regal shape of her hair would have shown it off finely. He imagined the splendid tiara of the bejeweled queen, Sophie, who, according to Lars, had radiated when it was placed on top of her regal head. He did what little he could. He gave Miss Mackey a card, a Hallmark card bought at the drugstore (fifteen cents), and wrote on it: *To the super custodian of the German-English dictionary, with affectionate thanks from a greedy user—Orson*. Miss Mackey leaned over and kissed him on the forehead. He returned with a lingering kiss on her aged hand.

The day's travel west brought him to the junction at which he would bear off from the Northern Pacific line in favor of the greater Santa Fe network of the Southwest. Aboard the southbound train, he sat on the straw matting in the empty half of the boxcar as the train rumbled down the track that paralleled the Rocky Mountains, heading for Utah. Now fully awake he felt a desire to talk. Most of his conversation, since leaving Ann Arbor, had been utilitarian. But in the six days in Billings, he had many hours with Brian, between long bouts at the library. He enjoyed the human company and now wondered for how long—weeks? months?—he would want to continue with the solitude of the past six months.

But it was prudent, he knew, to make allowances for sudden mood changes. In the early pages of the book Brian had given him, Kerouac wrote about a girl he had picked up. "I tried to tell her how excited I was about life and the things we could do together—saying that, and planning to leave Denver in two days." Kerouac knew what he was going to do. Orson didn't.

Kerouac had spent a lot of time on the road writing. He

appeared to be writing constantly. He was writing screenplays and poetry and a novel. Orson didn't do that. He wrote only when he was translating, and his letters to his mother, every week or so, but he found them hard going, in part because he didn't think it would interest her to recount what train he had taken, going from where to where, and she didn't welcome political ruminations, which he had, in any case, pretty well run out of. But then who did? Except for his little band at the university? And, sure, at a few other campuses—Tim had reported that there were stirrings at Columbia. And Lizzie had told of a determined little nucleus at Berkeley.

In the meantime, as always, there was a need to reflect; and to guard against the creeping cold.

22

Wyoming, October 1964

THE TRAIN STOPPED SOON AFTER CHEYENNE. A TRAIN engineer peered into the car and shone his flashlight on Orson, who was hunched at an angle to let the overhead light fall on his book.

He had had several such encounters. Sometimes the trainman made him get out of the car. When that happened, he simply had to make do. As long as he kept his eye on the time of year, he could maneuver to travel in clement weather and he was prepared, if necessary, to spend the night outdoors. There was always some way to protect against the rain. Kerouac, he was just now reading, said that if he found himself really in "deep shit," deep drafts of the weed provided solace. He was correct, Orson verified.

At Cheyenne the man behind the flashlight had said nothing, but an instant later the overhead light was switched off. If it had been much earlier, Orson would have groped his way to where the switch was and, after the train left the station, turned it back on.

But it was well into night, so he closed the dog-eared page in Kerouac and burrowed his hand into his sack feeling for his Zippo. He couldn't roll a joint and keep the Zippo lit at the same time. A small flashlight, gripped between his teeth, would have been useful. Now he would need to roll his joint by feel. When he first tried to do this, in St. Louis, he all but gave it up as impossible. But then the next day a fellow passenger, Burt, with whom he ended up sharing two days on the train, ridiculed the problem, raising his voice to be heard over the rattling of the wheels. "How do you think blind people roll joints?"

Orson was intrigued by the challenge presented in that perspective. "You see all right?" Burt asked. "Your glasses look like they're stuck on your face."

"I can see okay, but it's got to be with my glasses on."

Burt said: "Look, I'm going to close my own eyes." He reached in the deep pocket of his coat and brought out a pouch. He zipped it open and felt inside for the container. He drew out a rolling paper, shaped it with his finger, reached back into the pouch and with thumb and forefinger picked up a pinch.

"You gotta be prepared to lose some. But when you light up you can probably see what you spilled, pick it up, and put it back in the pouch." Burt ran his tongue down the paper and feelingly sealed it together. His eyes still shut, he reached once again into the pouch and brought out a lighter. Now he opened his eyes.

Orson was gingerly engaged in imitating Burt at Cheyenne when another flashlight shone on him. There had been silent boarders, toward the end of the ten-minute stop in Cheyenne.

"I'll give you a hand with that, dude."

Orson flicked off the lighter.

"Thanks." He heard a second voice, then a third. "Want some?"

There was no answer. The flashlight beam searched about the car for the switch box. The first man, locating it, trained his light on it. One of his companions perched his foot on the crossbeam, reached up, and now the overhead light was on them.

At that moment the train began to pull forward.

All three of the men wore cowboy boots and hats and were un-shaven. Cowhands, Orson supposed. A large, worn suitcase made up a table around which they positioned themselves. The third man took a slug from a whiskey bottle and passed it around.

Orson drew on his joint, inhaling deeply, waiting with some pleasurable anticipation for the snoozy lift he had gotten used to. He opened his eyes only to give himself the gratification of seeing his exhaled smoke snake up in the dim light. Then he would close his eyes, until it was time for the next drag. But the words he heard next intruded on his sleepy composure. He couldn't discern who was talking. But the words came in distinctly.

"I say fuck Cheyenne."

"What're we going to find in Denver that Cheyenne doesn't have?"

"A sleepier man at the switch. That guy back there must've had the alarm attached to his eyelids. He looked like he was still asleep when the alarm went off."

"Fuck it." The first man's voice was the voice of the leader, it was clear. The bottle went around again.

Then, "What about the kid here. Worth rolling him?"

"Doesn't look like he's traveling heavy. Might be worth it to see if he has a pretty ass down there, what you think, Gus?"

The flashlight shone on Orson's face.

"He looks a little like a girl. He must've shaved five minutes ago. Maybe he's never shaved." There was laughter.

"You go ahead. Me, I'll jerk off on this—"

Orson could see him unlatch the suitcase, reach inside, and bring up a magazine, which he unfolded.

Orson ground his joint out on the floor. His head suddenly felt light, his nerve ends were tingling. His eyes searched the darker end of the car for anything that might serve as a weapon. He could make out what looked like folding chairs lying on each other.

Again the voice of the second man.

"Hey, you there. Drop yer drawers. Let's see your pretty ass."

He would try to discourage them.

"Hey, guys. Cut it out, okay? You want a case of clap? Go ahead!" He thought to try putting a light side on it all.

There was a moment's silence.

Then again, "Come on pretty boy, I'll take my chances."

Orson rose and strode quickly to the end of the car. He pried up an aluminum chair. He held it up. "Okay, I said cut it out."

There was an exchange of words. Two of the men rose and moved toward him.

Orson swung the chair hard on the head of the nearest man. The second lunged at his feet.

From the third man. "*Sheeyit!* That fucker...hit me! Hit me hard."

The first man dropped his magazine and stood up. Orson could see a massive shape moving toward him. He aimed his fists at the man whose arms were closed around his legs.

"Okay, then," the leader spoke. "Let's teach him a little manners. Hang on to him, Heston."

Orson aimed his knee at the face of the man wrestling with his legs and fought himself free. The first drove his fist into Orson's stomach. Orson gasped for breath. The second man lunged at his chest and brought him down to the floor. He kicked Orson's side vigorously once, then repeatedly. "This little prick needs a going over." The first man grabbed Orson by the ears and knocked his head on the floor.

"Hey, wait a minute."

Orson didn't know who said that.

"Take off his glasses."

One man gripped Orson's hair, his knees holding down his arms. "Lem, take off his glasses." A pair of hands removed them.

Then they took turns, smashing him on the head and kicking him on his side.

Orson passed out.

He didn't know how much time had passed. Without his glasses he could barely discern the forms of the three men, but could tell that they were spread out around their suitcase, apparently asleep. With acute pain he pulled up his jeans. He reached about for his glasses. He was eternally grateful when he found them. It was painful to move any part of his body. Slowly his mind brought focus on the scene.

The train had stopped. If he had a gun, he thought, he would fire at their groins, one after another. Maybe two shots at the third man. Instead, he could only just manage to crawl to the door handle and open it.

He let his body slip over the side, falling down to the concrete of the platform, his backpack behind him, his body in agonizing pain. He inched his way across the adjacent track and tried to sleep, a bare ten feet away from an abandoned car, athwart the pain in his head, shoulders, sides, and back. He was relieved to make out the Cheyenne train pulling away.

23

Laramie, November 1964

HE WAS EIGHT DAYS IN LARAMIE. HE HAD MADE HIS way to the university's health center. The woman at the desk asked for his student ID. Orson shook his head and said "they" had taken everything. She asked no further questions; obviously he was a student, obviously in terrible distress. She sent him to daycare, and an elderly doctor looked him over, felt his bones, pronounced him "lucky" for being "in one piece," gave him a slip to take to radiography for an X-ray of his head, and handed him a score of painkillers. Orson pocketed these and some tubes of salve, thanked the doctor, and walked away. They'd want specific ID at the X-ray center, he suspected. He'd give that a pass. What he needed was sleep, a lot of sleep.

He surveilled students coming out of a dorm, found a room that was unoccupied, without furniture except for a bed and mattress, and slept for twenty hours. The next day he had no trouble insinuating himself in the line of students passing through the cafeteria: He presented his slip from the health center, saying he had lost all his IDs. No one, looking at him, was in a mood to deny him access to the food counter.

He made his way to the university library. There was no problem occupying one of its corner desks. And when he leaned over and slept, no one bothered him. The broad bandage over his head gave him welcome protection from curiosity, or unwelcome intervention. He gave blurred attention to random books, but did not read with understanding, or system. He needed, he knew, a single thing, the passage of time. The more of it the better. He needed to mend his wounds, but also to absorb them. He spent time walking about the expansive grounds of the university, and on the third day forced himself to exercise his arms and legs, and to breath deeply the mountain air. Back at the library he checked the foreign magazines and found himself gratefully immersed in French and German. On day six he opened the local newspaper, the *Laramie Daily Boomerang*, and noted that the presidential election had just come and gone. His bandage was off, his swellings gone. That night he spent the money to buy a movie ticket. His companions in the boxcar hadn't bothered to take his wallet and its thirty-two-dollar collection of fives and one-dollar bills. He saw the Beatles' *A Hard Day's Night* and felt cheered. He had eaten well at the cafeteria and went now to the local bar. After the second beer he decided to end the hiatus the following day, to go back on the road, but with less conviction than when he had set out from Ann Arbor six months before. At any rate he needed to earn some money and needed to move south, where it would be warmer.

Finding a boxcar late in the morning, he was bound for Denver, where Kerouac had spent so much time, and then Salt Lake City. He tried to chase the memory of the three men from his mind. He attempted to relate the violence to the capitalist system—property is theft, didn't everybody know? But he didn't put great effort into it. What he did was add a bowie knife to his knapsack equipment. A day later he was in Utah.

At Salt Lake City Orson left the railroad boxcar, disappointed that he had been deprived of the feel of the Rockies. He'd heard it described as the most beautiful ten-hour rail ride in America, Denver to Salt Lake City. What seemed a mile of wooden barrels, stuffed with steel 2.78 rods (so the stamped letters on the barrel described them) had been stuffed into the car minutes before departure from Laramie, leaving Orson and the two Mexican occupants with little more than breathing space. There was no view of the exterior, but Orson was grateful that the overhead light had been kept on, and he geared himself with equanimity to ten hours of sleeping, reading, eating his tightly packed sandwich, sipping the ginger ale from the can with the pop top, and spending one more night on the rails, shielded from the cold air of the Rockies.

He exchanged, as he had got used to doing, a few words with his fellow passengers, but the short, browned men in their thirties talked in Spanish and fiddled with their little portable radio, with an antenna that brought in a transmitter here and there on an alpine peak. The Mexican called Braulio offered Orson a slender, limp cigarillo, proffered with a knowing look and the only necessary introduction to it as "good stuff."

Orson shook his head, said "gracias." *Not tonight, thanks.*

He'd thought back to Elvis's occasional declamations against drugs, tobacco, and booze, and remembered benignly the hotel in Paris where Elvis offered his sleep-deprived companions one of his amphetamines. After passing the big bottle of pills to Lamar and Joe and Charlie, Elvis had yanked it away from Orson—who, after all, was subject to a curfew of 3:30 A.M. "You'd hardly need one of these, Killer. They're to keep you awake, but what you'll want is to sleep."

Marijuana, Orson knew now from practice, was different. The very idea of pot was good; altering one's mind, suspending one's tactile dependency on the world about you. He turned back to the book by Kerouac.

———

Arrived in Salt Lake City, he was grateful for the expansive facilities in the railroad station's men's room. And in the terminal he would not be disturbed at this late hour; he slept on one of the great waiting room benches, his backpack under his head. Early in the morning he passed through the station clean and shaven and curious to know something of the capital of U.S. Mormonism and (according to Judy Harris, back at Ann Arbor), the "cradle of soft-snow skiing."

He sipped his coffee, ate his sweet roll at the station's restaurant, and perused a discarded copy of the *Salt Lake City Tribune*. The headline spoke of President Johnson's launching of an antipoverty program at his ranch in Texas, where he was "resting from his triumphant victory over Senator Goldwater." He turned to the Help Wanted column and saw the ad: *Wanted, day-time laborers at highway construction site.* He was attracted to the entry-level wage, $2.15 per hour. Ah, capitalism and its vulgar market allocations! By digging ditches (or whatever other labor he'd be asked to do), he would earn more money per hour than by sitting at the Billings library putting into readable English an obdurate German text....On the other hand, he had to acknowledge, he was physically more comfortable at that table in the library than he'd no doubt be at Hagel's Construction, Inc. He looked again at the ad, memorizing the address on Sutter Street. So maybe it was fair that he'd be paid less for his work at the library than at the construction site.

At the railroad station and, in fact, everywhere in Salt Lake City, the hospitality of the Mormon community was active. The woman at the tourist information desk gave him full instructions on how to get to the building site at Sutter Street. Two bus rides and a half-mile walk, and he was there, reporting just before ten to the improvised office in front of a large area of upturned dirt, where, he'd soon find, a new access road to the highway was to be constructed.

He would not be deceitful, so he informed the bearded hiring agent that he was looking for work for only a few days.

Buzz, as the young girl in the inner office referred to her boss, made notations on a hiring slip and motioned Orson to follow him outside. "Take the calls while I'm gone," he instructed the girl, who nodded while bent over the desk. The early light caught her flaxen hair and illuminated her straw hat.

"That's Susan back there," Buzz said. "Thank God for college dropouts. Your job is to unpack the steel rods we'll be using with the cement."

Buzz led him to an outdoor toolshed and pointed vaguely to a collection of tools. Then, at the other end of the supply depot, to what seemed an endless supply of wooden barrels. Orson found himself face-to-face with the cargo that had accompanied him on his journey from Denver.

He was given no further instructions. "Just open up those barrels and lay the rods on the ground alongside." Buzz looked first at one of the barrels, then over to Orson. "You're a good, young husky guy. I figure...what? You can open up three of them in one hour? We've got eight hundred barrels out there. You'll need gloves and some sort of apron. You'll find all that stuff in the tool room." He looked down at his watch. "It's ten-twenty-one, but I'll put it down that you began work at ten."

At twelve Orson was sweating. He had gone at his job inventively, and by the time he got to the third barrel, had made some rudimentary calculations based on the configuration of hoops and staves and the placement of the nails. But there was no way to substitute for the need of brute force, however large the hammer and chisel, in loosening the hoops, opening up the staves and, finally, lifting the heavy rods into neat piles alongside.

He had only six barrels emptied when the girl came out—the November sun was hot now, and Orson wished he had pulled his dark glasses from the backpack parked in the coat room of the office. He looked up at her, shielding his eyes with his hand.

"I'm Susan," she said. Her voice was that of a very young girl. Too young, he later remembered thinking, to acquire any mannerisms.

"I'm Orson. It's hot."

"Yep. I figured maybe Buzz forgot to tell you that we get a half hour off at noon, with nothing docked from the pay. So you're free until 12:30, and I bet you're hungry. I am. I always pack enough for two. But let's eat in the shade."

She motioned toward a wooden structure over the parked truck, which gave a welcome shadow. She smiled at him, and he smiled back at the sweetness of her gesture. Her animation and smile were especially welcome after the hard exertions. "Let me see your bag. Otherwise I don't trust you that you packed for two."

She handed it over. "Go ahead. Rip it open."

"I'll open anything that doesn't require a large hammer, a claw, and a chisel."

He picked open the brown paper bag. There were four sandwiches wrapped in wax paper, two apples, and a container of Oreo cookies.

"You know," she said, unwrapping one sandwich, "I like your face. You're very handsome."

Orson looked at her. She was not the precocious beauty Priscilla was. Not the cute, appealing pixie of Lizzie Doyle from UM. He thought that she could only be a product of Mormon country, bright and direct, with the face of a girl whose freshness refracted as if from a pool of water.

"You're not so bad."

"I was wondering what you'd say. You know, I never said to anyone, to any boy—I have a handsome grandfather, and I said it to him once—that he's handsome. Actually, there are a lot of handsome boys in Salt Lake. We make beautiful people here."

"You're from here?"

"Yes. I've never actually traveled out of state, except once on the train to Denver—"

"I came on that trip yesterday."

"It's beautiful, isn't it?"

Should he tell her that where he was riding he couldn't see the outside? No.

"But I'm thinking to travel now," Susan said. "My Mom and Dad were killed in an auto accident two months ago, September fifteenth, and after the funeral I just decided to quit college. I can always go back."

"I'm sorry about them. About you. I quit too. Only I was expelled. I can also go back, but I'm not sure I will."

Susan seemed overjoyed at their common experience. But it was already 12:30, and Buzz called over to them. "Back to work, team."

He got up. "Thanks loads."

She gave him her fresh, delighted smile. "*Okay! Okay.*"

"We'll talk later?"

"Oh yes," she replied.

"Coming, Buzz," she called out.

24

Phoenix, November 1964

APPROACHING PHOENIX EIGHT DAYS LATER SUSAN said it would be nice to visit Senator Goldwater. Orson told her such impromptu visits with strangers just didn't happen, not with presidential candidates. She was not put off.

"If I was old enough to vote I would have voted for him. Mom and Dad liked him a lot, too. You're not old enough to vote either. Remind me—when will you be twenty-one?"

"Next January."

Orson thought to tell her about his birthday drama and the genesis of his surname, Killere. His impulse was to tell her all, and sometimes he reproached himself for talking to her in what seemed an almost breathless effort to catch her up on everything. But not now. He said nothing. Her head, with the light, loose hair, rested on his shoulder as the bus they boarded at Provo rolled down the highway. But he changed his mind. He put his arm around her and squeezed her hand: Yes, he'd tell her.

"You know," he tilted his head a little, "Elvis was born on January eighth—that's January eighth, 1935. Well, I came along on January ninth—1945. So when I was living in Germany I made Mother celebrate my birthday at midnight. Why? Because that meant that Elvis's birthday and mine were coinciding—for seven hours."

"I like that. I like everything you've said about Elvis." She raised her head and narrowed her eyes inquiringly.

"I'll tell you more about him one day."

"Why not today?"

"Because...it's a long story. And anyway, we're pulling into Phoenix. Ready to do some touring?"

"You bet. I've never toured, except in Utah. And that one day in Denver I told you about. Orson, could I ask you for just one thing?"

"You can ask me for anything you want."

"Can we rent a car? I've told you how rich I am."

With his left hand he reached over to her chin and brought her face up. Her eyes were closed now. There was just a trace of a smile on her lips. *Rich!* she had described herself.

"Oh, Susie. You're not *rich*. You said your trust gives you college tuition plus two hundred dollars per month. That's not rich. And, anyway, you're not *in* college right now."

"Yes, but I get the two hundred dollars even if I'm *not* in college. I've got a *ton* of money with me right now, in my bag."

"My mum has a college fund, too," Orson thought to recall. "But there isn't a monthly allowance that goes with it. So what we have is your two hundred dollars plus whatever I can bring in."

"You'll go to the post office. And you'll get your friend's chapter with another check, and you, too, will be rich. I want you to tell me about King Ludwig—"

"I'll do that. The whole story."

"Orson, honey, we can rent a car for five dollars. At least, you can rent a car for that in Salt Lake. And maybe for less, if we tell the dealer how much I like Senator Goldwater."

Orson laughed. There and then he rescinded his resolve to live every day like a Capuchin monk. He was nineteen years old, and he felt a huge store of energy stirring, and some of that would need indulging. He was blissful in her company. He would not forget his obligations—to Lars, to his mother, to Elvis—but for the duration of his work on the next chapter, he'd gratify himself. The chapter would be waiting for him, and while working on it he'd live under a roof, and bathe other than in public washrooms. A motel!

The bus nudged to a stop and Orson reached up for Susan's canvas bag and his backpack. She bounded into the aisle. Her golden hair was now tied behind her head in a bun. Her shirt had slipped down. She brought it up, and her firm little breasts moved up with the tension. She looked out through the window into the sun. "I think I'll like Phoenix. Let's ask where Senator Goldwater lives and maybe—with our rented car!—we can drive up there and just—wait and see if he comes out of his house?"

Orson wondered whether the Secret Service that had protected the presidential candidate during the campaign had been withdrawn—the national election was three weeks ago.

"We'll find out," he said indulgently. Orson climbed down the steps and turned to help Susie, but she had already bounded to the ground and stooped over to pick up her bag.

In the motel they registered as husband and wife.

Walking along the passageway toward their room, Orson betrayed his hesitation. He found himself asking: Would Susan prefer a separate room? Should he give her that alternative? The civilized thing to do? But could he bear it, that she should be other than at his side, that he should be other than one in her?

She read his mind. "No," she said, when he asked, leading the way to the assigned room number.

When, that morning, they walked into the hotel room at DuPont Place, they had not before shared a bed. Everything was novel. Everything that would become routine, after two or three nights together, was now improvised. He brought in the bags, placing them on the baggage rack and on the floor. Susan closed the door and drew down the window shade.

"I know what you're thinking, dear, dear Orson. My Orson. But I don't want to be funny about it. And, anyway, I've done this before, but never before with anybody I loved the way I love you."

She turned her head away. Orson could discern, in the darkened room with only the crack of light from the bottom of the shade, that she had discarded her shirt and let down her jeans. And now she was lying on the bed.

"Come," she said.

Lying naked at her side, he stroked and kissed her. She moved her hands about his body, coming to rest finally on his tremulous and worshipful sex. He hoped and prayed that it would last forever.

25

Phoenix, November 25, 1964

IT WAS THE WEDNESDAY BEFORE THANKSGIVING. THE night before there had been a banquet of the Arizona Republican Party, according to the *Arizona Republic*. And the honored speaker was: Senator Barry Goldwater, giving what was billed as his first speech since the sad end of his sad campaign. Susan hoped the Phoenix local television news channel would play an account of it, but she didn't want to wake Orson. He lay there, still naked, a day's growth of beard on his tanned face, almost unrecognizable without the little glasses that were so much a fixture—was he born with glasses on? She reminded herself, playfully, to ask him sometime.

She tiptoed to the television set, situated on the extended windowsill across the room. She thought to twist it about a bit, so that it wouldn't be aimed at the bed—aimed at Orson. It was, at this moment, pointed right at his face, right at his lips (she studied them), which were just slightly separated, the white teeth barely visible, the light brown hair of his head dangling at the side, over one eye.

Stealthily she turned the dial to channel 6, listed on the printed card thumbtacked to one side as the independent Phoenix station. She began to turn delicately the power knobs and had to remind herself that she wasn't in the business of adjusting volume control. The button on her finger would give her either on or off. So she pushed it down decisively, after establishing that the volume was turned down all the way. But no matter; Orson woke. He cocked his head up on the headboard.

"What you looking for, Susan?"

"I thought there might be something about the banquet last night with Senator Goldwater—*Shh!*"

Orson reached over to the night table for his glasses, raised the sheet over his legs, and listened to the newscaster. The screen showed a still photograph of the dais at the Hotel San Carlos. The news reader described the event:

> "...introduced by Congressman John J. Rhodes Jr. and received a standing ovation. The senator opened his remarks by saying, 'Where were all you people on election day?' and got a big laugh. Mrs. Tillich, party chairwoman, reported that the two hundred fifty diners, who paid twenty-two-fifty each, had contributed forty-three hundred dollars to the GOP coffers to help to retire Senator Goldwater's debt...In other news, J. Edgar Hoover, director of the FBI, responded critically to the Warren Commission's report on the FBI's role in Dallas at the time of the presidential assassination..."

Susan gave a half minute's attention to the news broadcast. "Turn it off and come back here," Orson said.

She did as asked. And added, "Maybe we can have some music."

"There's a radio right by me. What kind of music do you like?"

"You don't know, Orson Killere? You're running all over the

United States with a girlfriend, and you don't even know what kind of music she likes?"

Orson grunted, his eyes closed. "She likes the music I can make ... when ... I say how much I love her. When I"—Orson opened his eyes and smiled as lecherously as he knew how—"express myself on the subject."

Her panties were down. She stretched her hands up to his neck. "If *you* had run for president, I think *you* would have won."

"If I did, I'd appoint you—what?"

"I can't talk with your ... with you ... distracting me."

"I'll wait. You can tell me later. Only, whatever it is, you'd have to sleep in the White House with me."

"I'll sleep wherever you are, Orson Killere," she managed to say.

They had a map of Phoenix from the motel shop that sold papers and sundries, and Susan bought the special campaign shirt, which was on sale. The cashier gave them a brief orientation, and without much difficulty they triangulated their way to Barry Goldwater's house, up the hill in Paradise Valley. Susan's projected strategy was straightforward. "We'll just drive up there and say we want to see him. Orson, sometime you have to explain to me why you are a socialist, against everything Senator Goldwater—and I—and the freedom-loving world—"

"And the God-fearing world. You left that out."

She was cross, momentarily. "If he does come out, you just shut up, I'll do the talking."

"So I'm not supposed to act like the American people? And tell him to clam up?"

"The American people don't *necessarily* vote for the right person. So go on back to your—your socialism."

It was just 8:15 in the morning. They were able to drive the rented Chevy closer than Orson thought they'd get, right up to the small parking area opposite the wooden, stone-trimmed house. A plainclothesman stepped out from an area between the house and the garage. His expression was benevolent.

"Miss. Young man. This is private property."

Susan, in her jeans and her brand-new Goldwater-for-President sports shirt, the top two buttons unfastened, had opened the door and climbed out of the car. Orson followed suit. A determined freshness lit up her face. The highlights of her hair bounced off the early sun.

The guard raised his hand gently. "You can't come in any closer—Miss—?" His question was genial.

"Susan. Susan Young."

"Susan. And what's your boyfriend's name? Can't imagine either one of you was old enough to vote for the senator on Election Day—"

"I would have, if I could have...Would you just, maybe knock on the door?"

"*Susan,*" the guard's voice was now direct. "Senator Goldwater was running for president of the United States up till just three weeks ago, and he's got to be resting up, and he can't just see *everybody,* you know. Twenty-six million people voted for him. Now—what's your boyfriend's name?"

"Orson."

"*Orson?*"

"Yes. Like Orson Welles."

"Well now, Orson." The officer shifted his gaze from Susan. "Let's not make any trouble here." He signaled with his hand, and a second guard emerged from the garage and stood by, silent.

"Come on, Susan," Orson said. He turned to her and signaled his frustration by shrugging his shoulders. He addressed the guard. "We'll write to the senator and ask for an appointment."

"You do that, Orson."

The car door was open and Susan had slid one leg inside when they heard the voice.

"Henry? *Henry.* What you up to?"

The guard stiffened and turned his head to the main door, open now. "Senator, just looking out for you, sir."

He was dressed in khaki chinos and a sport shirt freckled with cactus plants. He peered over, examining Orson, who stood next to the Chevy, by the driver's door. Susan was on the passenger side, her left leg still inside the car.

Combined, their ages had to be less than forty, Goldwater thought. "Well, Henry, maybe you should carry an AK-47, for a tough assignment like this one."

When he stepped down to the driveway, he cast a long shadow that stretched to the yellow Chevrolet.

"What's your name, miss?"

Susan's face stretched wide. She withdrew her leg from the car.

"I'm Susan, senator."

"Well, now that you've pulled your leg out of the car, Susan, you can say hello. Who's the young feller?"

"This is Orson." She hesitated for a moment. "Orson Killere."

Goldwater stretched out his hand. "Welcome to my house, Orson." Susan came busily around and extended her own hand.

"We just wanted to stop by, senator. We're—I'm a big fan."

"You're not a big anything, Susan, you're a nice little lady. A very pretty little lady. Where you all from?"

Susan lowered her eyes. Her mind was reeling from the whole scene. *Talking with Senator Goldwater! Looking over, three feet away, at that noble, freckle-faced, that handsome man who— well, nearly—became president! Being told by him she was so pretty!*

She stammered, and Goldwater turned to Orson.

"You from this part of the world, son?"

Orson said, "No, sir. We're just sort of driving by."

"Well, I'm real glad you didn't glide by without landing here." He turned to Henry. "Henry, let's take our visitors into our hi-fi room, give them a Coca-Cola. Emil," he called out to the second plainclothesman. "Emil, tell Berta to bring on over some Cokes to the radio room."

He turned to Orson, motioning him to follow across the parking area, toward the garage. "That's my radio room, and I spend a lot of time here."

He brought up what seemed a cigarette lighter from his pocket, held it aloft, and the garage door creaked open. "That's my radio signal. Touch this here, it beams out instructions, the door opens. Got to keep up with modern times." He grinned, motioning them into the room. "I told that to the voting public, and you know what?" He turned and laughed. "They said, *No thanks.*"

They were in what looked to Orson like a recording studio. Goldwater eased himself into a reclining chair opposite a bank of wires and sockets. He motioned Orson and Susan to sit on the two studio chairs.

"You want to hear what they're saying on Radio Moscow?" He looked down at his watch. "It'll be just after seven there. Unless Karl Marx has changed the sidereal system." He consulted a shortwave registry, switched a patch cable to a different socket, and tuned the dial. A man's voice floated in from the speaker.

"You speak Russian?" he asked Orson teasingly.

Orson shook his head. Susan quickly broke in. "But Orson speaks perfect German and perfect French, senator."

"That's good," Goldwater smiled. "I can handle a little Spanish. Not as much as I pretended, during the campaign. *Un poco. Usted habla español?*"

Susan shook her head and accepted a Coca-Cola from an elderly Mexican servant woman. "Thanks." Orson took the second bottle, Goldwater reached for the third.

"Berta. This is Susan and Orson. Now get out of here, *mama-cita,* we old folks have to talk some foreign policy. Oh. Berta, tell Mrs. Goldwater I'll need to be eating early. Twelve o'clock. Got a college seminar at two o'clock."

Berta left with the empty tray. The droning Russian voice continued to come in on the radio. After a concentrated few seconds, Goldwater turned to Susan, shifted his eyes to Orson and back.

"Those bastards, you ever read the things they broadcast every night? Read what they're *saying?*"

He paused to turn down the volume. And then, to Orson, he went on. "I get reports, whenever I ask for them, on the text of what gets said. I've had them since way back before the presidential thing. Got them as a member of the intelligence committee. I'm kind of lonely these last few weeks. They don't denounce me anymore. Maybe they think I'm dead." He lifted the Coca-Cola to his lips. "Maybe I *am* dead!"

"Oh, senator," Susan objected. "Nobody can kill *you!*"

"Well, Miss Susan, they can sure do a good job of *pretending* to kill me. Shit. I mean shoot. The North Vietnamese are pushing pushing pushing. And we don't get the word from Johnson. President Johnson," he explained patiently to Susan, "is *incapable* of telling the truth. It would wreck his digestion. Lyndon Johnson could eat a barrel of chile jalapeños, no sweat. Tell the truth? His insides would explode. We don't find out what we're up to over there in Saigon. I tried to get him to come clean on that—"

He stopped himself short. "But the hell with that. I've got to get busy. You folks got other presidential candidates to visit? Let me see, where do you have to go for that? You got Nixon's address in California?"

Goldwater had risen, and his two guests followed suit. Then Susan struck.

"Senator." She fumbled with her canvas bag. "Sir, I have a camera. Could you *please* let Orson take a picture of us?"

Goldwater looked down at her Kodak. "You know, Susan, I'm like a professional photographer. Yep. I should have run for president of the National Photographers' Association. Well...but using one of my cameras wouldn't do *you* any good. Sure..." He paused. "Orson. If you want to be in the picture I can get Emil here to snap it."

Orson hesitated for the briefest moment. "Thanks, senator. Yes. I'd like that."

Susan handed her camera over to Emil.

"Let's go outside," Goldwater said, clicking his magical door opener. "Better light."

Afterward, they shook hands, and Goldwater stepped back into his radio room. "You show them out, Henry."

They drove down the driveway.

Susan was silent for a few moments, then looked cautiously over at Orson. She wouldn't push the subject. She said, "Let's see what it's like over there." She pointed to the adjacent mountain range.

"Okay." Orson stole a look at the map at his side. "You're wanting to stay in Phoenix?"

"Why not? We can tour a little, go down to Tucson, and to Nogales, in Mexico, and you can do your next chapter."

"While driving?"

"No. At night."

"I plan to be doing other things at night."

She grinned and nodded her head.

Two days later they were in Nogales. They had walked about on the Mexican side of the border in the afternoon. Susan bought a straw hat and a turquoise ring, frowning dismissively at Orson when he started to say something about the cost. The sun was down now, and they were eating tacos and tamales and tortillas and drinking Bohemia beer in the across-the-border-style restaurant, serapes fastened along the walls. "My mother used to cook Mexican meals, and I think they were better than this."

Orson, his mouth full, nodded.

"Mom was a Mormon, you know, I told you that. Dad, too. Dad was a little bit of a—rake."

Orson looked up. "You never told me that."

"Why should I?"

"Because you should tell me everything."

"I *have* told you everything, I've been talking to you like non-stop for what, ten days?"

"Nine."

"What do you want to know about me that you don't know now?"

Orson suspended the fork from his mouth long enough to say, "Well, did your father make out?"

"That's a filthy question. Yes, he did, and that was what kept making Mom plenty sore, and one time I heard him say to her, 'Alice, you just don't really understand the Mormon tradition. If you did, you wouldn't mind if I had two, maybe ten wives.'"

Orson was startled. He had read about the Mormons, but he thought the multiple-wife business was dead and gone, long ago. "So your old man just kept at it? That's kind of..." He drew his breath. He hadn't used the word before with Susan. "Shitty."

"It's worse than that. It's ... On the other hand, I don't know, Orson. My dad stuck with my mom even when she started to hit the bottle—"

"Hit the *bottle*? What kind of Mormon background are you talking about?"

"Mormons have problems, like everybody else. But Orson, that kind of thing wouldn't happen to us when we get married. We are going to marry, right?"

"I can't wait. Who'll be best man? Senator Goldwater?" He raised his beer glass and tipped it over toward her smiling face, but suddenly her expression was serious. He said apprehensively, "Well, there's no hurry, really, is there? I'll have to get a job."

"Yes, eventually. There's no hurry about that, either. You've got your chapters, and I have *tons* of money left."

"At the rate we're using it up, we can go only a few weeks. I told Lars to send the next chapter to Seattle, when we talked about cruising the northwest."

"When we get back to Phoenix," said Susan, "we'll check at the motel, and ask if there's any word about Senator Goldwater in the last few days."

"He's probably given a speech on how we ought to go to war in Vietnam."

"Orson Killere, you can be a stuck record on things, you know? If it wasn't for our military preparations—"

"Susie. Listen."

The strolling guitarist had come to them and was singing a folk song.

> *Te quiero muuuu-cho*
> *Tambien me quiiie-res*
> *Borrachitaaaa me voy*
> *Hasta la capitaaaal*
> *Que me mandaron lla-mmarr*
> *Ante—yyyyer.*

They were holding hands. "Did you get any of that, Orson?" He shook his head. "But it sounds nice."

"Everything sounds nice," Susan said.

BOOK THREE

26

Tacoma, January 1965

ORSON HAD BY NOW THE IMPRESSION HE WAS LIVING at the hospital, that the Grace-Tacoma Hospital was his home. Where else—going back how far?—had he spent so much time, so to speak, in residence? In the last week, he'd found himself sharing the waiting room with Phil Androtti. It was Androtti's young partner that Phil was so concerned about. He, too, had been in an automobile accident, Orson learned. Could it have been worse than Susan's broken leg, her concussion, and her loss of memory?

"His car was totaled. For a lot of people, losing your right hand is something that's hell, but you can put up with it," Phil Androtti explained, stretching out his own fingers. "Well, sure, Vladimir Horowitz would have a hell of a time if his right hand were chewed up in an accident. My Tom Bayliss is not a piano player, but in what we're trying to do, what he's been doing with his hand is—yeah, you can compare it to a brain surgeon. We're in the computer business, just starting out, beginning last July, not even six months. We're trying for a real beautiful new twist on the printing chip. It's secret, but"—he smiled grimly—"I doubt you'd understand even if I was dumb enough to tell you about it. You been to school, Orson?"

"A couple of years. Dropped out. University of Michigan, Ann Arbor."

"I was in school, eight, ten years ago. What are you doing now?"

"I'm waiting for my ... girl to get better."

"That's not a full-time job."

"I hope not."

The nurse came in. "Mr. Androtti, the doctor will see you now."

The next afternoon Orson walked back into the waiting room after a half-hour visit with Susan, who was sharing the starched hospital room with an elderly woman and two visiting daughters keeping a death watch. Orson was told by the nurse with a pencil tucked above her ear that he could come back in two hours. Susan would need to rest, the nurse told him. "She'll need to rest for a very long time, Mr. Killere."

Phil Androtti, wan, unshaven, was in the waiting room, a copy of the *Seattle Times* on his lap, still folded. He spoke up.

"They're going to operate on Tom. They're doing it right now. He's got a very special surgeon, specializes in hands. Orson, do you pray?"

"I used to."

"Well, would you do me a favor and start up again? And pray for Tom Bayliss?"

A woman sitting across from them kept her eyes on the magazine she was reading but said quietly, "There's a chapel in the hospital. Seventh floor."

Phil Androtti looked over desperately at Orson. "Orson, would you come with me? To the chapel?"

"Of course."

The older man led the way to the elevator. At the seventh floor they found their way to the chapel and entered the secluded room, which contained six chairs, two prie-dieux, some bookcases, and a white-clothed table holding three Bibles and the Book of Common Prayer. There were no windows. The lights were dim but bright enough to permit reading.

Phil spoke in a semiwhisper. "Tom and I teamed up two years ago. He's MIT, I'm Cornell. I'm thirty, Tom's twenty-eight. He's always tinkered. Me, too. I sold an idea for improving the electric typewriter to the Royal Typewriter Company. They paid a packet for it, and Tom was working there. We got to spend time together, because part of the deal was I'd supervise the reassembly to include my Albatron—that's what they call it. Tom said—I was at his apartment, having a beer or two—he said the future of printing wasn't *typewriter* keys. It's *impressions,* he said. Commanded by a computer brain. He explained his idea. *Really* nifty idea, Orson. Then he looked at me, I'll never forget. He said, 'Phil, are you rich?' I said, 'I'm a hell of a lot richer than I was two weeks ago.' He said, 'I know what they paid you. With that in the bank we could maybe set up shop, find out if my idea is any good.'"

He stopped.

"I just don't know, I just don't know whether Tom could continue those experiments without the use of his fingers. But, whatever, we've got to keep reports going out to our investors. There are only eight of them. Four of them are right here, in Seattle and Tacoma. They aren't technicians. They're speculators. Tom's very good with them. I'm going to say a prayer now."

He slid onto one of the prie-dieux. Orson knelt down next to him.

"Phil?"

Phil Androtti looked up.

"Would you say one for Susie?"

Phil nodded and looked over at the distressed figure next to him, with the young face and sad eyes.

After fifteen minutes Phil Androtti got up from his knees. "I'll go back now and see Tom."

"I'll stay on for a bit," Orson said. "I can't see Susan again until four."

He rose and walked to a chair and desk up against a small bookcase. He began looking over the library, which exhibited several editions of the Bible and a half-dozen devotional books. A middle-aged man in a dark linen suit, tall, angular, deeply tanned, came into the prayer room and walked quietly to a cupboard. He withdrew a half-dozen Bibles, placing them in his briefcase. He addressed Orson in a quiet tone of voice. "Is there anything I can do for you?"

Orson had got an idea five minutes before, when he was kneeling alongside Phil Androtti. "Could you sit with me a minute, Mr.—"

"Weems. I'm Robert Weems."

"But you're a minister?"

"Yes. And you're...?"

They found two chairs and sat down.

"My name is Orson Killere. And my girlfriend and I had an accident. She's very bad. And I've decided I want to marry her. Quickly."

"Impulsive marriages aren't usually a good idea."

"This isn't impulsive. I want her for the rest of my life, even if she lives to be a hundred."

"And—the girl? The young woman?"

"Her name is Susan, Susan Young."

"How is her state of mind? Is she—alert? Does she speak to you?"

"She is on-and-off-again conscious. Assuming she makes it, there's going to be a problem with her memory, Dr. Chafee says. That'll take a while."

"Orson, I have to ask this question: How can I marry you unless she tells me she wants to do it, in words I think reflect her own...deliberate mind?"

"Will you talk to her? I'll tell her first that you're going to do that. We had been planning to marry but didn't get around to it. We've been traveling. I can see her at four. She doesn't stay awake very long. How long are you here?"

"I'm here as long as I can be of any help."

"Where will you be after I talk with her, at four?"

"I'll be making the rounds but will make it a point to check in here every fifteen or twenty minutes. Does that sound all right?"

"Yes. I'll have to call my mother. I can't do that now. She's in Germany."

"And Susan's mother?"

"She's dead. Her father, too."

"How old is she?"

"Eighteen."

"How old are you?"

"I'll be twenty in—on January ninth."

"To get a marriage license you have to take a blood test."

"Well, there's blood all over this hospital. They can have mine."

The minister's lips parted in a half smile. "Assuming Susan's in shape for it, we're still talking about forty-eight hours, minimum. Blood test, analysis, state application, permit, in different parts of the city. Do you have a car?"

"Yes, thanks to the insurance company."

Robert Weems stood up and looked over at Orson. He found him appealing, and not to be confused with a teenage romantic. He thought to ask: Would you want to marry the girl if she was here for only routine medical help? Instead, he asked Orson if he played tennis.

"Actually, yes, I played in...I've played since I was a boy."

"I was wondering if, after hospital hours, you'd like to play a game. I have all the equipment—my son's your size, and he's away at college."

Orson blurted out that he'd really like that. "I can't see Susan after six. I'll get the blood test before then. Where do you want me to be?"

"Why don't we meet here at six? We can say a prayer together for Susan, and then you can follow me to the club. I have an honorary membership."

"You deserve one," Orson said impulsively.

A month later Orson met his appointment for breakfast in Tacoma with Dan Nettleton the next day. The session at the courthouse would be at ten. "LaVera's lawyers—I know Oliver Helms, and a couple of his partners—are very good at wasting time," Orson's lawyer warned.

"I guess they wouldn't call it that, Dan," Orson said. "As long as they're not out-of-pocket, they haven't wasted time."

"Yes, sure. And of course they're always looking for a settlement. They've got a special problem with you and Susan because you don't have a corporate body they can deal with. It's just *Killere and Young versus LaVera*—you and Susan against a very big trucking company. The motion today is, as you know, to hold Hertz responsible on account of Susan's seat belt not holding, and rule out the suit against the trucking company."

"But what would you need a seat belt for, except that their truck banged into us?"

"Their position is that the actual damage done to Susan wasn't because the truck ran up across you, but because of the braking and the collision. You had your seat belt fastened, your seat belt held, you weren't hurt. Susan had on her seat belt, the seat belt didn't hold, and she's..."

"Out of it."

"Out of it. Our position—we want LaVera to stay in there as a defendant, alongside Hertz—is that when the truck went up the hill—A: It didn't stop adequately at the stop sign; B: causing you to smash into it when it crossed in front of you; and C: causing Susan to snap her head forward into the glove compartment. And that, therefore, D: It's up to Hertz and LaVera to quarrel about what role the seat belt did or did not play in the accident, no concern of ours."

"Why do they need my testimony, in that case?"

"Because they want to say you were drunk. In which case you and Susan would need to depend on the State of Washington's no-fault law, but those benefits are limited to just actual damage, which means hospital costs. Nothing left over for—extended care or—"

"So what have I got working for me?"

"The police tests. They were taken within an hour of the accident. And they're pretty good. You came in with point-oh-eight. Intoxicated, in Washington, is point-one-oh. What they'll do now is—go into your background, grill you pretty good. But we've gone over all that ground. You know, Orson, they might try to bring Susan to the stand."

Orson looked up, teeth clenched, incredulous. "You're kidding."

"No. Susan probably wouldn't know what they're asking. But since we can't know what *she* would say, it's not something I'd look forward to."

They both accepted more coffee.

"You know something, Dan, I don't really remember all that clearly what Sue and I had to eat or drink before—what was the time of the accident?"

"The police were there at eight-twenty-seven. The people at the restaurant in Puyallup testified you left there just after seven. The supper bill shows two beers. The waitress said she didn't notice whether you each had one beer, or whether you drank both of them. If you drank them both, at normal rates of metabolism, you could have been intoxicated under the law."

"But wait a minute. My blood test says I wasn't!"

"But nobody can testify to exactly what moment the accident happened. The truck driver went off looking for a public phone. You were looking after Susan. And she was out cold. They've probably got a doctor at hand who'll say if the accident was as late as eight, and if you drank both beers, you could have been intoxicated by State of Washington standards. Your break is that Susan's parents' insurance coverage worked for her until six months after their death, and your accident was five months after the Youngs died."

Dan Nettleton was ever so tender as he began his examination, evidencing great concern for the witness. "We are so deeply sorry about what happened, Mr. Killere, but of course we have to get all the...facts."

"I understand."

"Now, that night at dinner at the Capriccio, the record shows that you and Ms. Young ordered two beers with your"—he stopped and looked at his notes—"with your hamburger steaks. Is that correct?"

"I don't remember, but I'm not challenging your account of it."

"Yes. Now, we need to know this: Does Ms. Young drink beer?"

"Yes. She does."

"Well, that night, did she—?"

"I've told you, I don't remember the meal." He paused. And then he added, "But I know, even if I can't remember, that she would not have had a beer that night."

"That means you drank *both* beers?"

"I guess so."

Dan Nettleton interrupted. "How can you be sure Ms. Young didn't have one of the bottles of beer?"

"Because she had morning sickness. She hadn't drunk a beer for a few weeks."

Oliver Helms looked over at Dan Nettleton. Dan looked down and then over at Orson, who came and sat beside him, without expression.

As they walked from the courthouse, Dan Nettleton did not disguise his rage. "You're such a fucking Boy Scout, Killere. You put both beers in your stomach when there was zero need to do so. And while you're at it, you tell the defendant that you had knocked up your co-plaintiff... Well... thank God for Susan's parents' insurance. Though..." Nettleton was calming down in the cool air of Tacoma. "We still have a pretty good case. What may happen is they'll do an experiment, make you drink two beers in the time it took you to have dinner, then run blood tests at intervals that correspond with the earliest the accident could have happened, and the latest."

Orson didn't comment. Telling the truth was one of Mr. Simon's rules. He had had to abandon a lot of Mr. Simon's ideas on how to live, but not all of them.

27

Los Potreros, November 1965

IN THE PAST SIXTY DAYS, IN THEIR TINY FURNISHED apartment, Orson several times told Susan what was going on. She would nod her head appreciatively, but clearly the news hadn't registered in her memory. She seemed to understand that she had left the hospital, that it would take a while before everything "was okay," that Orson had a job that kept him away during the day; but Orson couldn't be entirely confident that all of that was truly lodged in the permeable memory she now had.

But she was cheerful, mobile with her crutches, a willing custodian of the apartment, cleaning it and cooking supper. She tried to read a book but didn't succeed. When she got to the end of a chapter, she would begin it afresh. She kissed Orson passionately when he left for work at Androtti's laboratory in Tacoma and once asked how far it was from where they now were . . . to where they were before. Orson said he would write down their itinerary, beginning in Salt Lake, and she could look at it any time she wanted to. Then he drove to work at Albatron.

One day at noon Phil Androtti's secretary, who served also as switchboard operator, rang through to Orson. "There's a gentleman here—he's standing right by me—"

"In other words, Vicky, he can hear what you're saying?"

"That's right. Well, the gentleman wants to see you but doesn't want to say who he is." She addressed the short, crew-cutted figure standing in front of her. "That's correct, sir?"

The visitor nodded. He seemed to be pleasant enough.

"He says he's a very old friend."

"No sweat, Vicky. I'll come on over. I don't have *that* many old friends in this part of the world. I was just going out for lunch anyway."

Orson turned off the terminal and encoded his work. The papers on his desk he slipped into a manila envelope, placed it in the drawer, and locked it. He thought all this a little extreme, but he was not going to disobey Phil Androtti's instructions. Security was a big thing with Albatron. Maybe he would be more understanding, Phil told him when he smiled incredulously at specified security procedures, if he had had two years of his own work pirated. That, Phil said, had happened to him. The challenge—the dream—was to develop what Phil and Tom called a "chip" of silicon that could do what vacuum tubes and transistors had been doing; to produce one much smaller than the competition's, and cheaper. Orson walked out of the building, a converted shed in a decommissioned naval supply depot, and opened the door into the adjacent shed, where Vicky's desk was.

"Charlie!"

They embraced.

Orson stopped short and asked: "Charlie, is our boy in trouble?"

"Is he ever in trouble. Why d'ya think I'm here? Because you're my buddy? Well, you are of course, Killer. But, I mean, we could correspond, without my hauling my ass eight hundred miles away from L.A."

They walked out the door, and Orson led the way to the grill where he usually had lunch.

"Though you are my buddy, and who else knew you when you were fifteen, and saw you make out—naw, I didn't *see* you." Charlie laughed and reached up to put his hand on Orson's shoulder. "But the girl, that Brit chorus dancer, she talked about it later to us. We'll talk at lunch."

Charlie Hodge, guitarist and singer, had been praised in 1956 by his contemporary, Elvis Presley. They became friends and musical collaborators and when drafted, Charlie, by good luck, found himself in the same military detachment with Elvis. They did basic training together, and sailed the troop carrier that took the regiment abroad, ending at Friedberg. Charlie was a fixed part of the entourage, a senior member of the Memphis Mafia.

They sat at a booth. Charlie began to talk, but the waitress interrupted him. Charlie dismissed her, saying, "Two Cokes, two hamburgers. And anything else you want, Orson." He continued. Orson nodded at the waitress.

"Elvis has got two problems." The sonority of Charlie's voice suggested his profession, the melodic quality, the rhythmic cadences. "And on one of them, only you can help. Priscilla wants to go home."

The Cokes arrived.

"But let's catch up. Let's see. We're in November 1965. As you know, Priss came over to Graceland how many years ago? Three? There'd been all those lengthy negotiations with her mother and the captain. She would do this-and-that, not do this-and-that, et cetera, et cetera. But one thing was up front: She and Elvis would marry. Otherwise, what's the point?"

"That's right." Orson sipped his soda.

"And Elvis said it, more or less, to everybody—he certainly said it to me. The question was always: When? Well, Priscilla didn't expect *when* to be years away. She's what, nineteen now?"

The waitress delivered two hamburger plates.

"Twenty—maybe twenty-one," Orson corrected himself.

"So she's wondering: What's going on?"

"I know she's unhappy," Orson said, inspecting the gray hamburger perfunctorily. "I talked to her a couple of weeks ago. And my mum—remember Francie?—we talked a while back. She's living right in Camp Pershing now, married to General Hoffritz. You remember him? But you and Elvis weren't at Camp Pershing, you were at Friedberg. Anyway, Mum had a visit from Mrs. Beaulieu, and she cried a lot about the whole arrangement with Elvis. What's the *matter* with Elvis? Why doesn't he *marry* her—or send her home?"

"Killer, you may be the five-hundredth person who's asked that question. But nobody goes to Elvis to tell him to sort that out, because Elvis doesn't like people to talk about his problems. That problem or *any* problem."

"He's got others?"

"I need to tell *you*? He's got the problem of his career. Did you see *Frankie and Johnny*? And the shoots since then have gotten worse."

"Tell you the truth, Charlie, I avoided it. I haven't seen any of his movies since *Roustabout*. I saw *Love Me Tender* back in Wiesbaden, and I thought he was pretty good."

"He *is* pretty good, but they've been coming out with this dog shit they put him in. Just so they can make him sound off like a nickelodeon, singing every three minutes. The Colonel likes that. And you can never get Elvis to object any time a movie director, or for that matter, anybody else, says to him, 'Okay, Elvis, sing.'"

"Does he have the right to veto a song?"

"Yeah. But they argue with him, and they get the orchestra to make the notes sound real pretty and—Elvis gets carried away. Of course he can put over *any* song." Charlie sighed. "He could put over 'Baa, Baa, Black Sheep.'"

"That's nice music, that song, actually."

"You're right. Real nice harmonics." Charlie began the first bar, and with a bandleader's arm movements brought Orson in to sing the first bar as Charlie moved to the second. Orson was wobbly on the music line, but hung in there, and ended, 'Yes sir, yes sir, three bags full,' with merriment in the voice. The other diners turned their heads to see what was going on.

"Hasn't Elvis asked you if you saw *Frankie and Johnny?*"

"Yeah, he asked a couple of phone calls back. I told him it was scheduled here at Los Potreros but hadn't yet been shown. Can you guess what he said?"

Charlie leaned back and chuckled. "Well, he might have said he'd arrange to have the movie house do a special showing of it for you. Or he might have said he'd buy the movie house and have them run it for you."

"The King. Yep, he did actually talk about arranging a special showing. You can imagine how I fought to avoid that."

"Has he asked you to go down to L.A.? To see him?"

"He always talks about it and then sort of forgets, and then the talk gets distracted."

"Well listen, you can guess that coming up here to see you wasn't just my idea. Elvis asked me to come. He wants you to go see Priscilla."

Orson wasn't totally surprised. "No way I could say no to Elvis on that mission. But . . . I'd have to clear it with Priscilla. Did Elvis talk to her about my going out?"

"No. He said he thought it would work better if you just showed up."

"How come he didn't just call *me* and—"

"*Killer!* You know Elvis. He doesn't *work* that way. Was it Elvis asked your ma to let you go off with us to Paris? No, it was done through Vernon. And that was six years ago. Elvis doesn't change."

"That's good. And that's bad. Charlie, I'm going to have to

think about how to clear this with Priscilla. The Androttis are always ready to look after Susan for a day or two."

"Look, here's the current scene. Elvis had Priscilla come with us to Hollywood when we did *Spinout*. But she was sort of in the way. Elvis had to worry about her; she'd come and go. Then we all went back to Memphis—I know Elvis spoke to you from there, he told me so. Then Hollywood scheduled two more movies back-to-back: *Double Trouble* and *Easy Come, Easy Go*. That's going to take us until October. Elvis made it plain this time around he wanted Priscilla to stay home in Graceland. And that's what's pissed her off, so much that she says she's going home to Germany. All of that makes it right for you to fly on out there now. She's sad and lonely."

"I still think I ought to talk it over with her."

"Why don't you do it halfway? Go on out to Memphis and call her from downtown. Tell her, 'Priss, this is Orson. I'm here in Memphis, at the Peabody Hotel, and I want to come on over and say hello.'"

It was a wild idea, and for that reason, in part, appealing.

And so on Saturday afternoon, Priscilla Beaulieu got the call.

"Priss? This is Orson. I'm here in Memphis, at the Peabody Hotel, and I want to come on over and say hello."

28

Memphis, November 1965

ORSON PIECED TOGETHER EVERYTHING THAT HAD GONE on. The living arrangements had been worked out in some detail.

For two years after leaving the army in Germany, Elvis courted Priscilla by phone. He swore his eternal love and posted as evidence of his commitment that he was willing to wait until she was of marriageable age before consummating their union. And that until then, she would live in Graceland.

In the spring of 1962, Ann Beaulieu, weary of the tension, turned on her husband. "Priscilla won't do her work. She cries almost every night and writes endless letters to Elvis. I think what we have to do is—make an arrangement."

"An arrangement that involves delivering Priscilla to Memphis? Not on your life."

But Captain Beaulieu's resolution was wavering. Although Ann Beaulieu didn't bring up the matter, both she and the Captain were always aware that Priscilla was her child, not his— Priscilla's father had been killed when she was six months old, in a military air crash.

Though every effort was made to avert press coverage of the arrangements, Louella Parsons, the Hollywood columnist, broke the story. She commented that bringing Priscilla to Memphis merited comparison with the ancient protocol of sending a princess to a foreign court under strict supervision, pending the advent of puberty.

It was done. The chaplain at Camp Pershing was brought in for consultation; letters were exchanged with Vernon Presley and his wife and with Elvis's aged grandmother; and, finally, with Elvis himself.

Priscilla, at age seventeen, would move to Memphis in the fall. She would live with Vernon and his wife, Dee, in their house, a few yards from Graceland, occupying a large suite especially prepared for her. During the day, when Elvis was in residence, she would spend the time with him, but always there was to be a third presence in the room. Sometime after dinner she would be taken back to Vernon's house. On school days she attended the Immaculate Conception High School in Memphis. She had classes in dance and music. Transcripts of her work would be sent regularly to her parents.

Captain and Mrs. Beaulieu hadn't thought to set limits on what might be provided Priscilla in the way of clothes and finery. It was she herself who, soon after arriving, explained how she wanted her quarters decorated. Her tastes ran to velvet and gilt. She gave instructions that the two sofas should be embroidered with the initials *P.B.P.*, for Priscilla Beaulieu Presley. "That way we can just move them in to Graceland," she told Elvis happily, "without having to fuss over changing the initials after we've married." Elvis hadn't shown enthusiasm for the idea but said nothing.

"Do you have a car?" Priscilla asked Orson when he called.

"As a matter of fact I don't, Priss."

"Well, I'll send for you. Peabody, right? How about in, say, ten minutes?"

Orson laughed pleasurably. "How about sixteen minutes? I'm just off an airplane."

"I can't wait! I'll get the albums we had at Wiesbaden, at our fan club. We'll catch up on everything! What do you like to eat? I mean, just say it, they'll come up with anything I want."

Orson remembered their joint meals with Elvis in Wiesbaden. "Well," he said solemnly, "I'd like some fried chicken, some bacon well cooked, some honey biscuits, yams, beans, and some apple pie or peanut-brittle ice cream for dessert. Or both."

She giggled. "You'll have it all."

The car and driver brought him to the King's castle. It was nice, Orson thought gratefully, that the Presley family was there, standing outside the pillars to greet him: Vernon and Dee and even Grandma. He kissed the ladies and shook Vernon's hand. And there, just off to one side, was Priscilla—ravishing beyond memory, dressed in white and gold, the pleated skirt reaching just below her knee to show off her stately legs. She wore a broad leather belt studded with gold icons. Her neckline came down deep, the topmost button of her dress left open. A gold barrette held her dark hair in place. Her beauty had fulfilled the promise of 1962, when he'd last seen her, grown up and bronzed by the sun of Tennessee.

"I know you children want to visit together," Dee Presley said affably. "You'll be here a few days, right, Orson?"

"Well, ma'am"—he replied evasively—"I certainly wouldn't leave without visiting with you and Mr. Presley and Grandma."

The Presleys went back into their air-conditioned living room, and Priscilla led Orson down the long hallway to her own wing.

It was a snug few hours.

"The last time I saw you was at the airport, on your way to college," she reminded him.

"And then it was only a little bit after that that you left home and came here. It's been three years. All our telephoning isn't really a substitute, is it, Priss?"

"No. September 1962 was our last visit." Priscilla sat down on her velvet sofa and motioned Orson to her side. She reached over to the coffee table and depressed a button. An elderly black waiter, wearing a white jacket, came in.

"What can I bring you, Miss Priscilla?"

Miss Priscilla was elated. Both by Orson's presence and by what he was witness to: Priscilla Beaulieu, rescued from the prim, military-housing half duplex in Wiesbaden, sitting now in her opulent room, summoning a butler to do her bidding.

"I'm going to have a rum Coke. Jeff makes wonderful rum Cokes. One for you?"

"Sure," Orson nodded. After Jeff had left the room, he said, "I'm glad you're not mad at me for just showing up this way."

"I couldn't be mad at *you*, Orson. But I can guess why you're here."

"I figured you would. But I couldn't say no when he—when I was asked. You're my oldest friend, and he began as my idol and is now—"

"Is now what?" she wanted to know.

Orson looked up, quizzical.

"He is, I think, the number-one entertainer in America, and the most beautiful singing voice—ever."

"But no longer your idol?"

"I'm twenty years old. At my age we don't think of them as idols, exactly. He is a great artist and—I've told you this, sort of, on the phone—I love him. We talk often. And"—he might as well not postpone it—"he still wants to marry you."

She stood up and took her drink from the silver tray Jeff held out to her.

"Oh yes. He wants to marry me. Say it again. What's he waiting for? I gave him a deadline. I've given him *two* deadlines. But this one I'm keeping. Look." She walked over to a desk, opened a drawer, and pulled out an envelope. "Here is my ticket. July twentieth, Memphis-New York. Two days in New York. You remember Jane Robbins? Well, she's living there, married—there are other people who are married who were at school with us in 1962. But the . . . *King,* he wants to make his own decisions in his own way in his own time."

She flipped over a leaf of her ticket. "Anyway, then, July twenty-third, New York-Frankfurt. Mother will meet me, or Don—he's big now, and as handsome as you are. No, not quite *that* handsome." She smiled her flirtatious smile. "He's my brother, remember? And he comes on the phone every now and then when Mom calls. Up to a year or so back he'd ask when the wedding was going to be. Now he doesn't ask any longer." She stifled a sob.

"Because, Orson, I am a *laughingstock.* Not only in Memphis, for God's sake. Everywhere. Everybody knows everything about Elvis. I mean *everything.*"

She sat down and pulled out a newspaper clipping from her desk. "Listen to this—this is *Variety.* Everybody reads *Variety.* You've seen it?"

He shook his head.

"So"—she opened it—"here's a picture of Elvis. Sorry," she added, clearing her throat—"*the King.* He's dressed up in that—that black leather costume. And there—there's a picture of Ann-Margret. Looking *so* amorously over at Elvis. And the caption? *Why Elvis's protracted stay in Hollywood? Yes, he's making a lot of movies, but the other reason he doesn't want to go home is five-feet-three, sleepy-eyed, and blonde. Lots of pretty girls have tried to bust up the planned knot with the beauteous Priscilla, and it seems to be working.*"

She began to cry.

He talked to Priscilla quietly, soothing her. But he was trying to decide for himself, he suddenly thought, whether his heart was really in this mission. It had been a wonderful romance, his fourteen-year-old schoolmate and the great entertainer they both idolized. What he didn't doubt, and couldn't, was the sincerity of Elvis's desire for her. Why else ask Orson to go to Graceland to intercede?

But how to justify the so-frequent delays? *Why* these delays? This or that distraction in Elvis's life? Or temptation? Orson hadn't come to Memphis to deny Elvis's running liaisons. They were known to everyone in Hollywood. Besides, to handle the current crisis, all that Elvis needed to say to Priscilla was that he loved her and was willing to set a date for their marriage. At that point he could easily persuade her that any trip to Germany for any other public reason than to visit her parents would bring the inquisitive and skeptical press to their hearth. They would camp out here, and haunt her, and haunt Elvis. Haunt Orson's ex-little-girlfriend, and haunt the idol they had in common.

"Let's not talk about it any more tonight, it's getting late. Let's listen...Did Elvis tell you about the gospel album? It's very beautiful, especially 'How Great Thou Art.'"

She read down the list on the typewritten label on the album demo. "'Come What May,' 'Down in the Alley,' 'Fools Fall in Love,' 'Love Letters,' 'Tomorrow Is a Long Time,' 'How Great Thou Art,' 'By and By,' 'Farther Along,' 'If The Lord Wasn't Walking by My Side'—that one is especially beautiful. And then 'Somebody Bigger than You and I,' 'Where Could I Go But to the Lord.' And it ends with 'Without Him.'"

She began to cry again.

"Without him. No, I couldn't live without him."

29

Los Potreros, June 1966

EARLY IN THE SUMMER CHARLIE CALLED. "YOU WERE great with Priscilla, getting her to cancel the going-home-to-daddy business. Elvis is mighty glad—did you talk to him?"

"Yeah, a couple of weeks ago. But he didn't mention Priss, or that I had been there. We spoke about his movie contract. He wanted to know if I had noticed that it makes him the highest-paid star in Hollywood."

"I hope you said no, so he could have the satisfaction of telling you. The King. He really knows nothing about money, he just likes to have as much of it as he can spend, which is a lot."

"Spend and give away."

"You can't take that from him. He's more generous than Santa Claus."

"And works harder. Santa has only that one date every year."

"Listen. Elvis wants you to come down to Bel Air. He'll be there only another week. Then, the usual—the trek back to Graceland in our bus. He still insists on driving, won't fly these days. Sometimes he drives the bus himself. This time he says he's going to announce his formal engagement to Priscilla, only, I'll believe it when I see it. Anyway, what he wants to do is thank you personally and, as always happens—you know all about it—there has to be an intermediary. Me, because he knows we're pals.

"So that's invitation number one. Invite number two, which Elvis knows nothing about, is for you and me to siddown and talk about Elvis's career. What I was thinkin' was, why not come on down, spend the evening with Elvis, stay over, and we'll spend the next day on our own, jawing. I've got a nice apartment with a spare room. *And* I've got a sixteen-millimeter projector, and *all,* count 'em, *all* his films. And sure, a complete set of the albums. Remember that, in case the Smithsonian loses its collection: good ol' Charlie Hodge can always fill in."

"Okay. But let me think a little about the timing. My own work, and other...commitments."

"I never did ask about what was going on with Orson Killer, back when we visited in Potretos—"

"Potreros. Los Potreros."

"But we can cover that ground next...next what?"

"Like I said, Charlie, I've got to take a couple of soundings. What I'll try for is Friday for Elvis and Saturday for you. Is Elvis always free at night?"

"He's always free mostly between eleven P.M. and one A.M. They shoot late. And Elvis goes to sleep, as usual, like five, six A.M. All he has left with him at that point is the broads. We've all flaked out. Me, Lamar, Red, Joe. Some of us are around during the shoot and for a while after it. You know—no, probably you don't know. Your time together was kind of offbeat. Anyway, he likes the gang, or at least a few of us Mafia, to be there after the workday."

"I'll call you, Charlie."

"Thanks, Killer."

There'd be no problem at Albatron, not the way Phil Androtti ran things. Time clocks weren't kept there. Orson hadn't come to Albatron with technical skills, but he quickly picked up on the drift of things. The agenda was to experiment with semiconductors. The objective, to devise a supersmall silicon chip especially suitable for working accessories—printers, in particular, of the kind just starting to come out. Orson's special assignment was to lure investors otherwise grouping around larger, better-established companies, in order to come up with the money needed for the enterprise. Two weeks before, he had been asked by Eric Jessup, a young investor, to come around and talk to him and his financial adviser. Orson did so and persuasively spoke of the prospects of Albatron's possibilities. He told of a survey by the Royal Typewriter Company, the conclusion of which, according to a friend once intimate with the affairs of the company, was that typewriters were simply going out of favor. "Something else will have to do the work of typewriters," Orson recited, "and that's what we're trying to come up with, and we have big brains, inventive brains, at work on the problem." Eric Jessup invited Orson to stay on for lunch, and at lunch asked questions that were also personal: How had Orson acquired his sense of the industry? Had he majored in electrical engineering?

Orson looked at the wealthy investor, only a few years older than Orson; and told him he had been kicked out of college before he'd had any chance to learn about computers—courses on them were offered only to upperclassmen. "I ended college after sophomore year."

Jessup struggled in formulating his next question, but Orson relieved him of the pain. "You're asking why I was kicked out?"

Jessup nodded.

"Because I engaged in a demonstration against the university's trustees. It was a damn-fool demonstration—" He paused. Should he run the risk? Mr. Simon had counseled that the truth should be told, but he didn't say that the truth had to be courted. Orson could steer the question away; but chose not to. "I'm a socialist. Not just a plain socialist, as in the British Labour Government. A world revolutionary socialist as in the anarchist-revolutionists, of, well, 1900."

"Do you still feel that way, Orson?"

"Well, actually I do. It would be a better world, I think. But I don't go much for the halfway stuff. Theoretically, I could find myself voting Republican. My wife would have voted for Goldwater. If she had been twenty-one."

"How old are you?

"Twenty-one."

Eric liked that. Liked the whole thing. His honesty. The twenty-one-year-old college dropout revolutionary whipping up support for a new technology.

"I think we'll go with Albatron."

"That's great. I hope you—we—do well and make a mint."

He would hardly need to explain to Phil, or to Tom, why he wanted to be away for another couple of days: Orson was free to make his own schedule. All he had to do was cultivate the investors.

He'd need to see about looking after Susie. She hadn't seemed to notice when he went away to Graceland. This morning she was dressed, as usual, in a flowered shirt and loose-fitting blue cotton pants. Her hair was carelessly tended, and she wore no lipstick. She knew and cherished Orson but seemed not absolutely sure who he was, though she was much concerned to conceal her mindlessness. Orson encouraged her little interrogatories. A part of his role was to affect no knowledge of what she was trying to do. He had to proceed as though she knew everything, so that her questions would seem mere banter, not desperate attempts to grope with ignorance.

"That was a very nice hotel, wasn't it?" she asked now.

"It certainly was. The people were nice, and the room was nice."

"Yes." She was taking, now, an investigative step.

"The scenery was so nice, don't you think?"

"Terrific. I love it that way."

Susan looked up and said tentatively, "You mean the mountains?"

Orson pounced. "Yes, the mountains you can see in Phoenix, way back on the horizon."

Susan closed her eyes to digest it all. Hotel...food...service...mountains. Could she hazard the name of the city? Of even the state?

"I want to go there again, when I'm well. Orson, how long does it take to get there?"

He'd try to help her, but it was hard to do. They had been in Phoenix, and then Tucson, then back to Salt Lake. They were approaching Seattle when the accident happened. He'd have to be evasive. "Depends, darling, on how you travel. You know, we could fly, or drive—"

"Drive? I don't think they'd let me drive."

"Not now. I mean, when all that is behind you. Behind us."

"Orson, are we—"

He waited only a moment. Would she feel her way back to how it was?

"Are we best friends? Of course we are. And of course we are a lot more than that."

She could go wherever she wished with that information. But now the glaze came over her eyes, and the interrogatory was over.

But he'd attempt the concrete communication. "I'm going to be away for a couple of days, Susie. But Vicky knows how to reach me."

"I don't want you to go away." Her face clouded up, and she

propelled her wheelchair away from him, her most direct sign of displeasure.

"I'm not going away, Susan. I'm just going to be out of town a couple of days." She wouldn't know that that was the same thing.

"Well, will I see you tomorrow?"

It was safest to say, simply, "Of course you will, darling."

30

Hollywood, August 1966

"ASK FOR *ME*," CHARLIE HAD SAID. THE BIG SIGN WAS up: SILENCE: FILM SHOOTING. Charlie brought his index finger to his lips to signal *Be quiet!* and led Orson to a chair.

Elvis is onstage, dressed as a nightclub performer, Guy Lambert. He is seated behind a desk. A soldier in uniform walked over to him. "Guy—"

"CUT."

The director spoke to the actor playing the soldier: "Adrian. You're not nervous about anything, so don't *stare* at Elvis as though you expected he'd *eat you up*. You're just coming through the door with routine business. Back up and try it again. I won't shoot this time until we see how it goes."

"Sorry, Norm."

Adrian went back to the door, paused, turned around, reopened it, and walked over to Presley, this time affecting a casual demeanor. Elvis sat patiently. But the look on his face suggested his mind was elsewhere. Adrian got to the desk and began to speak.

"CUT. Okay. Let's try it now—for keeps."

Adrian once more returned to the door and went out.

"All right." The clapper board snapped shut and the voice called out, "SCENE FIFTY-FOUR: TAKE NINE." The cameras whirred. Adrian opened the door and sauntered up to the desk.

"Guy, I got to ask you something. A favor."

"Well"—Elvis, expressionless, responded—"what is it?"

"Well, Guy, this is my birthday. And what I was hoping was—you'd sing 'Old MacDonald.' I can get your guitar. I know where it is, in the closet."

Elvis smiles, with some effort. And then says in an accent not quite his own, "Well, what the hell. Birthdays don't come every day. Sure, bring in Bel Cando—"

"CUT. Elvis, the name you've given the guitar is Bel *Cant*o, not Bel *Cand*o. Back two lines. Say, 'What the hell,' and go on from there."

The clapper board snapped. "TAKE TEN."

Elvis repeats the lines to the satisfaction of Norman Taurog. Adrian walks back through the door and reemerges an instant later with a guitar. He walks with it to the desk—

"CUT. Adrian, you're *pleased*, see? Pleased because Elvis is going to sing for you. Don't bring in the guitar with a sour expression on your face. A little smile would be good. FIRST PLACES."

Adrian brings out the guitar again and hands it to Elvis. Elvis rises, turns his chair at an angle, and puts his right foot on it, nestling the guitar on his knee.

"CUT. All right." To the sound technician: "Go with song 21A. Play it regular volume. Elvis, same procedure. We've got it on tape. You can sing it if you want. If not, just lip-synch—with *feeling*. And—important—you missed this when you started out on 'Could I Fall in Love' yesterday. Be sure to move your right hand as if you were actually striking the chords on the guitar. All right—"

"SILENCE ON THE SET," the boom operator yelled out.

The music blares, Elvis comes through the soundtrack belting out "Old MacDonald." Elvis-onstage begins by humming the song, then moves his lips. When he reaches the words, *EE-EYE-EE-EYE-OH,* he raises his voice to performance level, his body vibrating with the music.

"CUT. That's good, Elvis. But I could tell the difference between when you did that last bit, the *EE-EYE-EE-EYE,* and what came before. Watch it. Play it, Al."

The camera whirrs on rewind, and on the screen to one side Elvis is seen taking up the guitar and singing the song.

"Now, watch the lips carefully, Elvis."

The lips move naturally, in sync with the music, but at the closing bar, Elvis's lips move apart more pronouncedly and his eyes take on a different look.

"See it? See what I mean, Elvis? Okay, let's go back. Begin at the beginning of the song."

The director calls a ten-minute break.

Orson wondered whether to go over and greet Elvis. To do so he'd have to walk onstage, past the dozen technicians moving about.

He decided against it. *I'll wait till it's over.* "How much they got left to shoot tonight?" he asked Charlie. It was after ten.

"I got the script here. Norm wants to get to page eighty-nine, to where Elvis puts in the phone call and speaks to Claire . . . Figure—eleven o'clock. Maybe eleven-fifteen."

Orson nodded. It was very exciting, he said to Charlie, seeing a movie actually being made.

Charlie, suspicious, paused. Then, "Glad you're liking it, Killer."

31

Bel Air, August 1966

"You ride with me, Killer. Red, Lamar, Joe, take the other car. I want to visit with my good old buddy from Germany!"

Orson shared the back seat of the Cadillac limousine with Elvis. The driver started up. Elvis reached to flip open the tortoiseshell lid at his side. He turned the switch, and a light shone down on an array of liquors. "How about a drink? You know me, I don't use the stuff hardly ever. But you prob'ly need something; you've come a long way—where *did* you come from, Killer? Remind me."

"It's up by Seattle, Elvis." He shook his head, he didn't want a drink, thanks. Elvis took a Tab.

"Yeah, I remember, you tol' me. But I owe you a lot. That trip you took to Graceland. That made a *lot* of difference. You probably know she called me the next day, tol' me she wouldn't say anything about travelin' to Germany, excep' to say she wanted to see her family for a bit, visit with them—nothing wrong about that..."

"She's very much in love with you, Elvis."

"And how about me? Killer, it was *me* who spotted her at age fourteen and announced I wanted to marry her. You should know better than *anybody*. I mean," Elvis laughed heartily, "I stole her away from you! She was *your* girlfriend. Oh my, I remember, when she came running over to your house to see me; I was then with you and your ma. Fanny?"

"Francie."

"And she just knocked me over, that li'l', beautiful girl. But it's gonna be all right."

The car pulled up at the front of the house. Elvis ran up the steps and depressed the bell button and simultaneously knocked loudly on the door. He didn't stop speaking.

To the driver he called: "G'night, Jessie, see you tomorrow. Don't forget to unload Mr. Killer's gear. Wait!" To Orson: "You need anybody to take you around tomorrow? Jessie is with me full-time. Yeah. Tell you what, Jessie, you can expect a call sometime tomorrow from Mr. Killer. Kill-AIR. Do whatever he wants you to do. Got that?"

"Yes sir, Mr. Presley." The driver reached into his pocket for a card. "I'll be there whenever you call, Mr. Killer."

The large living room was decorated in heavy, solid colors, Elvis's favorite, blue, predominating. Before long, Red and Joe and Lamar and Charlie came in. They ordered drinks. Elvis offered Orson one of his pills. "Don't know what I'd do without these, the schedule I have to keep."

Lamar said he, too, could use one tonight, otherwise he'd go right to sleep. He addressed the question to himself. "That's right, ain't it, Lamar?"

Elvis handed him the bottle. The butler approached Elvis in a whisper.

"Who is it?" Elvis asked. "Ah—well—tell her, Boykin, tell her I'll call her later." He turned to Orson. "Tell me about what y'all are doing up there, near Seattle. I haven't been there for a long, long time. Everything keeps workin' on me to stay here. One of these days I'm going to call the Colonel an' I'll say—"

The butler was back. He leaned over and whispered again.

"Dammit, tell her I *cayan't* talk now. Tell her I'm on a live broadcast to—to—Lamar, give me the name of a country," he laughed. "Yes, Afghanistan."

He turned back to Orson. "I was talkin' about—how'd you like the movie just now? Norm, he's a perfectionist. He works and works and works on a film sequence, he'll settle only for the best. And who am I to complain?"

"You set pretty high standards yourself," Red interrupted. "How many takes did you go on those RCA sessions just before the army service?"

"I done maybe fifty on 'Don'cha Think It's Time.' You remember that, don't you Charlie? Heck, I did more than twenty takes when I did *your* song. Orson, did you know that Charlie here wrote the song 'You'll Be Gone'? You heard it?"

Orson nodded.

"Great song. Boykin, when do we eat? Just put it all on the table there. I'm puttin' on a little weight, you notice, Killer? Y'all go ahead and eat." He gulped down his Tab, walked to the closet and came out with his guitar.

"I feel like singin'." He began with "All Shook Up." Everyone applauded, tapping single hands on their knees to avoid spilling their glasses. Orson was transfixed.

"That's a beautiful song, Elvis, really beautiful."

"You like it?" He beamed his pleasure. "Listen to this one." He sang again, stopping after a few bars. "Charlie? Charlie, give me a little drumbeat, will you?"

Charlie turned over an empty plate and took two tablespoons from the center of the buffet table array. He gave Elvis the beat and Elvis swung into "Kissin' Cousins."

Orson was carried back and away. He began beating the rhythm with his right foot, a smile of pleasure on his face. Would Elvis do one more?

"Elvis," Charlie interjected. "Play for Orson 'Tomorrow Is a Long Time.'" To Orson: "He recorded that song last week."

"Yeah. Yeah." Elvis nodded. And to Orson: "This is a Bob Dylan number. Here we go." He began to strum and to sing:

> *If today was not an endless highway*
> *If tonight was not a crooked trail*
> *If tomorrow wasn't such a long time*
> *Then lonesome would mean nothing to me at all.*

Again the makeshift applause.

Elvis sang until after one in the morning. Then he wolfed down some fried chicken and told the gang he had a movie for them. He motioned to Boykin to get the projector ready.

"This is good, Norm tells me. It's *In the Heat of the Night*."

It was four in the morning. Lamar and Red had slid out during the movie. Elvis said he didn't like the movie all that much; it was too damn-Yankee anti-Southern. He addressed Charlie. "Charlie, be a good boy, call Alice. Tell her to come on over. I couldn't talk to her earlier because"—his face brightened—"I was broadcasting to Afghanistan!

"Killer, you stay *here* tonight. Never mind your stuff downstairs. We got everything, pajamas, you name it. I got maybe five bedrooms here, and one of them is yours. You might wanna take the one with the red wallpaper and black silk. It's real nice, man, real nice. Charlie, you can stay too, if you want."

32

Bel Air, August 1966

CHARLIE HAD HIS OWN PLACE IN BEL AIR, SUBSTAN-
tial, if modest by contrast with that of the King. Orson arrived
there, as he had agreed to do, at one P.M. The alarm clock sounded
in Elvis's guest room at noon, only five hours after Orson had finally bid good night to Elvis, stretched out on the couch, Alice on
her knees, her head over his chest. With one eye on the television,
Elvis had called out, "Don't forget to phone me up, Killer. An'
come on back soon, will you? It's cool to see you, real cool."

In the general daze of the hour, at seven in the morning,
Orson had removed his clothes and thrown himself on the bed.
When the alarm clock rang, he was startled to examine the room
he had slept in, with the shredded red wallpaper and black silk
hangings along the walls. He moved to the bathroom. It was fully
equipped. A telephone squatted on a little protrusion from the
wall. He paused. Why not use it? He moved back to the bedroom
and searched out the card in the back pocket of his pants. He got
through to Jessie and asked to be picked up at 12:45.

He would need a fresh shirt and underwear from his bag.
Where had he left it? *Oh yes.*

He opened the door and walked down the staircase to the huge living room he had left only hours before. The lights were still lit. On the large coffee table were Coca-Cola bottles, some empty, others half empty. There were empty cocktail glasses, an ice container, large slabs of cheese and ham, sliced loaves of bread, butter, peanut butter, a jar of jam, and an opened box of chocolates. The television set was on, though soundless. He flicked it off.

In his shorts he walked into the wide coat closet and pushed aside two of Elvis's dress costumes, neatly insulated with tissue paper. He poked underneath, located his bag, and took it up to his room.

Dressed and ready to go, he wondered if Jessie had a key to the house. If not, Orson should wait for him outside—it would not do to have him ring the bell and maybe wake Elvis.

But, treading softly down the stairs, he saw that Boykin was there. Dressed in a T-shirt and black chino pants, he applied himself to restoring order to the room. Then Jessie came in. Orson slipped a ten-dollar bill into Boykin's hand and went out of the air-conditioned house into the smoggy heat of Bel Air, the sun now directly overhead as they climbed into the limousine. After one and a half blocks, the car stopped. This was Charlie's house.

"You should've told me, Jessie, it was only two minutes. I could have walked."

"I didn't know where you was going when you called, sir. Will there be anything else?"

"No. Thanks." Orson didn't know how much time he'd be with Charlie.

By the middle of the afternoon, Orson thought to take notes. He had listened now, interrupted by points Charlie wanted to stress, to twenty-eight Elvis songs.

"Let's back up a minute here," Charlie said, shoving Orson's pad of paper away. "What do we know? The first thing, real abbreviated now, is:

"At this point, Elvis doesn't know a good song from a bad song.

"Elvis knows how to make a song *really* work, especially if it's a song he *really* wants to swing with.

"The songs being handed to him by Hal Wallis and the gang are okay, some of them, but not many that Elvis really lights up with.

"Now, Elvis *needs* an audience. Cameras and technicians don't make an audience. Last night when he sang for us 'Tomorrow Is a Long Time'—that was the real Elvis. Who'd he have listening to him? Just you, me, Lamar, Red, and Joe. Only five people. But we weren't technicians. *That* was the King.

"The movie people think that movie watchers want a ton of backup when Elvis sings. What are they using now? Not just the bass of Bill Black, the guitar of Scotty Moore, drums by D. J. Fontana. Oh no. We get bass, guitars, drums, organs, violins (sometimes), synthesizers, and what I call the Heavenly Choir. Now, I'm not against a backup chorus. It can be okay. But when they don't let Elvis *move* without his Heavenly Choir, all you get is yard after yard of velvet.

"Also, Elvis is an innovator. He came on the scene in 1954, and we were hearing black music and the blues, and a God-in-heaven rock beat that tore us all apart. He had a kind of raunch that was real new when he came up with it, the thing that drives the girls *nuts*. It was like what the guy said, like a jug of corn syrup at a champagne party. But that doesn't happen in a studio..."

Orson stopped his note taking.

What was the purpose of it? All he had written down that he had any further practical use for were the names of the three songs he wanted to get, so he could play them for Susie.

"So what are you going to do about it, Charlie?"

"I think you mean, what are *we* going to do about it, Killer?"

So that was the idea, hatched by Charlie, enthusiastically endorsed ("the gang are really really counting on you") by Red and Lamar and Joe. Orson was to approach the King.

"Has anybody tried talking with the Colonel?"

"The Colonel does not listen to lesser folk. As long as Elvis is churning out the cash Tom Parker needs to live in the casinos, that's all he cares about."

Orson looked down at his notepad. "But you're telling me the *Harum Scarum* soundtrack didn't go above number eight on the charts?"

"And 'Blue Christmas' didn't score at all."

"Aren't those signals the Colonel would notice?"

"They're signals the Colonel *should* notice. But he hasn't noticed them."

"Why should I have any luck, if you all don't?"

"I'm not saying you can make it work. But we're thinking he'd *hear it* if you said it. He needs to *hear it* from somebody who isn't just a member of the gang. After all, we're—employees. But that guy—you—has to be..."

"An Elvis fan."

Charlie smiled. "An Elvis fan, Killer."

33

Los Potreros, 1966

"You bet, Killer, I'd be glad to see you again. I don't care that you were here a while ago. I'd like it if you came to see me every week, not every ten years."

"It wasn't exactly ten years ago, Your Majesty." Orson twigged him. "I was there in August. I'm going to be in town"— Orson thought it best not to give the impression that he was Elvis-bent on a mission in Los Angeles, yet he didn't want to be invited to stay the night. *What would Mr. Simon make of such improvisations as this?* "My Susan has to be at the UCLA clinic for a couple of tests and I'll have to be with her most of the time, but I'd like to visit for a couple of hours."

"A couple of days would be better. You talkin' about *this* Friday?"

Orson was guarded. He had privately checked out Elvis's schedule with Charlie. Elvis would be shooting on Friday and also on Saturday, so Friday night should be good. But if Elvis were to make an excuse, Orson could find himself talking about the succeeding Friday.

"I'll be working late on my new flick, *Easy Come, Easy Go.*

But you know all that stuff. You want to come to the set, meet me there?"

"Can we play that by ear? I'll be coming in from the clinic."

"Tell you what. I'll leave word with Boykin that if you get to my place ahead of me, just let you in and give you a drink. An' you can come on over to the studio if you're real early."

"That will be great."

The next problem would be to detach Elvis from his nightly entourage. He discussed the problem with Charlie. Orson was under no circumstances to let on that Elvis's own people were themselves demoralized. Obviously, then, he could not plead his case in front of Joe or Red or Charlie. They were co-conspirators, but they wanted to conceal their misgivings.

"You know, Charlie, this mission the Mafia has got me on labors under a pretty crippling burden. If it's true that Elvis is endangering his career, then why wouldn't that be something you people spot and are alarmed by? But, no, you've staged it where a twenty-one-year-old computer intern whose only credential is that he fell in love with Elvis as a kid of fourteen, comes in and says, King, never mind any reassurances you're getting from the Colonel, from RCA, from Hollywood, from your fifteen Mafia members, from your shrink, your spiritual adviser, your karate instructor, take it from me, you're doing lousy work."

Charlie was silent. "I didn't say it would be easy."

"But you didn't say it would be impossible. If it's going to be impossible, why do it?"

"To help Elvis."

Orson gritted his teeth and forced out a smile. "I'd guess you'd put it that way, Charlie. It goes: 'Orson, on account of your liking of this guy and your feelings about how important he and his music are—you can't say no. Even to an impossible assignment.' Well, okay. I'll have to play it carefully."

"Play it any way you want. We need the seeds dropped in his mind, that's what we need. The single and the album from *Frankie and Johnny* never even got off the ground, not by Elvis's standards. The so-called 'vacation special' the Colonel put out only got to number nineteen on the charts. The albums from *Paradise, Hawaiian Style* came in with sales of less than a quarter of a million copies. A new low. Elvis is in danger of losing his fans."

"Okay. Your job then, Charlie, is to clear the decks on Friday, so I can get to talk to him alone. How're you going to do that?"

"You know the house. Did you notice the room on the second floor that looks in over the living room? That's where I am most days, working on my music and the arrangements and helping Elvis out. You might get him up there, away from the others and his girl, then I could leave you two alone..."

"We'll have to see how it goes. This is Tuesday. Do you people know three days ahead which members of the Mafia are going to be in attendance on Friday?"

"I can figure that out, and we'll try to keep the number down."

"Yeah. Don't invite the Colonel."

Orson got there at ten, was let in, and at ten-thirty Elvis arrived. Joan, his girl that week, was with him, also Joe and Charlie. Orson shook hands all the way around. Elvis was exuberant. He gestured to Boykin for drinks for everybody. "Let me tell you about this movie, Killer. See, there's this buried treasure. Look at me." He opened his hands, putting one over his head, the other under his chin. He talked as if through scuba headgear. "I'm underwater nearly the whole time."

"Oh, come on," Red said, taking a swallow of scotch. "He means, Orson, the movie has a scene of the King going down for the buried treasure, et cetera, et cetera, only the whole thing's faked."

"Whaddaya mean, the whole thing's faked? You forget, Red, I went out with the crew for two days' shootin' at—where the hell was that fuckin' beach?"

"El Marino," Joan volunteered.

"What about the musical numbers, Elvis?" Orson interposed.

"Well. Some are better than others."

Red West broke in. "They've got the King recording on the fucking soundstage instead of the studio. Bad stuff."

Joe Esposito stepped in, treading cautiously. "The guy at *Billboard* said some of the songs on *Spinout* sounded like they were recorded in 'a giant tin can.'" So, Orson noted, it was okay to blame other people, as long as Elvis was protected.

Elvis's high mood quickly gave out. He didn't comment.

Red said he had to turn in early because in the morning he would be listening to some of the sound-track material. "I'm concerned about 'Long Legged Girl (with a Short Dress On).'"

Elvis said he hadn't thought much of that song. "It doesn't last long, though. That's one thing. How long does it go, Charlie?"

"One minute twenty-seven seconds."

Another silence. Untethered, somebody in the Mafia would have commented that that was a minute and twenty-seven seconds too long.

Red went to the door, and Joe said he'd also leave, make it an early night. Joan said she wanted to see *The Tonight Show.* Elvis snapped at her. "Go see it in the bedroom, don't want to break up the party." She went upstairs.

It was the moment. Charlie Hodge darted for the door, with complaints about something he had done, or forgotten to do.

Orson was alone with Elvis, after the King dispatched Boykin to make up some fried chicken.

Orson had resolved that only a direct approach would leave a mark. He took a deep breath and began. "You know something, Elvis, I'm afraid you're running the risk of losing your fans."

Elvis looked up, his nostrils flared.

"There's just no two ways about it." Orson had dug in his feet. "Some of the songs you're singing in the movies aren't worthy of you. And people come in to see the King, and they leave with a sense, well, that either *they've* had it, or *you've* lost it."

Elvis's legs descended from the couch. Orson didn't stop. "Like that 'Long Legged Girl' song the boys were talking about, the one you said you didn't like. I haven't heard it, but I'll take your word for it that it was no good. What I want to know is: Elvis, what are you up to? Where does the Colonel think you're going? Why aren't you singing to—the people who worship you? The people who made you the King? I mean, people like me. And Priscilla."

Now Elvis stood up.

"What you doin', kid, tellin' me what's right for my career? Tellin' me what Priscilla is sayin' about me—"

"I didn't say that, Elvis. I just said Priscilla was an example of your early fans."

"Early fans!" Elvis's voice was raised. "You know what they're payin', what Hollywood is payin' for my last three pictures?"

"I'm just saying, Elvis, that the talent Hollywood bought into is being shredded by the product Hollywood is coming out with, and that the corpse that matters isn't MGM's profits—who cares about that? The danger is—it'll be yours. You need to go back to Memphis, I'd say, and do more of the great, great music you're, well, the King of, and go play to people who can see you in the flesh, not on the screen—"

"Killer. My driver is outside. I told him to stay, 'cause you said you'd be goin' home. You go now, understand?"

Well, Orson thought, *that's done it.* He would leave by saying the truth. "Elvis, I think you make the most beautiful music of anybody who ever lived. And I'll add to that that you're still my personal hero."

Elvis looked to one side. Orson walked to the door.

34

Memphis, December 1966

ON INSTRUCTION, THE CADILLAC MOVED SLOWLY. "Slow down some more, Leroy."

"What's the matter, honey? You forgot something at the Stilimans?"

Elvis pecked Priscilla on the chin. "No, didn't forget nothin'. Just wanted you to see somethin' I've arranged, see it in a special way, when the light's 'specially right. Leroy, I got a better idea. Just drive one time around the park. That ought to delay us about seven, eight minutes."

Elvis was peering at the twilight and checking his clock. "Twilight's scheduled for 5:22. They ain't never late, twilights, are they?"

Priscilla laughed and Elvis followed suit.

After a few minutes it was darker. "Okay, I guess it's safe. Take us on to Graceland, Leroy." The words were said with pride and anticipation.

Moments later, turning the corner, they saw the lights of the castle. Priscilla shrieked with glee. "Oh, Elvis, it's *so-oh* beautiful the way you have it lit for tonight! It's just like the White House!

Oh, I've got to have a picture of that and send it to Mom and Dad."

"I'll get that done for you, Priss."

Soon they were walking about the interior, decorated with Christmas trees and crepe and silver paper and stockings hung over the fireplace. He took her hand and sat her down opposite a large illuminated tree. "I got a Christmas present for you."

She put her hand out.

"No, it's not nothin' I got in my hand. It's something I got in my heart."

"Oh, Elvis." She reached to touch his hand.

"Tomorrow, on Christmas Day, I'm gonna announce that we are engaged."

She hugged him, and tears came to her eyes.

"Yep, announce it on Christmas Day, and we'll have in a few people on New Year's Eve for an official celebration. Meanwhile, just in case between now and tomorrow you feel different, I've got somethin' to tie you down with." He reached into his jacket and brought out a box. There was a ring. A brilliant three-and-a-half–carat diamond encircled by a row of smaller diamonds, detachable from the ring.

"See," said Elvis, picking off two of the little stones. "You can put them anywhere, ears, chest, and they all light up together. Like Graceland!"

Priscilla pronounced it the most beautiful ring she had ever seen. "I think it looks bigger than Elizabeth Taylor's." Elvis didn't want to tell her that Elizabeth Taylor's ring was the Krupp diamond, and the Krupp diamond, he knew, weighed thirty-three carats.

Dinner was served, set on trays in front of their sofa. They had sliced turkey and yams and corn bread and stewed tomatoes.

"Why don't you just try some of the champagne?" Priscilla urged him.

"Okay. Don't mind if I do. After all, tonight is a special occasion." He motioned to the butler to pour the champagne—not into the champagne glass but into his large water glass, now drained. "May as well not fool around, if we're going to take champagne, eh, Priss?"

He elevated the glass and began, in a soft voice, to sing "It's Now or Never." *"It's now or never, my love won't wait,"* it concluded.

"Now, the press is gonna get the announcement tomorrow, and we'll schedule our New Year's Eve at the Manhattan Club."

He walked over to the desk and came back with pad and pencil, which he handed to Priscilla. "Let's write down a few names, people we got to invite. Leave out Memphis. We'll let Dee and Vernon do all those. Just think about out-of-towners we want to invite."

"How about the Beatles?"

Elvis furrowed his brow. "I don't know whether those dudes are in the country. Hell, they could come from London, after all. Yep, put them down."

"What about President Johnson?"

"No, that would be bad taste, I think. There're guys getting killed in Vietnam right now. I'd invite Bob Hope, excep' he'll be out, good old boy, out there entertaining them. Lemme think a minute. We've got to invite the musicians. Bill's gone, poor guy, it was real fast, but Scotty, of course—put down Scotty Moore. And Sam Phillips and Dewey Phillips. And Deejay—D. J. Fontana, Jones Blackwood, Johnny Cash—"

Priss scribbled away.

"Oh, ah, yes. Now take these down carefully." Elvis stood and walked across the room, facing his desk, hands clutched behind him. "We got to invite, ah, Natalie Wood... Anita Wood... Elisabeth Stefaniak... Ann-Margret... Shelley Fabares..."

There was a sound from behind, a scream. He turned. Yelling

and sobbing, Priscilla removed her ring and thrust it into the fireplace.

"*Hey wait a minute!*" He shouted out, "Leroy! Alma! *Come here!*" He reached for the pitcher on the dinner tray and poured water into the fire. He spotted the ring. With the poker he dragged it out. He touched it, but pulled back his finger. Using the poker he maneuvered the ring into a water glass. There was a sizzle. Then it was safe to pick it up.

"Not a scratch. Real stuff. Priss, that was a dumb, stupid, shitty thing you did."

"That was a dumb, shitty thing *you* did, thinking to invite all your whores!"

Elvis flushed. His lips parted, baring his teeth, but not in the endearing way they did at concerts and in movies. Slowly they re-arranged themselves into a smile, a forgiving smile. Then he said, in indulgent tones, "All right. Let's get on with the list."

He resolved simply not to reveal to her the names of every-body he'd invite.

The calm resumed, and Priscilla said in matter-of-fact tones, "We have to invite Orson."

"Not Orson!"

"He's my best friend. Remember, it was Orson who kept me here that time I was going home a couple of years ago."

"If you heard what Orson said about my movies and about my music—"

"Darling, he was just trying *to tell you* a few things a few people are saying. He couldn't have meant he loves you or your music any less."

Elvis was silent. "I haven't talked with him since then. You know where he is?"

"Yes. He's with Susie."

"Who's Susie?"

"He's married to Susie."

"I didn't remember that. I haven't called him since that night he lef' my house, after eatin' my ass about my music..."

Again, Elvis's face recomposed itself. "*Awrright.* Go ahead and invite him."

In fact, Orson could not have gotten away to be at Graceland on New Year's Eve, 1966. Susan was scheduled for three days of psychiatric tests over that weekend, and he needed to be with her twice a day, to ward off any alarm.

It was just as well, he reflected on reading about it in *Variety.* The engagement party turned out to be a genuine full-blown Elvis extravaganza. The Manhattan Club in Memphis was so crowded, the story said, the police finally gave up trying to make way even for Elvis and his fiancée to get into the building. They were driven back to Graceland. There, too, crowds assembled and, right into midnight, crooned out their love for Elvis, who opened the large windowed doors on the second floor, blew out kisses, and hoisted up Priscilla's hand, pointing dramatically to her engagement ring. At his second appearance he had a large flashlight in hand, and shone it on the diamond. This brought *oohs* and *aahhs* from the crowd. They begged him for a song. Elvis hesitated. Priscilla joined the clamor. Charlie brought him a guitar. There was, suddenly, a total silence. "Hey, it's midnight!" a girl's voice rang out. Elvis raised his hand for silence, returned to the guitar, and sang:

> *Should auld acquaintance be forgot,*
> *And never brought to min'?*
> *Should auld acquaintance be forgot,*
> *And days o' auld lang syne?*

He raised both hands to summon the crowd to join him, and together they brought in the New Year:

> *For auld lang syne, my dear,*
> *For auld lang syne,*
> *We'll take a cup o' kindness yet*
> *For auld lang syne!*

35

Los Potreros, 1966

PHIL ANDROTTI ALWAYS ARRIVED EARLY AT HIS OF-
fice earlier than any of his thirty employees; but today Orson was
ahead of him. It was 7:30. Dressed, as usual, in khaki pants, a
sports shirt, and a light gray sweater, Orson was sitting on a
chair in the waiting room reading yesterday's *Wall Street Journal.*

"What you doing here, Orson?"

"I need to talk to you."

"Grab some coffee—need a dime? I want some, too." He approached the vending machine and gave it what Vicky called
"Phil's ritual kick."

"Yes, thanks, I'll take that dime." Orson brought his coffee
into Phil's office and sat down. He sipped and said, "Phil, I got to
leave the company."

Phil Androtti looked up sharply. "You don't mean—leave Albatron? After ten months and two raises? Your work is fine.
Why?"

"It's this. The doctor thinks Susie is ready now to make big
strides. She needs to get gradually coaxed into a return of her
memory. He says what would be ideal would be to take her someplace that maybe had a beach, someplace cheap, obviously—I was

thinking of Cabo San Lucas, in Baja—a place we could be to-gether, hour after hour, day after day, trying to ease her memory back."

"How long would that be?"

"That's the trouble, Phil. I just don't know. The place I'm talking about, offtrack Mexican, room and board, is only twelve dollars a day. I can swing that for a good while. Hell, if we win out in this lawsuit, we could *retire* there."

Orson lowered his head. He looked up then at his boss. "Phil, I know you well by now. And I know you understand. If, after we find out how it's going to be with Susan, you want me back, I'd really like to do that."

Androtti got up. "You've done very good work. We'll really miss you. But my guess is that—whenever it is, we'll want you back. Unless we're broke. Unless Tom breaks his other hand—is it going to be all right with Susan?"

"I don't know. But there's hope."

They had a staff party for Orson the next night, the day before he would leave for Baja California. Phil had asked him earlier in the day if he would do his routine for them. Orson had worked on it, had done it a month before for Phil's birthday party.

It was patterned after what he had heard at the Montana fra-ternity party nearly two years ago, a medley of Elvis songs with Orson the ostensible singer, the true voice of the King coming in through speakers. In years to come such performances would be routine, the Elvis impersonator. But in the summer of 1965, no-body was really impersonating Elvis, because nobody really could. Orson had to rely on a carefully assembled tape of Elvis singing. He began his little act by imitating Elvis introducing a song, and swung into "Hound Dog," quickly followed by "Jailhouse Rock," all of this performed with exaggerated facial expressions and body movements. What most amused the staff was the *huge* ovation Orson gave himself, turning the volume all the way up when the canned applause broke in.

Orson was feeling fine.

36

Cabo San Lucas, 1966

THE PAPAGAYO HOTEL AT CABO SAN LUCAS, A FEW miles from the luxurious La Paz, was an informal hostelry, entirely maintained by its owners, Carmen and Cecilio—Carmen squat and officious, Cecilio tall and vague. They did everything for the guests occupying their six thatched huts. Carmen prepared the basic foods, rice, beans, corn, and tortillas, and Cecilio served from the buffet table. On Mondays, Wednesdays, and Fridays, Carmen came into the beach huts and made the beds and checked the mosquito screens—there were no windows at Papagayo, and no electricity. Cecilio, alternating with Carmen, did it all on the odd days. Each of the huts (they were called paradores) had an oil lantern, checked every other day by Cecilio.

Orson had brought with him a portable radio. It tipped him off to the big gladiatorial event and, in the fourth week, he and Susan walked down the sandy street to the restaurant to see on television the great prizefight. Muhammad Ali knocked out Cleveland Williams. "Nobody can beat Muhammad Ali," Susan opined, then looked up questioningly at Orson. "Has he...actually...in the past...ever been beaten?"

Susan was very talkative now. She had given up trying to conceal her loss of memory, and her efforts at reconstruction had become more systematic. For a full day she talked to Orson about her mother, Flo, and her father, Mugsy. She laughed on recalling that her grandmother had forbidden anyone in the house to use the word "Mugsy." His real name was Morgan. "But it didn't work."

"Did he care, your dad?"

"I think he cared probably when he was at school, because, Mom told me once—" Susan stopped suddenly. "What did my mom tell me?"

"You mean, about Mugsy?"

"Yes, about Mugsy. What was I talking about?" Her eyes filled up, and Orson quickly said, "Let's talk about whether you're going to try to sail in that beat-up old Sailfish Cecilio is pushing on us."

"Is that part of the Papagayo? I mean, do we get that free, Orson?" She sat up and extended her hand, describing an arc from the right, where the Papagayo central thatch hut was—the office with Carmen and Cecilio, and the kitchen and outdoor dining room—all the way to the left, the far corner of the beach. "Orson, how are we managing to pay for all this? Is my allowance enough for this?"

"Darling, we're in Mexico, you know that. And this is a very, very inexpensive place." He thought to twit her. "Are you saying you want to move to where you get television and air-conditioning?"

She ran her fingers over the sand, then looked up at Orson. "No. I wouldn't want anything else. I want to be here—at Papagayo—a lot."

In the fifth week she had begun to read from one of Orson's paperback books. "You know," she commented, "I've read a lot of these. Of Agatha Christie. I began reading detective stories when I was fourteen, and I ate them up. Have you read *The Murder of Roger Ackroyd?*"

Indeed he had, Orson said.

"You remember who the killer was in that book?" Susan laughed with pleasure at the surprise ending. "It was the *narrator*! That was a dirty trick on the reader, making him think it was one of the other people...You know, I was thinking the other day of Senator Goldwater. You know, what I thought—I think... He's still in the Senate, isn't he?"

"Actually not. He had to pull out when he ran for president. But he's going to run again for the Senate."

"Well, I thought he was terrific in the Senate. I liked his face, too. I know you weren't very high on him because of your dirty Marxist past. But that's over, isn't it, Orson?"

"I'm not planning any revolution. Not this week. Not this decade, I guess it's safe to say."

"Would you like it if it were—a socialist world?"

"Yes, I would. But a lot of things would have to be different."

"Like human nature?"

"That would be a good start."

In early December Susan said she would like to write a story. Fine, Orson said, he would write it down as she dictated it.

She sat back. "Maybe what I'll do instead is—an autobiography." She looked at him, inquisitively, trustingly.

"Not a bad idea. That helps, too, with the whole memory business."

Susan shut her eyes now and said, in a voice that sounded distant, as if she were speaking words she had framed in her mind to ask him, "Orson, Carmen and Cecilio call me *señora*. Darling... are we married?"

Orson was glad the Reverend Weems wasn't within hearing.

"Yes, my darling. We're married. We married in the hospital. When you said you wanted to marry, and said 'I do' to the minister, I really thought you knew what was going on."

"Maybe I did. That doesn't mean I mightn't have forgotten. After all, there's this...problem. But I'm getting a lot better, aren't I, Orson?"

"You're the top of the world. And in no time you'll be going on quiz shows."

That night they made love. She liked to have the oil lantern on, very low, at the corner of the parador, so that nobody walking on the beach could see the profile of their bodies interacting. She embraced him ardently, and Orson fantasized that Susan was with him in the boxcar, just the two of them, there was this big mattress, and the sounds of the train chugging along, and all the time in the world, no interruptions, no deadlines; just Susan and him.

Later she stroked his hair.

"Orson, tell me something."

"Anything."

"Did I have a baby? I think I did."

"Yes."

"What happened? To her? Him? What happened to it?"

"Carla is a very beautiful little girl, and she is safe at home in Germany with my mother."

Then she cried with happiness, as Orson did.

37

Memphis, May 1968

NOBODY, ESPECIALLY NOT CHARLIE, SAID ANYTHING at all about the big, offbeat show now scheduled. It would be billed simply as—Elvis Returning! Returning as the King of Rock 'n' Roll.

And why not? he commented to Priscilla. It had been nine years since his last time out in the world of television performances as the star of rock 'n' roll. In the interval, he liked to remind reporters—speaking now with Jill Peterson of the *St. Petersburg Times*—he had made twenty-eight movies and had forty-two gold records. Gold records tallied actual sales, not merely appearances on the chart, Jill Peterson reminded him, remarking that Elvis hadn't topped the chart at number one in six years, and that his last two movie sound tracks hadn't even made their way onto the charts at all. He hadn't had a number-one single in six years, a number-one album in three. His most recent significant success was one more compilation of old hits, *Elvis's Gold Records*. How did he account for this?

Elvis dodged the question. He sensed a great many things going on, or not going on, and he was now telling Red and Joe and Lamar, along about December, that he had truly tired of

Hollywood, that he would give it a lot of thought before accepting another Hollywood commission.

Everything, as usual, rested with the Colonel, who was in Las Vegas. And the Colonel, reflecting in his hotel suite between prolonged bouts at the casino, meditated on his tidy notations.

He had made some projections. Measured as a piece of the pie, the Colonel's interest was well protected. Bit by bit he had increased his take on all Elvis activity to fifty percent. Even so, his figures—and Tom Parker was very good at figures—revealed that at this rate of attrition, Elvis would stop earning *any* money seven and a half years down the line. That was intolerable. The Colonel was very loyal. He would not look at another client, not since he'd taken on Elvis, in 1955. But he didn't intend any sacrifices. Life was expensive.

Hollywood had had enough of Elvis as a reliable-but-waning agent of best-selling movies. Hollywood wasn't panting at the door for one more Elvis flick. Even though Elvis had himself grown restless and bored, the diminished enthusiasm for more Elvis movies had to be communicated to him delicately.

It was in January that the Colonel said, "Y'know, Elvis, we really should do a television special. Include, maybe, one or two new songs, but bring back those great numbers. Be fine for your fans to hear you tackle 'Heartbreak Hotel,' and 'Hound Dog,' 'Blue Suede Shoes,' all those songs you made legendary—"

"Why should I do that, Tom? Why not just re-release the old versions, like we been doin' for ten years or so?"

"Publicity, kid. Give 'em something old, but tell 'em it's new."

It took a lot of arranging, but arranging was the Colonel's specialty. He gave the impression, on the days he met with his staff to plan it step by step, that he was undecided about exactly when the show should be broadcast, and by whom it should be sponsored. He had in fact made a deal with NBC. It would go out as a ninety-minute special in the fall, the exact date to be decided on later. Charlie, brimming with enthusiasm, spoke over the phone with Orson.

"He's going to sing *live*! Not a huge auditorium audience, just maybe a hundred fifty, two hundred people, seated around him. Half the songs will be sung campfire-style, Elvis sitting there with his guitar, Scotty and another guitarist on his right, a bass player and a drummer...And Elvis! It's going to be *real* informal—"

"How's Elvis looking?"

"He could lose some weight. Maybe he will, with this show in front of him. But let me tell you, Orson, this boy hasn't lost his magic. He's the King, and he'll prove it...Shit."

"What's the matter."

"At the rate he's taking those pills, he may not sleep again until studio time."

"When is that?"

"June twenty-seventh and twenty-ninth."

"How many...sittings?"

"We can't plan exactly. We're thinking a total of four, and we'd like to do two every night. But every show will have a fresh audience. Golden tickets, for this set of concerts."

"What's the...title it'll go out under?"

"Remind me, Killer, how does it go in French? Gracie and I were there, Versailles, a while back, a long time after you and Elvis were out there. The big inscription in the Hall of Mirrors?"

"You asked the right person. I was eight the first time I saw it. I couldn't understand it. What it says is: '*Le roi gouverne par lui-même.*' 'The King runs things.'"

"Is that a good translation, Killer?"

"That, Charlie," Orson said, "is a perfect translation."

BOOK FOUR

38

Tacoma, June 1968

"THE PHONE'S FOR YOU." BESSIE ANDROTTI CALLED up to Orson in the guest room of her and Phil's house, where Orson was boarding. "But better watch out," she continued. "The gal on the phone says Elvis Presley is calling."

Orson drew a deep breath. He closed the door, picked up the telephone, and spoke with Elvis for the first time in a long time. Somehow Lydia had tracked him down.

"*Killer!* I wanted you to be the *first one* to know, on account of, you know, that little fallin' out we had back there. Well, let me tell you somethin'. I did the *first* part of my television special tonight, you know, the TV show comin' up? And they went *wild!* Everybody. The audience, of course. But also the Colonel. Also Charlie. Also the RCA people."

"That's wonderful, Elvis. Terrific. How long did it go?"

"'Bout an hour. The special, when the editin's done, will be ninety minutes. Now, listen, Killer, listen real hard. The second half hour will be filmed live *the day after tomorrow.* Thursday. *You gotta be there.* I just feel...feel it in mah bones, you've got to be there. You're my good-luck piece on this special special.

Now, don' say nothin'. I talked to the Colonel, told him you had to be there and he'd have to send a plane up there for you."

Orson felt the excitement of long ago. Susan's health was so good that she was off to Germany with her little girl to visit Francie. It was way, way back in Paris that he had last been directly caught up in Elvis's whirl. ...How on earth did Elvis *find* him at Phil Androtti's? Orson reminded himself that Elvis's Lydia would locate anybody Elvis wanted to talk to.

"Gee whiz! Elvis. But it's a long way, Tacoma to L.A."

"We'll tell the pilot to bring plenty of gas, Killer."

"Well. *Sure!* When do you want me there?"

"Studio time is eight P.M. sharp. I want you to have a little good-luck dinner with me at six. At my place. You stay with me. Can you stay on a bit? After the taping?"

"You mean, stay over Friday?"

"Stay on fifty Fridays in a row!"

Orson laughed. "I got a job."

"I'll talk to your boss."

"*Elvis!* Sober up, King. Well, I could stay the weekend. Should be back at work on Monday."

"Maybe I can persuade you. You got a girl, Killer?"

"Yeah. My wife. Susan. But she's not here right now."

"Where is she?" This was the old Elvis, the telephone marathoner. He was in no hurry.

"She's in Germany, visiting with my mother."

"Ms. Francie?"

"You remember!"

"Sure, she an' Priscilla's ma, they were together all the time. Like you and Priss. She okay, your baby?"

"She's great. We got a little girl."

"Well, so do Priss an' me! She's Lisa Marie. Probably Priss has told you. Say, Killer, let me ask you somethin'. You know anything about karate?"

"Absolutely nothing, Elvis."

"Well, you should. I started doin' it a bit back in Germany, and since I went to Hawaii las' month I've been gettin' back involved in it. It's great stuff, man, real great stuff. Not only teaches you how to look after yourself, it teaches you, you know, to *feel* good. It's a great substitute for the drugs and liquor all the kids are doin'. That's really terrible. Half the kids in San Francisco are on dope. Anyway, I work out an hour practically every day. Very first thing, about three, four in the afternoon... Yeah, yeah," Elvis called out, to whoever was attempting to get his attention on the other end. "I'm talking to Orson, be with you in a bit."

He came back on the phone.

"Now, what I'm sayin' here is, Killer, you got to start up with karate. If you're gonna be here the weekend, how 'bout I have my teacher, his name is Ed Parker, give you an introduction? Say, one hour on Saturday, another one on Sunday? An' if I can talk you into stayin' over, you can have one every day. You'll stay at my place, unnerstan'? I already said that."

"Elvis. It's a good idea. But it won't work, I don't think, unless you do it, unless I could do it, like, you know, on a regular basis. Tell you what. I'll poke around here—"

"You mean in your city? Where you work?"

"Yep. Tacoma. I'll find out if anybody around here teaches karate. If I find a teacher, I'll take you up on it. That okay?"

"That's good. Now don' *forget* to do that. Have you heard 'Nothingville'? I picked that up a while ago, song written by Billy Strange and Mac Davis. I'm gonna include it in my special. That'll be on the high stage, not the campfire. We'll have the Blossoms backin' me up. Scotty'll be there. An' a few extras. I'm just gonna sing my heart out."

"You always do."

"Yeah, that's right... Though maybe—on the Hollywood business—maybe you had a point. It'll be great to see you. You be in touch with Joe about the airplane and stuff. So long, Killer."

"So long, Elvis."

Get a call from him! Signaling a truce! More than that, he's going to fly me by private plane! Fly me to hear him perform!

All of Orson's engines of enthusiasm revved up. He felt like he was setting out by bus for Columbia, South Carolina, to buy the first Elvis record he'd ever owned.

"Well," Bessie Androtti said when Orson came down. "So that was Elvis Presley calling, I bet."

"Actually it was, Bessie." What purpose was there in concealing the friendship any longer? "Elvis and I are old friends. I got to know him in Germany when I was fourteen."

He told the Androttis the story.

"He must be quite a guy," Phil said.

"Yes. He is. Quite a guy."

39

Tacoma, June 1968

ORSON WAS BACK LATE ON SUNDAY AND LET HIMSELF into Phil Androtti's house. He had left the office early on Friday and thought now to make up missing work, so he set the alarm an hour earlier than usual.

He'd be happy to reoccupy his own apartment. With Susan away for a month, he had impulsively offered it for use by the elder Androttis, who were coming to Tacoma to visit with their son. They didn't want to share a house with their son, didn't want to pay for a hotel room, and didn't want to visit for less than a full month, so this was the arrangement. It was a strain for Orson, though, to have to tiptoe about early for fear of waking Bessie or Phil.

The morning weather was sticky. He felt the damp in the newspaper he brought in from the porch. While the coffee perked he unfolded the paper on the kitchen table. The headlines spoke of a nuclear-proliferation treaty. The lead editorial was an argument directed at California Governor Ronald Reagan. The editor, Orson read listlessly, was pleading with Reagan not to enter the race for the GOP nomination in 1968. *Let's go with Nixon for unity against the Democrats,* wrote the editor.

Orson was singing "Nothingville" to himself, fresh in memory from Friday night. When he'd told Elvis—after the taping—after dinner and reminiscences—how struck he had been by it, Elvis had reached for his guitar, told the Colonel and Red to shut up, and began to stroke the opening chord. He then stopped and announced: "This is for Orson." It had been very beautiful, the whole thing, the show, the song—Elvis.

Most of the talk in the paper was about who would get the Republican nomination—Nixon or Rockefeller or Reagan? *Who cares?* He wondered, Would Mr. Simon, in Wiesbaden, be paying any attention to American politics? What was Lizzie up to? And Eleanor and Barry Schmidt and Elsie, the old gang from the Students for Democratic Peace? Tom Bayliss once told him a story about the meeting of the executive committee on ethics of the AFL-CIO in 1958. After they had been in consultation for two days, CIO boss John L. Lewis asked, "Have they discovered any ethics yet?"

Poor Lizzie, Eleanor, Barry. Had they discovered any democratic peace yet? The students at Berkeley didn't seem to have found any, to gather from the commotion there. Nationwide, colleges were erratically shutting down and postponing commencements. But the war in Vietnam, from which, as a married father, Orson was safe, was still going on, and just what good would nonproliferation do, when the world was already teeming with nuclear bombs?

Phil Androtti didn't appear at the office that day. He called home to Bessie to say he would be spending the night in Seattle. "Something's going on," Bessie nodded to Orson, on her way to take her in-laws out to dinner.

Nor did Androtti come in on the second day. Tom Bayliss was in, but closeted himself in his corner office. By then rumors were circulating. The giant firm of Hewlett-Packard was now a live presence in the two-barrack offices of Albatron.

Orson found himself in the washroom with Tom alongside. Without turning his head, Tom said: "I guess we should've known. Hewlett-Packard wasn't about to let anybody upstage them on computer printing devices."

"They're moving in, Tom?"

"Yep."

Phil Androtti gave Orson the news formally. He did it that night at home, after Orson had got back from dinner with Susan's doctor and his wife. The takeover would be confirmed the following day.

The next afternoon, Orson met with Henry Salter, personnel manager for Hewlett-Packard. Salter had scheduled meetings with ten key employees of Albatron, beginning at ten A.M. and stretching through the afternoon.

Salter seemed a pleasant man, middle sized, in his forties. He spoke softly and did not remove his jacket, the mugginess of the weather notwithstanding. He told Orson that the company was impressed by what Orson had accomplished for Albatron, that Mr. Androtti and Mr. Bayliss had spoken warmly about the knowledge Orson had absorbed, and of his natural flair for communicating with investors and encouraging interest in the company.

Mr. Salter had projected future demands on Hewlett-Packard and had consulted with the vice president in charge of planning. The firm of Hewlett-Packard would welcome a long association with Orson Killere, but required that he attend business school. Mr. Salter summed up. "The place for you to learn what we'd want you to learn is USC."

"I don't have a college degree."

"I know that. We do a lot of business with USC. They'll work out a program, catch you up at the same time on the B.A. work. We'd require a two-year commitment from you, after you complete the degree. We are prepared to pay university expenses and to continue you on your present salary."

The news was breathtakingly reassuring. Orson said that he'd need to call his wife. He smiled a boyish smile of relief and pleasure. "It's late in Germany to call her—but not *too* late."

"Let us hear from you."

Henry Salter looked down at his watch. It was time for the next employee.

Susan listened. "What did they do with Phil Androtti?" she asked.

"He's out—with some sort of buyout package. Tom Bayliss is being promoted. About half the guys are going to the firm in San Francisco, and a whole lot to Los Angeles."

"Honey, that's not the worst news in the world. So they want to educate you? Maybe I'll go back to school at the same time! We've got to stay ahead of Carla. She's gurgling in German. We'll be with you in a week, unless this means we ought to stay over a bit."

"I'll figure it out. I miss you, doll. Let me have a word with my mom."

Francie Killere expressed her delight with the company of her daughter-in-law and granddaughter. She said then, "Did you get my letter, with the clipping?"

"No. About what, mum?"

"About Mr. Simon."

Orson paused. "What's up?"

"He died last week, on Tuesday. It was very sudden. He had his classes right through the spring term. Two weeks later we all got the bulletin from Major Brennan about the funeral service on Saturday."

"Did you go?"

"Yes, darling. I remember how nice he was to you."

Orson began to ask what Mr. Simon had died from but stopped himself. He talked about his little girl, and then about the renewed threat by Khrushchev to Czechoslovakia.

"Yes. We're very concerned about that at HQ. With President Johnson pulling out, that and the Vietnam business, foreign policy is going to need shoring up. You well, darling? I'll get your news from Susan. She's terrific, wonderful, I'm so happy for you."

Lou Ehrlich came to Orson's door.

"What do you say we get the fuck out of this place. Let's go to Seattle, let off steam."

"I'm all for it." Orson slammed shut his folder and locked it in his desk.

Lou Ehrlich was a pretty big deal at Albatron. At age twenty-eight he had already spent eight years in the computer world. A tall, rangy figure with brown eyes that locked in with obsessive concern on whatever he was dealing with. He kept no regular hours, laboring sometimes around the clock in Albatron's laboratory. Lou, silently, led Orson to the Thunderbird in the parking lot.

At eighty miles per hour on the highway he spoke as offhandedly as if at a coffee table. "I didn't tell you, or anybody else. I own—owned—five percent of Albatron."

Orson knew intimately the structure of the company, dealing as he regularly did with the investors and the banks. He tried in his mind to place which pseudonymous entity in the corporation's books might have been Lou's. There were six five-percent owners.

"Are you maybe the same person as the, er, 'Hillman Brothers Fund'?"

"That's me. But I've got no brothers. I've got a father. He's a small-time banker, in Parson's Creek. He thought I was full of shit when I asked for ten grand to put into Albatron." He chuckled. "I bet Dad'll wish he had invested it, instead of just lending me the money."

Again Orson was calculating. He knew the details of the company, its assets, its debts. What he didn't know was how much Hewlett-Packard had agreed to pay in exchange, in cash and stock, for the patents and pending research. Or how much for the invaluable Tom Bayliss, and the equally indispensable Stu Davenport. And what about the future of Lou Ehrlich?

"I can't figure out"—Orson grinned over at Lou, hoping not to distract him from the highway—"what five percent netted you. Tell you what, Lou. You can pay for tonight."

"That's a whopping commitment, Orson, because tonight is going to be...expensive!"

"Does tonight maybe include looking in on Jefferson Airplane?" Orson was much attracted to the new rock sensation.

"Why not! We'll take in the early show. After that I got to introduce you to a pair of *really* lovely ladies."

After the three drinks and the wine and the uproar of Jefferson Airplane, with their psychedelic, surreal music, and the great, booming caterwaul of Grace Slick, Orson's resolution weakened. It was a good-time couple of hours, after a nerve-wracking twenty-four hours, very different from Elvis hours at the recording studio. This, combined with a change in career and the prospect of going back to college, had a narcotic effect.

Lou went to the phone at dinnertime, and now he said: "Follow me, Orson. You get fifty percent of the action tonight."

An hour and a half later, Orson was asking himself: *What's dogging you? The whole experience, 1956 to tonight, was about what Elvis's music was telling everybody. Do it.* It didn't mean he couldn't marry Priss and have little Prisses. Hell, Orson had proved he'd do anything for Susan—and he would, he thought, tears coming to his eyes. He would die for her.

No reason, was there, not to have a little extramural—diversion? "*I can't get no satisfaction...,*" the band had played, replicating the famous Rolling Stones lament, the lament of the excluded guy. That excluded guy wasn't Orson Killere, not tonight.

There was soft light in the luxuriously appointed bedroom. Pictures hung on the walls, most prominently a fake Toulouse-Lautrec. Or maybe it *wasn't* a fake?! Tonight Orson would believe anything. It showed a graphic, multicrayoned view of a half-dressed girl and a young bearded man in midcopulation. *I can't get no girl reaction, 'cause I try, and I...try and I try and I try...,* he thought hungrily, stroking the welcoming, embracing torso...transported by the in-and-outness, which gave—now—*huge* satisfaction. *Huge satisfaction.*

He eased further down on the bed. Becky, fondling him, said she too loved to hum when she did it.

40

Las Vegas, July 1969

FINALLY, AFTER ALMOST FIVE YEARS OF HEARING ABOUT him, Susan would see Elvis Presley in the flesh. These were golden tickets, to the heralded opening of Elvis's show in Las Vegas. January's television program, now commonly dubbed "The Comeback Special," had been an enormous success. And now Parker/Presley had resolved to return to the original, pre-Hollywood regimen: public performances and regular record releases.

Elvis Presley, Inc., had begun the year with concentrated work on a new album. *From Elvis in Memphis* had twenty songs, many of them new. Elvis was buoyed by the success of his TV special, and the Colonel caught the signal. One month after the *Memphis* release, the Colonel had concluded a contract with the International Hotel in Las Vegas for month-long appearances—two shows every night, except opening night. On opening nights the glamour of the event called for a single exposure.

The Colonel devoted all his resources to promoting the Vegas opening. Even though the initial show was quickly sold out, the Colonel drenched the city with radio and television ads calling attention to it. *First time in ten years! Elvis onstage! International*

Hotel! New promotional ventures were launched almost daily. The Colonel rented advertising space on Vegas taxis. Elvis, Inc., was now pushing Elvis belts, scarves, skirts, jeans, lipstick, charm bracelets, statuettes, publications, and ties (Western). Elvis surveyed the activity and thought it all fine, truly fine. "Leave it to the Colonel!" he exclaimed happily to Charlie Hodge.

But then Elvis drew the wrong kind of attention to himself with that fucking interview. On a sleepy afternoon, just one week before the opening, he had yielded to an ingratiating reporter and spoken about...money. About everything.

The Colonel had exploded when he read it. He set out on foot to Elvis's headquarters, two blocks away. He found the King relaxed in his suite, a guitar in his arms, the guys sitting about, a couple of them reading the papers, Joe Esposito tackling a crossword puzzle.

The Colonel opened fire. "Of all the *stupid* things to say..." The row was still going on at full steam when the telephone rang for Charlie.

"Let me get on another phone," Charlie said.

Orson waited. Moments later, short of breath, Charlie's voice came in and somebody downstairs clicked the first phone off.

"Boy, is this a relief! Elvis and Tom are downstairs, screaming at each other about the interview."

"What interview?"

"You haven't seen it?"

"No. You got it in front of you? Interview with whom? About what?"

"I got it here. Stuffed it into my pocket this morning. If I could steal every copy, I'd do that, believe me."

"Got time to read it to me?"

"Sure. Kays Gary, of the *Charlotte Observer,* did the interview. It's titled 'Elvis Defends Low-Down Style' and talks at the beginning about how Elvis makes out with all the girls. But here's what the fire's about. Presley said he does what he does because, I'm quoting him, 'this is what is making money...and after all, the music's been around forever.' The Colonel doesn't like that, A, because of the money orientation and, B, because he likes for Elvis to be thought of as an original."

"I kind of admire Elvis, saying that—"

"Hang on. The interview quotes him some more. 'The colored folks been singing it and playing it just like I'm doin' now, man, for more years than I know. They played it like that in the shanties and in their juke joints, and nobody paid it no mind till I goosed it up. I got it from *them*. Down in Tupelo, Mississippi, I used to hear old Arthur Crudup bang his box the way I do now, and I said if I ever got to the place where I could feel all old Arthur felt, I'd be a music man like nobody ever saw.'"

Orson broke in to express his glee. "It's *too* good—"

"Hang on, not quite over. The reporter asks Elvis if he agrees that his music is often dirty. Elvis answers: 'Yep, some of the music is low-down.' But Elvis didn't want that to mean he agreed with the criticism of the kind of people who don't want him to shake his legs. So Elvis goes on: 'There is low-down people and high-up people, but all of them get the kind of feelin' this rock 'n' roll music tells about.'

"The reporter then asked him about the future of his music. Elvis said he doesn't know how long rock and roll will last. 'When it's gone,' he said, 'I'll switch to something else. I like to sing ballads the way Eddie Fisher does and the way Perry Como does. But the way I'm singing now is what makes the money. Would you change if you was me?' That's what got the Colonel—"

"Elvis's grammar?" Orson asked delightedly. He was holding the phone cocked on his shoulder, so that he could take notes for Susie.

Charlie laughed apprehensively. "The business about money. That's what really offended the boss. But let me give you Elvis's closing line, which I think is terrific. It has to do with Elvis-the-sex-stimulant." Charlie attempted to imitate Elvis's voice. "'When I sang hymns back home with Mom and Pop, I stood still and I looked like you feel when you sing a hymn. When I sing this rock 'n' roll, my eyes won't stay open and my legs won't stand still. I don't care what they say, it ain't nasty.'"

Orson was silent. Then he spoke. "What the Colonel has is— Elvis. If it was anybody else, it wouldn't be Elvis. And the Colonel wouldn't be rich."

"But the Colonel has a point about the critics. Probably everybody will throw it at him now: 'Elvis Says It's Just for the Money.' 'If that's right, Elvis, how can you look so sad? How can you warble the way you do?'"

Orson said, "Charlie, did I ever tell you my theory about... money? Oh never mind—"

Charlie interjected: "Hang on. Got to check the door...It's okay. They're still downstairs, wrangling.

"On the PR problem, Elvis had a taste of it yesterday, coming into the hotel. I was there. Some woman shouted at him that he was corrupting children. Elvis stopped and said, 'Ma'am, if I did think it was bad for people I would go back to driving a truck, an' I really mean this—'"

"Charlie, what matters is that Elvis *really does* believe it. We don't have to go any further than that, do we? In that way he *is* different. You take the Colonel. If Tom Parker got a higher bid from the Hotel Whorehouse than from the International Hotel, *that's* where Elvis would be opening."

"Probably you're right, Killer. Anyway, Las Vegas is all ready for you, and I'm sure anxious to meet Mrs. Killere."

Orson liked that, and let it rest a bit before correcting him. "It's Susan. Or, if you like, Susie. I didn't want it to happen, her meeting you, back in '66, till she was all well." He paused. "She's all well now."

41

Los Angeles, December 20, 1970

Lydia put Elvis on the line.

"I need your help, Killer. I want to see the president."

"The president of the United States?"

"Yes, him."

"Elvis, I don't *know* the president."

"You know one of his assistants. You told me that one time."

"Well, yes, Bud Krogh was at Ann Arbor when I was going to school there. He was an assistant to the dean who kicked me out, back when I raised all that hell. And now he's an assistant to the president."

"Once a friend of Orson, always a friend of Orson, that's my rule."

"Never mind Bud Krogh. What is it you want to see President Nixon about?"

"Dope. It's all over the place. A national plague. An' I want to do somethin' about it, take a public stand. I want you to go with me to Washington, to hep' me get in to see the president. Tell you the truth, Killer, I got a lot of friends here an' they help me out a lot but I'm not about to take Lamar into the White House, he'd hardly fit through the gate. And Red's a hell of a guy, but he wouldn't be right to, you know, do the interviewin' I'd have to do, on the dope issue. Nor would Joe. We don't have to go down the list of the—they all call it the Memphis Mafia. You know that. I've tried to do you a favor or two, haven't I, Killer?"

"You've been terrific and generous."

Orson was composing his thoughts. There would be no trouble missing classes for a couple of sessions at the business school. Susan was busy at college during the day, and looking after Carla at night. "When did you want to go?"

"Tonight, on the last plane out. My own plane is out of commission."

"You mean on the red-eye?"

"Yep. Leaves at eleven. What do I care? We care? We're up nights, mostly. We can talk about the drug business on the plane an' I'll give you my plan."

Orson agreed with Susan that it was a crazy idea. On the other hand it was hard to think of anybody, even the president, who would flat out refuse to see Elvis Presley; though Susan was skeptical. "All Nixon has to worry about is the Vietnam War, NATO, the collapse of gold, Cambodia..."

"You're probably right. On the other hand, Susie, goofy ideas can also be *fun*. Like impromptu trips to Paris. And I wouldn't mind a free trip to Washington."

Susan gestured. She raised her right hand and wiggled a few fingers, repeating the gesture she had absentmindedly used when she was an invalid. That was her way of saying: Okay. Susan liked the continuing friendship, Orson and Elvis. Elvis had been wonderfully warm when they'd spent a few minutes together in Las Vegas after the opening.

Sitting with Orson in the first-class section of the TWA 737, Elvis recounted his concerns. He had done an in-depth study, he said, of drug abuse and communist brainwashing techniques. What he wanted, Elvis had resolved, was official status of some sort. With that, he could give talks about drugs and counsel agents actively engaged in the detection of illegal drugs. "That kind of thing. I want to give this my Elvis-all."

"What kind of official recognition do you have in mind?"

"I want a badge. Exactly like what they give you at the Bureau of Narcotics and Dangerous Drugs—"

The stewardess handed him a note. "Sorry to interrupt you, Mr. Presley. This is from Senator Murphy. Senator George Murphy. He's sitting in the coach section, just wants to pay his respects."

"George Murphy! I've seen him in old movies, Killer. *Great* dancer. He's now a United States senator."

Elvis rose. The stewardess led him back to where Senator Murphy was sitting.

Elvis extended his hand. The middle seat, next to the senator, was empty. "Mind if I sit down a minute, senator?"

Elvis was gone almost an hour.

"What a *great* guy, Killer! He told me one funny story then another and he's a great fan, says he has all my records. But—no ma'am, no drinks for me. Orson, you want some booze? Go ahead." Orson ordered a second scotch and soda. "What's most important is, Senator Murphy said he'd try to get word in to the president about how important it is to see me. I showed him"—Elvis beamed, drawing the envelope from his breast pocket—"the letter I've written to the president. When we land we're goin' directly to the White House an' I'll drop it off. Want me to read it to you?"

Orson encouraged him to do so.

When he got home, Orson would repeat the opening lines to Susie. He loved it. So did she. *Dear Mr. President. First, I would*

*like to introduce myself. I am Elvis Presley and admire you and
have great respect for your office.*

Elvis's letter then spoke of his concern for the country and his
eagerness to use his public station to alert people to the dangers
of drugs.

At 6:30 in the morning, Whittaker was there to meet him. He
was the elderly black driver who looked after Elvis when he was
in Washington. He drove, as directed, to Pennsylvania Avenue,
and stopped opposite the West Gate of the White House.

Elvis jumped out of the car, signaling Orson to follow him.
He presented himself to the police officer at the sentry booth. The
uniformed agent didn't immediately recognize him. This seldom
happened to Elvis. He angled his face a little, this way and then
that way, to give the officer a better chance to recognize the familiar features. That finally worked.

"Mr. Presley, I'll see that your letter is in the White House as
soon as business begins. That'll be in one hour."

They checked in at the Washington Hotel, into adjacent suites
with a connecting door. Orson drew the shades and lay down
to rest.

At ten Elvis banged on his door. Orson emerged in shorts and
T-shirt, eyes blinking.

"I'm going off now to see the director of the Bureau of Narcotics and Dangerous Drugs," Elvis said. "Senator Murphy said
he'd call him and tell him I wanted to see him. His name—" Elvis
removed a memo pad from his pocket. "His name is John
Ingersoll."

Orson stepped back and surveyed Elvis. He was wearing his
new jeweled, oversize glasses. He had on a dark Edwardian jacket
with brass buttons. It draped like a cape around his shoulders,

above a purple velvet V-neck tunic with matching pants. These were set off by the massive gold belt the International Hotel had given him in tribute to his record-setting string of performances. Over a high-collared, open-necked white shirt, he wore the gold lion's-head pendant he had recently purchased from Sol Schwartz, his favorite jeweler, in Beverly Hills.

"I look okay?"

"Elvis...," Orson began. But stopped himself.

It would be great, it flashed through to him. If ever he contrived to get into the Oval Office. Elvis and Nixon. Elvis looking *just this way.*

Orson promised that while Elvis was talking with John Ingersoll, Orson would go to the executive offices of the White House and present the case for an interview to Bud Krogh, his Ann Arbor friend of six years ago.

Deputy counsel to the president, Egil Krogh, told the clerk to admit Orson Killere. Krogh hadn't changed, though the sport coat was missing, replaced by the executive-wing suit. They reminisced briefly about Ann Arbor in 1964.

"Mr. Revercomb was a pretty intimidating gentleman."

"Well, Orson, you certainly aroused his intimidating side. Since the president of U of M has passed on, I don't mind telling you—working here gets you used to passing nuggets like this along—that he *personally* ordered John Revercomb to boot your ass out of Ann Arbor."

"Well, I guess I had it coming."

"You still up to—overthrowing the world? If so, I'd appreciate your taking a vacation from that line of work as long as you're visiting the White House."

"Good point, Bud. I hereby declare a two-day armistice. But you'd better climb back into your air raid shelter beginning on

Wednesday, when I leave town. Now listen, I told you what I wanted to...get you to expedite. Elvis wants to do some good for a cause the president is identified with."

Orson spoke of how important a presidential audience was for Elvis. He told of the worldwide audience of the King and observed that in this tight season for President Nixon, with the widening student protests, it might be useful for the president to be photographed with this idolized figure, so associated with youth, youth pleasures, youth understanding—youth's love and ambitions.

"Hold it, Orson. Youth isn't the president's favorite thing right now. By the way, I'm glad to see where you're coming in these days on student protests. But anyway, you're right: Elvis is an important world figure. And the president should encourage this impulse in Elvis, to warn about drugs. I'll send along a recommendation. Where is Elvis right now?"

"Senator Murphy got him in to see Mr.... Ingersoll? Bureau of Narcotics and...Illegal Substances and—" Orson stumbled over the full name of the agency.

"Dangerous Drugs. I know Ingersoll. Tough hombre."

"Elvis wants that badge from the bureau. I've never known him to want anything more than he wants that badge."

"Well maybe Ingersoll will give it to him. In any case I'll get back to you at the Washington."

Egil Krogh stood up. Orson caught the signal. Time to get out of the way of the assistant to the president.

For the hell of it, Orson gave Krogh the victory symbol, right hand hoisted, two fingers separated. He could see Krogh wondering whether Orson was summoning the spirit of Churchill, or the spirit of student bomb throwers.

"Thanks, Bud. Nice to see you again."

Orson wouldn't go any further in teasing Krogh, wouldn't do anything to distract from his present inclinations, to bring the King to the president.

42

Washington, December 1970

ELVIS PRESLEY HAD BEEN SPOTTED GOING INTO THE
temporary offices of the Bureau of Narcotics and Dangerous
Drugs on Connecticut Avenue. By the time he came out, a half
hour later, thirty high schoolers had gathered, coming in excit-
edly from the adjacent high school as the magical word got
around: *The King is here!*

Laying eyes on him they began to shout and sing out and
plead. The security officer stationed at the entrance picked up his
telephone and zip-dialed the D.C. police. "*Elvis Presley is here.
He's been upstairs with the director. His limo is surrounded. Got
to be thirty, forty kids out there. Oh gee! One girl—I can just
make her out through the door... She's thrown herself on the
drive in front of the limo... No *way* that limo can just plain drive
Elvis away... You better send somebody. Better send *two or three*
somebodies.*"

A police car drove up in minutes. Elvis was signing auto-
graphs, and now he was pleading to be let into his car. "*Sing,
Elvis, sing!*" The roar began. One policeman physically removed
the redheaded girl on the drive while another officer, with the
help of an agent from the drug bureau, groped Elvis's way

through the crowd and tunneled him into the car. The police parted the students, gently but resolutely, to one side. A way was cleared, the limo inched forward and, finally, Whittaker eased it down the driveway and onto Connecticut Avenue.

"Take me back to the hotel," Elvis directed.

He said nothing more during the ten-minute drive. Whittaker was surprised. He had driven a half-dozen times for Elvis Presley in the past. Customarily there was another passenger, usually two or three, to talk with him in the rear seat. But on the one occasion when Mr. Presley had been alone, he had chatted with Whittaker about this and that. Not today.

The police had got word to the hotel, where a plainclothes officer waited for him. Elvis was led into the elevator and up to his suite. He walked across the living room and flung open Orson's door. Orson was on the telephone.

"I got to talk to you, Orson."

Orson cupped his hand over the receiver. "Be right with you. I'm talking to Bud Krogh, White House." He made a note on the pad and said, "Thanks, Bud. I'll get you that background." He hung up and walked to where the costumed figure stood waiting.

Elvis Aaron Presley shouted out his rage. "Who the fuck does *John Ingersoll* think he is? I mean, what did I ask him for? The State of Texas? A Cabinet post? No, just an ordinary badge. He just said *no!* Said *only* agents of the fucking BNDD could have a badge. I *explained* to him the good I could do for the program. But no! *No, no, no!*"

Elvis hurled himself onto the couch. Then he got up, removed his cape and his tunic, unclasped his belt, threw it down on the floor, and plopped himself back down. A moment later he bounded up and strode into his bedroom, reemerging with a bottle of pills. He walked to where the pitcher of water was, dug into the bottle, removed some pills, and gulped them down with the water. "That oughta help."

He sat down on the sofa and looked up at Orson, who was standing, his back to the bookcase. "Did you get anywhere? Any messages from the White House? What did your boyfriend tell you?"

Orson let the language pass. "I had a good talk with Bud Krogh, and he says he's going to put in for a meeting with the president."

"I'm not sure I want to see him." Elvis was sulking.

"That was Bud Krogh on the phone when you came in. White House security people need a couple of things, you know, like your address, that kind of thing."

"My *address*? Did you tell them Graceland is maybe bigger than the White House?"

Orson tried to console him. "Come on, Elvis. It'll work out. I think it will. I know it will. By the way, there are a couple of messages here from Lydia."

"I don't want to talk to nobody."

"The Colonel's son—Andrew Jackson Parker—called. He lives here—I didn't know that. He wants to take us to dinner."

"Andy Parker? Nice enough guy. Nicer than his fucking father, who practically owns me...Well, we're goin' to have to eat somewhere. Any music in town?"

"I'll ask him."

"I was at the Warwick Hotel a couple of years ago, there was a band. Tell Andy."

Elvis was in a better mood when they set out. "If we get an appointment, I hope it's not for too early. The pills are gonna keep me up the usual hours, so I won't be gettin' to sleep till...late."

"I'll wake you up if the president is waiting."

Elvis soured again at his reminder of the federal bureaucracy. At dinner he was less than responsive in talk with Andy Parker and his wife, Hester. He twice complained to Andy about his treatment at the drug bureau. "It was like they want me to sign up as a full-time Treasury agent before they give me a badge," he snorted. "Maybe your dad can draw up a contract, me and the drug bureau, full-time work."

At ten, the emcee introduced the band. "Let's listen to the Chicago Round Table!" he exclaimed, urging, with his outstretched hands, a show of enthusiasm. The applause was only polite.

The band began with the languorous notes of "Unchained Melody." At the cadence the piano eased into a memorable musical line, quickly joined by the guitar and the bass, the drummer egging them on. The two hundred diners were suddenly listening to intimations of "Love Me Tender." In moments it was known that the King was in the room, and the entire audience was on its feet, looking over at Elvis.

"What the hell?" Elvis glanced at Orson. Orson smiled and lifted the palm of his hand slightly, in encouragement.

Orson knew what was going on in Elvis's mind. He had suffered a face-to-face rejection that morning, and rejection wasn't something Elvis had experienced in a very long time. He still suffered when reminded, as happened on occasion, of his rejection as a candidate for serious attention by the Grand Ole Opry. Journalists plowing over his career for one of their portraits liked to recall that in 1954, the managers of the Opry were unimpressed by his trial performance. But that was sixteen years ago, and since then no audience—no studio, no record company, no television feature—had denied him. When he was in the army, Elvis had been privately advised by Captain Haley Laswell that some care would be taken to avoid confrontations with military superiors, and he was never denied. What Elvis needed right here and now was to restore his self-image—as the King. To do this meant to sing. Nobody would deny him, after hearing him sing.

He made a feigned show of reluctance, then rose and walked over to the microphone. He pointed to the guitarist and beckoned with his fingers. The guitarist instantly unstrapped the instrument and handed it over to Elvis.

He strummed a few chords. And then, with a broad smile: "Let's get this one right, okay, guys?" And he gave them "Love Me Tender." "Love Me Tender" as it should sound.

The audience begged for more, but didn't need to. Elvis's face was now lit up and he began to strum "Are You Lonesome Tonight?" The diners were transported by the unexpected treat and the pleasure of it all, and so was Elvis, who sang three more songs, the accompaniments picked up by bass drummer and second guitarist. Then, still grinning, and gesturing with his hands to both sides of the dining area, he rejoined Andy and Hester and Orson.

"That was beautiful," Orson said.

Whatever Elvis's psychological needs, he was consecrated, at his best, to his mission to please, to transport those who heard him sing his songs.

43

Los Angeles, December 1970

SUSAN, FROM LOS ANGELES, TALKED WITH ORSON ON the phone before his dinner. It was seven, Washington time, late afternoon in California.

She reported that she had had a call from Priscilla. "She wanted to know how come we hadn't answered her invitation. I said what invitation? While she was on the phone, I pawed over the letters tray with your mail in it. It was there, an invite from the Colonel's office, a handwritten note from Priscilla on it."

"Invitation to what?"

"To what they call an 'impromptu screening' in Hollywood of a couple of Elvis's live performances in Las Vegas. Not the opening night we saw, later ones. Did you know that the Colonel filmed every single one of them? I don't know what they're thinking about with this particular screening. And of course Elvis is in Washington with you. So if what they're looking for is reactions to it and they want Elvis's, they'll have to play it again for him."

"But you're going?"

"Oh sure, I'll do that. I told Priss I'd go. Elsie can stay on with Carla. She never minds. She likes the extra pay."

"And likes Carlita!"

"Who wouldn't? After a few months of pre-kindergarten she's ready for the stage. This morning, before I went to school, she said something that sounded like—"

"Our mother tongue, I hope."

"Cut it out. Your teasing doesn't help her trouble, whatever it is, putting words together, but you always know what she's—meaning to say."

"She is my true love. After you. Who else is going to be at the screening, besides Priss and the Colonel?"

"I don't know. I'll tell you tomorrow. How're you doing on your Nixon mission?"

"We've got the White House surrounded. They're just pleading for a little time. Tell the Colonel that Andy—Andy's his son—is taking me and Elvis to dinner tonight."

"Elvis behaving?"

"Mmm."

"I see what you mean."

"You got any messages for Nixon?"

"Yes. Tell him to make Senator Goldwater Secretary of Defense."

"I'll do that."

Susan was surprised, coming into the luxurious little screening room with deep leather armchairs suitable for Hollywood vice presidents, when Priscilla, after kissing her in greeting, ran her fingers down Susan's arm, sliding a piece of paper into her hand. Susan acknowledged the furtiveness of the approach, reacting instinctively by looking straight at Priss, ignoring the disguised note.

She was guided to one of the armchairs by Charlie, who sat down next to her. She brought the note discreetly to her waist and opened it. *Can you have dinner with me after the screening? Important. XXPriss.*

From the front row, seated next to the Colonel, Priscilla Presley was looking over at her. Susan nodded: Yes, she'd go with Priss.

But why the covert maneuver? And how would they manage to leave together, if it was intended that they should disguise their rendezvous? She'd wait for a cue.

It came two hours later, after the screening. The Colonel got up and said that he proposed to trim a total of 50 minutes from the 110 minutes the amalgamated shows had run, in the version they had just seen. "We'll trim the repeats, there are a few of those. And of course the applause, bring it way down. But we are leaving enough of it to communicate the enthusiasm of the people there. Elvis, you probably know, broke all Las Vegas records, with a gross of $1.5 million. I'm—we're—deciding what to pull out for a television special. I'm glad to have reactions. Charlie? Where's Charlie Hodge?"

"Right here, Tom."

"Charlie, you're an expert. Tell me if you see any differences, plus or minus, on the repeat songs we've left in. You got a pad and pencil?" Everybody was supposed to have a pad and pencil for comments.

"Yeah, Tom. I'm all set."

Elvis had begun with "All Shook Up." He followed it with "Johnny B. Goode" and then "In the Ghetto"; but for no clear reason, he had dropped the opening words, catching himself up a few bars down the line. Susan noticed that Charlie had been making notes. Elvis had gone then to a familiar two-song routine, "Jailhouse Rock" followed by "Don't Be Cruel." At the end, following a diapasonal "Can't Help Falling in Love," accompanied by the heavenly choir of the Sweet Inspirations, who swelled the harmony to the breaking point, the nightclub audience had stood up to applaud wildly.

The Colonel thanked the auditioners for coming, asked Charlie to collect the notes, and then approached Priscilla. "Ready to go to dinner, Priss?"

"Tom, I'm going to beg off. Got a little . . . I don't know what it is, but I thought I'd just go home."

"Okay, okay. Actually, I'm going to be trying my luck at a friendly poker game. Call me in the morning, tell me what Elvis is up to."

"I'll do that, Tom."

She winked at Susan, and they followed a half-dozen technicians and viewers into the elevator.

Her car was waiting. At age twenty-five Priscilla Beaulieu Presley's beauty was in full bloom, enhanced by designer dresses regularly commented on by the showbiz press. Her profile was illuminated by the car's headlights. With a show of conspicuous spontaneity, she turned to Susan. "Let me drop you home, okay?"

"Thanks. That would be nice." She followed Priscilla into the limousine. Inside the car she whispered. "I'll tell you about it when we get to Bel Air." She then chatted about the screening.

Susan agreed that it had been a spirited show, combining the two Las Vegas hours. "He did only the one show on opening night, remember? I don't know how he could manage two shows every night beginning the very next day."

"Have you ever worked, Susan? I forget, if I ever knew."

"Yes. Sure I worked. I quit college—you know my mom and dad were killed in a car accident. Car accidents run in the family. I quit college and went to work for a construction company, there in Salt Lake. I ran—at age eighteen—the personnel office. Kept in-out work hours for twenty, as many as twenty-five workers. I had a long working day because I had to be there to clock the first man in—he came at six-thirty—and the last guy out, at six P.M."

"*I* never had a job," Priscilla said as the car door opened at the Presley house on Rocca Place. "But Elvis did." She beckoned Susan to follow her out. "He was a truck driver. And he kept whatever hours the trucking people told him to keep. Maybe that's why he never complains about long hours in the studio, or about doing two shows in one night."

The front door was opened. She said to Perkins, the butler, "I'll have a scotch on the rocks." She gestured to Susan. "What will you have, honey? See how I've picked up the language of Graceland? In Germany if you said *honey* to a girl they'd think you were queer."

Susan brightened. "I'd like a gin and tonic."

It wasn't until after dinner, when they were seated alone, that Priscilla finally disclosed her mission. At dinner she had finished a bottle of wine, and now she had a crème de menthe with the coffee. "I want your help. Actually, it's Orson's help I need most, because he's got that special relationship with me *and* with Elvis. He's not an employee, he's not just one more fan. He is a very old friend, Elvis relies on him more and more, even though they don't see each other all that often."

"Priss, tell me. What do you want Orson to do?"

"I want him to tell Elvis this: I'll be going back to Graceland in a couple of days. I know that the *minute* I go back, Elvis is going to take up again with Ella. And if not Ella, it'll be somebody else. I mean, he's—insatiable. He told *everybody* he was going to straighten out after we were married. Then he told everybody the same thing when Lisa Marie was born."

Susan said nothing. She wasn't going to feign surprise, but she wasn't going to contribute more names to the collection.

"What I want Orson to tell him is that he knows it from you, because you got it from me here tonight: *I'm not going to put up with it*. He does it? I'll do it. So he's big and famous, so he thinks he's the only one with—appetites? I have appetites, too. I bet you do, too, no, Susie?"

Susan was born candid, Orson had once teased. "Sure I do."

"Does Orson give you...everything you want?"

"Whoa there, Priss. You wanted to talk to me about *your* troubles. I didn't tell you I wanted to talk to you about my troubles. Maybe I don't have any, that ever occur to you?"

Priscilla put down her liqueur glass. "Does that mean you don't want to help me?"

"No. I'll help you, and I know Orson would like to help you. But we'd better talk about personal problems, yours and Elvis's. Not about, you know, problems everybody has, because of human nature."

Priscilla looked up, one of her studiedly ingratiating looks. "I understand, hon. So look, tell Orson to talk to Elvis. To say to Elvis: *Cut it out!*" She swallowed hard. "You know something, honey, he's not *going* to cut it out. He's just—not *going* to..."

Susan was not prepared to volunteer a conclusion to the syllogistic challenge. One: Priscilla would no longer put up with it. Two: Elvis was never going to stop doing it. Therefore? What then?

Let Priscilla face it. She should draw the conclusion, or step back and modify a premise.

Priscilla was droning on, filling her liqueur glass again.

Susan said she'd have to be going home. "Elsie—that's our baby-sitter—doesn't like to have to stay past eleven."

"Do you want me to send Jessie to take her home?"

"No, doll, you're a sweet friend. But if Jessie's still around, he can take *me* home."

Priscilla rose with a little effort.

"I understand, honey. I completely understand. And you'll speak to Orson?"

Susan did the best she could. "I'll tell Orson we've had this conversation."

"Tell Orson I love him, will you?"

"I certainly will. And you know he loves you. Ever since you were kids."

They exchanged kisses good night.

In the car Susan gritted her teeth. What was Orson supposed to do that would alter the basic situation—if the basic situation was as Priscilla described? What right did Priscilla have to be so offended? So betrayed? How was Elvis now different from the man she pursued for five years?

It's too bad, Susan thought. And Priscilla was right about one thing, you couldn't just blame it on human nature. Human nature is there to be contended with.

It did not occur to her what *she* would do if she found herself in that kind of a situation with Orson. But she never would.

Would Orson?

44

Washington, December 1970

WORD WAS WAITING FOR THEM AT THE HOTEL WHEN they got in at midnight. The president would see Mr. Elvis Presley at 12:30 the following day.

"Whee! I knew they'd come to their senses!"

"That's good, Elvis. Now what you ought to do is try to get some sleep."

"I don't feel like that, like sleepin'."

"You've got sleeping pills in that mix of yours, don't you?"

"Yeah. Yeah I do, Killer. So you goin' to shove one up my ass?"

"Come on. I tell you what, I'm going to wake you up at ten o'clock in the morning. You'll just have to get up, like it or not. I'll have some breakfast ready. You know there's a gym in this hotel. You could go down—fourth floor—and take a steam bath, a swim, a karate workout, whatever."

"Me go to a public gym? You kidding? I'll be all right, Killer. You go ahead and turn in. I'm goin' to watch a little TV. Has Johnny Carson come and gone?"

"Yeah. It's after midnight. See you, Elvis."

"See you, Killer."

Orson hoped Elvis would tone down yesterday's ensemble, but he wouldn't say anything. When dressed, though, he walked into the living room, and Elvis saw the dismay on Orson's face. "Look, I'm Elvis, I got to dress like Elvis, and I got to put on a good show for my people." Orson thought to comment, as Elvis adjusted his huge, golden-buckled belt, that President Nixon was not exactly one of Elvis's "people." But he said nothing, not until Elvis reached into his suitcase and brought out a package, and bared it.

"This is my gift for the president."

Orson stared in disbelief. "Elvis! You are *not* going to take a . . . great big . . . *pistol* into the White House! Are you crazy?"

Elvis was chagrined. "It's not loaded, you know, Killer."

"I *know* it's not loaded, but the Secret Service is not going to let you into the White House with a—what is it?"

"A Colt forty-five. I paid two grand for it. Here, look at the stock, hand carved."

"Okay. Now, Elvis, when you get out of the car there, at the White House gate, tell Perkins to go to that first guard and tell him you have a gift for the president, that it's an antique pistol, and how does the guard want to handle that? They can come to the car and take it from you. Okay?"

"I'd like to give it to President Nixon myself."

"If the guard and all those people say yes, then go ahead. But do it my way, will you?"

"Okay."

"I got a better idea. I'll ride with you. *I'll* step out and tell the guard."

"I kind of thought you'd like to meet the president."

"I'm not talking about meeting the president. I'm talking about meeting the guard."

"Maybe the president will want to say hello."

Orson smiled. "Elvis . . . tell you what. I'll sit in the car, and they can send for me if they want."

"Good. I *hope* he'll let you in. But what *I got to have* is that badge. I'm gonna flat out tell him I think it's only fair, if I take a lot of trouble to make the drug case, I should have that—"

"Badge."

"Yes."

"Elvis, let me suggest just one thing. Don't bad-mouth Ingersoll. Just say they ran into a bureaucratic problem at the Bureau of Drugs, etc."

"Okay. I'm not into revenge. You know that, Killer."

When Elvis was admitted through the west gate at 12:20, an aide motioned the chauffeur to take the car into the West Wing parking lot and wait there for Mr. Presley. Orson sat in the backseat reading the *Washington Post*. The big foreign item was a German threat to motor traffic into West Berlin. He waited. It was 12:40...then 12:50. At 12:55 an aide approached the car. "Mr. Killere?" He pronounced it properly, Kill-air.

"That's me."

"Would you come with me, please?"

He was led directly into the hall, to the elevator up to the second floor, down another hall, and into the Oval Office. They all rose. The president, his assistant Bud Krogh, and Elvis Presley.

"Mr. President, this is my old pal Orson Killere."

Nixon shook hands, smiled, said he had had a good talk with Elvis Presley, whom he very much admired. He told Elvis he was very glad to have met him and to have spent a little time with him and would like to present him with a pair of presidential cuff links.

He looked over at Orson. He opened a second drawer. "And I'd like to give you something here, Mr. Killere, for your—"

"Wife," Elvis interjected. "A beautiful girl, Mr. President."

"I'm sure she is."

In 1970, President Richard Nixon presented
Presley with a badge designating him an official
of the Federal Drug Enforcement Bureau.
WHITE HOUSE PHOTO

Orson accepted the brooch and offered his thanks. The president turned to his assistant, bringing to a close the matter at hand. "Bud, can you see any reason why we can't get Mr. Presley a BNDD badge?"

Bud Krogh said he couldn't think of any reason, but there were those rules—

"Well, we can see our way through *federal* rules, can't we Bud?" President Nixon, Orson thought, had given due weight to the division of powers.

Elvis smiled broadly.

The president rose and extended his hand. Orson shook hands also with Bud Krogh. An aide materialized.

The president said, "I've arranged for a tour of the White House for Mr. Presley—"

"Elvis, sir. Ain't heard *Mr. Presley,* like, maybe, *never!*"

"Elvis, and for you, Mr. Killere. I want to thank you again for your support of our war on drugs, Elvis."

The aide showed them the way out.

45

Las Vegas, 1971

ALL WAS NOT SMOOTH BETWEEN ELVIS AND TOM Parker. The Colonel was not often on the scene, but there was never anything he did not know, affect, encourage, veto, consciously ignore or forget, and that had been true since the Colonel more or less acquired Elvis in 1955, sixteen years before. When Patricia Painter, a waitress in North Hollywood, filed a paternity suit against Elvis, the Colonel assigned the job of looking into it to John O'Grady, now full-time investigator for Elvis, Inc. O'Grady reported back after a few days that it was pretty much established that Patricia and Elvis had spent an evening or two together. He counseled the Colonel just to wait. "Maybe the blood tests won't check out." Elvis told the Colonel he hadn't slept with Patricia Painter. "Didn't even want to." The Colonel took the occasion to deplore Elvis's carelessness.

Then there was the trouble in Las Vegas in January, another lapse in the long sequence of Elvis's engagements at the International Hotel. Elvis said he had been sick. He refused to see the doctor the hotel management hysterically tried to get him to consult. *No strange doctors,* Elvis decreed. He did arrange to fly in Dr. Nick Nichopoulos from Memphis, and was soon back on his feet.

"But you missed over *one-half* the shows," the Colonel thundered at the other end of the phone line. "What's that Greek voodoo quack doing to you? I bet he's just feeding you more pills. You're going to die of pills, Elvis, if you don't look out."

"You afraid if I die you'll have to go back to work?"

Elvis had taken recently to a confrontational style with the Colonel. He was especially vexed, in that period of the early seventies, by the Colonel's failure to nail down a European tour. Elvis wanted badly to do the big cities in Europe. He would include a free concert for the soldiers at Friedberg, the army camp he had served in. The Colonel kept telling him the time wasn't right.

"Which is horse shit, Tom," Elvis replied. "Why *isn't* it right? In September last year I went out on the first concert tour *since 1958.* Risky? It was a sellout, you know that—you organized it. Sellout in St. Louis, in Detroit, in Miami, in Tampa, in Mobile. I got another movie scheduled, the documentary. And there's the new RCA album. And just incidentally, at the same time all *that's* going on, I'm meetin' with the president of the United States about drug policy. If this isn't the right time, what is?"

The Colonel reminded him he was already booked through 1971. "You're booked, like, two, three times a month, and of course the Vegas gig is nightly, five weeks." He maneuvered to change the direction of the conversation.

"I got this bulletin," the Colonel said. "It's very confidential. They're going to give you at Vegas in August the Bing Crosby Award. That's about the biggest statement that can be made, recognizing you as a, well, as a *classical* popular artist."

"Who else has got it?"

The Colonel was ready for the question. "Well, Bing Crosby, of course. And Frank Sinatra, Duke Ellington, Ella Fitzgerald, and Irving Berlin."

"That's good stuff. I like that." Elvis had been covetous on the matter of his standing in the world of big musicians. He didn't mind the inevitable press references to his batting down his foot and continuing to swivel his hips—he did that naturally, as he had several times said to interviewers. But it wasn't that that entranced his audiences. It was his *artistry*. He wanted that certified by as many authorities as possible.

"Why's it so secret, the award?"

"As a matter of courtesy they want to inform everybody who has already got the award."

"You mean get their okay? Is Bing Crosby gonna say yes? You remember when he said that, well, that critical thing—"

"That was in 1954."

"Yeah, I guess so...No trouble with Frank, or Ella. They like me. I've never met Irving Berlin."

"He's never rejected the royalties from the songs by him you've sung."

"That's true."

The conversation had got off the subject of a European trip, and the Colonel remembered that he had another engagement.

But a month later the Colonel was on the phone again. "Tell me, goddamit, I want to hear it from *you*. What happened last night?"

"There was confusion. I admit it."

"I'm told the band just *stopped dead* at one point. Had no idea what in the hell you were going to sing."

Elvis wasn't combative on the question. "I tol' you, there was lack of *coordination*. I take the responsibility, but it's Charlie, y'know, who's supposed to coordinate those things."

The Colonel took advantage of Elvis's conciliatory mood. "You know, Elvis, I never took it up with you, what you did in Nashville, actually *walking out*—"

Elvis regained the offensive. "Fuck it, Tom, you weren't even *there* when the singer, the tenor backup, came in off pitch. I stopped, of course, and we did another take, this may be our one hundredth take, and fuck if he didn't come in wrong *one more time*. Whaddyou expect for me—stay on and give him singin' lessons? I told Felton to call me after he got the band and back-ups lined up, I wasn't gonna stay there all night, givin' the guy what, a tuning fork?"

"That wasn't exactly the way Felton told me it went."

"There isn't anybody I like workin' with better than Felton Jarvis, and we been workin' together a long time. But if he didn't hear the screwup, then all I got to say, Tom, is I have a better ear than Felton Jarvis." He thought about it. "Better ear, maybe, than *anybody*."

The Colonel let it go. This was not the time to talk to Elvis about the secondary glaucoma the doctor had diagnosed in Nashville. He'd end on an upbeat. "So they're going to call that road in Memphis the *Elvis Presley Highway*. That's nice."

"Yeah, that's *real* nice. Wish mom were alive to see it. To drive down it." Elvis chuckled. "I figure if I drive on it once in every car I own, it'll take me till Christmas."

"Okay, Elvis. Stay well. Stay good."

"You too, Tom."

46

Los Angeles, May 1972

ORSON AND SUSAN CELEBRATED THEIR JOINT GRADU-
ation—an M.B.A. for him, for her, a B.A. She dressed specially
for the occasion. Orson had never before seen her in the red silk,
with the long pleated skirt and the tight black leather belt with
the turquoise. "Take a close look." She pointed to her belt. He
looked down at the lettering spelled out by the light blue stones.
To the left of the buckle he could discern *B.A.*, to the right,
M.B.A.

"Oh gee!" was all that Orson could think to say.

"I thought you'd like it."

He went to the drawer and pulled out his new Polaroid.
"Hang on. I want to get close enough to see the lettering." He
stepped forward. "I can't focus. I'll take you first, then the belt."

Carla opened the nursery door. The television quacked out
Donald Duck's concern. "Here, Mommy. I'll take the picture.
Move over, Dad."

They went out into the Ford station wagon. With his left hand
on the wheel, he clutched Susan's with his right. It had taken a lot
of time before she could ride seated in the front, without involuntarily closing her eyes. One night, in bed, she'd told him that she

could now bring back the scene, the hard rain, the sudden braking, the great truck smashing up in front of her. "The next thing I really remember was our—parador."

"Papagayo?"

"Yes. The golden eye-opener. How long was it? A couple of weeks?"

"It was like a year."

"Oh yes." Susan bit her lips. "Of course, because Carla came, and I had no memory of it...But"—she smiled broadly—"who cares now?"

They drove up to the Four Seasons. Orson turned the car over to the valet-parking attendant. He reflected gratefully on their good fortune. The academic degrees of course. But besides, he had been productively at work for over a year, completing his schoolwork at night and on weekends. His good academic work had helped him get, from the aggressive firm of Hewlett-Packard—so determined to dominate so much in the new world of computers—a substantial rise in his salary.

An hour later, in a little leathery booth, their wine glasses prominent on the small, dimly lit table, Orson looked up, responding to his name. "I can't see you very well. Who is it?"

"Mike." He moved into the light. Orson recognized him.

"Mike. How're you doing? Susie, this is Mike Stone."

"Mike Stone? I recognize the name. You're the dangerous guy who's been teaching Orson karate."

"That's me," Mike said. "And you better be good to Orson. He's gotten to be a *real*—killer!" Mike Stone was greatly amused by his pun.

They laughed. "I'd ask you to sit down, Mike, except there's obviously no place here."

"No, no. I know that. I'm off at the corner table. I'm waiting for Priscilla."

Orson said nothing.

Susan broke in. "Well, give Priss our best, okay?"

"Will do. Will most certainly do. Orson, don't forget your exercises. I haven't had you in the gym for a few weeks. Elvis gets better every day. Don't pick a quarrel with him!"

"I'll see you, Mike."

"Nice to meet you, Susie."

They didn't speak when he left. Then Susan broke the silence. "I guess you know about it?"

"Who doesn't, after that column."

"The Hedda Hopper?"

"Yeah. Have there been *other* columns about, ho ho, Priscilla's 'self-defense' karate teacher?"

"I don't know."

He was silent.

"You remember what I told you about that dinner I had with Priscilla?"

"When I was in Washington?"

"Yes. When she said, 'If he can do it, I can do it.' "

"It didn't take her long. Well, she and Elvis are through. There isn't anything can be done about it, that I can think of. You know, Elvis is terribly unhappy."

"I think I can sense that, and I've run into a couple of his Mafia people lately, at the cafeteria." Susan was working for RCA in personnel. "God, Elvis looks awful. I don't believe it, that he's going to do a live special from Hawaii carrying all that weight?" She paused.

"Orson?"

"Yeah, hon."

Susan looked down.

"What is it?"

"You. Are you... taking something?"

Orson paused. She looked up into his eyes, through the close-up eyeglasses that melted into his hazel-brown eyes. Her gaze was steadfast. Orson's eyes retreated.

"Yes. Elvis asked me to try them. Pills."

"Would that have been about Easter time?"

"I guess."

"What *are* they?"

"Uppers. Those were long days. You know. The academic work and the work for Hewlett-Packard at night. First it was the uppers. Then," he scratched his fork over the tablecloth, a series of Xs—"the coke. I've been snorting a little coke...What did you...especially notice?"

"Your mood. Intense highs. Your cheeks flush when you come in. Your visits at night to check the garage. Have you tried to quit?"

"I keep telling myself I'll quit tomorrow."

"Tomorrow is the day after tonight's celebration."

Orson smiled wanly. "You know, I'll try."

"That's not good enough."

"*So what do you want me to do? Goddamit, Susan!*" He looked about him. Nobody had overheard, but he lowered his voice. "Guarantee from this minute on I'll give it up?"

"Yes, exactly."

Orson got up and walked out the front door. "No," he said to the valet-parking attendant, he didn't want the car yet, he was just getting a little air.

He walked down to the end of the driveway, avoiding the curbside lights. He brought out a small plastic bag, dipped his fingers into it, and inhaled deeply. His mood quickly revived.

He waited a few minutes and reentered the restaurant.

She was sitting there, wine and dessert untouched. She looked so beautiful with her honey hair and the lightly daubed lips, the blue eyes slightly shaded as she stared down at the untouched food.

He sat down beside her. She extended her hand.

"I've read about the problem," Susan said. "It can be tough. But it isn't like giving up, well, heroin. But it's tougher for some people than for others. Orson, I've got an idea."

"What is it?"

"If you can't lick it, then we'll go back. To Papagayo. I'll look after you, this time around."

Orson leaned back against the padded backrest, to hide the tears.

Susan said nothing, but gripped his hand tightly.

47

Honolulu, January 1973

COMING DOWN AT THE AIRPORT IN HONOLULU, ELVIS braced himself. He was certainly used to crowds. In the last few months, they seemed to him diminished in size, but the auditoriums were full. In four consecutive appearances he had filled Madison Square Garden. And Hawaii wasn't so habituated to phenomena like Elvis and the Beatles and the Rolling Stones as to have become incurious. Elvis had been frequently in Hawaii, but as a vacationer; on such trips he'd managed to stay incognito. Moreover, the Colonel was giving this Hawaii arrival full-time attention, like an opening at Las Vegas. The Colonel was planning nothing less than the first musical event ever to be broadcast by satellite to the entire world.

The crowd at the airport was as predicted. Elvis had signaled his boys to precede him down the gangway. On the plane he'd explained the procedure to the newest member of his Mafia, his stepbrother David Stanley. David and his older brother, Rick, were sons of Dee Presley (now Elvis's stepmother) by a previous husband. Elvis had recruited him, David, age seventeen, as a supplementary bodyguard.

"For one thing, David," Elvis, still seated, said, "it's not a bad idea, in case there's a lot of people there, you know, tryin' to get in the way, not a bad idea to have a little traffic control. Besides, that's also how the queen of England does it. She comes out of her airplane first—but after security. So if it's good enough for the queen, why not the King?"

David chuckled appreciatively.

One of the dozen newspaper people on the scene at the airport devoted his popular weekly column, "Aloha to You," to the arrival. He wrote,

> Elvis, getting off his special plane, looked pretty tired. Colonel Parker's rep passed the word that he's lost weight the past few months. He needs to lose weight the *next* few months. You have to remember about the King, he is a very beautiful human specimen. Or anyway...he certainly was that. Would be a pity if he loses that, even if he hangs on to his voice, which he's done. But he doesn't let up. In addition to all the recordings, he's been on the concert road almost nonstop. In November he did Tucson, El Paso, San Bernardino, and Long Beach. Mrs. Presley and daughter Lisa Marie, age five, are expected to be in town for the concert. Elvis's friend Linda Thompson is not expected. Hard to wrench her away from Graceland.

It was out, and all over: Elvis and Priscilla had filed for divorce and separation. But they continued to see each other, except at Graceland, which was reserved for Priscilla's connubial successor.

Hawaii, vacation land or not, was all work for Elvis, Inc., preparing for the great event. Joan Deary, the expert coordinator, had been an entire week at the arena. Everything had to be perfect, the Colonel had insisted.

Three "rehearsals" were scheduled. Elvis had once before worked with James Burton and John Wilkinson, two guitarists living in Honolulu who played well with him. From the Mafia itself he had Charlie Hodge, guitarist, vocalist, and composer, though none of Charlie's songs was scheduled; as bassist, there was Jerry Scheff striving, always, to do the work of the late Bill Black, and pretty much succeeding, in Joan's opinion. Elvis agreed. On the drums, Ronnie Tutt, filling in for the good, reliable D. J. Fontana. Glen Hardin would do piano; J. D. Sumner, whom Elvis especially enjoyed working with, would do the accompanying vocals, backed up by the Stamps. Elvis's female backups were the reliable Sweet Inspirations, featuring high-soprano Kathy Westmoreland. The orchestra was under the lead of Joe Guercio. At the dress rehearsals the audience members were selectively invited and limited in number to six thousand.

Colonel Parker was nervous, yet confident that everything was going as planned. Elvis was agreeably compliant, and once in stride, sang out his special blend of life, joy, sadness, and hope, making it clear to everybody why they were all there—the participating musicians, the coordinating technicians, the select audience just sat there, entranced.

Elvis made a few demands after leaving the auditorium session to return to his suite. He wanted his friends with him, of course. He carved out a half hour for Lisa Marie. Priscilla dropped their daughter at the door, went off in the car on an errand, and came back to pick her up. She and Elvis exchanged conventional greetings, he even giving her a kiss on the cheek.

He would have dinner with his guys, sometimes listening to a new recording—he was always curious about the reaction of his Mafia to the work of other artists. Sonny and Red were enthusiastic about the Allman Brothers Band, less so Lamar and Charlie. At about eleven Elvis said it was time for his karate. He liked to do his exercises before midnight, and he was advanced enough to keep his karate instructor Khang Rhee, now a regular member of his Mafia, alert. "Watch your right jab," Elvis said to him the night before the concert. Khang had to remind him that it was Elvis who was the amateur, not Khang Rhee. "Maybe you can prove that," Elvis said proudly.

The broadcast was all that the Colonel could possibly have hoped for. He scheduled a news conference for noon the next day at the Hilton Hawaiian Village. He hoped Elvis would turn up for it but was not surprised that he didn't. Having looked over at what seemed to be a pile of Telexes, the Colonel announced that over one billion people listened to the concert. "That's one billion, ladies and gentlemen. That's not one hundred million people but one *thousand* million...lucky people! The proceeds from the live audience, as you've been told, will go to the Honolulu Cancer Society, and they exceed fifty thousand dollars!"

What were the immediate plans for Elvis?

"We're going to go to the Hilton in Las Vegas this time around. Give the competition a chance!" He smiled broadly.

Would Mrs. Presley be accompanying him?

The Colonel knew there'd be no way of avoiding that question, especially with Linda Thompson so prominent in the Elvis household. He couldn't act surprised that such questions were asked, or feign indignation. For one thing Tom Parker didn't believe in being indignant with the press—except when they sort of expected it, and maybe would be disappointed without it. (Was Elvis a little off his stride last night? Elvis off his stride! Was Old Faithful off *its* stride?) On this question, though, he had carefully rehearsed his words.

"Gen'l'men, ladies. Come on, they may be havin' li'l disagreements, like a lot of couples who really love each other and want to get on in the long run. So let's just give them a chance, right? Next question."

Elvis slept on without being disturbed, not even by young David Stanley, who looked in on his famous stepbrother every two hours with progressive concern. He was relieved when, just before midnight, Elvis at last woke. He had been asleep for twenty-four hours. He reached into a pouch near the bed and withdrew some pills.

"David?"

"Yes, brother." Elvis liked that, and encouraged the use of the word.

"Jus' to begin with, call downstairs and order the same thing they served me last night. Then, call Sonny, Lamar, Red, Joe, Larry. Especially Charlie. Tell 'em to come on over. Three, get me the morning papers, see what they said about last night. Four, where is Lydia? She mindin' the board at Graceland? I want to be connected with Linda. And then I want to talk to Orson. I'll go shower."

A half hour later they were all there, celebrating. Elvis went off to use the telephone in the side room. They were all used to the long bouts on the phone that interrupted everything in Elvis's life, and proceeded as usual, to talk, mostly music, and to eat and drink.

He got Linda on the phone and told her it had been a smash hit, and she agreed, and said that *all* of Graceland agreed. When he got Orson he asked, "How was the reception in Los Angeles?"

Orson hated himself for doing it, but he lied to Elvis. Orson had slept foggily through the Honolulu broadcast, waking only to sneak in another snort.

"It was sensational," he told him. "Susie and I had people in to view it. Like a party."

"Didja like the close?"

Happily, Elvis didn't wait for an answer.

"And how do you like my tossin' my scarves to the crowd? They *loved* it, Killer...How *you* doin'?"

Orson said he and Sue were doing just fine and thanks a million for calling.

Elvis went happily back to the celebration; Orson, to his own deep concerns.

48

Santa Ana, Spring 1973

TOM BAYLISS OBSERVED ORSON CAREFULLY. WITH HIS prosthetic right hand, Bayliss worked the zooming device, directing the focus of the remote camera down on the select work area in Bureau A. That kind of scrutiny was routine at Hewlett-Packard. There were security cameras overhead, not unlike those that banks and even convenience stores now had; they were cheap and, at certain moments, critically useful.

This particular division of H-P at Santa Ana was testing and developing, model after model, probing chip-circuit alignments. Much hung on the enterprise at Bureau A. Their own lawyers had disapproved patent applications, one after another. "You've got to introduce an X factor—something nobody else has and isn't a derivative of what they have, protected under the patent laws," Tom Bayliss was told. "You get that, you can get a patent; then you can run with it."

Tom Bayliss was in charge of the research office in Los Angeles. He had known Orson from the day he and Phil Androtti had shared their separate worries in the same hospital waiting room. That was eight years ago, back with Albatron. Tom Bayliss was glad that H-P had kept Orson on, sending him to business school. He was proving out well as a general idea man and was popular with investors as well as fellow employees.

Orson's salary—Bayliss opened the second drawer in his desk and pulled out the ledger—was now thirty-five thousand dollars. Pretty big-time dough, Tom told himself. On top of that, like most key employees, Orson had been given stock options, ten thousand shares at the 1970 market price, over two years ago. The company hadn't gone public, so there was no trading of the options and no one could say with assurance what they were worth. But Tom Bayliss had some idea of what they were worth. A lot of money.

Up until three months ago, he'd thought it entirely possible that Orson might himself come up with that patentable component, the missing X factor. In September Orson had come up with the idea of combining the resources of two chip connectors, intending a symbiosis that would be useful and original. Tom was intrigued. But once again the lawyers had said no—too close to what Electrosignals already had.

But these past days Orson seemed—odd. Going back to Christmas, even. He'd talk during meetings extendedly, sometimes not advancing any point coherently. Normally Orson, however genial, was somewhat retiring. Now he was engaging everyone in conversation. It was last Thursday that Tom first had the terrible thought. *Could it be?*

That night he instructed the technician who worked on H-P security to alter slightly the angle of the camera in the Bureau A lab. Tom was not indirect. "I want, when I want to, to be able to look down on Orson Killere. You know where his desk is?"

"Yes, sir."

"Can you do it tonight?"

"Sure."

Now he was looking at the screen. Orson, in shirtsleeves, was sketching a design on his desktop, making notes on the right margin. He saw Orson pick up the telephone. Tom had no way of telling whether it was an outgoing or an incoming call. He turned to the memorandum he was himself typing with deft use of four fingers of his left hand, two of his artificial hand. Ten minutes later he looked over at the television screen and was astonished to see that Orson was still on the phone.

Tom studied his movements. Orson leaned over his desk, the telephone still up against his ear. Tom saw him reach into a drawer and angle his body counterclockwise. No one else in Bureau A had him in line of sight. Orson brought his fingers to his nostril. He then put down the telephone and leaned back slightly, his curly hair reaching, Tom suddenly noticed, right over his ear, hippie growth.

The son of a bitch is on coke.

Tom Bayliss was impatient by nature. But this wasn't something to be impatient about. Not for Tom's sake, not for Orson's, not for Hewlett-Packard's. He was fond of Orson, but he was no sentimentalist.

It wouldn't be as easy as just plain firing him.

He thought suddenly of Lou. Lou Ehrlich, who had worked alongside Orson at Albatron—Lou would give useful advice. He had struggled with the same problem for a whole year after Hewlett-Packard had bought Albatron.

He put in the call. He couldn't quite understand why his eyes were still riveted to the television screen, bringing in the camera at Bureau A, zoomed to the back of Orson's curly hair.

The all-American boy. Shit.

49

Los Angeles, Mid-1973

"LYDIA?" ELVIS RATTLED THE TELEPHONE HOOK. TO David he called: "Why the fuck doesn't she come on the line? Somebody else usin' my—*my* operator?"

Lifting his eyes from his newspaper, Joe Esposito spoke. Of all the Mafia Diamond Joe, as Elvis referred to him, was the most calming in tight dealings with the King. Joe had been with Elvis since they were soldiers together in the army, and continued with Elvis after their discharge, serving as tour director, bodyguard, and discreet procurer. Now he said, "Elvis, the Colonel's operating out of Memphis this week. He probably has Lydia connecting him up with the tour people. You've always said it's okay to use Lydia when he's working out of Memphis."

"He should get his own operator, what I pay him. David? Get on the other line in the bedroom. If Linda's still sleepin' tell her to get her ass out of bed. It's almost—supper time. Get on the phone, call the outside line at Graceland, tell whoever answers to walk over to my office; it's all of one flight of stairs down. Tell Lydia to call me when she's through—through suckin' up to the Colonel."

David left the living room and walked to the staircase. Elvis paused, cocked his ear. "Linda's obviously still sleepin', David oughta bang the door open. Charlie? *Charlie?*"

The guitar in the next room stopped strumming.

"Yeah, Elvis."

"How often you got to sound those chords? If you cayan't come up with anything why don't you stop *tryin'* to write tunes? It's been—how long?—since I sung that one song of yours?"

"Sorry, Elvis. Didn't know I was disturbing anybody. I'll shut the door."

Elvis got up and began his karate exercises.

"Not bad, Joe. That seventh karate belt they gave me." He swung his arms and moved his legs, forward, then sideways, against his imaginary opponent. "You know how many people have earned themselves a seventh karate belt?"

"I don't, actually. Not many, I'd guess."

"I'm thinkin'. In the next act we're settin' up for Vegas, I might jus' give them a couple of minutes of—" He mimicked a grim karate exercise. "There. He's *out*! Gone! No referee anywhere in the world, not even in the pay of"—he shot his arm out again—"that poor fucker I just *destroyed,* would say anythin' different, right Joe? Lamar? Red?"

"Looks like a clean win to me, Elvis."

"I wouldn't mind if it *was* a dirty win. I'll take the referee on, if he says anythin' different—"

The phone rang. Elvis moved to the sofa and picked up the receiver.

"Lydia? Where—where you been, li'l' girl? I been waitin' like maybe *one hour*...Well, you tell the Colonel, next time he ties you up, you tell him, tell him you can't keep—the King waitin' *all day long*! Sorry, honey. I know, I know, not your fault. Now look, I want to talk to Orson. I told you yesterday to get him. No. I tol' you like *day before yesterday* to get him on the line... Can't find him? Li'l' girl, you're supposed to *find* people. Like, I mean, call him at home...No answer at home? Sh—I mean, he's got a wife and a daughter. *Somebody's* got to answer...Okay, okay. Keep tryin'."

He slammed down the receiver.

"Charlie? CHARLIE?"

Charlie Hodge opened the door.

"Where the fuck is Orson? You guys are always talkin' together. You know where he is?"

Charlie stood outside the door of his makeshift office. "Elvis, I got to tell you something."

"Somethin' about Orson? I suppose he's run off with Priscilla. She got tired of that—gigolo karate lover of hers? I was an *asshole* to give in on the settlement she put in for. Siddown, Charlie. What's up with Orson?"

Charlie remained standing. "Elvis, Orson's been fired."

"Been fired? From his company? *Fired?*"

"Yup."

"Wha'd he do? Nobody *half sane* would fire Orson."

"He was fired for taking drugs."

Elvis stopped. He stared at Charlie, then over at Lamar Fike.

"Is that right, Lamar?"

"That's right, Elvis."

"When that happen?"

"A couple of weeks ago."

"Why didn't nobody tell me?" His voice was quiet.

"Didn't want to talk about it, Elvis, with the divorce and everything, and the new stand in Vegas."

Elvis looked down.

"Where's he gone?"

Charlie spoke. "Mexico, I believe. Yes, Mexico."

"Did you know about that, David?"

"Yes, sir, I did."

"Oh shit." Elvis got up and walked out to his study, and shut the door behind him, quietly.

50

Cabo San Lucas, November 1973

"YOU KNOW WHAT THE TEACHER CALLS ME, DADDY?"

"What, dear?"

"She calls me *Huerita*. Why doesn't she call me Carlita?"

Orson looked over at Susan. They were grouped under a broad, faded awning that had once been green and white, extending out from their cottage. The unending beach stretched out on either side. Susan had seated herself in the sun, removed from the awning's protection, though she wore a straw hat and sunglasses. Orson was there, but in the shade, working his way through technical journals, his ballpoint pen in hand.

"Susan. You're the Spanish student. Answer Carlita's question."

Susan put her book down on her lap. "Darling, *huerita* means 'blondie' in Spanish. It's a very nice term. You have blond hair, so sometimes they'll call you 'blondie.'"

"Señorita Paula has black hair. What's Spanish for blackie?"

Susan suppressed a laugh. "It doesn't quite work that way. There aren't always ways of—saying things that are—you know, the opposite. Like, you know, Uncle Charlie? They call him *Shorty*. But they wouldn't call Mr. Ehrlich '*Tal-ly*.' In Spanish, blond isn't the *opposite* of black or brown."

Carla sighed. "I wish they all spoke English."

"But you're doing wonderfully, Carlita, after only three months."

"I can understand pretty well, Mom."

Susan looked over at Orson. "You thinking of a swim, Orson? Or you want a Pepsi first?"

"Sure. Even though, if I have one, I'll have to put it in my log for my big Monday meeting with Doc Schuster."

"So that's not a real hardship. You objecting to that?"

"No. Of course not. But the Salvador regimen—I've told you this—requires putting down *everything*. Every medicine you take, even an aspirin, everything you eat that has caffeine, all the exercise you take—" He interrupted himself, looking down at Carla, who was constructing a moat around her sand castle. Never mind, Carla wouldn't understand, wouldn't pick it up. All she knew was that they were living in Cabo San Lucas because daddy had business reasons for being here.

"We've got every reason to be grateful to the Salvador people."

"Honey, I'm not denying that. And the Monday meeting completes the three months I'm committed to. I have a feeling Herr Doktor Schuster would like to keep me here another three months, just so he can have somebody to talk German to."

"Can you say—it's definitely worked?"

"You know the old saw about alcoholism: You never say you're cured, because the whole philosophy holds that you can't count on being cured. All I can say is—I think I'd kill myself before snorting again. I mean really kill myself."

"When will they let you have a drink? It's been pretty dry here at Killere's Beach Paradise."

"He said I could have a beer in a couple of months. But also that I should go to AA meetings when I get back."

"Remind me, I forget. When I was—here, did I drink wine? Or beer?"

"You had a sip of wine on your birthday. I had to explain to you about birthdays, and why this was your birthday."

Susan picked up her book and blew the sand from it. "This is an exciting book, *The Making of the President, 1972.* I know you've already read it. Theodore White on presidential campaigns, hard to beat. The reader doesn't know till election day, the way Teddy White tells it—they call him Teddy—that George McGovern never had a chance. I know you didn't vote in November '72. Darling, when are you going to get over that business?"

"You know I don't talk about it. But I took that pledge when I was eighteen, at Ann Arbor, with my little political group—"

"Students for Democratic Peace."

"Yep. We all took a *pledge,*" Orson smiled slightly at the memory, but not derisively. "A pledge not to vote until the great revolutionary opportunity came. Like Mr. Simon's great dream for October 1917."

"You still have that itch? Even when we live off those glorious Hewlett-Packard options?"

"And that nice accident settlement by the insurance people—but, Susie—it isn't exactly fair to bring that up. I've worked within the U.S. political system and probably always will. But that doesn't mean I have to renounce my dream of common property."

"Yes, dear," she teased. "Common property. And everybody loves everybody, et cetera, et cetera."

Orson's chin jerked up.

"I'm not making fun of you," Susan quickly added. "And I'm not expecting you to become politically—well, you know, active. I should've said, activist. But what Elvis did to you back in 1956, that stopped you dead. You told me so—"

"Yes. Elvis the rock-and-roller liberator"—Orson paused a moment—"the man who wanted just his own woman, wanted not to be lonely, wanted no heartbreak hotels in his life. The line *Do what you want*—that line of thinking advanced a lot further pretty damn soon after Elvis's early years. Just a little while and we have John Lennon and Mick Jagger. They want all those things—plus it's just fine if everyone drops out in a drug haze.

"Right." Orson rattled on, as if to himself. "And Elvis never preached that, quite right. The public Elvis is the one-hundred-percent American. The man with the badge to enforce drug prevention—who is shot full of drugs. The one-woman man—who changes his girls with the laundry—"

"When you spoke with Charlie yesterday and he caught you up on Elvis in Vegas, did he say anything about—the problem?"

"Charlie's wonderful. He knows my situation, and even with Elvis there as the center of his life, he's always worrying about other people. He says he and his friends, all those Hollywood connections, plus the Colonel, they can come up with a good job when I pull out of here, *no question*. I told him that thanks to H-P and insurance, I wasn't all that worried. Besides, an idea has been going through my mind. For a *very* private company. All I want, I told him, was to be damn sure it won't happen again. That and"—he turned his head to Carlita—"that and to be with you, and Huerita."

Susan drew a heart on the sand, then an arrow going through it, feather at her end, the point reaching to Orson's toe. He wiggled it seductively, moved his journals from his lap, and said what Carlita liked to hear most in all this world.

"I'll beat you to the water, bet you five cents!"

Carlita was on her feet bounding down to the water's edge. She always won, but her Daddy was right behind her. It was *very* close, a matter of *inches*.

51

Las Vegas, Early 1975

ELVIS WAS IN HIGH GOOD HUMOR. TONIGHT WOULD end his current Vegas engagement. He was now looking on the split-pant episode early in the year not as a reproach on his being overweight, but as providence beckoning him toward a new style of attire.

The jumpsuit! Elvis accepted it as a new trademark and had a dozen of them made up. The structural design called for a high-collar, low-cut, V-style top, a high waist. No pockets—Elvis didn't want anything that might so much as intimate a greater girth than was inexorably there. (His regimen called on him to diet down to a maximum of 220 pounds before his concerts. One-seventy was his weight in the army, and he liked to go down to 210.) He had brought in three designers to make the stitching unique, and a few months later, he had twenty different suits. Their themes included American Eagle, Blue Prehistoric Bird, Burning Love, Flame, Indian, Sundial, King of Spades, Mad Tiger, Red Lion, Tiffany, Inca Gold Leaf, White Eagle, and White Prehistoric Bird. Each had its own cape and was worn with a long silk scarf.

He'd wear, at tonight's close at the Hilton, the Inca Gold Leaf, with a necklace to match. His dressing was a feat of the so-called wrecking crew. They handled him as a matador is handled by his cuadrilla. He need do nothing except extend his arms and, on signal, rotate his body. In minutes he was a splendid, tailored King.

"What do you think, Red? Joe?"

Red West and Joe Esposito had done their job. The King was dressed.

"I think you look great," Joe said. "And *everybody's* out there tonight. Including Tom Jones. He's opening tomorrow at Caesar's Palace."

Elvis got up and exercised his shoulders. He began to go with some karate movements, but Red said no, no, Elvis, that might mess up the suit. He stopped, then drew his scarf through his hand feigning sadness over his imminent dispossession of it. Elvis had accidentally dropped a scarf at his Hawaiian special. Reaching down to pick it up, he heard the plaintive cry of a girl in the front row. "Elvis! Elvis! Can I have it? *Please!*" As he tended to do, Elvis indulged his generous nature and tossed the scarf out.

That was now an Elvis trademark: dropping scarves down on petitioners in the assembly. Joe Esposito had a dozen prepared for each of Elvis's concerts, and handed them out to him from backstage as required. After Elvis had dispatched the incumbent scarf he would sidle to the rear of the stage, reaching out in the darkness beyond the stage lights. Joe's hand would be there, hidden from the crowd, with the new scarf, which Elvis would grab with his right hand, his left hand on his mike. Now he had a fresh scarf to run over his perspiring face, and one more royal benefaction for his ravenous, adoring, grateful fans.

The closing show went as planned, and at the end of the evening, Elvis acknowledged the special festivity that attaches to a closing. His high mood and that of the audience elicited three more songs than he had scheduled. Red West, always there with his stopwatch, advised Elvis when he finally emerged that he had been on stage 114 minutes.

"And you used up eight scarves," Joe added plaintively.

One reason for Elvis's good mood these days was the airplane. He had bid on a Boeing 707, but the Colonel's lawyer, Tim Draper, had phoned to warn that the financier Robert Vesco, from whom the aircraft had been seized by Internal Revenue, was lying in wait to lay claim to it if ever it landed in a foreign airport.

Elvis was undeterred. "Tell Tom landin' in a foreign airport's hardly a threat, the way he closes me in, refuses to book me in Europe. *Or* in Australia. A million dollars, I got wind of—not from the Colonel, from an Australian newspaper—they been speakin' of a cool million for a two-week tour—"

"Elvis, Elvis, you know I don't get into these things," Tim Draper interjected. "My job was just to tell you about the danger in buying Vesco's jet." Draper didn't want any further conversation. He certainly didn't want to involve himself in complaints about the Colonel, so he got off the line quickly, with "so long, Elvis."

But three months later, Elvis had bought his own Convair 880. Elvis had carefully specified the *Lisa Marie*'s interior layout. The queen-size bed, the walnut paneling, the large bathroom with gold fixtures. He'd be surrounded by artifacts and decorations reflecting in tone, if not in size, those in his bedroom at Graceland.

"Whee!" he exulted to the Mafia members waiting for him in the dressing room. Tonight Elvis and the crew would fly home to Memphis in the new plane. "I won't know whether I'm in the air or at home."

The three limos, assembled by his three personal bodyguards and the eight policemen provided by the city of Las Vegas, were at hand. In twenty minutes he was there. Waiting for him were the usual photographers. It rather surprised Joe and Red that Elvis didn't then do what was expected of him, and what had been habitual: invite the press in. Elvis had perceptibly changed. He didn't want people, except for the gang—and even them, selectively—in his quarters. And on the Convair he specified new rules. Nobody was invited aft to his spacious stateroom, except for Linda.

The plane revved up. Seated in the luxury cabin, forward, Red said to Joe, "He's going to need a lot of pills to get to sleep tonight."

When they arrived in Memphis, Elvis was sound asleep. Linda had attached the large safety belt over his prostrate body. Still strapped in, he woke at noon in high spirits. He showered on the plane, and donned a jumpsuit of workaday design. It was a carefully tailored imitation of a working man's overalls, with deftly plied stripes of black velvet. He emerged from the plane and told Red he wanted to go to the car dealer's.

They drove him into the lot of the Tulloch Mercury franchise. In one hour Elvis had inspected the new models. He bought the entire stock of Lincoln Continentals, six cars. He kept one for himself and specified the new owners of the other five.

Jack Tulloch, an experienced grin on his face, asked, "Usual arrangements, Elvis?"

"Yes, sir. Usual arrangements. Charge all the licensin' fees to me. Just give my daddy the bill." Vernon, who kept Elvis's exchequer, would pay.

"If there's any money left, after the Convair," Elvis joked.

He was driven to Graceland and found waiting for him there the new Harley motorcycle he'd ordered. He turned to his stepbrother.

"Lemme show you how this thing works, David."

David was positioned in the rear, his hands on Elvis's shoulders. Elvis zoomed off happily.

They were gone an hour, drawing up in midafternoon under the portico. David dismounted with some relief.

"You like, boy?"

"It's really—terrific," David said, "brother."

52

Los Angeles, 1975

ORSON, WORKING IN THE CORNER OF THE LIVING ROOM
he had made over into a study, closely examined his projections.
It was there that he had spent his time, in the year after his return
from Mexico. "Let me show you what I came up with after six
months' operation." He motioned to Susan.

"Honey, I'm not so good with these things."

But Susan stared down soberly at the columns of figures.
"You have under *overhead* ... How is it set up, with Ferdy Gon-
zalez? Is he going to be a stockholder? Is that how come you have
him down for ... only eleven thousand for a year's salary?"

"Yep. He'll get a probationary ten percent of the stock going
in—provided he's still working for Cybercom in January 1976, a
year from now. Then he gets ten percent equity and ten percent of
any net increase in net income—"

"Do you have the right to dismiss him?"

"Unequivocal right to do that as long as we're running a
deficit. If we're running at a profit, he gets severance pay—here,
it's all spelled out in the footnotes."

"How many subscriptions are you counting on Ferdy to bring
in—I mean, right away?"

"His column at UCLA on the rise of the industry was very popular. I think we have a crack at two-point-five percent of the graduating class of 'seventy-five—"

"Two-point-five percent? Orson, that's—*peanuts*. That's one out of—"

"Forty," Orson obliged.

"That translates to—fifteen people in a class of six hundred."

"Yes, but if you look over here, three months down the line, I'm looking at *five* percent on a mailing to go out about that time."

That reminded him of something. He scratched out a note on his memo pad.

"Ferdy has a good style for what we're going to take on. He writes informatively, with a hint of mystery and surprise. But the editorial material, that's my job. I'm nicely wired into the campus scene: a year in Tacoma with Albatron, four years at school here, six years, from the beginning, with Hewlett-Packard. I know a whole lot of people in the trade, and some of them are busting to tell or leak their stories, or to do a little corporate speculation. We'll make that possible—and exciting."

Susan called out to Carla. "Come here, darling. I want to take a picture with my new camera." She turned to Orson: "I'll label this picture *Carla and Daddy before Daddy became rich.*"

Carla called back. "I can't come till the end of *Wild Kingdom.* It just started."

Orson looked at his watch. "That's twenty minutes from now. I know what we can do in twenty minutes."

Susan giggled, returned his kiss, took his hand, and followed him to their room.

Orson and Ferdy agreed on the terms of the partnership. With the debut publication of their report now a mere ten weeks off, what they needed above all was a superefficient and superliterate secretary and proofreader, and Orson knew who would be ideal. Gladys Schmidt had worked alongside him at Hewlett-Packard, Bureau A. Back then her hours were 2 P.M. until whenever she finished the day's work. Her assignment then was to read and transcribe the notes dictated and scribbled down by the technicians. The folder she prepared would go up to Tom Bayliss and, when appropriate, and after careful editing, on up even to Messrs. Hewlett and Packard themselves.

Her work at Bureau A had been something of a challenge for Ms. Schmidt because the material fed in to her in the afternoon was densely technical and the penmanship of some of the technicians obscure. Maybe the strain of work in those long and lonely hours brought on, or exacerbated, Gladys's problem. Orson, who had been fired in August, hadn't even known that there *was* a problem, or even that she had left Hewlett-Packard. Not until he ran into her at the AA meeting.

On Dr. Schuster's recommendation, Orson had undertaken to attend Alcoholics Anonymous for at least two years. "Alcohol, specifically, isn't your problem, Orson. But the mind-set of AA people isn't very far removed from that of people who end up with the problem you've had."

Gladys Schmidt told her story to her fellow addicts at the meeting—how, little by little, she had taken to drinking more and more, and attempting more and more furtively to cover her tracks. But one day the all-seeing Tom Bayliss had caught up with her and her concealed bottle of vodka. At AA she happily joined her old colleague, Orson Killere, after the meeting, for coffee. He told her about his enterprise and there and then asked if she was willing to come to work for Cybercom. He outlined his plans for a weekly bulletin that would be "indispensable to everyone in the field."

Gladys, restless with her freelance work, enthusiastically agreed. She could wrap up her part-time jobs in a week or so.

"Shall we drink to that?"

Orson smiled. "We can have a toke on it."

It was time, he thought, to call on Tom Bayliss.

Orson was cordially received in that eyrie above the working bureaus, with its special camera; so much so that, for a minute or two, Orson was afraid Tom was going to offer to hire him back.

"You have to be careful about that," Susan had warned. "You're a pretty able guy, Orson. Now that you're, well, cured, why wouldn't they want you back on the team?"

Orson acknowledged he'd have felt an obligation, if re-recruited, to an organization that had paid his way through college. Orson sidetracked the question by immediately revealing to Tom that he had entrepreneurial ideas of his own—"ideas I can afford to play with, thanks to those Hewlett-Packard options." He told Tom he had hired Gladys Schmidt.

Tom nodded. "Fine lady."

"I've got an idea or two I want to experiment with, and Gladys will be perfect for me, but this is just to tell you I'm not poaching, and that I'll be coming to you with ideas, and maybe with ideas you'd like to hear."

Tom wished him luck and said he would always be glad to hear from him. "And whatever you do." He smiled. "Don't forget to install an overhead security camera."

He didn't install a camera, but one room in the office was reserved, no telephone, no visitors allowed, for the files he and Ferdy accumulated. From these came the lively, sixteen-page Cybercom weekly newsletter. It was from Cybercom that the greater world learned about Texas Instruments and its plan for across-the-board coverage for their sixteen-bit microprocessors. And when affected subscribers began to call in, panting, to know more about Univac's "Project Acorn," Orson and Ferdy just sat it all out in their sealed-off room, revealing nothing in the next issue about the source of their information; making no comment on the angry comment of Univac's president.

Orson came home from the office with the year-end books.

"It's one year of publishing, with the issue that went to bed this afternoon. We have thirty-eight thousand subscribers *annnd*"—he stretched the word out till Susan clawed her impatience on his cheeks—"we went into black ink with—"

"Let me guess. Fifteen subscribers?"

Orson closed his ledger happily. "Can I have a drink?"

"You can have one beer."

"One beer for every month we've had a profit?"

"One beer until the next monthly statement."

53

Los Angeles, October 1975

ORSON HAD NEVER LAID EYES ON TOM PARKER, FOR all that the Colonel was ubiquitous in the life of Elvis Presley, Inc., and, tangentially, in the lives of all for whom Elvis was an inspiration, a burden, a companion, a consultant, a chat pal on the telephone, a provider. But Orson would not refuse to see the Colonel, not after being told by him over the phone, at seven in the morning, "Elvis is truly sick."

They made a date for two that afternoon at the Colonel's office in Los Angeles. After hanging up the phone, Orson called Charlie and told him about the appointment. "Charlie, I've heard a lot of wild things about this guy. And now I'm actually going to meet him. That's confidential. Elvis is not to know about it— the Colonel made a point of that. Can you give me just a couple of straight sentences on him? I know he was born in Europe. Everybody says he started life as a dogcatcher, ha ha—"

"Well, yes, he did."

"You mean literally?"

"I mean, *as a dogcatcher*. That's somebody who catches dogs when they're loose or lost. That didn't last for too long because our illustrious friend then founded the Great Parker Pony Circus.

From there he got into promotion. He was born in Holland and spent three years in the army, 1929 to 1932."

"You mean he made colonel in 1932?"

"Hell no. Somebody in Louisiana called him colonel, like in a joke, and he liked it, and *that* was that. Colonel Thomas Parker. Everybody goes along."

"Well, I've got no quarrel with that."

"Why did he say he wanted to see you? Something to do with Elvis, obviously."

"He's not going to propose a singing career for me. Yes. He's worried about Elvis."

"He should be. We all are. Last night Elvis left the stage in Detroit, just walked out—halfway through his act. On the other hand, the Colonel's working him to death. Did Elvis tell you the reason for his checking into the Baptist Hospital in Memphis, the day he called you from there?"

"Last November? He told me it was a sinus checkup."

"Well, it was a straight detox hospitalization. Second time in twelve months. They got him in there to try to drain the drugs out of his system."

"Does the Colonel know all that?"

"The Colonel knows *everything*."

"Does he know about...me?"

"That's probably why he called you, because you've had your own drug problem. That, and he knows how Elvis...put it this way, you're probably the only guy Elvis hasn't screamed at in the last year."

"No, Elvis has never done that. Though he did ask me to leave his house, that time I spoke to him about Hollywood."

"I know. And that was an important thing you did, might have been critical in bringing on his successful comeback. But that's unique, excepting maybe Priss—he's never screamed at her, that I know of. Her and you. Speaking of Priss, he did try to get her friend Mike Stone bumped off—"

"Come on!"

"Yeah. No shit. While you were in Mexico. He got so pissed off about Mike Stone he called in Red and Sonny—you know Sonny?"

"Can't remember meeting him. You're talking about Red's cousin?"

"He called them in and said he wanted Mike Stone *wasted*."

"Charlie, I wouldn't tell that story around."

"I don't tell it, excep' to you—"

"I mean, it must have been a tantrum. Just sort of a *horseplay*, I'll-bust-his-ass sort of thing."

"Orson. Remind me to tell you about the guy from Detroit who came onstage with a gun."

"I didn't know about that."

"Only three of us know. But what happened was more than a tantrum."

Orson paused. "Well, next time I see you, Charlie, tell me about it... Charlie, next time I see you, will you play me one of your nice songs on the guitar?"

"Sure will, Killer." Charlie softened. "Let me know how it goes."

The office was an unpretentious ground-floor suite near the RCA studios. A harried-looking elderly woman wearing heavy thick glasses opened the door and looked up at Orson's face.

"You're Mr. Killere?"

"Yes ma'am."

"The Colonel's expecting you. He's on the phone. Please sit down."

On the coffee table were bound magazine articles about Elvis and order forms for Elvis albums from Sam Goody Music Stores.

The door to the inner office opened, and the Colonel walked out. He was clean-shaven, balding, with heavy pudge under his chin, his shoulders unnaturally elevated. He wore a string tie and a light, summer-brown suit. It was easy to believe, viewing the bulk in the door frame, that he actually weighed the three hundred legendary pounds people wrote about.

The Colonel seated Orson in one of the three armchairs opposite his desk. Would Orson like an iced tea? A Coca-Cola? He reached to a pile on the side of his desk. "I'm sure you'd like to have *this*. The *latest* prerelease." He handed the acetate to Orson.

He came then quickly to the point. "Elvis is choking himself to death with drugs. And you've been a drug addict, and you are maybe Elvis's closest male friend outside the gang. You can take it from there, can't you, Mr. Killere?"

"Orson."

"Okay, Orson."

Orson said he had guessed the subject of their talk. "I'll try. But I wouldn't anticipate any success. I haven't seen him since I was...sent down to Mexico, by my wife. But we've spoken. In fact, we've spoken a lot."

"I know how often he calls you."

Orson half smiled. "I suppose Lydia reports on all calls?"

"Orson, I've been doing nothing except tending to Elvis since 1955. That's twenty years. And one of my jobs is to keep records. Yes, records on everything. Phone calls, McDonald's hamburgers ordered up, Cadillacs given away to friends. You know about the last one—"

"You mean the six Continentals?"

"Oh no! That was Elvis being moderate. He managed to buy fourteen Cadillacs at Wilson's Dealership in Vegas on"—the

Colonel looked down on his desk and flipped the pages of a ledger—"July twenty-fourth."

"Is that because he's sick, or is that just because he's... generous?"

The Colonel stared at Orson. "You don't buy fourteen Cadillacs impulsively for friends. You know who one of the recipients was? I mean, who got *one whole* Cadillac? It was the bank teller. Joe Esposito goes from the car dealer's to the bank across the street to tell them it *really is* Elvis Presley down at the dealer doin' business, and the bank teller should check Vernon Presley, telephone 901-377-7200, if he wants to verify that the bank balance is there, sitting around, to pay for fourteen Cadillacs, and the guy says, sure, sure, Mr. Esposito—Joe had handed him a card—don't you-all worry, not for a minute. So Joe says, that's real nice and obliging of you because Mr. Presley—Elvis—don't like to just sort of hang around, waiting. So while the backroom people check the credit at the home office, Joe says to him, come across the street and say hello to Elvis. And he does, and Joe tells Elvis how nice he's been and Elvis—you know what? Elvis asks the guy for his card, hands the card over to the car dealer, and says, 'Here, make out one of those Caddies for Mr.'—I forget what that lucky bastard's name is, though I'd have it here in my ledger if I looked." The Colonel pointed to the ledger.

Orson decided to yank a little harder on that line about Elvis's being sick or was he just... good-natured. "Is that thing he did, giving away fourteen Cadillacs, something you think would be, oughta be, reported to the health people?"

The Colonel jolted up out of his chair. He was now in stentorian voice. "You think that's *not* a health problem? Giving away a *hundred thousand dollars of Cadillacs in one afternoon*? To strangers?"

Orson rejected the Colonel's aggression. *Fuck him.* Orson

knew how to fight back. "Is that more—or less—than you let yourself drop at the casino in a night, Tom?"

Parker sat down. He said nothing for a moment.

"Let's cut this out, this kind of thing. I may be a little heavy on cards. But I don't take, like, twenty-five pills at night. I don't choke up in the middle of a performance. I don't have a giggling fit onstage. I don't threaten to have anybody *killed*."

Orson said, "Look. I'll try. I've got a bad feeling about it. But what can I say, that I *won't* try?"

"He's in midtour right now." The Colonel looked down to trace the itinerary. "Jacksonville, Tampa, Lakeland, Murfreesboro, Atlantic, Monroe, Lake Charles, Jackson, back to Murfreesboro—and then he'll be in Memphis for three weeks."

"What happens after that?"

"The second leg. Huntsville—five days in Huntsville—then Mobile, Tuscaloosa, et cetera, et cetera. I figured with, like, practically a whole month in Memphis, maybe that would be a good time for you to go over to Graceland and visit, unless you could catch up with him earlier, maybe Vegas the next week. I don't mind telling you the expense is on me, for you and Mrs. Killere."

Orson got up.

"I'll suggest a date to him. That's January he'll be in Memphis?"

"Last three weeks."

"Linda with him?"

"Yeah. She doesn't help, he's so out of it. He don't even fuck her anymore."

"You got that in your book?"

The Colonel lowered his eyes. "Sorry about that." He stood and walked Orson to the door.

"Let's just pray for a miracle, Orson. Maybe you're part of it."

They shook hands.

54

Las Vegas, November 1975

"I TELL YOU WHAT, KILLER. I'M OPENING AGAIN IN Vegas on...on...right after Thanksgiving—on November twenty-seventh. Why don't you come on up there and we'll visit. Or you can come here to Graceland anytime in the next couple of weeks. I'd send the *Lisa Marie* for you except it's being overhauled. When you get your own jet plane, Killer, don't ever forget to have it overhauled. Every million miles. Or maybe it's a hundred thousand miles, I forget. I figure the pilots are gonna do the rememberin' for us. I mean, when you're flyin', before *you* get killed, *they* get killed. 'Specially if your cabin is like mine, at the way back of the airplane. I don' allow no one back there, but that wouldn't apply to you, Killer. You can come see me *anywhere, anytime.*"

"Thanks, Elvis, that's cool, hearing you say that, and it's been a long time—"

"Yeah, for a while there I couldn't reach you even on the telephone. I was *real* sorry about that, Killer. Did you get a chance to listen to my *Today* record? You know somethin'...Now, I can trust you, I know that. *I didn't like it at all.* Those words, they don't add up to nothin', 'cept the usual I-love-you-you-love-me,

I'm-going-to-*dyyyeeeh*-without-you, you're-gonna-*dyyyeeeh*-without-me. But the Colonel said I had to sing it. The Hollywood people...
Yes, I'm thinkin' 'bout maybe doin' another movie. But, you know, they're not sure how much I'd be *singin'* in this one. Now, Killer, can I count on you?"

"Well, I hope so. After what, sixteen years?"

"I'm thinkin' of playin' opposite Barbra Streisand in *A Star Is Born.* You like that idea?"

"Sounds great. Only I don't remember the story well enough, remember whether it's right for you—is it right for a *lot* of your songs?"

"Anything that has Barbra in it is right for a lot of songs."

"But you said they wanted you to do that 'T-R-O-U-B-L-E' song for Hollywood?"

"Yeah, but not necessarily for *that* movie. You know, there's always so much goin' on, an' so mixed up. Anyway, even though I put my heart in that record—"

"Elvis, you always do that. You give every song everything you've got."

"Yeah, I guess I do do that. But that don't mean I like every song the same, and maybe people can tell the difference. For instance, look at 'Help Me Make It Through the Night,' 'For the Good Times,' 'Why Me, Lord?' Kris Kristofferson songs. Now, those are out-and-out *great* music. I sometimes wish I could say to the audience, 'Ladies, gen'l'men, this song comin' up is B-plus. The one just after that is, like, C-minus.'" He chortled. "Wouldn't the Colonel just *love* that! How you doin', Killer?"

"Elvis, I'll tell you about all that stuff. And I'll be there for sure. I'll get there, like, November twenty-fifth. That sound right?"

"Hey! I got a great idea! Priscilla called me, tole me Lisa Marie wanted to come to see daddy perform at the Vegas opening. So I said sure, I'd send the plane for her and Priscilla. Lisa

Marie's first ride on the *Lisa Marie*! Now, what I'm gettin' to is: Why not Susan come with—with—"

"Carla."

"Carla. Isn't that a great idea?"

"That would be great. The Saturday after Thanksgiving, I'll make it."

"Right. Now you come on up with the gang, and the next day—there's no shows on Sunday—you and me will catch up together. How's that sound?"

"That sounds great."

"I'll make all the arrangements. You come on out for the show and stay over. But *any*time you come is all right by me, Killer. We'll have a real family night on openin' night."

Orson met with Charlie at Huevos Rancheros in downtown Los Angeles. "What'll I have? I guess I'll have *huevos rancheros*," Charlie said. Orson nodded his okay, he'd have the same thing. "Add a bottle of beer." Orson was proud of his liberation. It was judged he could have beer without being tempted back onto drugs.

"I'll have a bourbon old-fashioned," Charlie said.

Orson told in some detail about the conversation with the Colonel.

"All I can say is—good luck, Killer. I said that to you a few years ago, when you went into the lion's den on the musical mission. You're a real, true, reliable friend, Orson. Elvis is lucky to have you as a friend. On the other hand you better watch out."

"You were going to tell me something about a guy in Detroit."

Charlie looked down at his old-fashioned and turned the whiskey around in the glass.

"It was at the Silverdome in Pontiac. A couple of months ago.

The show's going along, and I hear Elvis stop in the middle of a song. Then the orchestra stops. I look up. A guy's lumbering in with something or other in his hand. David shoots out onstage and lands some sort of a haymaker on the guy. He is out like a light. It turns out that what was in his hand was a pistol. They carried him offstage and the show went on. Elvis is never afraid of anything—what he was was *pissed off*. I thought after a few days he had forgotten about it."

"The guy with the pistol. Was the pistol loaded?"

"Turns out it wasn't. But how the hell would he *expect* us to act, running up toward the stage with a gun in his hand?"

"A kid?"

"Hell no, like maybe he's thirty, forty."

"Then what?"

"Turns out Elvis is really fuming about it. And the night I'm talking about I was with him. It was like maybe two in the morning, at the hotel suite in Houston. He asked me to stay on, after the others left, but didn't say why. Then he told me. He wanted me to try to get the guy from Detroit on the phone—Elvis knew he was out on bail. The police report came in to us saying that. I said, 'Elvis, what do you want to talk to that crazy guy for?'

"'Just get him on the phone,' he said.

"I didn't want to do that, but Elvis was all 'luded up, and so I had to try. He was right there in the room, and so I called up Detroit information—and got the guy's number. So I rang the number. There was an answer, and I turned the phone over to Elvis. Elvis said—I'll never forget what he said—he said, 'Hey, buddy. You know who this is? This is Elvis. I'm your worst nightmare. I'm gonna blow your brains out.'

"He just kep' saying that in a louder and louder voice, and finally I just grabbed the phone away from him. I said, 'Elvis, you're gettin' yourself in a *heap* of trouble.' So Elvis then says to me: 'Call my plane. I'm gonna fly to Detroit.'

"I stalled. Then I told him it was snowing outside and nobody was flyin'. He said it again and again, he wanted his plane, and I kept puttin' him off."

"And?"

"The pills went to work, finally. Elvis passed out."

"Charlie, I mean, that's bad stuff. But it doesn't affect me. Elvis is hardly going to treat *me* that way."

"Of course not. He likes you a lot, Killer. But you're settin' up to tell him tomorrow the one thing he refuses to talk about, that he's a—a drug addict."

"I know it won't be, well…easy, but I do have that one special thing going for me."

"Yeah, that's right. The addiction. *You* had it. And *you* licked it."

"I hope I licked it. You going to be in Vegas after opening night? Can I get through to you?"

"What time's your date with Elvis?"

"He said come anytime, and he talked about the day after the opening."

"Go early. Go like maybe supper time."

"Does he always eat alone?"

"He pretty much does now. Linda might be there. But he just tells us all to shove off. Oh shit, Killer, it's awful, really awful."

"You got any song you like a lot?"

Charlie smiled. "I got *two*. I'll play them for you. Maybe tomorrow, why don't you come on into my suite sometime in the morning, or in the afternoon. I don't care."

"I'll see you. Tomorrow, with the opening, it'll be a crowded day, especially with Priscilla and Lisa Marie, and my Susan and Carla."

"Good ho." Charlie stood up. He paid the bill.

"I'll be there," Orson said.

55

Las Vegas, November 1975

ELVIS HAD GIVEN INSTRUCTIONS. THE FAMILIES SHOULD be seated ringside, yes, but off to one end of the club. There were rules against ten-year-olds in nightclubs. Those rules were routinely waived for families of the performers, but management reasonably requested they be placed in less-than-central seating.

Lisa Marie and Carlita, seated side by side at the right end of the table, were wild with excitement. Priscilla sat next to her daughter, placing Orson between her and Susan. The announcer, in black tie, came out and introduced the first act to polite general applause. After they performed, Kathy Westmoreland, the Sweet Inspirations, and the Stamps were cordially received. But what the audience was waiting for was Elvis, dressed in his tiger jumpsuit, his bulging neck spilling into the collar.

When he appeared the applause was loud and sustained. Lisa Marie not only joined in it, she stood up in her blue silk dress with the padded shoulders, her blond hair descending to the middle of her back.

"Lisa Marie!" her mother whispered, pressing down on her daughter's shoulder. *"Sit down!"* Lisa Marie looked up, her face flushed. She hissed at her mother: "Just because you're *divorced*, you can't...shut me up!"

Priscilla gasped and looked over at the crowded tables. On her right were two couples and a girl in her late teens wearing a polyester T-shirt and velvet bell-bottoms. She was looking up at Elvis, adoringly. He had begun to beat out "Catchin' on Fast." Priscilla leaned forward on the table. That way, Lisa Marie's tantrum would play out hidden from the direct view of the table so close by.

Elvis sang along, through "Got a Lot o' Livin' to Do." The piano player was given a riff, then the bass player, then the drummer, and applause was nicely enthusiastic.

Elvis was several bars into "I Forgot to Remember to Forget" when his mouth stopped framing the words, and now he was singing monosyllables. His left hand kept the mike by his lips, but his right hand gyrated, gaining in tempo, progressively out of rhythm with the confused orchestra players. The bandleader, Joe Guercio, trying to accommodate soloist and accompanists, looked over at Elvis, perplexed, then distraught, then paralyzed. Elvis was sweating. He looked to the stage entrance as if expecting something, somebody. David, as though he caught a cue, ran forward with an upright chair in his hands for Elvis to sit down on. Elvis looked over at the bandleader. Joe stopped the music.

There was total silence. Joe whispered out the word, and the orchestra swung into the theme from *2001*. Elvis sat on the chair, his head bent down, his face turned away from the audience. On the closing bars he stood up, leaned over to Joe, and turned his head around to face the audience. There was a pause, and Joe gave the signal. Together, Elvis and the players celebrated the spirited favorite "Teddy Bear."

Elvis was quickly back in form. His eyelids drooped down, he had his squinting, inquisitive look, his lips in the curiosity mode, savoring the implications of the lyrics he sang. The audience, shaken from the interruption, waited tentatively until after Elvis had sailed into "Good Luck Charm"; then they applauded lustily, as if to compensate for their probationary silence.

Elvis began singing again.

Susan leaned over and whispered to Orson. "Is it going to be okay?"

"I think so," he ventured. Lisa Marie had clutched her mother's hand when Elvis paused. But now she was jubilant again, applauding happily after every song. Priscilla leaned over to Orson. "Something has to be done about Elvis."

"I'm going to be seeing him tomorrow."

The final song was the irresistible "Can't Help Falling in Love." Now the crowd had been restored to confident good humor.

Walking away from the table, past the transfixed girl in the bell-bottom pants, Lisa Marie grabbed Carlita on the shoulder. "Carlita!" she said. "Carlita. Tell that girl that he's my Daddy! I'm too shy to do it."

Carlita looked up at her father for guidance.

"Go ahead, honey."

The neighboring girl was dazzled by the information and relayed it to her mother and father.

56

Las Vegas, November 1975

ORSON WALKED THROUGH THE LOBBY OF THE HILTON. It was eight o'clock, and the place was bustling. The slot machines were in constant motion, the angular arms pulled down and released, down up, down up, down up, in quest of the magical jackpots, causing the magical sound, the unremitting whir, interrupted by the yelp of elation. The woman closest to the concierge leapt up from her stool. "Aaron!" she turned to her companion, who was working the machine on the left. "Look! Look!" She turned to the next gambler in the row. "Look! Come here, look!" On her right she spotted Orson, walking toward the front desk. "Come. Mister, come look!" Orson obliged, congratulated her, and walked on to the concierge.

"I'm here to see Mr. Presley."

The balding clerk looked up at Orson, his face drawn. He ducked his half-eaten sandwich under the counter.

"Mr. Presley is not staying here."

"Yes, he is. Please tell him Mr. Killere is here, to meet his appointment. Yes, Kill-air. K-i-l-l-e-r-e."

"He's not here, sir."

"Please call the manager."

From behind the partition a man wearing pince-nez appeared. He looked at the young man, paused, then beckoned him to come around the counter to the inner office.

"I understand all these precautions, Mr. —" Orson looked at the identification badge on the manager. "Mr. Cohn. I know about these things. Please ring up to his suite. Ask for Mr. Stanley or Mr. Esposito or Mr. West or Mr. Hodge. Tell them Orson is here. Mr. Presley is expecting me."

"Please wait a minute, sir."

He was back after a minute or two. "I will escort you up."

To go to the ninth floor required a special key on the elevator console. A plainclothes policeman was on duty outside the elevator.

The manager motioned to him. "This is Mr. Killere." He pronounced it Killery.

"Yes. He's expected. This way."

Orson followed him down the hall to the Eisenhower Suite. The officer knocked. David Stanley opened the door.

"Hey there, Orson. How you doing?"

"Good, thanks." And to the manager, "Thanks very much."

David led Orson to the far end of the suite. The lights of Las Vegas blared into the penthouse. He opened the door. Elvis was in the room, practicing karate movements.

"Hey there, Killer. Come in. David, get Orson a drink. What are you . . . *killing* yourself with these days—*Killer!*"

Orson laughed. "A beer would be fine."

"Make that *six* beers—that's what the boys up here always order. Lamar would faint if I ordered up only one beer for him."

They sat down in opposite armchairs. Orson looked sadly on the bloat—on what had been the perfectly shaped young man who had appeared at Wiesbaden, with the Greek god's young face.

"Now, Killer, I know about your bad luck, but we won't talk about that. That's over."

Orson had to say something about the nightclub performance. "That was tough luck, last night, but you got through it just fine. Those things happen. Susan was so happy to take it all in, and so was Carla. She became, like, best friends with Lisa Marie. Did you hear what Lisa did on the way out?"

"No!" Elvis was avidly curious.

"Well, there was a noisy fan of yours at the next table, a teenager, and Lisa couldn't stand for her not to know that Lisa was *Lisa Presley*. But she was too timid to tell her—herself. So she asked my Carlita to tell her!"

Elvis beamed with pride. "She's a beautiful little girl. I'm sure y'all feel that way about your girl. Gee, it's great, isn't it, to have a little girl? Wish they could just stay frozen at that age." He looked to one side. "On the other hand I guess we *all* wish we could stay frozen at—at back then. But you've been through a little pain. Ah heard about it. Booze will kill you."

"It wasn't booze."

"The other stuff, too."

"Actually, Elvis, that's what I wanted to talk to you about. I mean, just to tell you something about what happened to *me*—"

"Cocaine? Yes, *bad* stuff. I would never never take that stuff myself, though, you know, looks like everybody else does, looks like. You know John Lennon, of course?"

"No, I don't, Elvis."

"Well, you know Mick Jagger?"

"I don't. Elvis, I only know *you*."

Elvis liked that. " 'Only Know You.' That would make a great song...Let's see: *Only know* you... *Beautiful you*... *You only know me*... *Tam-te tamtam you*... *Heavenly tum tum dew*... No, that's not very good. You want me to try it on the guitar?"

"Elvis. Let me just say it. I worry about you—"

"I like that. My mom used to say she worried about me. You didn't know Mom? My real mom, Gladys?"

"No. But I know about her."

"But of course you know my dad, Vernon."

"Of course. Everybody knows Vernon."

"I'll tell you somethin' really sad, Killer. My dad is not doin' so well suddenly with Dee. Dee is David's mother. An' Rick's mother, too. I never quite understand it, and even if Vernon is like my older brother, he's still my dad, and so he doesn't tell me, you know, things that would make me sad."

Orson lost patience. "Do you tell your dad things that would make *him* sad?"

Elvis looked up, his eyelids lowered, the inquisitive grin on his face. Then: "Not *that*. Don't go there. Killer, you're not gonna give me a lecture about Dr. Nick's pills, are you? If you kep' my hours, you'd understan' I got to have some help, keepin' those hours."

"Elvis, you're poisoning yourself. There isn't any *point* in your saying what kind of relief for this or for that the pills do, not if those same pills are pulling you down in the long haul—"

"In the long haul? Killer, we got to live in the short haul. I mean, I got to perform, like, tomorrow night, like, last night, like, night after tomorrow, so who's gonna tell me I cain't get a certified medical doctor to tell me how to live with that schedule—"

"*Certified medical doctor?* A certified medical doctor *I'd* listen to was somebody who loves you a lot. That doctor wouldn't let you take stuff that makes you older and *endangers* your health—"

Elvis stood up. He had a second's trouble in balancing his frame. "Fuck this fuckin' business, this tellin' me what I can do an' what I can*not* do. Who invited you to be my doctor? I mean, can't I run my own life?" He turned to the fireplace.

Orson got up.

"I had to try, Elvis."

He heard nothing from Elvis, who had turned his back. Orson started to walk to the door. He stopped, arrested by the sound of convulsive sobs. He looked around. Elvis turned, walked over to Orson, and threw his arms around him, his shoulders heaving.

"Now go, Killer," he said hoarsely. "Go. An'...thanks. Thanks anyway."

Orson returned the embrace, opened the door quietly, and closed it behind him. David was playing cards, still serving as gatekeeper. Orson nodded curtly, turning his head to one side to hide his tears. "See you," he managed, and walked to the elevator.

57

Oklahoma City, July 1976

IT WOULD BE THE THIRD TOUR OF THE YEAR, THIS ONE beginning in Oklahoma City. Elvis didn't complain. He was quickly reestablished in a routine that had been worked out for him since resuming his concert life.

His day began, as usual, at four in the afternoon. He always needed to be nudged awake. This was usually done by David, in the two years since the nineteen-year-old had joined his Mafia.

Elvis liked to eat as soon as he got up and to be given his regular breakfast, which was two cheese omelets, one pound of bacon very, very crisp, a cantaloupe, and black coffee. He would watch television while he ate. He liked quiz shows especially, especially the *Match Game*. Without looking about to see which members of the gang were there, he'd challenge them to compete with him on the right answer to the puzzle on the screen. "Joe, I say the answer's DiMaggio. That's a buck I'm betting, one buck...Shee-yit. It's Mickey Mantle. I owe you—" He reached over and lowered the volume. "I owe you one buck, Joe."

"Joe's not here," David said.

"Well, tell him when he gets back I owe him a buck."

At eight Elvis walked into his bedroom. There the wrecking crew assembled, five men led by Al Strada, the wardrobe manager. Elvis took time to deliberate the selection of that night's ensemble.

"Let's go with Mad Tiger... Don't be 'fraid of the tiger, boys," he teased. "Pussy, pussy, com'on over to Elvis, you been lonely a *loonnng* time." He began to hum.

The tiger jumpsuit was withdrawn from the huge closet. The entire remaining wardrobe would need now to be transported to the hotel at Terre Haute for the next concert. Elvis liked to be free to choose from the whole inventory of costumes every night.

When he was dressed he drew in his breath and looked at himself in the mirror. The boys around him jawed a little. Red talked about how well Elvis had done the night before. "It's a great act," Charlie agreed.

At 8:30 exactly they walked to the elevator. There'd be police escorts waiting in the lobby for him, and Elvis's crew concerted to get him down on schedule. In the elevator, Elvis suddenly pushed the Emergency Stop button. An alarm began to sound. The elevator froze.

"David, go back to the suite. I forgot to bring my Drug Enforcement badge to show to the troops that'll be escortin' us to the party."

"Well, yes, Elvis. But you got to move this elevator on down before I can get out and go back up."

"Oh yeah, sure." Elvis pushed the Garage Floor button and the alarm signal stopped ringing. Arrived at the basement level, David scooted out and signaled for the adjacent elevator. He entered it and went back up to the eighth floor.

"We'll wait here for David to get back with the badge. Then we'll go on to the main floor," Elvis commented.

Joe looked at his watch.

"Nervous in the service, Red? We used to say that in the army—*nervous in the servus.*"

"I know, Elvis. I was in the army with you, remember?"

"Yeah, yeah, I remember. I remember, too, you were with us in Paris."

"That was one hell of a trip. I'm sure Orson thought so, too!"

"Yeah, Orson lost his cherry on that one. He was a nice kid back then. I sometimes wondered, did he tell Priscilla what happened when he got back to Germany? I think maybe he didn't tell her, maybe didn't tell anyone. What the *hell*'s the matter with David? Get lost havin' to go all the way from garage to floor eight back to garage?"

The elevator door opened. David was there with the badge. Elvis grabbed it and walked into the elevator, followed by his team.

On the main floor everybody was waiting for them. Tonight it was twelve city policemen and Elvis's five personal bodyguards. The limousines were outside, engines on. Elvis climbed into the first one. The motorcycle policemen ahead were given the signal and the caravan moved out.

Elvis walked into his dressing room at the Myriad Convention Center at 8:48. He could hear the applause for J. D. Sumner, the warm-up singer. J. D. was helped out by the Stamps, the five-man white male backup group, which combined with Kathy Westmoreland, a white singer who led the Sweet Inspirations, black women who made their name backing up Aretha Franklin. The two groups were melding white gospel and black soul.

At nine exactly, Elvis walked onstage, flourishing a red scarf. He angled his head slightly to shield his burgeoning neck, and the lights frayed over his torso, focusing brightly on his resolute smile and the motion of his hands. The crowd erupted, and he

swung into "C.C. Rider." At 9:58 he finished with his final offer-
ing, "I Can't Help Falling in Love with You."

His bodyguards went quickly into action. What they dis-
trusted most was those stages that didn't rise high enough off
floor level. When the elevation was a mere three or four feet,
aggressive fans sometimes hurled themselves up onto the stage,
necessitating quick protective action by Elvis's human cordon.
Tonight the designated forward guards were David Stanley and
brother Ricky. Backing them up was Ed Parker, Elvis's karate
coach, and Jerry Schilling, sometime film editor and personnel
manager for Elvis since 1964. Red West and his cousin Sonny
were there, too, for protection. Elvis was well shielded, and Oklahoma City was easy. The stage there rose eight feet above the
floor.

Once again, the lead limousine, the motorcycle cops, and
the two trailing limousines. The caravan proceeded straight to the
airport, right up to the *Lisa Marie*'s gangway.

Boarding the plane, Elvis heads aft to his bedroom and the
fourteen-thousand-dollar queen-size bed. Dr. Nick is there, and
Elvis's wrecking crew has to put off disrobing until the doc pulls
out Quaaludes, Percodan, and Dilaudid, expedient to decom-
press Elvis from his concert high. Then he submits to his han-
dlers, who wiggle him out of his costume and give him pajamas
and a robe. Food is waiting in the bedroom and Elvis begins immediately to eat, alone.

The flight to Terre Haute is just over two hours. Once again,
the limousines and the police. They all drive to the hotel and go
up to the hotel suite. Colonel Parker is there with the advance
men who have checked things out. The window of the suite is
blackened and keys are in place in all the doors. The Colonel and
the advance men leave to fly to Cleveland, tomorrow's date, to
look in on things.

Dr. Nick comes in again and ministers to Elvis. Elvis eats the cheeseburgers and ribs and signals David to bring in Ginger.

Lying on the bed next to her, he spends hours with his reading, including his special books, the Bible, Cheiro's *Book of Numbers,* Kahlil Gibran's *The Prophet,* and Joseph Berner's *The Impersonal Life.*

At five the pills take hold. He sleeps until awakened, at four in the afternoon, to prepare for that night's concert in Terre Haute.

BOOK FIVE

58

Memphis, August 16, 1977

WHEN AT 3:55 THE RESUSCITATION DOCTORS AT THE
Baptist Memorial Hospital in Memphis formally abandoned
hope, Joe Esposito asked to be taken to the adjacent trauma
room, which had a phone. Using it, he tracked down the Colonel,
in Portland. Tom Parker heard the news and for an unprece-
dented moment was silent. Then, "I should talk to Vernon."

"Vernon's at Graceland. He can hardly stand up. Charlie's
going over there to tell him, to tell him, I mean, that it's official."

"So the word hasn't gotten out?"

"We're waiting till Vernon gets the official word. The press
people are downstairs, they've been streaming in ever since Elvis
got here. That was less than an hour ago. I'm going to talk to
them as soon as Charlie phones in from Graceland to let me
know that Vernon's been told."

"Joe, now listen—Joe, you got to *stop bawling.* Now listen
hard. I got some thinking to do. I'll need to talk to you after I've
done that, maybe also talk with Vernon—"

"No way you can talk with Vernon, the shape he's in, Tom—"

"All *right.* But, Joe. Joe! *You got to stop crying,* I'm telling
you. You'll be in charge of things there, I mean with Vernon, you

and Vernon. But there are things I'll have to think about hard and real fast, and then I'll need to talk with you. That'll be *urgent*."

"Lydia's coming on duty. I'll fix it so she can find me."

Joe Esposito hung up and tried to control himself. He walked into Trauma Room 1 where Elvis lay, a linen sheet pulled up over his head. There were five, maybe six doctors there, half of them still clad in their medical gowns. Joe singled out Dr. Nichopoulos. "Nick. Come here a minute."

He led him back into the adjacent trauma room and closed the door. There were no chairs, only the operating table and two instrument trays.

Nick threw himself over the table and sobbed convulsively. Joe gripped him on the shoulders. "Jeezus *Christ*, Nick. I mean, I was going to ask *you* to give *me* some goddam pill to—"

But Joe himself couldn't go on. He bent over the other end of the operating bed and sobbed for a moment with the doctor, but then arrested himself, stood up, and kicked Nick hard on the back of one of his knees.

"Get up, goddamit. There's things to do. There's God knows how many of them down there by now—"

The phone rang. It was Lydia, crying through her words.

"Joe, it's Charlie for you."

"Yeah, Charlie. Vernon been told?"

"Yes," Charlie said.

"I'm going to need you here with me."

"Coming. Vernon wants you to take over the arrangements. But to check with him. I've got through to Priscilla in Los Angeles."

"The thing to do is send the plane for her. I'll attend to that."

"She asked a couple of things, but couldn't go on, broke down. She wanted to know about Lisa. I had to tell her Lisa was there outside Elvis's bathroom when they dragged him out into the ambulance."

"Charlie. Stop everything and get over here!"

"You reached the Colonel?"

"Charlie. Shut up and get your ass over here. And flick the phone now for Lydia, okay?"

"What about Orson?"

"I'm going to hang up on you. I'll dial for Lydia on my own."

Dr. Nichopoulos was back on his feet. He went out into the death chamber and came back carrying the black doctor's kit he had left there.

Joe was on the telephone, dialing Graceland.

"Lydia?"

Wordlessly, Nick handed him a pill. "I'll get you some water."

Turning his head from the phone, Joe muttered, "I don't need water—Lydia?—I'll swallow it." He put the pill in his mouth. "Lydia, the Colonel will be calling for me. I'll need to speak to him. I expect to be here at the hospital, but if I'm not, you'll have to track me down."

"I've got like fifty calls to make..." She was sobbing again.

"*Whoever* you need to interrupt, put the Colonel through. I'll leave word with the operator downstairs. I'll be with Charlie, when he gets here, for a bit, before we go with the press. But put the Colonel through—I know, I know, dear. It's like the end of the world. The end of the world."

59

Memphis, August 16, 1977

THERE WASN'T ENOUGH SPACE IN THE HOSPITAL'S WAIT-
ing room. The newly arrived TV reporter, followed by his crew,
tried to make his way into the crowded room, puffing from his
exertions. Through the half-open door he spotted his friend and
rival, Stoopsie, and whispered, "Have they said it yet, said the
word?"

"Nothing yet," Stoopsie spoke into his friend's ear. "But there
can't be any doubt. The King is gone."

There was no alternative, the hospital administrator, Maurice
Elliott, decided: The crowd would have to be allowed into the
main lobby where there was ample room. He passed the word on.

As people poured silently into the lobby, out of the tight little
waiting room, more of the press kept coming in but also just curious spectators. Elliott grabbed a nurse going off duty. "Hilda.
Hold everything. Station yourself there." He pointed to the hospital entrance. "And don't let one person through the door who
doesn't have press credentials."

"Give us a break," one reporter called out, addressing Maurice Elliott, "is Elvis..." But everyone in the room turned on
him. "*Shh! Quiet!*"

There was silence. In minutes, even the lobby was crowded. Hilda had barred many who wanted to come in from outside, but the company was now swelled by hospital personnel gathering in the lobby, doctors, nurses, laboratory technicians. Elliott spotted patients making their way down the staircase, some clad in pajamas.

Elliott groped his way into the main trauma room. Charlie was there with Joe and a half dozen pathologists. Charlie handed the officiating doctor the formal request, signed by Vernon Presley: *Proceed with an autopsy.* The brilliant overhead operating floodlight had been dimmed. A beam from the lamp next to the door cast the profile of Elvis's shrouded face as a shadow on the opposite wall. Charlie could discern the line of Elvis's nose and lips. He jolted his head away.

"All right," Joe said, motioning to Charlie. "Let's get on with it." They were escorted to the elevator and went down to the lobby.

Their somber appearance as they stepped out of the elevator alerted the cameras. There was total quiet.

Joe Esposito cleared his throat. "Gentlemen, ladies, I—" He stopped, his shoulders began to heave.

He tried again, again without success. He turned then to Charlie and in an undertone said, "You tell 'em."

Charlie Hodge tried, but he also failed.

Sizing up the situation, Maurice Elliott whispered questioningly to Joe, who motioned him to proceed. The only sound was of cameras whirring.

"On behalf of the Baptist Memorial Hospital, it is my sad duty to report that Elvis Presley died—"

"Of what?" one reporter broke in. A chorus echoed his question.

"—died of a suspected massive arrhythmic cardiac arrest. Further details will be released after an autopsy is completed."

A hospital attendant groped her way behind Elliott to Joe Esposito. "It's a Colonel Parker on the phone. He says it's a matter
of life and death. You want to take it in the admissions office?"
Joe nodded and left the turbulent room with the staccato click of
camera lights, the reporters talking now mostly to each other.
One approached Mr. Elliott and requested setting up some kind
of orderly file to the two public telephones everyone wanted access to.

Joe Esposito, in the admissions office, took the telephone and
began to make notes.

He was—the Colonel barked out—to get from Vernon—
"even a nod of the head is good enough"—confirmation of the
Colonel's authority to cope with the myriad problems they faced.

The tour scheduled to have begun on Wednesday was an important priority.

But most important, the Colonel emphasized to Joe, was to
discourage any attempt by any private group to reproduce for
public sale anything related to Elvis—"nothing, Joe, nothing...."

"And here's something else. I've had phone calls from radio
stations. They want an okay to play Elvis's songs without paying
any royalty. Negative. Double negative. Don't give Vernon any of
these details. Just tell him you've spoken with me and that I'll
take care of everything. Just get him to nod his head, that's all.

"The press taken care of?"

Joe reported that the press had been notified just then, "like
five minutes ago."

"All right, now here's the next thing. Get word to the hospital
authority that no, repeat, no coroner is to be asked to come in.
What we have to okay is an autopsy. Get Vernon—"

"He's done that, Tom. Charlie brought in his signature on the
request for an autopsy."

"That's to be a *private* autopsy report. All we need is for the press to be told that Elvis has an entire toxic pharmacy in his stomach."

The Colonel paused. "Oh shit. Poor, dumb, stupid, beautiful son of a bitch, forty-two years old, you believe it?"

"I gotta believe it, Tom," Joe said.

60

Los Angeles, August 16, 1977

ON TUESDAY, AUGUST 16, IT WAS NEARLY SEVEN WHEN Orson and Ferdy emerged from their cloistered research and writing room. Gladys had already gone home, leaving a dozen message slips that Orson thrust into his pocket.

He drove down the freeway, always a slow and tedious journey, even two hours after the rush hour was officially over. The crowds had gone home. As he approached the great racetrack, the going got better and he turned to his house in Santa Ana, on the leafy street not far from the huge, now empty parking lot. He opened the door to see Susan seated on the chair opposite the door, facing the entrance. The sound of Carlita's television set in the bedroom, her door closed, came through only faintly. He looked, exploringly, at Susan, alarmed by the disarray in her features.

"What's up, honey?"

Susan knew that meant he hadn't heard. "Elvis is dead."

Orson extended his hand to the side of the doorway, groping for balance. Susan came to him. His eyes were flooded with tears. She moved her hands up to his head and, tenderly, removed the glasses.

"Come and sit down."

She told him about it. Just after two, Priscilla had called. "She reached me at work. I had to call her back, she was so—upset. What she said was—well, that Lisa Marie had been there at Graceland, seen it all. She saw him taken away to the hospital. At that point Priscilla got a little garbled. She did say that the Colonel was sending Elvis's plane to pick her up. Her and others. That's when she asked if you'd ride out to Memphis with her— she figures the *Lisa Marie* would be ready to take off about eleven tonight. She didn't know, at that point, how many others would be on the plane with her."

"What did you say?"

"I knew you wouldn't want to take that trip, with all the, all Elvis's... people. What I said was you couldn't be reached and I just didn't know when you'd get back, sometimes you stayed real late in the office. She said she wanted you to sit with her at the funeral services. That's day after tomorrow, Thursday. At Graceland."

Susan had acted. "I've booked you on the eight A.M. to Atlanta. The connection gets you to Memphis at eight Memphis time. During the day they're going to expose the body. The funeral will be the next day."

"Did Priss tell you anything about the arrangements?"

"Only that Vernon and Joe are looking after things."

"Did you see anything on television? Did they catch Elvis, like, going to the hospital? When was the announcement made—"

"I didn't turn on the television. My guess is there's nothing else on *except* Elvis. Do you want it on?"

"I don't think so."

They struggled, when Carlita bounded in to say good night, to be cheerful. Orson picked her up, squeezed her, and, holding her legs, had her upside down until the ritual giggle, "Daddy! Are you going to leave me upside down *all night long*?"

After she had been put to bed, they talked.

Susan let him wander down his memory lane, without any thought to guide him. He jumped around. He wondered about the doctors in Memphis. "What did they do to try to save him? Was there anything that *could* have been done? Elvis must have had a million doctors. Did you ever meet Dr. Nick? What a jerk. What did they find? What did they actually *report,* or haven't they done that yet? The Colonel, where was he in all of this? Do you know anything about the scheduled tour? No. Of course you don't. What are they doing about that? Elvis knew it had to come. That last time I saw him, there was no other way to read off on how he acted. Charlie, where was Charlie? Was he there? And Joe?—forget it. You already told me Priss said he was on the scene, also Vernon, poor Vernon. He'll be in charge. I wonder about David...and Billy. And Lamar and Larry. Maybe some of them are here and will be flying out with Priscilla."

He left his half-eaten fish and absentmindedly scraped the dishes and put them in the washer.

He went then to his records. "Do you mind?"

"Of course not. I was his fan too, remember?"

Orson put on "Can't Help Falling in Love." Then, in rapid succession, without comment, "I Forgot to Remember to Forget" and "The Wonder of You." And then "All Shook Up." Now he commented, "That was on the charts for a long time. His top seller was 'Heartbreak Hotel,' I think."

"Wasn't it 'Hound Dog'?"

"I hope not. I got tired of 'Hound Dog.' I'm probably wrong. Let's try it. I've got...four different recordings of it."

And much later. "I wish Dr. Schuster hadn't said no sleeping pills."

"I think tonight you'll have to have one. I'll overrule Dr. Schuster."

Susan walked into the bathroom and was back with a glass of water and the pill. "I'll wake you at six."

"I think I want to watch the television news."

"Not till after you swallow that pill." Susan handed him the water and flicked on the television. It was five minutes after the hour, and the reporter was reporting that Premier Brezhnev had approved President Carter's call to endorse the Panama Canal Treaty. The eleven P.M. news had already run. Orson didn't want to stay up for Johnny Carson. "Though probably he'll be talking about Elvis...He liked Elvis. Practically everybody liked Elvis. Paul McCartney said he was the Beatles' greatest idol. Yes, everybody liked Elvis."

"Like you."

"Yes." He paused for a moment. "And like you, too, Susan." She nodded.

On Orson's second leg, Atlanta to Memphis, the plane was full. After they landed he looked anxiously about, and was relieved to see Billy Stanley there, grave and handsome at twenty-four, eighteen years younger than his dead stepbrother.

"Charlie told me to be here, Orson, to bring you on over to Graceland. I'm glad you're here; it's been a while. In Graceland it's like—it's not like—well, like anything ever. The whole world, it looked like, showed up for the viewing. Vernon had to extend the closing hour he had set. There are tons of people outside. We don't know what's going to make them go on home. There's got to be an acre of flowers around the house."

"Where is Priscilla?"

"They took her to—the room."

"Elvis's room?"

"Yes. They got Ginger the hell out of the way. It was Ginger who found him, in the bathroom."

"When?"

"Two-twenty-two P.M."

In the car Orson said: "Charlie's waiting for me, right?"

Billy nodded.

"The Colonel there?"

"Oh yes. He's met a couple of times with the press. Told them the funeral would be at Graceland, private, invitation only, then we'd all drive to the burial ground. He said the autopsy report would take a while. And he said that radio and TV couldn't just treat Elvis's records like, you know—"

"I know. Like common property."

Charlie and Orson were up late. They sat in the corner of the Pool Room on the Louis XV chairs, the heavily decorated cotton fabric overhead and on all sides of the room surrounding the pool table.

Orson told Charlie, after drinking a beer, that one beer was his limit. Charlie signaled for more for himself and they talked about him, their memories of him, recent and not-so-recent, and Charlie said that Elvis had mentioned Orson Killer from time to time and was always saying he was going to call him on the telephone. "Did he, ever?"

Orson shook his head. "Not since I told him what the Colonel told me to tell him."

"That doesn't mean he changed...about you."

"I know," Orson said, and they talked on. At one in the morning a young man unfamiliar to him said his car was ready, the car Charlie had ordered to take Orson on to the hotel.

Priscilla, dressed in black, a veil over her face, escorted Lisa Marie, clutching her hand, to the front row of the crowded living room, and sat down. Orson was standing against the wall, to one side of the marble fireplace. She beckoned him to come to the front row and pointed him to the chair next to Vernon, on her left. Lisa Marie smiled wanly at Orson.

The service began. Kathy Westmoreland sang "Heavenly Father." Kathy singing that same hymn was a standard at Elvis's performances. James Blackwood, who had performed at Gladys's funeral in August, just nineteen years ago, sang Elvis's signature piece, "How Great Thou Art." Jake Hess, so greatly admired by Elvis, recreated "Known Only to Him," a song Elvis had recorded in explicit tribute to Hess himself. Elvis's favorite, J. D. Sumner, with, as always, the Stamps to accompany him, sang several hymns, most of them hymns that had been sung at Elvis's shows. There were two eulogies, and Orson forgot to listen, after the opening words, which said what he knew would be said about Elvis. But words were incapable of rendering Elvis, only Elvis could do that, and that was the point of the service, that Elvis wouldn't be able to do that anymore.

As the speakers went on, Orson was thinking of the first sight of Elvis at Friedberg, the explosive generosity of the twenty-one-year-old icon; thought of him in the snug private smoking car of the train chugging through the German forest toward Paris, singing "Twinkle, Twinkle, Little Star," and authorizing fifteen-year-old Orson to have his first beer at the same time that he was instructing the gang that, on arriving in Paris, Orson was to be sheltered beginning at three in the morning. Then he tried a composite in his mind of the phone calls—so many of them, for so many years, received in so many places—until the time almost two years back when Elvis stopped calling because, Orson had figured it out, to call would deny the true brotherly love Elvis had admitted to by embracing Orson and confessing that Orson was right to say that Elvis was killing himself. He'd wait until he had actually done so, wait until now, and speak now only in song to

Orson, and to a world shaken by the thought that he would never sing to them again alive; but the songs were there, would always be there, and the songbird would always lodge in the memory, and in the heart of the fourteen-year-old boy whom Elvis delighted to address as Killer, and did so right to the end; the end of time, Orson thought, the hymnal's lines blurring as he struggled to join the mourners in one more song.

If you enjoyed *Elvis in the Morning,*
look for these other titles by WILLIAM F. BUCKLEY JR.

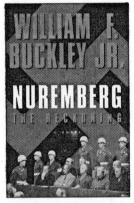

Nuremburg: The Reckoning
0-15-100679-2 HC
$25.00 (Higher in Canada)

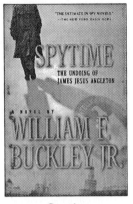

Spytime
0-15-601124-7 PB
$13.00 (Higher in Canada)
0-15-100513-3 HC
$25.00 (Higher in Canada)

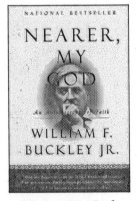

Nearer, My God
0-15-600618-9 PB
$14.00 (Higher in Canada)

Brothers No More
0-15-600476-3 PB
$12.00 (Higher in Canada)

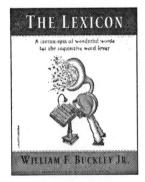

The Lexicon
0-15-600616-2 PB
$10.00 (Higher in Canada)

The Right Word
0-15-600569-7 PB
$15.00 (Higher in Canada)

Available wherever books are sold